THE LADY IN THE RED SHAWL

an Erotic Thriller by

Nicolle Vaughn

Artwork by Joyce D'Annibale

2nd Edition, edition by Debbe Johnson

Dedicated to ~

The givers of this world who always reach for goodness.

...And the monsters who preserve it.

Epigraph

~Her face in my mind drives me crazy.

How I remember every detail, how I hate seeing it there.

In the depths of my soul, I still find her.

Her soul is my soul, I have been carrying it over the entirety of all lifetimes.

At the end of my mind, I see her standing there to mock my thoughts.

She warps my image of content, leaving me blank to soak in her distortion of 'real.'

She sits, exemplary and unscathed, preserved by the sanctity of my memory.

I am forever trapped in the embrace of her wasted spirit and surrounded by an epiphany of her never-ending, sought-after dreams.

At the end of my mind, I reach out to her.

But in a grasp of regret, she drowns me and yet still, at the end of my mind, all of her remains.

She is now, somehow, the sanity in-between.

She is the lady in the red shawl. ~

Introduction
The Ranger Medic
Operation Iraqi Freedom

"Secure that fucking area!" Sergeant Will Hartmann's team leader shouted from the other side of the vehicle as he ran along the building.

Sounds of gunfire overwhelmed the senses. Ragged breaths rushed through clenched teeth as focused brains defied flight responses. Each of them immersed in adrenaline, pushing past the high-pressured sting of ocean waves that drowned eardrums in the dry desert air.

Moving as fast as muscles would exert, they ran towards the danger.

Bravery was harsh. It took so much out of a person. Stole their innocence, stole their belief in safety forever. Not one of these soldiers would ever get that back. They would never get back any true form of trust in their fellow man.

Not one of them could ever be able to put the weight of this down. The heaviness of bravery they would carry forever replacing almost everything else a human being should ever feel.

Will's breathing accelerated. His chest filling up with a rush, the same as it would after hitting a high jump on a snowboard and realizing your angle was off. He remembered that feeling from hitting the slopes as a kid with his father.

The one fucking thing they ever did together.

Random memories seeped through his focused mind. He pushed them down deep into his gut, because sentiment only weighs you down. Running with heavy steps, his gear weighted him down. Each stomp of his boots crushed into the gravel below him. The aid bag thumped against his back as he moved, his Kevlar slipping into his line of vision as it shifted slightly with every motion. Sweat poured down his face.

Will gripped his weapon securely in combat proficient hands, trigger finger outstretched at the ready. Staff Sergeant Fuller moved in front of him, weaving through the labyrinth of foreign lives as they ran, shouting commands. All of it was alien to them, they were the invaders.

Duck and cover

The gunfire sounds continued to grow louder as they reached closer to the threat.

Up ahead, the path turned a corner around a building, and a man darted towards them.

Pop pop

SSG Fuller opened fire.

The man dropped. Another, with a woman holding the hand of a child wrapped in a dirty red blanket, came running around the corner.

Will yelled out, "Halt! Stop!"

Pop pop

The man hit the ground, while the woman became frantic, screaming, and flailing. The child reached down into the man's bag to retrieve something.

"Don't, don't grab that!"

Before the command could leave his lips, SSG Fuller fell to the ground, shot through the neck.

Pop Pop, Pop Pop

Will fired.

Four shots, four shots to drop a woman and a child. He plopped down next to SSG Fuller, the blood gushing from his neck. His eyes frantic as Will tried to push his hand over the wound.

"Press down!" Will ordered him.

Another round hit the wall beside them.

Sniper!

With his weapon propped out, Will used his free arm to awkwardly drag Fuller down behind the wall. He couldn't stop himself from glancing down at the dead family as he shuffled past them, dragging his brother in arms.

It was a doll. She was grabbing a fucking doll. Christ! I just killed a little girl.

His breathing sped up. He was going to vomit.

Pop Pop Pop

More shots fired.

Will dropped SSG Fuller, throwing his own back against the wall. He scrambled for a bandage from his aid bag.

Fuck, Fuck I just killed a little girl.

The bile was rising in his throat. It burned as his mouth filled with the metallic taste of the blood and the dry sand air.

It burned. It burned down into his gut, over to his chest.

It burned through into his heart.

It burned him up, hotter and hotter.

SSG Fuller's blood pouring over his hands was hot, too.

It burned his skin.

It burned Will's eyes, looking into his dying brother, seeing his fear of death.

It burned him up. It burned him where he knelt, and it burned away all that he felt.

All the guilt.

All the fear.

All the pain...it burned him up to ashes inside.

He watched the life leave SSG Fuller's face, watched it leave his body as his army brother's blood soaked into the earth. It soaked into the same ground as the family down the path from him.

They all bled into the ground together while Will burned in his boots where he stood over them.

Chapter 1

Four Years Later
The Dishonorably Discharged Ranger Medic Veteran
Tacoma, Washington

"Will?" Jessa's voice sounded hesitant as she knocked slightly on the door but dared not open it. "I don't know what you want me to do? Do you want me to leave?"

No, I don't want you to leave. I want you to help me forget. Didn't you know that you're a distraction? He thought.

His wife had just surprised him with coffee. In an effort to reconcile, to talk about what they needed to do to fix their marriage, she just let herself into his apartment. The apartment she insisted he get during their *trial separation.* She sauntered in with coffee and was so shocked to find a half-naked Jessa wearing nothing but a t-shirt walk out of the bedroom that she threw the coffee into the air.

Hot coffee flying all over the place.

Women shrieking.

It was a fucking mess.

This was the end. He knew it. She yelled to him she wanted a divorce, that this was it, she couldn't take it anymore.

He just lost it all.

"Will, I said, do you want me to leave?" Jessa whined from the other side of the door.

Slowly rising to his feet, he opened the bedroom to her.

"Come in here, baby."

Without allowing a moment to think about anything else, he grabbed the hem of her t-shirt and pulled it over her pretty head.

"I was so confused, and I didn't know what was going on?" she sobbed. Tears trickled down her face.

God, she's so weak.

She wouldn't survive in a life outside this sheltered world created for her.

Created by men like me.

"Shhh, just stop talking." He ran his thumb down her cheek and across her tears before leaning in to taste them.

Tasting the tears on her quivering mouth, knowing how much she didn't deserve those tears, made a part of him hate her. She was just the girl he picked up the night before, the kind of girl who would follow him home and spread her lovely legs for him without even knowing his last name.

He really didn't give a fuck if she cried.

Besides, what the fuck does this girl have to cry over?

I'll take all the pleasure I want from her he thought, pushing the image of Nikki... his now ex-wife... who wanted to bring him coffee... away from him. *And never feel the worse for tossing this distraction aside when I've had my fill.*

He kissed Jessa's mouth hard, craving all she could give to him in this moment.

Walking into her, Will sucked on her lip, pushing her naked body backwards towards the bed while holding her head, her hair laced between his fingers. When her knees hit the mattress, he braced her elbows with his controlled grip and spun her around.

Very slowly, his hands moved up the front of her naked body, grasping her large, ripe breasts.

Too large for her frame, he thought. *She bought these for men like me to enjoy.*

Rolling her nipple around in his fingers, she moaned, leaning into his touch, as Will delicately pushed her long hair over one shoulder. With her neck exposed, bending down to brush his lips along her throat was easily accomplished. The move was meant as a distraction, to take her focus off his free hand, sneaking to hold her wrist down at her side.

Gently, his teeth sunk into the soft flesh of her neck while pulling her arm swiftly up behind her back like he would an insurgent in Iraq. The forward motion of his body was enough pressure to force her over onto the mattress below them.

With Jessa bent over, incapacitated in front of him, he trailed his fingers down her perfect spine. Then he allowed his mind to dissect her.

Not a single stretch mark or blemish. Not one scar or indent. Not one burn mark or scratch.

His touch lingered at her wanton ass, tracing a pattern along her tan-line free cheek.

It's the same shade as the rest of her perfectly delicate skin.

He wanted to find an imperfection, to find something that made her *less* somehow, but her skin was impeccable.

I want it to be flawed, he thought as he brought down a slap onto her ass of perfection.

She cried out with pleasure.

Will reeled back to deliver another harsh blow onto her now slightly pink flesh.

She cried out again.

The spot was reddening the flesh around it, making one flawed spot for him to focus on as he pulled his erect cock out of his pajama pants. It annoyed him he couldn't find this experience worth the effort of taking them off.

Bringing down another well-placed blow, he sighed in agitation before lunging into her wet, waiting snatch. Jessa cried out into the mattress as her body pulsed around him, finding her release the very moment he entered her.

Will's thrusts pushed past her rocking orgasm to seek his own. His drive to get off pinned her down, demanding the visual of the red flesh bouncing under his touch as mental fuel to plow harder into her again and again.

After his endurance lingered long enough for her body to collapse on the mattress beneath him, he flung her arm free to get a better grip on both sides of her hips. Desperate to slam deeper still. Anything to try to find his orgasm.

His relentless rhythm had her moaning and crying out, grasping the sheets... but he needed more. He needed to push her, to have her writhing away from her perfection. He wanted to take it from her, to push her past it.

Killer's hands seized her flesh more securely as he charged on. Feeling her muscles build inside her again annoyed him. Those muscles worked for nothing, and now they wanted to burst and quiver around him?

One hand raised up to slap her ass hard again while thrusting. The repetitive motion and the harsh, well delivered blows became her undoing. This time, her spasm of pleasure brought him close to climaxing with her. So close to release...

Instead, he lost it.

His erection was gone. The discolored flesh of her well-beaten ass wasn't enough.

The sight and feelings were gratifying enough. *How the fuck did it disappear?*

Frustrated, he whipped himself out, rolling down next to her onto the bed to catch his breath.

Fuck, it wasn't enough.

He lay pissed, thinking about how best to rid himself of the pleasure box lying next to him. Her worth consumed, Will was now tired of Jessa. She reached out an arm, no doubt to snuggle up to him, but he abruptly scooted up off the bed.

"I'll get you a washcloth," he announced.

Will knew he was in no shape to deal with her tears. God, if she started crying in front of him again, he'd probably punch her in the mouth.

It was best to lie, make plans, and break them. Hopefully, she would get the hint. If he gave her rejection, she'd grow angry instead of hurting, and that suited him much better.

I'd rather her hate me than cry at me.

Will sauntered back over to where she lay on the bed with his red handprint branding her ass. It made him smile at how delectable that imperfection looked on her, especially knowing he had put it there.

Very gently, Will moved the warm washcloth across her freshly beaten skin. "Let's have breakfast and then you head home. You can clean up and get all pretty again," he leaned in to kiss her shoulder, "and then I'll pick you up later to go out to the clubs or something."

She tilted her head to the side and gave him a wide smile, "That was amazing."

"Thank you." He threw her a wink.

On the other side of the bedroom doorway, Will froze mid-stride when faced with Nikki's coffee offering all over the kitchen. It served well in reminding him once again of the shock and hurt he watched skitter across her sweet face because of him.

"Do you want me to make pancakes?" The cum-box Jessa's voice was bubbly and happy.

God, I fucked everything up. I fucked it all up even worse.

"Did you hear me?" she called out again.

The way she bounced into view made him want to smash his fist into her face. He wanted her to feel pain, to feel pain like his. He couldn't stand for her to breathe the air in the plastic little world she lived in for one more fucking second. That world he gave to her by sacrificing everything good in his. He lost everything for her!

Now he decided, rashly in the moment, that she was going to lose everything too.

"No, you know what, why don't you hop in the shower, and we'll try for a round two?" Will shot her his beautiful, dazzling, disarming smile. The one he knew always got him his way. "Head on in, I'll be right behind you."

She giggled in compliance, bouncing away towards the bathroom.

He was going to hurt her.

No. He was going to make her bleed everything, too. Thinking of her terror later when she realized why he was holding her in the shower, how panicked and afraid she would be when she realized it was a knife he held in his hand. Imagining how her warm blood would feel as it flowed down his naked flesh, draining from her perfect skin.

The thought brought a disturbing smirk to his lips.

Sauntering over to the fridge, Will retrieved the milk to suck down a few gulps from the carton. For the briefest of moments, guilt invaded. Who knew why he wanted this girl to feel hurt, why he wanted Jessa to feel pain, why he wanted to end her perfect undeserving life? Even *he* couldn't understand what she could have possibly done to make him want to hurt her. Nothing he thought, that's the point. She has never done anything.

"Go ahead and get in, I'm right behind you." He put the milk carton back and shut the refrigerator door.

Hearing her obediently turn the water on, Will walked over to the nightstand to plug the phone into his speakers. Loud techno music filled the room as he moved to the dresser drawer to retrieve his marine corps issued KA-BAR, given to him by a special operation's marine who once saved his life. It would serve perfectly for this occasion.

Steam was already pouring out from behind the curtain when he walked into the bathroom. Will shut the door behind him and stripped-down naked to step into the cascade of hot water behind her.

With the KA-BAR in one hand, he wrapped his free hand around her wet naked perfect flesh, sliding his body up as close to hers as he could get. She leaned back into him.

Will could feel the smile on her smug face as Jessa rested her head against his chest, closed her eyes, and moaned. Surprisingly, he loved hearing that moan. Owning her pleasure before her death was deplorable of him. It was perfect, and *this* was what he needed.

His fingers ran up her side, resting on her neck, her small, pretty little neck. Slowly, he began kissing her shoulder, moving his large, strong hand closer and closer to her mouth and nose. He sucked the delicate flesh along her throat, bending her slightly forward as she fell deeper into him. It was exhilarating, knowing what was coming, knowing the pain he was about to inflict.

His erection was aching. He felt as if the carnal urges bubbling up under his flesh were burning him, boiling, roaring over the surface of the façade he had become.

Will was a purposely molded monster. Used up in war for the job that was needed. Told to do terrible inhumane things to protect what was good. Now draped in the flesh of the man he was before.

Under the flesh, he was an empty shell. Every motion he went through in life he did, feeling nothing. Existing and numb. He was empty. An empty, numb shell covered in the flesh of the man he once was.

But now, Will decided, *I deserve to feel.*

This made him feel desire... he slid his cock inside her. This made him feel powerful... he wrapped his hand tightly around her mouth and nose. This made him feel her fear... he held tighter as she tried to pull her face away. This made him feel hatred... he slashed the KA-BAR across her stomach. This was his counterattack... his reprisal.

She screamed through his fingers.

Will slashed her thigh. Her arms flailed out, trying to get away, trying to make him stop. He slashed across her breasts.

For all he had done for her, for this county... he slashed her stomach again.

Only to come home without anywhere to find peace, without a single night without the screams... he slashed under her hips.

The only comfort, the only release of pain, was smoked through a pipe, which cast him out of the army dishonorably... he slashed across her rib cage.

Now to lose his wife.

He thrust his anger into her over and over as she bled and thrashed around in his arms. The warm water and warm blood washed over his fury as he found his pleasure deep inside her mangled body.

Finally, release.

Slumping against her, forcing her sliced frame into the wall, cupping her head down into his chest, Will found his breath.

She gurgled, gasping breaths, as he caught his.

Satisfied, for the first time in years, he felt appeased. His limbs felt light, his adrenaline had spiked so high it was like being in battle again. The aftermath of that rush tingled through his veins, and he felt relieved to feel it again.

Backing away, her body fell into the bathtub beneath him. Will reached forward to turn the water cooler, stepping over the bloody mass to get directly under the showerhead's flow. It felt refreshing, and he felt rejuvenated, clean.

Grabbing his shampoo, he washed his hair, and then reached for his loofah and body wash to clean off the blood as her near lifeless hand weakly grasped hold of his ankle.

Will shook it off in disgust before turning off the water and getting out of the shower to towel off.

Today was going to be a good day, after all.

Will sat at the kitchen table. He had cleaned up the coffee mess and made a sandwich. Now sitting with the empty plate in front of him, he was faced with the decision of what to do next. He had to be smart about this. It was the only way to not get caught. He needed to think through strategically what to do next.

Getting rid of the body was, of course, going to be the biggest challenge, but not impossible.

He had her car out front.

Driving off a cliff seemed feasible.

That wouldn't be foolproof, though. He couldn't be sure all the evidence would be destroyed. If they did a proper autopsy, they would probably still be able to see the slash marks on her body.

So that's out.

He got up to wash his plate.

Intruder in her home could possibly work. If he could stage it right. His semen was inside her, but that could be explained away by a casual sex encounter with him the night before. But there would be a lot of questions though, a lot of police spotlight.

No, no police involvement was better. She didn't even know his name when they left the club, so no one else knew his name either. Unless they found his semen in her and identified it, there would be no one to trace her back to him.

Really, the only option here was that no one find her body. She disappears.

The car would be easy. He knew enough people in low places from the drugged-out scene up north. Not one of them would ask questions, and he'd make enough money off it to leave town for good.

He couldn't help but think how having a deep freezer would have been ideal in this situation, but hindsight is always 20/20, and he'd really have to plan better next time.

There would be a next time.

He had made the decision. Just like they trained him to, he would hurt and destroy. He'd get the thrill of living again and he would do it by taking away undeserved perfect lives.

He wouldn't need to kill them all. He could just ruin some, take their money, destroy their trust in people, and create horrible reputations.

Killing would only come with great planning from now on.

It was just too easy to get caught nowadays. This time he got lucky, because this girl had absolutely zero connections to him. No one would ever link her back to him unless they found her.

He sighed. The best option would be to keep her in the tub until the blood drains. Cut her into sections and dump them separately.

Still without his clothing, he sauntered back into the bathroom. Standing in front of the bathroom mirror he applied his deodorant, methodically counting the number of swipes each armpit got. He held his body spray out a full arms-length away and closed his eyes before counting the squirts he delivered down his body. *1... 2... 3....* Walking over to the toilet he glanced down into the tub, her naked body was slumped over, still breathing.

What the fuck? "God, you're taking a long time to die." he said out loud before sitting down. Taking out his phone, he began to search through YouTube, to create an ambience for her death.

"Oh, this is a good one. Have you ever heard of a band called Bright Eyes?" The music filled up the small space. "This will be decent to die to."

With calming music filling the room, he finished, flushed, washed his hands, and sat his naked body down on the cold tile next to the tub. Resting his arms on the bathtub's edge, his chin dropped down into his hands while watching her chest rise and fall.

Life was so delicate. The breath and the blood held such power over us, so much life contained in such fragile necessities. So easily lost.

Her blood was so beautiful against the white porcelain, gliding down to the drain with swirls of the rich, dark, rose-color steadily and confidently pouring. Just as it once flowed through her veins, now it flowed away with her life. Her blood held beauty now as it escaped her.

He hoped her heart would pump until the very last drop flowed through it. Such a dedicated organ to the body, beating from the second the cells formed in the womb, until the last moment it clung to life. It worked so hard for her, every second of every day of her entire life, enduring all.

It never faltered or skipped, never gave up or fell. That heart has beat through it all, birthday parties, celebrations, lovemaking, dancing.

Every night that she slept peacefully, that heart beat. Even now it beat, as the blood it pumped poured out in lovely swirls of beauty covering her skin with its silky glide.

Part of him felt guilty for taking away her heart's purpose, for giving it a reason to give up. Maybe it was mercy. Maybe the heart was exhausted from working so hard for so long, and he allowed it to be released from the misery of constant beating.

He would honor her body for the job it had done in keeping her alive and healthy for so long. The fragile system of organs that work together as the perfect machine to fight against all we expose it to just so we can stay living should be honored.

Just like the military.

He watched with reverence as her systems gave up.

The lungs stilled in her chest. The blood stopped pumping through her powerful heart. He sat for a minute, listening to the melody filling the bathroom around him, enjoying the peace her stillness gave him. She looked beautiful there on the bottom of the tub, with her hair wet and her makeup still perfect on her face, with blood all around her flawless white skin.

This should be art.

Respecting the body laying still, and appreciating its beauty in death. She was so much more beautiful than every other dead body he'd seen. So much more beautiful than the sweaty screaming soldiers with legs blown off. The meat of their muscles mangled like a beef steak fought over by dogs.

No, *this* was lovely.

There was no dirt or sand. No torn fabrics of brown and tan. No sounds of gunfire or yelling orders. No cries of "Medic!"

Just peace and beauty in death.

This was art. He reached out and slid his finger down her arm, swirling a pattern in the blood as he went.

This felt so right. This is what he was meant for.

With newfound purpose, he jumped up and moved to the kitchen to retrieve his butcher knife and a box of zip lock bags.

Returning to the bathroom, Will chose the sharpest little knife he had to open the skin on her chest. Carefully cutting through the muscle and tissue delicately, he located the still heart under her ribs. Ever so gently, Will removed it from its protected cavity and rinsed it under the flow of running bath water.

Holding her heart in his hand, he was overwhelmed with a sensation of pride. He felt honored to have it in his hand. How small it looked in his grasp, knowing how powerful it had once been, knowing how easily he overcame its power. It filled him with satisfaction beyond anything he could imagine holding her heart. Like a fisherman after the hard struggle put up by the fish he hooked on his line. He wanted to hold it up with pride.

But there was also a part of him that wished he could release it back into the stream and watch it swim away. Knowing that he defeated it, but showing mercy after the fight, by allowing it to live.

Her heart, not her. Jessa's choices led her on the path of the undeserving. Her heart had no say in that.

He put the heart into a Ziploc bag and placed it next to him on the bathroom floor. He would figure out what to do with it later.

Most of her organs he wanted to take out and save out of respect. They deserved his recognition for the fight they put up for so many years, just to keep her alive. There was such honor in life. Will remembered every single patient he gave to death in the war. One minute, their bodies would be superb specimens of strength and endurance, pushing the human form to the extremes with willpower and perseverance. And then they would just stop. The systems would fail and life would end. Will would realize that his every effort to thwart death was for naught, and instantly they became a dead body to be removed instead of the brother who once stood strong beside him. No longer the friend who laughed with him in the barracks the night before.

The permeance of death could not be processed on the battlefield. The loss and the hurt and burden of it all was too great for any man to feel while also being ruthless enough to continue fighting the war.

Turning off your humanity is the only way to keep the trigger finger outstretched at the ready. You are trained to override such fight-or-flight response, to bury the sadness of loss and guilt.

Who turns it back on?

Sitting naked on the bathroom floor, Will carefully dissected Jessa, pulling out what he felt deserving of his retention.

Music filled the small room as he used his gloved hands to place the dismembered pieces of her into several heavy duty black garbage bags. He sealed them individually with duct tape before triple bagging each. With bleach, he meticulously cleaned out the tub and the surrounding area of the bathroom. He dressed in a cheap dark blue sweatsuit before pouring Epsom salt into the bathtub and delicately burying the organs. Egyptians preserved organs this way thousands of years ago. It seemed appropriate.

Washing his hands again before pulling on socks and a pair of old running shoes, he completed his look with a baseball cap, and packed a plastic grocery bag with a change of clothing and shoes.

It was dark as he carried the garbage down for disposal. Driving around the city to different dumpsters, depositing the bags one at a time as he went, brought the adrenaline again. It was a rush he desperately craved for so many hours, of so many days, since returning from war.

Eventually, after ridding himself of all the bags, he drove to meet his connection to sell the vehicle. A woman he knew from his drug days, who would have the car stripped and sold for profit.

He kissed her mouth in parting after she paid him for the stolen vehicle, and with no questions asked. Will changed clothing and shoes before walking down to the bar a few blocks over, disposing of the sweat suit, sneakers, and ball cap along the way.

Sitting at the bar, adrenaline fading from his veins, he planned his life.

He would leave here, sell his car, sell his furniture, put the rest of his belongings into storage, and go find a small cabin on the other side of the country. In the mountains. Somewhere that it snowed. He loved the snow. Set it up as his base camp, his home of operations.

It would be easy to find women online, men too, if the circumstance arose. He would bait them, and then determine what they deserved from him.

Death, respect, or ruination.

He would become the judge and jury of the superficial selfish parasites that expect everything from a life they never earned.

This is how he would live without feeling dead inside. This is how he would take back all that was stolen from him.

He sat at the bar, sipping a light beer, knowing the organs of a dead girl sat at home in his bathtub. The thought had him smirking, and he felt relieved inside for the first time in years.

Sitting on a high shelf above the bar, Will noticed a row of beautifully decorated vases. So delicate that one swift blow could smash them to pieces, but ornate enough to justify the risk.

Vases. He would keep his girls in vases, pieces of his girls, anyway. He could travel the country collecting the lovely décor to store the organs of the undeserving in as reparations.

A display of retribution.

Chapter 2

The Two Army Medic Veterans
Gettysburg, Pennsylvania
2 years later

They parked on the street corner in front of a small restaurant nestled into a quaint storefront facing the main street in town. Vivian had driven past it many times without ever noticing it was there.

"You'll love this place." Will put his hand on the swell of her back gently, barely touching, to lead her onto the sidewalk, "I came here all skeptical, because it's a hole in the wall, but the food is just divine."

"Divine, huh?" she still had doubts about the restaurant as they walked through the door. It was a cramped little room with diner like tables and chairs all crammed in too close together. The waiter seated them in the center of the room. It made her feel exposed and crowded. The uncomfortable feeling had her on edge. She held her shoulders straighter in places like this, on alert.

"I love that dress on you. Did I tell you that?" Will's voice hummed. But she was focused on all her uneasy feelings. Putting effort into trying to maintain composure to mask her inner unease with an outward facade of put-togetherness. Instinctively, she looked up at the ceiling.

Noticing ceilings had become a habit, a silly way to gather herself when she felt scattered.

Looking up when she was nervous forced her mind to center her thoughts in new places. It kept her from looking at the odd set up that occupied the rest of the small room, and forced her to notice something ordinary.

"Hmmm? What did you say?" She met his eyes across the table, finally responding to his words.

He appeared annoyed, agitated by her question.

"I was giving you a compliment. I said you look nice in that dress." Will's voice was laced in polite annoyance.

"Oh, I think this dress would make anyone look nice." She smoothed down the fabric of the simple, black, form fitting dress she had picked to wear to their medic's group meeting earlier in the day.

"No, I think *you* are pretty in the dress. Why do you dismiss what I mean when I compliment you?" He held in irrational anger, composed, sitting perfectly in his chair across the table. "Do you think I'm a liar? When I compliment you, just say 'thank you.' You're my friend now." A rare manifestation for them both. "I get to compliment you if I want, and you should respect me enough to believe me."

She wanted to hide from his sight. "I'm sorry, I didn't mean to make you feel that way." Vivian suddenly felt small. She had only known Will a few short weeks. He showed up to a dinner she had helped organize to form an all medics and corpsman local support group in their area. She had served in the army, as a medic, before being discharged because of her war injuries.

Though she had been out five years now, she couldn't put it all down and it was getting too heavy to carry alone. A few months ago, she decided to do something about that, and brought the medics together so maybe they could all carry it together. Unfortunately, the club didn't seem to be as involved as she had hoped. Not many medics and corpsman in the area.

"I don't like to have my sincerity doubted, it's rude." He spoke as if he were one of the wounded now.

She looked up to meet his eyes, "Thank you for complimenting me on my dress."

"You're welcome." His fake smile lit up his face to hide the angered annoyance he had briefly allowed to creep out.

The waiter appeared with water glasses on cue, asking if they still needed a minute to look over the menu.

"No." Will replied sharply, without so much as an opportunity for her to respond, "We will both share the asparagus salad with the sherry vinaigrette, as well as the shrimp orzo. Just bring out the two orders with extra plates, please."

Vivian's brow furrowed, and she crumpled her nose at his audacity, shocked.

What in the actual fuck? she thought.

No one had ever taken her lunch choice away before. Not even as a child, her parents always let her make her own decision about what to eat at a restaurant. She barely knew this man. He had only been around her a handful of times, and he just ordered her food without so much as a glance in her direction for permission or compliance. She only invited him to go to lunch after the meeting because he seemed lonely, and she was trying to be nice.

Will nonchalantly took a sip of his water and set the glass down delicately on the table before finally noticing her expression.

"Did you just order for me?" She asked, her tone completely dumbfounded, laced with a hint of irritation.

His smirk hitched up the corner of his perfect mouth, "You just heard me order the food, Vivian."

She couldn't form words, "Wha, why... why would you order my food?"

Cocked head to the side, Will's smirk held firmly in place. "I don't understand your confusion. I've eaten here before, you have not. So, I know what's good." He shrugged his shoulders as if that explanation made perfect sense.

"You barely know me, Will. You don't know what I like or don't like. Even if we were married twenty years, you still wouldn't know what I wanted to eat *today*, right now."

He blinked at her, his composure held, looking ever so slightly unsteady. He paused, collecting himself, teeth clenched for a moment, as he swallowed hard. Will appeared almost pained as he smiled brilliantly. His voice a placating tone, "I apologize, I must simply have been raised in a different manner than you. I saw no harm in picking the meal."

Different manner?

"You grew up ordering food for people you didn't know?"

"No, Vivian, I grew up with people who appreciated when someone did them the favor of making sure they would have the best food on the menu." His eyes bore into hers. "I'll call the waiter over and cancel our order if you like. We can inconvenience the entire wait staff so that you may pick something sub-par for your selfish need to have what you want."

Whoa, how did this turn to me being selfish?

"That's not what I meant." His words twisted her meaning.

"So, you do want the food I ordered?"

"What? I don't understand how being weirded out that a near stranger ordered my food makes me selfish."

"I'm surprised someone as easily confused as you is even able to order food for herself." He laughed, dismissing her interpretation of the moment. "Honestly, I'm sorry if I offended you. Is it really that big of deal? I promise, you'll love what I ordered, it's the best food on the menu."

She was really confused now. Was she making a big deal out of nothing? He made her feel embarrassed for even bringing it up. "I guess it's not a big deal."

Triumph lit up his face. "See? Isn't it a relief to not have to worry over trivial things?"

Before she could respond, the waiter returned with the water. She watched as he filled her glass back up and assured them their food would be out shortly. Both medic veterans smiled brightly and thanked him as he walked away.

Vivian's eyes followed the waiter as he retreated, slowly moving attention back to her lunch companion. His were already on her.

"Near stranger?" He played with the words in his mouth as if they hurt him, "I know we only just met, but we're not strangers, you know that."

She couldn't think of a way to reply, so she broke away from his gaze and looked down at her own place setting. They both had the same blood on their hands. That's what he meant. She paused for a moment, thinking of how to reply.

"I do love asparagus. Not that you knew that."

"I assumed you would, actually."

"Oh please, there is no way you could assume that someone likes asparagus, it's not like a popular vegetable."

Her comment genuinely amused him, and she caught sight of his *real* smile. Not the fake one he used to disarm.

"A popular vegetable?" Will laughed, "What makes a vegetable popular?"

"You know, the normal veggies served at middle class American tables across the county. Corn, broccoli, peas. Asparagus isn't a popular pick," she shrugged.

"That's ridiculous. You're saying if I had ordered corn, it wouldn't have even been an issue because it's popular?"

"I'm just saying more people like corn than asparagus."

"Says who?" He laughed again. The sound was winsome.

She rolled her eyes, laughing out loud too. "That's not the point. How could you know I like asparagus is the question?"

"You've been to a lot of exotic countries," he shrugged. "Anyone who has experienced other cultures is usually more open to different flavors. I assumed that you're adventurous with your palate."

"Well, I guess we'll see, won't we." Vivian flashed him her grin in return.

"Enough, this vegetable discussion is silly."

"What would you rather discuss?"

"You're married. Your husband is okay with you going out on lunch dates with other men?"

Her hands clenched together under the table. "He doesn't care what I do anymore."

"Ahhh. Estranged husband then."

"You could say that. What about you? Are you married? Have a girlfriend?" *Subject changed.*

"I was married. We're divorced. I was living with a girl, though I got bored with her. She's smart, has a prestigious career, and makes an ostentatious amount of money." He rolled his eyes and said, "But she really started getting under my skin with what she felt she deserves."

"What does she feel she deserves?"

"Me." His smile dazzled again. "I have no interest in being her arm candy or allow her to call me her boyfriend and post pictures of the two of us smiling for all her friends to see. Wanting me to bring her flowers and beg her for her love, feel worshiped."

"Isn't that what most women want when they're in a relationship?"

"You tell me? Is that what you want?"

“No,” she answered instantly, “I would never expect anyone to see me as a prize they won.”

“Why not?”

“Because I know the truth of what I am. The horrible things I've done.” She looked up into his gaze, “Besides, I don't think I should expect anything more than someone is willing to give me.”

“What’s the most horrible thing you've ever done?” His words were as calm as if he were asking her favorite flavor of ice cream.

Vivian stared into his eyes, only to see unmeltable icebergs floating in the sea of hell's burning rivers.

He wasn't asking the question for the same reason civilians asked it. She could remember every time some asshole would ask her that question. People who never experienced war asked it for the same reason people slow down and hang their necks out the window to see a car accident. The horror and gruesome nature of war was something that entertained them, intrigued them, not something that invaded their brain and took over their soul.

When civilians asked her those questions, she always replied by informing them it wasn't okay to ask war veterans those questions. That didn't stop the truth from screaming behind her own eyes, though. Only Will was different.

He wasn't asking so he could rubberneck inside her memories from Hell. He had been there too.

This was just conversation, two medics saying out loud the moments that haunted them.

The waiter arrived with the food. “Here you are. Two plates and two meals. Can I get you anything else?”

“No, thank you.” Will's words, laced with irritation, interrupted her thoughts.

“Enjoy your meal!” The waiter quickly refilled the water glass before scurrying away.

"We'll resume this conversation another time." Will declared, "Let's enjoy our meal."

That smile lit up his face again. The bright one that felt like an Indian summer during the dead of winter when the sunshine feels warm on your cold face. When you walk out in your sweater, and put your face to the sky, craving its warmth because you've been so cold for so long and its warmth brings you happiness and comfort. Only, there's a part of you that knows it's not real summer, it's a façade. A trick, and when it's over, the winter you're trapped in will burn you with the bite of bitter cold for being so foolish.

"So, you came all the way from Washington state to live with this girl, and it didn't work. So now what?"

"No idea." He spoke with a mouth full of food.

"Well, where are you staying?"

"At the homeless shelter. I'm homeless now."

Vivian stopped midbite. "You're serious?"

"Unfortunately. Do you like the meal?"

"Yes, very much." She used the napkin to wipe her mouth. A worried furrow in her brow taking over her features. "Why didn't you just go to a hotel until you could find an apartment?"

Mid bite he answered her question. "I don't have enough money for a hotel or an apartment. Also I don't have any income and can't hold a job because of my mental state from the war." Will speared an asparagus, holding it on his fork but never taking his eyes from his lunch guest. "I guess six tours to Iraq and Afghanistan with over two hundred special ops missions contributing to the apprehension of over sixty high value targets will do that to man." Will snickered bitterly. "I knew you'd like it. Here," he held up the plate and moved it over to her, "Put the last of this on your plate."

Vivian held up her hand, “Oh, no, there is no way I can eat all that. I doubt I'll be able to finish everything already on my plate. Why aren't you receiving compensation from the VA?”

“Don't waste your food, Vivian. If you're not going to eat it, I'll have the waiter box it up for me to take for lunch tomorrow. Because I was dishonorably discharged, I can't receive anything from the VA, not even medical or mental services.”

“That's horseshit.”

Her anger surprised him. He laughed, “Usually I tell someone that I was kicked out of the army, and they immediately want to know what horrible thing I did to not deserve to get help.”

She shook her head. “No, there’s nothing you could have done that’s bad enough to exclude you from getting help to deal with the emotional trauma we experienced in war. Nothing.”

The waiter returned, interrupting them, and asked, “Should I box this up for you?”

“Yes, please.” Vivian responded and quickly took the check from his hand. “Today is on me.” She beamed her smile at the waiter while quickly handing over her card, not wanting to allow Will a chance to protest. When the waiter left, she dared to peek at Will and caught that already familiar smirk of genuine amusement on his face.

“You have a fake face too.”

Vivian rolled her eyes, focusing on putting her wallet back into her purse instead of looking at the grin on his perfect lips.

After signing the receipt, and gathering the boxes of leftover food, Will got up from his chair and moved around the table to pull hers out for her.

“Thank you.” She could barely get out the words loud enough to be audible, as his chivalry embarrassed her.

"You're blushing." He whispered, so close behind her that his breath tickled her neck. As they left, he held her elbow, leading her out.

"I'm not used to anyone guiding me in and out of rooms or pulling out my chair." She felt the tingle of his closeness up her spine. Almost forgetting what it felt like to shiver when a man stood close. It was something she'd forgotten how to respond to, something she had turned herself off from ever feeling again.

She had become blank, and still, frozen, as if sitting in the chill of a dull winter's day with snow and ice as her only companions. Just dead trees without leaves and freezing temperatures, as she sat in the snow with gray skies. Numb.

Finding comfort in the deep of winter, she was frozen in the snow, feeling nothing in the quiet alone, where no one speaks and no one sees, and no one knows.

Only now, Will entered into the room, and he could see her truth and feel the cold of her numb bones.

He marched in with heavy boots, straight into her snow. His hands pushed clouds apart, sending warm bright sunshine down onto her frozen face. His sun hit her body, and she wanted to close her eyes and just relish the moment of warmth, but she didn't dare.

His touch would warm, just like the brightness of his Indian Summer smile. Becoming only a single day sneaking into the wrong season, a small pleasure only passing through.

She knew that if she allowed herself to feel any of it, she'd wish for more.

He broke her silent mental dialog. "Men don't open doors for you? Hmmm. That's revolting for me to think about."

"Well, it's *revolting* for me to think about you being in a homeless shelter, and not getting compensation from the VA."

Vivian stopped on the street corner and turned to face him, her elbow still in his grasp. Her eyes wide and pleading with hope.

"Will, let me help you. I'm probably the biggest dork you'll ever meet. I read policies and find loopholes. I'm good at it. Let me go over your paperwork and see if I can find a way to get you benefits. Please?"

His large breath in made his chest feel closer to hers, when he looked down at her, assessing her intentions as she held his eyes waiting for a response.

"Why do you want to help me, Vivian?"

Her answer mattered. She knew he didn't want her pity. He wouldn't want her to help him because she thought she was better, or that she thought he needed her.

"You're my army brother. We stand by each other. It's just what we do."

It was a good reason. Will decided he liked her, though she annoyed him. But God, if he didn't like being around her.

"Okay. I'll take your offer and allow it."

"Oh good! Please let me get you a hotel room too. You shouldn't be in the homeless shelter." She did this odd little resemblance of a bounce, with radiance beaming from her eyes.

Was this Vivian happy?

Will paused. Her financial offer genuinely shocked him. "Why would you spend your money on me?"

"I have it, and you need it. That's it. I don't expect any of it back if that's what worries you," she shrugged.

"No one does anything for nothing." Will knew he didn't need the money, actually. Really, he was only in the homeless shelter for anonymity, but her offer of a hotel room was intriguing. He wondered about her intentions, if she was a rare genuine person, or better at hiding ulterior motives than most.

"It's not for nothing. I don't give a fuck about money, and I do give a fuck about your well-being." She shrugged again.

"You don't expect anything for helping me?"

"Nope."

"That's extremely naive of you," Will snickered.

"Then I'll be naive. You're in my path now, if you fall, I fall."

"You're ridiculous." He laughed, expecting her to defend herself with a mushy lecture on moral obligation and devotion, but instead Vivian laughed too.

"I guess I am, huh. Well, feel free to take advantage. I am a doormat for you to rest your feet." Her arms went out wide as she smiled in jest.

His eyes rolled in response, "You're embarrassing to be out in public with, that's what you are." Will pushed her arms down, the genuine smile back on his face. "You know what you get in return?"

"What?" she asked.

"The opportunity to look at my beautiful face and hang on my muscular arm." He winked down at her, smirk in place.

She laughed again, "Oh lucky me!"

"And I'm an Army *Ranger*. Did I say that yet?" he teased.

"Only about a hundred times since I met you." She weaved her arm through his, "Come on, hot ranger boy, let's get you a hotel."

They walked back to her car, arm in arm. He opened the driver-side door for her, helping her into her seat.

"Thank you." Her voice rang louder, with her gratitude this time.

He might need to make this his challenge. Getting Vivian comfortable with being taken care of.

"You're welcome." Closing her door gently, he walked over to the passenger side to get in. "The ex never said thank you when I did stuff like that. None of them did actually."

"Really? That's pretty fucked up."

"I think they just expected it. Expected that I have to earn them or something."

She shook her head as she drove, "I don't think two people who love each other should ever stop appreciating the little things. I'm sorry they stopped appreciating you."

"Naive Vivian." He chuckled, "They never began appreciating me."

"So why would you want a girl like that?"

"I have never dated a girl who wasn't drop dead gorgeous with a tiny little model's body."

"Of course." That seemed to make all the sense in the world to her.

"What does that mean?"

"Just you're all model perfection, so of course you would have a model perfection girlfriend. The two of you could probably have been in an Abercrombie and Finch ad together." She laughed, still looking at the road. "I guess only us plain, plump girls say thank you for chivalry."

"Plain, plump girls?" He looked over to assess her sitting in the driver's seat. Her hair was golden blonde with tiny hidden streaks of white. She had it pinned back into a bun at the base of her neck. Her skin was pale, but her features were appealing. She didn't airbrush her skin with makeup to erase all its flaws. He could tell she didn't have her eyebrows professionally waxed. They didn't point at the top like the stylish girls he usually noticed.

They should be shaped better.

He doubted very much they had ever been shaped at all.

But her eyes. Her eyes below those unshaped brows were strikingly beautiful. A piercing shade of blue that seemed gray when she was caught in a moment of thought that he could tell brought her mind somewhere sad. Her infinite eyes went deep down into her soul, and it helped that they were shaped nicely for her face. She didn't wear fake lashes. Their lavishness was natural, only delicately painted with mascara.

Probably bought from Walmart. He doubted she ever spent much money on herself.

Her nose fit her face, a nice European nose with a straight, angled slope, not overly big or too small, and her lips sat perfectly centered underneath. She didn't wear lipstick. Her natural lips had only a pale blush of faded pink to them. They weren't particularly luscious, but he had an undeniable urge to pull her lower lip in-between his teeth and bite down.

She was a pretty girl. He couldn't help but wonder what she looked like before the army got her. What her eyes would have looked like with the brightness of those who have never seen writhing men.

God, what it would feel like to crush the light out of those eyes.

Her forehead and eyes had wrinkles to show the worry, and pain, and happiness of her years. Not many, not enough to make her seem older than she was, but too many to ignore. For some reason, he liked that he could see her skin's imperfections. So different from all the flawlessly painted girls he usually gazed upon.

It made her real. He never wanted to see her all dolled up like the women he normally dated.

Her neck was slender, leading down to a defined collar bone and shoulder line. A long, slender scar wrapped down her throat, falling below her clothing. She didn't wear any jewelry, but he didn't think she needed it, and he liked that the dress she wore went up high on her chest.

She didn't show off her breasts to distract men.

They were defiantly plump! Round, large breasts that pulled the fabric taut as she sucked in every breath. Below them she had a small belly pooch that he could imagine made her feel fat and unattractive. Her hips were wide, and her ass round and big. Her thighs had meat on them too, giving her the hourglass shape that made her choice of a pencil dress perfect for her figure.

She probably looked in the mirror and saw every curve as an unattractive bulge, not realizing that men looked at her and saw the softness they could grab hold of, and rest on, lying next to in bed after a long and exhausting day.

She had a comforting beauty. The kind of beauty that made a man want to surprise her with hands plowed into her hair, holding her head in place, to plunge into her mouth, to own her.

Will felt the stir of an erection begin to throb in his tight jeans.

He could imagine her large breasts bouncing over him, doing the work to please him, wanting to give him pleasure, instead of expecting him to give it.

God, he needed to masturbate.

He tried to adjust the uncomfortable throbbing cock in his pants, shifting in his seat trying to shield her view.

Her golden hair would fall around her shoulders, all messy and out of place. Nothing about her would be perfect in that moment. She would be absolutely awry.

"You're not plain or plump," he proclaimed.

The returning protesting laugh annoyed him, "Oh, I'm *sure* I just turn you on with all my *not* plainness."

Her jesting mocking stopped with a gasp when he reached and grabbed her hand, pulling it over to feel his erect manhood.

"You do turn me on, Vivian. Don't put yourself down again."

She went awkwardly silent as Will threw her hand back over to her lap, irritated at her low self-esteem. "Change the subject," he snapped.

A moment of uncomfortable silence filled the car. He could hear the pantyhose slide as she clenched her thighs and moved around in her seat. She swallowed hard, and he smirked at the realization that he had her wanting.

Her voice pierced through his inappropriate thoughts, "What did you do to get dishonorably discharged?"

Well done, Vivian, he thought.

Controlling herself, asking the awkward question in the uncomfortable moment he created for her. He decided to be blunt and honest instead of the usual dance he made around the truth.

"Drugs. The nightmares were too much," he shrugged and spoke matter-of-factly. "I was terrified of sleeping, so I turned to meth. I could stay up for days and was still a stellar soldier. At that time, it seemed like my only option. You go crying about nightmares in the army and they treat you like a broke pussy ass bitch, you know that.... so it was either meth or swallowing a bullet."

He waited for her reply. The pause went on too long. Will found himself genuinely concerned about her reaction, about her response to his downfall.

"That's it?" She seemed almost disappointed.

"What do you mean 'that's it'?"

"What did you just tell me in the restaurant? You did six tours. You were on hundreds of special ops missions, personally responsible for the apprehension of over sixty high priority bad guys, and they fucking shunned you over drugs?"

Holy fuck, she gets it.

"Well, when you put it like *that*," he laughed.

"Don't laugh! It's not fucking funny." Her knuckles were white gripping the steering wheel, "They use us up, turning us into these emotionless 'machines of war' that have to do ruthless things to make our side the winning side, and then, when we come back all fucked up, and can't fit back into the mold of the suburban nine to five desk-job-working, fourth-of-fucking-July-burger-flipper, they turn their backs, and blame YOU for trying to deal with it on your own so you didn't swallow a bullet? Fuck them!"

"Fuck who exactly?" he asked calmly, trying hard not to laugh at her intensity.

"All of them! Every single fucker who benefited from your six tours. Every mother who gets to tuck her kids in bed all peaceful without worrying that the bad guys are going to come sneaking in our back door in the night. Every businessman who gets a fat paycheck for all the oil and imports and exports because the Middle East is now in our pocket. Every football lover whose biggest fear is their team losing the game on Sunday and having to face office teasing on Monday morning. Fuck them all!"

Will decided he enjoyed her all worked up.

"Boy, that's going to be a lot of fucking." His lips smirked up at the side as he watched her try not to laugh, her smile eventually breaking through as the intensity dissipated.

"Well, it just so happens," she glanced over at him, smirk tautly in place, "I was just recently informed that I am considered fuckable."

He shook his head, "God, you're so annoying." Laughing as he spoke.

"How can I be fuckable and annoying at the same time?"

"You're only fuckable when your mouth is shut."

They both laughed as she drove to pick up his belongings from the homeless shelter.

After loading his suitcases into the trunk, he hopped back in the car and she started driving towards the hotel.

"Where are we headed now?" he asked.

"I booked you a room for two weeks."

"You already booked it?"

"Yes, on my phone. I'll drop you off and then come by when you're settled. Maybe tomorrow? To look over your paperwork. You have it, don't you?"

"Of course I have it."

"Good, I was nervous you didn't." She peeked over at him, "The room is at the Days Inn. I know it's not the best, but they have free breakfast."

"The Days Inn is fine Vivian, honestly, I don't know why you would worry that I'd snub my nose up at it." He wished he could tell her he was only *not* in a hotel to hide any record of his presence.

"Well, you are a *Ranger*. I figure you snub your nose up to a lot of things."

He smirked to match hers. "Did I mention I was a Ranger? Or could you just tell by my amazingly good looks and killer toned body?"

"Oh, I think you mentioned it. You know, once or twice."

"Are you going to come up to the room?" He wondered what her answer would be, and then he wondered what he wanted her answer to be.

"No, I'm sure you want time to get settled and stuff."

"You're sure of that, are you?" Turns out it was 'yes.' He had wanted her answer to be yes.

He could tell the flat tone of his words caught her off guard. "Oh, did you want me to come up?" She sounded nervous.

"It would be nice to not have to make two trips. One with all my bags and the other for the leftovers." A sound reason to make her not nervous. For some reason, he didn't want her anxious around him.

"I didn't think of that. Of course, I'll help you carry your stuff."

The excuse had the desired effect. The car came to a stop outside the check-in office.

Fuck.

Did she put the name in his real name? "Is it in my name or yours?"

"Your name. That was an option on the website, a different name for check in than card holder. Do you need me to come in and help you?" Her sincerity was evident. It brought out the guilt in him, and was irritating. Now that his real name was recorded at the Days Inn down the road from his next planned kill made him downright angry.

"I'm not a child, Vivian." Using her for unnecessary help made him upset. Her untainted reasons for wanting to help him in the first place made him mad. That his name was now on record made him fucking angry. Worst of all, that he had wanted her to come up to his room, but she didn't, pissed him off most. He slammed the door.

Sitting waiting in the car for Will to return, Vivian looked out across the empty parking lot next to the hotel, trying not to wonder why he was suddenly so angry. Then she noticed a young mother pushing a stroller with a little baby towards the shopping center, holding the hand of a small toddler next to her. The little boy at her side had a head of dark brown curly hair that bounced as he walked.

It was such a normal thing to see, a mother with her children, yet the sight brought a deafening buzzing roar to Vivian's ears. The scene stirred memories, confusing her own realities behind her eyes. Vivian's neck ached and horrible guilt pierced through her chest. The mother and her child, they were walking alone. They were walking in the field.

Vivian's breath became heavy and the muscles in her arms and legs clenched with tension.

They were in danger. The parking lot was an uncleared minefield, and the mother was in shock because the child she walked with wasn't walking, he was dead in her arms. His dark brown curly hair blew in the wind, but he was still. The flashback allowed the stench of his rotting flesh and putrid seeping fluids to be carried on the wind after touching his brown, bouncing curly hair. She yelled to the woman to stop. She shouted for her to stop moving, that they would get her. But the words meant nothing, the minefield meant nothing, to live or to die meant nothing. The mother was dead already.

Slam

"Pull around to the side here and we'll take the stairs up."

She jumped back to the current reality she was in, with Will in her car. Her eyes closed as she contained her breathing. Will noticed the state she was in, confusion and concern flashed across his features. He brushed his fingertips against the back of Vivian's arm. *To what? Comfort her?*

"Are you all right? You look pale. What happened?"

"Nothing, it's nothing." She opened her eyes to watch the mother push the stroller across the empty parking lot with her brown curly haired American boy, alive and healthy. "I was just remembering something."

"What were you remembering, Vivian?"

"A boy I killed. A little baby." She followed the boy and his mother with her eyes as they walked towards the store. "She doesn't even know how lucky she is, does she?"

Will followed where her eyes led him to the mother with her children in the parking lot. "No, she does not."

"I'm sorry." Vivian took a deep breath and smiled. "That happens sometimes; I confuse realities and feel things I felt before."

"Did you kill a child?"

"A lot of them, actually. Not with a bullet, but they are dead by my hand, so yes."

"Is that why you don't have children?"

"No," she shook her head, her hand moving unconsciously to her abdomen. "I can't have any. I was wounded. I thought I told you?" *No uterus, no babies?* She shrugged her shoulders again. "So no children for me. Probably better that way."

"Why would you say it's better that way?"

"If I had my own, I'd constantly fear that horrible things would happen to them to punish me. You know, like why should I get to love something so beautiful without experiencing the crushing loss that I brought to so many?"

"It's not yours."

She looked over to him, confused. "What?"

"The death doesn't belong to you. You don't get to hold on to it and feel it every day you're alive. You were asked to do a job, and you did it. Would you change your decision? If you could go back to the same moment and make a different decision, would you?"

"No." Her answer was firm and instant. "No, the decision was the right decision."

"There were no good or bad choices, Viv, just the gray areas in between."

"Where did you say the room was?"

"I'm serious. No one else knows what it's like to have to make those choices. Only us. We were given permission to play God, to take lives and give life back as we saw fit. Rules of war are different from the rules of humanity, you know that. Maybe you didn't when you first got there, but I bet you learned *real* fast." He snickered, "You did a job, Vivian, a *job*, that's it. You didn't kill babies, you decided where to invest assets. If the child didn't have evidence of thriving, you didn't invest. It's as simple as that. Let it go. Now drive over there to the right and park on the end."

She didn't respond. She thought of his words. He was right that they were given permission to play God. Allowing soldiers to use their own judgment on who should die. If your judgment found that person to be a threat to the mission, you were justified to take their life.

Playing God.

But having that kind of power without owning it was dangerous. Life is too precious to become void of the guilt you carry for taking it away. That was the difference between the two of them.

Vivian would hold on to the lives inside her for the rest of her life. Their deaths belonged to her, and she would carry them. Will was wrong to be so distant from it. His detachment would crush whatever humanity he had left. Maybe that was why he traveled alone, jumped from superficial woman to superficial woman, and distanced himself from anyone he might love.

To feel anything deeply would make him feel everything deeply.

She wanted to tell him, take his hands and say, *I'm numb too! I don't feel because it's too much.* Instead, she unbuckled her seat belt and simply asked what he would like for her to carry up to the lonely hotel room he would live in for the next two weeks. Who knows, maybe she was the wrong one.

With his backpack on and the leftovers in her hands, she followed him up the stairs. Will opened the door, and they both stepped into the dark hotel room. It was okay, clean, a little outdated, but nice enough. She walked over to the desk and put the leftovers down before removing the backpack to set it carefully on the chair. Opening the mini fridge, she moved the food to the middle shelf and shut the refrigerator door. Standing up straight, she noticed him leaning against the wall, watching her intently.

"What?" she asked as he stared at her.

"How tall are you?"

"Five-feet-four. Why?"

"That's all? You seem taller when you move about somehow." He turned his body, so his back was up against the edge of the wall that stuck out. "I like watching you make yourself useful without being asked. It's refreshing." He slid himself vertically up and down the wall edge, trying to relieve the itch in his back.

"Well come here, let me make myself useful since it amuses you." She moved towards him casually, "I'll scratch your back before I go."

Without hesitation, Will turned his back to her, and her skin sliding up his shirt made him jump. He hadn't expected her hands on his bare back He never thought she would be so bold. Then again, she was practical to a fault, and it didn't make sense to scratch someone's back over their clothing. Before she could protest, he pulled the shirt over his head and laid belly down on the floor at her feet.

"Never look a gift horse in the mouth." He mumbled from the side of his mouth on the carpet.

She knelt beside him, careful to tuck her legs to the side with her dress covering as much of them as she could.

"I never understood that saying." He moaned with pleasure as her fingernails dragged over his shoulder blades. Both hands across the top of his back, scratching his skin as they moved.

After a few strokes, his eyes closed and Vivian couldn't help but notice how vulnerable he looked laying there without his shirt, face down on the carpet, beneath her hands. He either trusted her already, or he was so sure of his tactical skills that he wasn't concerned in the slightest that she could hurt him even if she wanted to.

She moved her hands down to itch along the sides and he clenched his stomach up tight, laughter bursting out from deep down in his chest.

Vivian froze, a smile creeping up the side of her mouth.

"Did that tickle?" She teased before doing the same motion again.

"What a stupid thing to ask!" The uncensored laugh broke out again.

His jerking movements continued as Vivian drug her nails up and down his sides, causing him to laugh out loud like a child, but he did nothing to stop her. His laughter infecting her with laughter, as they both let out sounds that had been hidden from their own ears for some time.

In her professional black dress and pantyhose, she kept up with his clenching and rolling, tickling his back with her nails as they bellowed out unrestrained laughter into the stillness of the lonely, outdated hotel room.

Wisps of her hair fell from the constraints of the bun she controlled it in. He felt them dance along his naked skin. The sensation of their caress brought him back to the realization that he should be in control of himself.

Where had this come from?

Regaining composure, Will flexed his abs and flipped abruptly over onto his back, catching Vivian by her wrists as she fell over him with the quick, unexpected motion.

She looked disheveled. Younger somehow. Her blue eyes were so bright, shining from inside her in a way they hadn't before.

From where? he wondered. *Where was this hidden place she locked her brightness up in? How did he get to be there with her?*

They both caught their breath from laughing and he watched as the brightness retreated, watched as she closed him off from that place deep inside that she protected. *Did she protect it from everyone? Or just against men like him.*

"It's teeth." he said, "Something about the way they grow, or change with age. Looking in the mouth lets the farmer know how old they are."

"What?" Vivian pulled her brow into that little confused furrow he was coming to recognize on her face when she was thinking too hard.

"The gift horse. You should just be grateful to get a free horse regardless of its age." He pushed her ever so gently until she sat back on her heels, allowing him to right himself to a sitting postilion.

"Huh, how do you know that?" She sounded embarrassed by their tickle session.

"I'm not sure, really. I know a lot of things." Will jumped fluidly to his feet, drastically shifting to a seductive persona to fuel her flustered state. "Would you like me to show you some of them?" He held his hands out to offer her assistance in standing.

"Don't do that." She put both her hands into his without a second thought as he pulled her to her feet.

As soon as Vivian was standing, she retracted her hands and used them to straighten the fabric down the front of her dress.

"Don't do what?" He questioned, walking over to grab a bottle of water from his bag.

Will's eyes stayed on her as she walked to the long mirror on the wall. She leaned into her reflection, forcing the free wisps of hair back into the conformity of her control.

He thought of her for a moment, imagining her hair down, walking barefoot down a beach with the wind lifting the golden strands making them dance in the salty air all around her head as she moved. Through the curtain of gold, he would see glimpses of the habitual smile she wore without effort as she strolled next to the ocean waves. With her flowing dress floating around her to the same dance on the wind that the golden hair twirled to. Her toes would squish down in the wet sand with each step, leaving only a delicate little footprint behind to wash away with the tide. She would laugh and twirl as she jumped over the small bursts of cool ocean water that trickled up far enough to kiss her skin. Her flowy dress would be gathered up in her arms as she ventured further out into the salty blue water.

But she didn't wear a dress. It was a uniform.

Vivian's hair was contained. Every strand was trapped to her head securely as she stepped heavy on the sand in booted feet that ran in frantic pursuit of the agonizing screams that cascaded across the wind. Her smile was wrested into a pursed, chapped line of vexation. Lips disuniting only to articulate the intake and output of the hot, still, dry, air desperately needed for her heaving lungs. The tan and brown uniform designed for the masculine muscle structure lay at the wrong places on her body. Elbow padding on forearms and knee padding on shins. The unprotected skin underneath painted in bruises displayed in hues of sapphire, sable, and plum. Salt from the perspiration dripping down her face, would dampen her lips as she stomped her heavy permanent boot prints into the dry hot sand next to his...

"Patronize me. I'm not drop dead gorgeous. I don't have a tiny little model's body. And I know you don't *want* me."

Will snapped himself back to the hotel room, with Vivian in the black dress and ugly shoes.

"Good to know you listen when I talk to you. That's the second time you've recalled something I said to you earlier in the day." He took another swig of water.

However, I told you I only dated girls who were drop dead gorgeous with tiny model's bodies. I never said anything about who I fuck.

He decided to keep the mental observation to himself. Better to prevent the blush from crawling up her cheeks. It might fluster her enough to make her leave, and strangely, he didn't want her to leave.

Will chuckled to himself at the thought that he liked her, and actually enjoyed being around her.

He didn't want to fuck her and then have her too embarrassed to call him back. Or worse, getting thoughts of love and romance. "Can you come by tomorrow to go over my paperwork?"

Can I take you to the beach to walk barefoot on the sand?

"Sure." She pulled her shoulders back straighter, her head higher. "Or I could just bring your paperwork home with me."

"No. I don't trust my important documentation to be out of my line of sight. No offense." The bright, placating smile lit up his face.

"Well, you have my number." Her words, dismissive and swift, were accompanied by pursed lips and averted eyes. Vivian then whisked across the small space towards the desk to retrieve her car keys.

"Are you irritated with me?"

Will's smirk held firmly, awaiting her response. He knew his long stride and strong grasp could have her contained in a heartbeat. If he truly decided he didn't want her to leave, well, then Vivian was simply not leaving. He wanted to know what brought on such a drastic drop of spirit in the space of but a few words, and by God, she would tell him.

"Yes," Her chin went higher, eyes straight into his, "you lied to me *and* questioned my integrity."

What audacious bravery. Well done, Vivian! And all on her own.

"What!? When did I lie to you?" *Oh, but this was enjoyable.*

"You told me in the car I was fuckable, and then retracted your opinion. Right before accusing me of being shady enough to steal your paperwork." She held up her hand "I'm not arguing. Call me tomorrow and I'll come back."

Drawing in a deep breath, he let her move past him toward the door. He didn't want her to go. Will wanted to keep her, but for what? Companionship? What did he want with this little wounded bird?

She pulled down the handle of the door, but Will's hand slammed above hers, pushing the door closed under his weight. Vivian gasped as he spun her around, pinning her up against the hard wood.

The gasp from her lips brought delight to Will's senses when the prick of shock and the briefest twinge of fear skittered across her features. Would her eyes dance with excitement or fear if he wrapped her throat up in his grip? Or would she wiggle like a little worm, slowly pierced by the hook of a fisherman's line? Of that, he was certain. He was also completely sure that her head would mush like an apple if he smashed it hard enough against the wooden door. With each bashing, her wiggle would slow, same as the wiggle of the worm as it sinks to the bottom of the lake tethered to the hook on the line.

What he wasn't sure of though, what he couldn't chance, was that her eyes would not dance but instead scream gratitude for being at the bottom of the lake as a lifeless worm on the fisherman's hook.

Reaching beyond her throat, he grabbed the ponytail holder that held the controlled bun instead. Without taking his eyes from hers, he savagely ripped it from around her golden hair. Vivian winced, an audible escape of air releasing from her surprised lips, hands instinctively rising. To what? Protect herself?

Smoothing the golden strains into submission around her face, Will leaned down into her. His lips a whisper above hers so she could feel the heat of his breath on her mouth.

"Don't wear your hair up tomorrow, Vivian."

With a quick peck on cheek, he stepped back, opening the door wide as he did.

Flustered, she moved through it without a word in return. He listened as her ugly wedge heels clicked on the concrete down the outdoor staircase.

Will stayed in the doorway, playing with the hair tie pulled from her golden locks in his fingers. The elasticity was her control. The need to bend it and contort what she believed it to be tingled across his skin. He could bind her up, to give her the control that she didn't need to wield herself.

Control these thoughts, his mind cautioned him.

He needed to hold life in his hands, but not hers.

Chapter 3

The List

As soon as he watched Vivian swoop down into her driver's seat, he shut the hotel room door and went to his backpack to retrieve his *other* cell phone. The one he used for his special girls.

She answered on the second ring.

"Hey babe, why don't you come pick me up. I miss your beautiful face."

The voice on the other line giggled with an annoyance that permeated under his skin. He felt his fist clench at his side. She agreed quickly, and he gave her the address of the fancy Sheraton he had spotted on the drive to the Days Inn. As soon as they hung up, he jumped in the shower to freshen up, and then put his clothes on and got his backpack ready for the night.

"Serena, Serena." He said her name, playing around with how it sounded coming off his tongue. She had been an internet find. Flawless and beautiful. Every picture she posted showed her skin bronzed shining in the sun. Her lips were always perfectly painted, plump and made to look ripe for sucking on. He researched her family, rich and mostly absent from her existence. She lived in a luxury apartment in a nearby city.

After the first few conversations, he realized that she found fault with everyone who did anything for her. Refused to pump her own gas. Refused to open her own door. Was proud to tell the world that she was entitled and was to being taken care of.

She was perfect for his next girl.

He tried to find some redeeming quality. Something that made her worth all he had done for her by going to war.

He asked her so many questions, gave her so many opportunities to show him even the tiniest glimmer of empathy and respect for others. He always tried to find a reason to let them live. Hell, one of them he let live because she loved animals so selflessly. She'd go volunteer at the animal shelter with those fancy nails petting gross flea infested, ungroomed, unwanted dogs and cats.

A redemptive quality to make it worth it. That's all he was looking for, one single redeeming quality. *What was her name? Carla or Carleen?*

He couldn't remember, but she didn't die because she washed unwanted dogs on the weekends.

Serena wouldn't touch a dog in need, she wouldn't touch a human in need either. For her entitlement, Will had come to this town to kill Serena.

He had been living in Louisiana before this with the ostentatious money maker he told Vivian about. Well, former ostentation money maker. Will ruined that for her.

Through his fake dating account, Serena invited him to come up for a wild night of drinking and sex. She very explicitly detailed what she wanted to do to him sexually and what she would allow him to do to her body for his pleasure. Even sent him money for the trip. When he first got to town, they met up for an amazing night out. He had decided to stay at the homeless shelter, under an alias, to plan her murder. He was simply going to meet up with her at a hotel, kill her, harvest her for his new vase, dispose of her, and move on.

Only when he got to Pennsylvania, he saw a flyer for the medics and corpsmen group meeting with a free meal. It intrigued him, because he wanted to be around others like him, eat a free meal among veterans.

He had walked to the meeting from the shelter, and there *she* was, blue eyes worn down of their shine, Vivian.

She rested her eyes on him for only half a second, not a smirk or an enticing smile, not even a head nod of acknowledgment.

Her eyes brushed his and immediately moved along.

But Will's eyes lingered on her, watching her movements, her facial expressions. He caught sight of a scar wrapping up around her neck, sneaking out of her shirt. Something in him wanted that scar to be his hands, wrapped around her throat.

But not to hurt her.

To hold her. The same way the scar held her.

The scar owned her, and he needed to know who put it there. He had to ask her where it came from, how it ended up for the rest of her life decorating her pale neck with its sharp edge.

When she made her way over to the coffee bar, he followed. He watched her pour coffee into a mug. Then she added only cream, no sugar, and stirred the hell out it. Looking for a place to dispose of her wooden stirrer she looked up, noticing him there and smiled. "Would you like some coffee?"

Abandoning her own first sip of hot coffee, she reached for a second mug before he could respond.

She didn't know his name, nor did she offer up hers. She just figured he had walked up for coffee, and she'd get it for him. To be what, kind, hospitable, flirtatious?

"How do you take it?"

"I'm sorry? What?" That was the first thing he said to her. A ridiculous question.

"Your coffee. How do you take your coffee?" A bottomless compassion flowed out of her naturally.

She was being genuine. What a conundrum of sorts.

He quickly gathered himself. "Sugar and cream please," beaming his disarming smile at her, but she simply set about making his coffee without any response.

Looking at her face, he knew she had to still be in her early thirties, but her soul was aged and exhausted. No doubt a repercussion of how much of herself she gave up accomplishing even the smallest of achievements for others. Even making this cup of coffee for him held every ounce of her attention. Her mind was completely focused on this small, mediocre task. Meanwhile her own coffee was abandoned, growing cold. *What would it be like to have that attention focused on me?*

He had been so distracted by his attraction to this simply dressed ordinary looking woman with the scar that he didn't realize he stood too close to her at the table. She looked up gently to whisper, "excuse me" before leaning across him to grab packets of sugar. As her movements stirred the air around him, he smelled vanilla and chocolate from her skin. It made him smile inside. *How does she smell of both vanilla and chocolate?*

He decided that maybe he could extend his time here a little bit. It was dangerous, making himself more known in the area, meeting people who could recognize him, but it seemed worth it to find out about the scar on the neck of the woman who now handed him a cup of coffee.

Never mind that it had been three weeks now, and he had yet to ask her about the scar. Almost as if asking her about it and finally getting the answer would leave him with no reason to want to be around her.

He came up with so many scenarios in his head. Did an ex-boyfriend do it in a fit of rage? Was she held hostage by bank robbers who held a knife to her throat as the swat team shot them dead? Maybe her father was abusive to her as a child and burned her with acid? The possibilities seemed endless, and endlessly intriguing. Practically, knowing he met her at a medic's group, it was most likely simply a military injury. He had scars himself that lacked intrigue. Yet this scar, on this woman. He couldn't keep it from appearing behind his eyes when he closed them.

It was time, though. He felt the urge bellowing up from his gut, overflowing his senses. There was no way he could be around Vivian while having the uncontrollable urge to hold and control life in his hands.

This recent encounter with Vivian at the door made that apparent, as she didn't deserve his wrath. He had to get it out of his system if they were to get to know each other, become friends. God, he hadn't had a real friend in so long.

Serena would scratch the itch. He would walk down to the Sheraton and have her pick him up. They could drive to the city and he'd convince her to get a hotel room with a balcony that overlooked the river.

He grabbed his sunglasses and put the backpack on before heading out the hotel room door. The same door Vivian had just hurried out of all flustered. The thought made him smirk. He affected her more than she let on, he knew he did.

"Focus now, Will, no mistakes."

Chapter 4

Two Army Medic Veterans at the Days Inn

It was a cold, rainy morning. The drive over made her shiver, she never waited for the car to warm up before just driving off. It used to make her husband insane. Her body couldn't handle the extremes anymore. The extreme cold shook her, and the extreme heat depleted her. It always used to worry him. She wished it had worried him enough to make him stay.

Her hands were frozen on the steering wheel and she swore under her breath for just getting in the car to head over to Will without receiving confirmation that he knew she was coming. Though she had tried calling him, his phone didn't even ring, just went straight to voicemail. She wondered if he forgot his charger and the phone died in the night. Or she worried that maybe he needed something and had no way to reach out. There was no way he knew her phone number by heart, and if his phone were dead, well, how would he reach her?

At ten-thirty a.m. she decided to drive over, knock on the door, and pretend like she thought they had agreed on eleven as their time to meet to do paperwork.

Now that she had pulled into the parking spot, she couldn't help but feel stupid. Maybe he turned his phone off on purpose. Maybe he really didn't want her to come and was politely blowing her off by not calling her.

Turning the keys to shut off the car, she sat in the stillness for a few moments. With the motor silenced, she could hear the normal buzzing sounds of life going on around her. Over the dull drum of traffic on the main road, she heard a bird singing a solitary wintery tune from high on a tree branch.

She wondered how the birds stayed warm enough to still find the motivation to sing from the treetops during the winter. Where did they live? How did they find food with the ground frozen and the bushes all bare? Were these birds so domesticated from the bird feeders hung in backyards and front porches they stayed to fare the frigid temperatures and snow simply on faith and trust in humans feeding them?

Her head fell against the back of her seat and she closed her eyes, listening to the lone bird singing above the parking lot.

God, she was tired. Sleeping had not been an option for her last night. Nightmares ripped her from sleep over and over.

Sometimes the nightmares were senseless panic, others were reliving real life over again behind closed eyelids. Some nights, it was a mix of her current reality and old realities of war. Those were the worst, waking up confused, wondering if what you just dreamed about was real or not.

With her head resting back against the seat and her eyes shut, she fell asleep. With the car off, in a Pennsylvania winter, listening to the bird's song in the Days Inn parking lot, all alone she drifted off.

Vivian swore she had only closed her eyes for a moment when she was startled awake.

A pounding noise woke her, and she jumped up in the seat.

"Open the fucking door!"

Will was screaming at her car window, pounding on it as hard as he could.

Her muscles were clenched, and her lips were shivering. As she pressed the unlock button on the car door, her hands shook.

He yanked it open immediately. "I thought you were dead." His hands reached over and released her seatbelt. As soon as it was unlatched, Will was pulling her up into his arms.

"My god you're frozen," his hands rubbed up and down her frame. "Come. Upstairs now." Pulling her into his chest, his hands slid along her back, leading her where he wanted her to go.

Vivian complied without protest.

She moved with him as he held her close to his warm, strong body.

When they entered the hotel room, he ushered her into the bathroom and the heavy wooden door banged shut behind them. The sudden noise made her shoulders hunch forward, startled.

"You're not awake yet, are you? Allowing your reflexes to overpower your rational thought." He shrugged, "Happens to the best of us sometimes."

"I can't believe I did that." Vivian spoke through her shivering lips. Her body wouldn't stop shaking.

"We'll get you warm." Will reached in to turn on the shower.

"I'm not getting in the shower. I don't need to be bathed, I'm just cold."

"I didn't think you'd allow it. Although I shouldn't care about your compliance. Falling asleep in a cold car in an empty hotel parking lot screams you are incapable of making sound choices for your own wellbeing and asserts that maybe I should just make them for you." The hot steam filled the small space. "The steam will warm you and I'll make some hotel room tea for you to drink."

He opened the door just wide enough to go out and exited quickly.

With his fists clenched at his sides, he wanted to punch through the wall. He was furious. *How could she be so careless?*

Will ripped the plastic off the hotel room cup and filled it with water, pouring it into the coffee pot. What would have happened if he hadn't been just coming back? If he hadn't spotted her car?

He allowed one fist to slam into the wall. *I still have blood on my hands, for fuck's sake!*

Serena had been a fun divergence the night before. She died well, on the balcony overlooking the city, just as he had planned. He held his hands over her mouth and nose, forcing her to watch the city below them as he smothered the life from her body.

It was the first time he had decided to use that death tactic and was surprised by how long it takes a person to expire from asphyxiation. She was such a tiny thing; it was incredibly easy to just hold the back of her head to his chest as he smothered her breathing holes shut. But by god it took a long time. She struggled, of course, that was to be expected, but she had to have been anorexic or bulimic for sure, barely weighed anything and showed little force behind her protest of being murdered.

She barely ate anything at dinner either, mainly pushed food around on her plate. Maybe most men didn't notice such things, but Will did. Almost made him feel pity for her, but then the busboy dropped a plate nearby and she spoke out in disgust for the incompetence of the brown people and their invasion of white America for a solid twenty minutes. He didn't even want sexual gratification from her after listening to her spew racial hate speech out of her pie hole for an entire evening.

As soon as they walked into the hotel suite, he suggested music. With techno music playing loudly from his iPod, he ushered her gently to the balcony in order to see the sites of the city below and then to feel her life leave under his hands.

The last words she heard were his hopeful declaration that the garbage men, who would throw her into the dump, after he cut her pretty little body into pieces, were all *brown*.

Cutting her up was a lot easier than the others, seemed like less blood from such a small structure. He found it disappointing. Her poor heart looked damaged under her ribs. She had abused her organs, pushed them to extremes to maintain a slender image and to seek fun above all else. Although damaged, he packaged the heart and liver in a freezer bag full of Epsom salts carried in his backpack, cuddled next to his precious military discharge paperwork.

He would need to shop for a new vase. He had seen a photograph of a human heart on display in a museum that was pure white after having been drained of all blood. Will had wanted desperately to experiment with this idea for Serena's heart, but he didn't want to waste such a perfect specimen. Also, he would need to wait until he could obtain a permanent residence. It would be foolish to attempt such a challenge using something so precious without a workstation and proper research. So, for now, a delicate vase would need to suffice for both of them.

Will had a knack for finding pretty ones at thrift stores. He would search out the perfect one to fill up with Serena's organs, a reward to them for their refusal to die for so many years, even as she poisoned them.

He had cleaned the hotel room meticulously, bagged up every bit of evidence, but noticed after depositing the last of the triple bagged black garbage bags around the city that he had neglected to get some of her blood from around the nail on his right hand. He held the contaminated finger out straight, to remind himself to clean it immediately after getting back to the room. When glancing over, he saw a young woman with the same golden straw-colored hair as Vivian. Her head was limply hanging against the headrest of her car in the frigid parking lot. After his eyes registered that it *was* Vivian, he abandoned all obsessive attention for his bloodied fingernail. Then his need for self-preservation was replaced with an immense and overbearing rush to save her life.

An unpleasant conundrum. He would need to examine in himself.

Later

In this moment, he only needed to get Vivian warm.

After the foam cup filled, he poured a sugar packet in the hot tea water and swirled it gently around before slipping through the smallest crack in the door to avoid cold air contamination. The small room had filled up nicely in the short time he had stepped out. He found her in the cloud of steam leaning against the wall, moving her fingers to get the sluggish blood flowing.

Will extended the cup. "Drink this."

Vivian wouldn't meet his eyes with hers. But thanked him for the cup quietly and obeyed him by bringing the cup instantly to her lips to take a sip.

Was she embarrassed?

He watched her nose twitch in surprise as her tongue first touched the tea.

"Too hot?"

"Oh, no it's fine, thank you." She took in another sip with less surprise, but her nose twitched in that funny way again as she drank. He wanted to see her eyes, to make sure she was alert and not groggy, to ensure she didn't have any effects from hypothermia. Her eyes still evaded him. The cup went to her lips once more and her nose again twitched.

"Why are you doing that?"

"Doing what?" She answered his question with a question.

Her face was intensely focused on her hands. Her eyes still staring at the cup she held, were fixated on the liquid that for whatever reason made her face twitch when she drank it.

Annoyed, Will reached out to tip her chin up so her eyes were forced to meet his.

"Scrunching up your nose when you take sips."

"It's just a little sweet, but it's warm and I need it, because I was stupid."

"No sugar in your tea either?"

"Will, I... I'm sorry. I didn't mean to scare you, to make you panic like that." Vivian's eyes bore into his now with sincerity elusive to him when looking into the gaze of most people. "I know how situations like *this* make us," she paused, "off."

Her lips began to shiver again, and her muscles tightened up. "I was foolish and stupid, and made you suffer."

Her eyes were the palest of blue against her light skin, and her golden hair looked so bright around her face. Her lips faintly painted with a natural tinge of pink. He wanted to taste them, to put them between his teeth and taste her gasp of surprise as it rushed out from her mouth into his. He could stop her shiver with the warmth of his tongue swirling around inside her mouth as her breathing increased, and she melted against him for comfort and warmth. Instead, he noticed her put her arms tight against her own body.

"That's it." With a swift movement, he pulled his own shirt over his head. Then leaned over to feel the water coming out of the shower head with his hand. "It's hot but not scalding. Come."

Vivian stood frozen to the wall, trembling all over from the cold. "I'm fine, really."

He pulled his feet out of his shoes and peeled his socks off. Then unbuttoned his pants to shed them.

"Will," she shivered, wanting to protest his stripping in front of her, but he gave her no chance to finish. Reaching forward, he pulled her by both wrists against him and began taking off her clothes.

"It's not practical, but since you're embarrassed about your body, we'll shower in our underwear. Bathing suits are no different, Vivvie." He chastised her for modesty while he undressed her in his boxer-briefs as they stood in the hot steam-filled bathroom.

Vivvie? She was Vivvie now, huh?

He unbuttoned her jeans and wiggled them down over her hips before bending to remove each old scuffed-up boot. Were all her shoes horrible and old? If she were his, the very first thing he would do was take her shoe shopping at an actual shoe store. Not the bargain basement of some second-hand charity event.

Her feet were frozen underneath her socks, and even with the icy skin under her clothing, she still let out an annoyed huff before he managed to pull the jeans completely off.

"Easy for you to say. You are like Jacques-Louis David standing there while I am a Botero model."

Will paused in the middle of peeling off her shirt, her face stuck in the blue cotton fabric that he was pulling over her head. An impetuous boisterous laugh escaped his chest loudly, "Wait? Jacques-Louis David, the *painter*?" He removed the garment from her head so he could look down into her pale blue eyes. "You think I look like a famous piece of art?"

Saying he was impressed at her knowledge of famous art was an understatement. Finding a woman with an equal level of art knowledge and love was a rare thing. Jacques-Louis David created such stunning paintings, hung in all Will's favorite art galleries, but the painter's name was not well known. Botero's art, however, with chubby cartoon like humans never struck Will's particular fancy.

An art worthy smile lit up his stern face, white teeth perfectly in a row, gleaming down at her.

"No," she shivered, "Him, the painter himself, he was said to be excessively attractive."

Will pulled her tightly into his arms.

"Oh." She was surprised at the effortless manner he hiked her up over the edge of the bathtub.

Her audible response to his strength made him chuckle, until the hot water shocked her cold body, and then a small yelp escaped her.

Will was around her in a heartbeat, wrapping his body around hers, shielding her from the hot water but allowing it to gently cascade off his skin onto hers. Instantly she succumbed to his immediate comfort, resting her head against his chest, allowing the water and his hands to soothe her.

"I'm excessively attractive, huh?" No doubt she could feel his smile against the top of her hair as they stood holding each other in the shower. "And you pick Jacques-Louis David, a dead artist from Napoleon days, so a *really* dead artist to describe me." He laughed again, a real laugh that made his chest rumble beneath her cheek.

"He just popped into my mind."

"Oh, but I do enjoy you." He chuckled so hard that his arms clenched around her, holding her tighter still. "Not Brad Pitt, or even old man Sean Connery, or any desirable man from the last oh, I don't know, hundred years or so."

Vivian laughed with him. "You look like him."

"You're serious?" He laughed harder, his chest moving with joy in a way he couldn't remember. *Yes, he could.* Just the other night before, she made him laugh this authentically, and she seemed to be making laughter a habit.

"I can't breathe. Oh, shit, Vivvie, you're too much." Will took a deep, steadying breath. "Oh... fuck... it's worth your scare for this, you know." His hands rubbed up and down her skin and he felt a rush of desire to press her up against the wall of the shower, thrust himself into her and make his home inside this body... *Where did that thought come from?*

"How do you even know what he looks like?" Will worked to collect himself, waiting for her answer, pushing away thoughts of being inside her. He didn't want to lose interest in her yet and he sure as hell didn't trust himself not to kill her. So far, his world was better with her in it.

With Vivian's face pressed so firmly to his chest, he could feel her smile against his skin as she admitted to being the true dork she was, "I love art and history. The books all say he was an intense and attractive man. He was involved in the French revolution, so he must have been brave. He refused to sit idly by in the face of injustice. Though he didn't have to be involved in the revolution, he was. I respect that, which makes him attractive in my mind already. Plus, he had a passion for art and beauty, and had a fierceness in his eyes. I saw a self-portrait." She shrugged, "I don't know why he is who popped in my mind, but there you are."

"Jacques-Louis David. Best compliment I've ever received in my life. Thank you, Vivian." He kissed the top of her head. "Warmer?"

"Yes, very much. Thank you. For getting me out of the car and for forcing me into the shower." She tried to drop her arms from him, but he tightened his grasp and held her securely.

"We're not ready to get out yet." He commanded without room for her opinion on the matter. "I don't understand it really myself, but this feels too good to end."

"I need to wipe my face. My makeup is ruined."

Will gently tried to pull her face up. "Let me see."

"No!" She tucked it down firmer to hide from him. "I don't want you seeing me with makeup smeared down my face."

His large killer's hands gripped her chin, "Let me see. You have no idea how important this is to me."

"You can't just man-handle me into making me do what you want, Will. Stop."

"Oh, but I can. See, I'm doing it right now." He turned her face to him. Streaks of mascara were running down her cheeks. Vivian brought her other arm up to attempt to move his hand off her face, but he was there, grabbing her by the wrist. "Shhh. Viv, I'm just looking. I've never seen a woman this disheveled before. With makeup I mean. The girls I'm with are so fake, so plastic. They never smear. It's maddening to me."

"I want to get out of the shower now." Vivian was not pleased with him forcing her to do anything.

Well, she was going to need to get used to *that*.

Will gazed down at her face. The black paint drizzled down from her eyes like blood crying from the eyes of the Madonna statue in a catholic church. He wanted to wipe it off her face, to scrub down to her real eyes and her real face, to see her without the crying blood covering her. His brow furrowed as he used his thumb to try and rub the paint away, but it only smudged it across her cheek.

Will let go of her wrist and reached for the washcloth hanging on the drying bar. He wiped the paint away and was relieved as it transferred off her skin onto the cloth. As the makeup disappeared and her facial lines showed from beneath, he felt his mouth curl at the corner. When he saw the first imperfection, his breath hitched. God, but her beautiful eyes had tiny little lines at the crease, and between her eyebrows there sat a little scar.

He touched it with this finger. "This?" he asked her.

"Chicken Pox, when I was twelve."

He washed the makeup from her chin and neck. Without the concealer, her scar was wicked and angry looking wrapping around her throat. It weaved down her chest and disappeared under the wet fabric of her bra. He touched his fingers to the mangled skin and felt her tense all over.

"Does it hurt?"

Looking off beyond his face, her answer was but a whisper, "Always."

Will stilled his fingers where they lay lightly over her scar. He wanted to ask her more. How she got it, how it hurt. Did it hurt her physically or was she describing the same burning that always lived under his skin, too? Those would need to wait for another day. The water began feeling chilled on his neck.

"The water is going cold. Come. We can't have you getting chilly again. Thank you for letting me see you."

"I didn't let you. You stole it."

He placed a kiss on her forehead. "I know it wasn't the worst thing anyone has ever stolen from you. I doubt it will even be the worst I'll ever steal."

She looked confused but did not object, and that small little concession had him laughing yet again. "Come on pretty, Vivvie, let's go get you under my covers and we'll tackle the paperwork while your bra and undies dry."

He turned off the shower before hopping out to get a towel for Vivian. She tried hiding behind the curtain so he wouldn't see her body without clothes. Up until this point, he had held her so close she knew he wouldn't have been able to see the full extent of her scars or her curves. She had never been thin, but by no means would she consider herself fat, and although she knew most men enjoined her curves, Will's perfection made her embarrassed to show him her imperfect body.

"Stop acting like a child, Vivian. We are not only both adults, we were both medics. A body is just a body." He chastised her while he held the towel open for her to climb into.

Hesitantly, her hand pushed the curtain aside, then quickly retreated to join the other in front of her stomach, a slight protection from his stare. Vivian stepped out of the bathtub. She paid close attention to his reaction as his eyes registered the mangle of scarred flesh ripping across her belly. She sometimes looked at herself in the mirror and studied them. The small horizontal surgical incision scars ran in contrast to the long, jagged ugly scars where the metal had ripped her open. Her flesh around them had become rippled and grotesque.

The scars were an array of colors, purple and crimson and white, some slate, some smooth, some upraised, and each one of them still had the nerve tinges that drove her near insanity when she moved too suddenly or stretched too far. Will's face gave nothing away. She would have almost thought he had no reaction at all to the vision of her trauma standing before him if not for the hard-swallowed lump she noticed work down his throat as she approached. She waited for the question burning on his tongue. *What happened to you?* But his words were different.

"Take off your wet stuff under the towel and I'll get you a t-shirt to wear while it dries. You're short enough, everything will be covered." Without mention of her scars at all, he left her standing in the bathroom wrapped in a towel.

Will escaped out of the bathroom, murderous rage bubbling in his blood. She shouldn't look so mangled. She shouldn't have painful angry scars painted all over her body, and she shouldn't have shame in her eyes when her body is exposed. Will wished he could kill everyone of his girls all over again for it.

He peeled his wet boxer briefs off and left them on the floor, where he dropped them. Naked, he marched his un-mangled body over to the suitcase on the table to get her a t-shirt before pulling down the covers on the king-size bed.

The sight of her shame invaded him, driving him to stop for a minute, to gather himself. Hands in his hair, Will closed his eyes and took in a steadying breath before walking back towards the bathroom to hand her the shirt.

"Here. Put this on and quickly get in the bed."

She complied. Scurrying out of the bathroom with his white t-shirt just barely covering her round, ripe ass. As she jumped into the covers, he caught a tiny glimpse of the bare skin beneath the hem.

No scars there.

"Will, why are you naked?"

He was standing stark naked in the room. His cock with a small chub just from seeing her ass under the hem of his t-shirt. He hadn't thought about it really, putting on clothes or not putting on clothes, as he was very comfortable in his skin. Unlike Vivian, his scars and jagged flesh, with its magnitude of grotesque colors and pain, were only on display under his skin.

"Do you enjoy it?" He teased her as he moved over to the suitcase, grabbing a pair of gym shorts, and leisurely putting them on. "No need to answer, I know you do."

"Get your paperwork please and bring it to me." She ignored his implication.

"Later." Will moved the covers back on the other side of the bed and climbed in with her. "I need a nap. Come over here so I can warm you. It'll be a rare indulgence for both of us to sleep all entwined with someone new."

Vivian thought about how nice it would be to just close her eyes for a little while, feeling his warm body next to hers. "I am tired. Just for a little while?"

"Just a minute or two. Come."

He scooted over towards her as she met him in the center of the bed. He tucked her into him, relishing at how easily she fit, how soft and pliable she was. Vivian's cheek rested on his bare chest and the skin to skin was enough to undo him. "I don't remember the last time I lay with a woman on my chest."

"That seems unrealistic to me."

"Why? Because you see me as a sex raving god who gets women every time I go out in public, even the grocery store?"

"I like how your voice rumbles in your chest when you talk."

The proclamation made him smile and run his hand down the top of her head where it lay on his chest. "Just close your eyes now. A nap. For just a few minutes. When we wake up, we can put our clothes back on all proper and conduct business. Hell, I'll even wear a tie if you want me to."

"No, no tie." The words were a whisper on her breath as she fell asleep in the warm bed, curled up next to the warm man who pet her head and cooed to her in soft soothing tones.

Chapter 5

The Army Medic and the Marine
Years Past

The smell of vodka punched her in the face as soon as she opened the door. Vodka might not even be the right scent, more like "vodka seepage," that smell of an alcoholic, one who has so much booze in their system that it passes through their pores and seeps into the air to fill up the space around them.

Jason was sprawled out on the couch. He didn't even sit up to check who was coming in, meaning he was already in a bad fucking place. There was a huge chunk of glass on the floor. Vivian did a quick scan for blood.

Relief. No blood.

She put the bananas and Gatorade that she figured he would need on the counter. When the plastic bag rustled, he sat straight up on the couch, finally realizing she was there.

His vigilance slipping like that made her chest tighten. This badass mother fucker could probably sense a Haji from a block and a half over in the pitch black of night, but he didn't notice his own front door opening and someone walking in.

Vulnerable.

That's the word she was reaching for, that's the word that made her want to hold this elite broken Marine and weep with him.

Fucking War.

He sat up, all irritated and confused.

Vivian peeled one of the bananas, "Here you probably need the potassium." Wrong thing to say, apparently. Jason plucked the banana from her hand and threw it across the room into the kitchen.

Without thinking, her lips hitched up into a smirk. It was funny as fuck. *Who the fuck throws bananas?*

The entire bunch of bananas was next. He smashed the shit out of them.

Vivian threw her hands up in defeat, mumbling under her breath about wasting money so he could throw a fucking tantrum as she headed into the kitchen to clean up his mess.

When he realized what she was doing, it made him upset enough to get up and stumble over to her. Using the wall to steady himself, he reached over to take the paper towels out of her hands and put the cleaning supplies down.

He grumbled, "Please, please, just come sit with me."

Leaving the mess on the floor, Vivian became his walking cane as they shuffled across the room.

As soon as they were seated on the couch, he got his giant bottle of vodka and his chaser in hand. With an open bottle in each hand, he prepared himself to drink it without throwing up.

Steadying himself, Jason took a deep breath before he was able to take a swig.

He held it in to relish the burn, and to force himself not to barf, and then swallowed it down with the chaser. Hawaiian Punch.

Most people would look at him and think, *'Why the fuck put yourself through that?'* but Vivian knew why.

Because the burn was worth it.

When she scooted over to grab the bottle from him. He death glared at her for getting closer. Then he pulled away from her like she might poison him if her skin touched his. His mean glares would scare the shit out of most. Not Vivian. She didn't move, only smirked, reaching again for the bottle.

Realization hit that she was not trying to touch him, only trying to take a drink from his vodka bottle. He smiled at her and handed it over willingly.

Vivian loved when she first brought the bottle to her lips. The taste, the burn, the promise of being able to feel. It burned her nostrils as she breathed in, closing her eyes to take a swig before handing it back.

"That's my girl," he chuckled while putting the tops on the bottles, placing them back on the floor before switching roles again. Without warning, Jason grabbed her arm and pulled her roughly to him. She would have fingerprint bruises where his hands clenched her. He didn't mean to hurt her, just the opposite. It was desperation. A need to push into her flesh to feel it under his grip. The permeance of holding her, the gasp of surprise she let out, feeling the *real* she represented.

Pulling her into him tightly, tucking her close, he wanted her to be part of him deep into the place that held him in darkness.

Once she was firmly settled against him in hell, he began to ramble.

"I can't contain it, Viv. It's like this constant itch under my skin that I can never scratch." Jason pulled her even closer to his chest. "I have these things that I thought I would have, who I should be. And then here you are, bringing me bananas." He kissed the top of her head. "You are this wonderful bright light that holds me up and fills me up. You sustain me and I don't deserve you, really Viv, but with you, *this* is what I am, and I can't stop thinking about who I could be if I can just put all of it down."

"What are you saying, Jason?" Confused, she tried to twist up into a sitting position to talk to him, but he held her tight enough to keep her still. "Are you telling me that you don't want me in your life anymore?"

"No, no, God, no. It's just I don't want to be the *me* that I am with you. Fuck, I have no idea how to say any of this without hurting you. I don't want to hurt you. I have never wanted to hurt you. You are the only one to lie with me in the dark, Viv. You can't even know how much that means to me. It's just, I don't know. God, I'm just so fucking under, you know?

I keep thinking about before the corps, when I was just a kid looking forward to the rest of my life; I never saw any of this. In high school down in Nash, there was this girl in my friends' group. Sweet girl with long brown silky hair and these big rabbit looking eyes, almost the same shade as her hair. She was shy and quiet, had this plain love for God and the church, and was so content with the *ordinary.* Though she wasn't even that pretty, almost flat chested really, nothing sexy or special, average. She was like a million other girls. You know the one, the girl that wears brown suede boots to her knees over jeans and a plaid shirt with a cream sweater over top in the fall to football games and holds hot chocolate and talks about going to youth group dances and shit.

I knew she had a crush on me, but I didn't want that at the time because I thought it was boring and safe. Only now, now I wonder all the time what it would be like to have planned the perfect proposal at a wine vineyard with all of our friends and family hiding behind the grape bushes. I'd ask her to be my wife and she would cry and put her hands over her mouth in happy shock and then pop her foot up because she is the kind of woman who watches fucking Hallmark channel movies with a box of tissues in hand while her friends would all squeal and want to see the ring. Then we'd have a picture perfect wedding with all the cheesy fucking toasts and go on to have nine-to-five jobs in the city. We'd buy a house in the suburbs to raise kids, go to soccer games, get excited for football parties and go for drinks with our couple friends we met in college. We would talk about our frat stories and how rowdy and cool we were and it would be perfect and boring."

"Jason, why can't you accept that you're a different man than who everyone else wanted you to become? You are not your brothers. You wouldn't even be happy in that boring, predictable life."

"God damn it but I would! I wouldn't know any different! I wouldn't have felt anything different!" He shouted in a frustrated growl, digging his fingers into her flesh. "I would have got my fucking thrills with stupid college boy beer pong glory and then would have found my fucking self-worth in a suit job and be fucking content with a cookie cutter house and a cookie cutter wife who buys me a stupid fucking tie every fucking birthday that I have to pretend to love and then have some boring fucking kids who dress up in matching outfits to make cards to send out at Christmas."

"With a sheltered reality made by people like us? You burn too bright to ever be satisfied in a life like that. Your eyes are fucking open, Jason, and you can never close them again!"

"I want the fucking tie, Vivian!"

Chapter 6

The Two Army Medics in the Days Inn

Her eyes opened as she gasped in air. Confusion pricked her mind as it took in the room around her. She was in the hotel with Will. Looking at Will next to her, she thought of how much younger he looked in sleep. Curled up on his side like a little boy making small snoring noises as he slumbered. She decided to move soundlessly so he could sleep.

Getting out of the bed, she went first to the bathroom to check if her underwear had dried. It was still damp. His shirt was plenty big for preserving her modesty. Not that she still had any left around him. But she put the damp underwear on anyway, leaving the bra to dry more.

In the bathroom, alone, she emptied her bladder and checked her clean makeup free face in the mirror. Viv had spent years in the army without makeup around a lot of men, so she shouldn't even be self-conscious about it at all. Why even try to impress him with a painted face?

Vivian splashed some water on her unimpressive face and crept out to find his paperwork. No doubt in the backpack he never let out of his sight.

Unzipping the backpack quietly seemed impossible. Yet he stayed sleeping. Peeking inside, she knew the folder must be what she was looking for. Gingerly, she reached down, moving a bag of salt away from the folder so she could pull it out.

Why on earth does he carry around a bag of salt?

Maybe he had dropped a cell phone in water.

No, wet cellphones went in bags of rice, not salt.

Vivian held the folder tucked into her arm and stared at the large bag of salt, wondering why it was there in his bag of valuable things. What was inside the bag with the salt? Part of her wanted to reach down and open the bag, slip a finger down inside the salt to feel if there was something else there, something valuable or precious. Rather quickly, though, she decided against investigating further. It wasn't her oddity to explore. He didn't belong to her, and neither did his bag of salt.

Zipping up the backpack, she plopped down on the desk, pushing the suitcase to the edge to make room for her work. The hotel notepad came in handy for her brainstorming as she meticulously searched through his records, jotting down dates, incidents, and conditions. She realized that he had two separate discharges. The first was an honorable discharge, but he reenlisted for another term. That term ending with the dishonorable discharge.

Looking further into the documents, she found pages and pages of legal documents from a military court martial. He hit his lieutenant with his car while fleeing from the unit when they wanted to drug test him. The thought of it made her giggle. *God, I wish I could have hit some of my officers with my car.*

It took an entire SWAT team to apprehend him. For one man. Not a man, though, a monster of war.

They called him a hero when it suited them to, then used a SWAT team to drag him to jail when it didn't.

The medical notes from the psych unit they brought him to before standing trial read like a horror novel. Uniformed soldiers forced him down on a bed while a nurse shoved a catheter into his penis for a urine sample. They locked him away in a crazy hospital for over a year before the trial even began. No contact with the outside world. No lawyer, no phone calls, no letters. He sat in a small room trapped alone with his own insanity while it burned him alive. They treated him like a traitor to the uniform for seeking an escape from his own mind.

Though the case got thrown out because of due process, the army still gave him a dishonorable discharge for the meth. She wondered where he went after they let him leave. Did he go home to his wife? Would he even want to go home to a woman who abandoned him in the nuthouse? Vivian put all those documents in a pile and continued searching for something she could use, something that would allow her to service connect his current medical and mental health conditions.

Then, as if finding a four-leaf clover on a hillside covered in unlucky three leafed ones, a letter of eligibility for educational benefits.

It was dated after his second discharge.

How could he qualify for educational benefits?

"The dates of eligibility." A smile lit up her face. "He is entitled to benefits from his first enlistment." She could file his claim for his first enlistment. Everything would need to be worded just right, but she knew she could make it happen. It was an open claim too, from years prior. That would mean thousands of dollars from the VA in back pay, free health care, and a monthly compensation amount. He could have the comfortable life he earned by keeping the wolf from our doors.

"How did you get my paperwork?"

Will's voice bursting through the private mental conversation she was in startled her, and she jumped in the chair.

"Fuck, Will, you scared me."

He was at her arm, turning her chair on wheels so she faced him. "Did you go in my backpack?"

"Well, yes, I figured that's where you kept it. You were sleeping and I..."

"WHY THE FUCK WOULD YOU DO THAT!" He screamed the words into her face. "What did you see?"

Vivian sat, baffled, pressed up against the back of the chair in the cage of his arms. "I, I read it all. I saw your history and the medical notes, and the court hearing. I thought it was okay. I thought you wanted me to help you?"

"No, Vivian, I don't give a shit what you read. What did you see in the backpack?"

She didn't know how to answer. What could possibly have him this furious, this ferocious? "The salt? You didn't want me to see that you carry salt with you? Will, I'm so sorry, I didn't know you'd be so upset that I saw your salt. I don't care what it's for, or why you have it. I swear I didn't touch it. I left it alone because it wasn't mine and it's none of my business."

"You didn't open it?"

"No."

"Listen to me, Vivian. You will forget that bag of salt in my backpack and you will never ask me about it, or wonder about it, or imagine it for any possible reason in your smart little mind about why I might have it. Is that clear?"

"Crystal." She swallowed hard.

The light switch behind his eyes flipped. "Good. Now, tell me, what have you found about my claim?" He spun her chair on wheels back around and leaned his naked chest over her shoulder as if nothing odd or frightening had just transpired in the Days Inn hotel room between the two veteran Army medics.

Vivian released the breath she had been holding as quietly as she could, took in steadying breaths as unnoticeable as possible.

She explained what she found and how she would appeal the decision based on dates of eligibility. He was elated, and she saw hope in his face for the first time since she had met him.

And it made her feel good for the first time in years.

They decided to order a pizza and watch *The Golden Girls* in the bed together like real friends while they ate. After the pizza was gone, Vivian got dressed in her dry bra and slipped her feet into her outdated boots to journey back home.

"Have you ever seen a Jacques-Louis David painting in person?"

The question caught her by surprise. "No, I haven't been to many art museums."

"Would you want to?"

"Of course I would. I would love to see his art in person."

"Then tomorrow, let's go tomorrow. I'll get an Uber to your house in the morning, and we can have breakfast and then drive to Philadelphia to the Barnes Foundation."

"I'll send an Uber to pick you up in the morning. We can arrange it now before I go even." Vivian took out her phone and pulled up the app to schedule a pickup that would gather him up and deliver him to her doorstep in the morning.

"Done. Although, Will, I can't understand why you'd want to spend another day with me."

"Maybe I'm just using you."

"For my VA brain and my damsel in distress episode?"

"I'm not entirely sure, to be honest. For now, don't ruin it. Come. I'll walk you to your car."

The drive home wasn't as foreboding as usual, knowing that she had plans in the morning to actually go do something fun with someone who knew what the screams sounded like.

He scared her, but he also comforted her. At least, both made her feel something, and that was much better than feeling nothing at all.

Chapter 7

The Two Army Medic Veterans Go to the Museum

He knocked on the door for the second time. She knew he was coming over, so why wouldn't she be waiting at the door? *She paid for the damn Uber for Christ's sake!* Not that he had really needed her to. The money thing was making him feel a little guilty. She shouldn't be spending her money on him, but he couldn't chance her finding out that he had money in his own bank accounts.

The house was a brick two-story with a wraparound porch. She had pretty little potted planters all around, but without plants inside them. Like she had tried to start making it the perfect little porch, but quit. He knocked again. He didn't have patience. If she knew he was coming over, she should be at the door when he arrived.

Fuck this. He reached for the knob and opened the unlocked door.

She is a woman, alone in a house, with the door unlocked. The thought infuriated him. *How could she not know how dangerous that was? Did she not realize how easy it would be for a monster to creep into her personal space and take over, making her home the scene of a horror movie?*

The house was an instant cocoon of comfort, and the second he stepped inside, he felt her everywhere. The rich earth tone color schemes that seemed to flow throughout the home like a mountain river valley. Paintings hung on the walls, mirrors, and unique amber colored glass lamps shone golden tones across the floor. The end tables against the walls had art statues and vases, accent pillows decorating the furniture and throw rugs matching the large artwork choice of each particular room.

He wanted to be in this house. No, it wasn't the house, it was the home. She created a home in the space, and he wanted to be in her home, with her. Not just right now. He wanted to belong there, always.

Walking through each room, he'd catch a larger glimpse inside her with each trinket or table runner he noticed. Seeing what she picked to go in each spot and understanding why she wanted it there.

This was intimacy.

Being alone in the space she made for herself. Touching the things she placed for her own pleasure.

He let his fingertips brush along the curtain that hung against the hallway window. When his fingers traced the detailed pattern woven in gold against the mauve blue, he could feel its soft delicateness against his skin.

He wanted to own her intimacy, to have her give it to him, for her space to be inside his, for her delicate hidden place to reside where he could lock it away from the rest of the world who didn't deserve to see it.

When he stood at the bottom of the staircase leading up to the bedrooms, he noticed the wall up the stairs lined with small, framed paintings of tulips in a field. Each frame different. One golden with leaves swirled around the outside edge, another with delicate little flowers shaped in an oval. She must have picked each frame individually at separate times, knowing in her mind how they would all flow together on the wall.

The steps creaked under his feet as he mounted them. Slowly he moved up, almost tactically, looking at each flower painting as he went, listening for sounds of movement in the rooms above him.

Not one photograph.

The thought hit him as he reached the landing, turning to climb the rest of the stairs. Why would she fill her home with paintings and art, trinkets and carefully carved frames, no doubt each piece loved by the creator who made it? But not one picture of someone she loved or who loved her?

He knew the answer was because deep under her skin, she existed alone, just like him.

The smell of her wafted down the hallway as soon as he turned the corner. Slowly, he followed the soft fragrance in the air to a bedroom with the door cracked open. He moved quietly to mask his presence.

He wanted to see her in her home, wanted to watch her in it without her knowing she was being seen. *Unlocked doors let the monsters in Vivian.*

Leaning against the open-door frame, he listened for her movements. Her quiet humming caught him off guard. No music. No television. She sat in the stillness of quiet, at the edge of an unmade bed.

Only one side had been slept on.

Her hair wet from a shower or bath, she wore a plain pale blue dress, an ugly brown sweater lay draped over the pillow, a bottle of lotion next to her on the nightstand. She hummed as she slid the lotion up and down her skin. He snickered, realizing that the coco-butter she now lathered onto herself explained the soft hint of vanilla and coco that traveled around her as she moved.

The small sound caught her attention, and she jumped, instantly realizing he was standing at her bedroom door peering into the snow globe she moved round inside of.

"Holy fuck, Will!" her hand shot to her chest. "You scared me." The lotion bottle crashed to the floor.

Will pushed the door open, irritated that he had been caught. He had wanted to keep watching her, to hear her hum the quiet tune that was just for her ears.

"You *should* be scared. You left your door unlocked, a woman alone in an unsecured house. What if I had wanted to murder you, Viv? Do you know how easy you would have made it for me?"

She rolled her eyes. "No one would want to murder me."

"How do you know that?" He felt a bursting surge to make her know how much her safety mattered, so his voice got deeper, "I could have opened your door and pulled a knife from your pretty little butcher block on the kitchen counter on my way up." He moved closer to her, boxing her in against the bed and nightstand. "I could have startled you in your room, pulled your arm up and stabbed you in the chest." He grabbed hold of her arm and pressed her up against the nightstand as he mimicked the stabbing motion of a knife into her gut.

She sucked in air at his proximity and looked up, startled, into his intense eyes. "I'll lock it from now on." Her hand went up to his chest, "I promise. I'll lock it okay?"

But now I'll be locked out, too.

The thought sent a surge of disappointment through him. *Fuck.* "Why don't you have any pictures up?"

"What?" She was confused, and the confusion irritated him.

"Your house, you don't have any photographs up, of anyone."

"I don't know. I just don't." She tried to step back, but her heels were as far back as she could move. "Will, I'm not ready to go.

You surprised me in my bedroom and now you want to know why I don't have pictures up?"

He swallowed. Collecting himself again. He ran a hand through his hair, feeling panicked. The thought of her door being locked to him, the thought of another man walking through with a knife in his hand, her blood surging out of her body soaking down onto the floor, never hearing the song she had been humming. The intruder knowing how silky and smooth her warm blood would feel running down through his hands.

But I won't know how hers feels. I don't want to know how hers feels.

He couldn't breathe. He felt frantic. Out of control. His hands knotted in his hair, his breath heaved sharply in and out in rapid shallow bursts. He stepped back, confused. His eyes darted around the room. *Someone is here to kill her.*

His mind raced ahead of his now moving stride as he threw the closet door open.

Where is he hiding?

He heard his name.

"Will," she said again, "Will, please, look at me."

The smell of vanilla and chocolate. Her skin.

His mind snapped back. He got control of his breathing, slowly. Just breathe in and out.

Was he thinking it, or was she saying those words?

"Slowly, breathe with me." He heard her voice say the words. "Just in.... and out."

He focused his eyes on her face in front of him. Her hair wet and unbrushed, her bare shoulders with goose bumps on them. He felt her hand resting gently on his shoulder and knew he looked frightening. He would be intimidating like this, a trained killer on the hunt, out of control.

She touched him anyway.

He knew she had to be afraid, must be terrified of him. He was a monster, a murderous beast hidden behind the beautiful face of perfection. She stood in bare feet, no makeup, alone in her bedroom. She stood only five foot four inches tall in front of his wall of six feet one looming muscles. Though she saw the monster inside him, she touched him anyway.

Her brow creased with concern. Not a hint of fear in her eyes. *Medic eyes,* he thought. *She is looking at me with medic eyes.* Those were not meant for him. He was supposed to be the one in control.

He was in control.

His hand came up and pinched the crease between her brows. "You're going to have ugly wrinkles here because you make this face."

She exhaled a slight laugh of relief.

"It's not funny, I have to look at your face and be seen with you out in public." He tapped her nose. "It's bad enough I have to look at you without your makeup on right now." Her shoulders relaxed, and he watched as a small smirk crawled across her features.

"Well, I didn't invite you into my bedroom before I was done getting ready."

He moved away from her, turned, and plopped onto her bed. "By all means, continue."

Flip of a light switch, his mood changed.

She looked so confused and small, standing in the middle of her room in her little blue dress.

I want to show her how to feel again, he thought.

Will looked over to the door, wondering if it had a lock.

No, not here, not in her home. Not in a place she shares with another man.

Confusion pricked in the back of his own mind. Where was the man that supposedly lived here? Where were his clothes? He looked over into the bathroom. There was only one toothbrush on the counter. No other towel hanging up.

She moved over to grab the ugly brown sweater. "You can wait for me downstairs." He was being dismissed. "I won't take long."

"Why don't you come onto me?" Will blurted out the words.

She froze, looking up, confused. Honestly bewildered. The confusion irritated him again.

"Are you really that stupid? We're alone in your bedroom. You could drop the ugly sweater, prowl over to where I'm sitting on the bed and entice me to fuck you until you can't walk. But the thought never crossed your mind, did it?"

She stood baffled holding her ugly brown sweater.

"Why Vivian? Why don't you flirt with me?"

She was taken by surprise. Completely off guard. *Holy shit. This girl really doesn't think she's worth wanting.*

"Are you asking me to flirt with you?" She wondered out loud, softly.

"No" He stood up, angry now at the realization that she had never once flirted with him. "I'm asking why you don't flirt with me. Why?"

She looked down again. He was over to her in two strides across the small room. "Look up at me and tell me why?"

"Oh, come on, Will." She pushed her shoulders back and faced up to him. "Don't act stupid, like you don't know how hot you are."

"Wait, so you don't come on to me because you think I'm hot?" He shook his head with a laugh. "That makes zero sense. Zero."

"It makes EVERY sense! I am completely vulnerable, alone in my bedroom, and YOU didn't even try to come on to me! Did you notice that? I am not hot. I am not want-able. I'm not lovable. No one wants me."

Her raw honesty made him smile. He brought his hand up to her face, and she didn't move away or flinch. His thumb ran over her lips.

"Tell me why you don't think I'd want you?" Will whispered in her ear. His free hand wandered up her side, sliding along her ribs, slowly up higher still they climbed sweeping over her breast. "Tell me."

"Because *no one* does." She admitted softly.

"Your husband doesn't want you." His mouth grazed up her hairline as he exhaled the truth out loud and wrapped her in his arms. "He doesn't want you anymore, he wants someone else."

She stiffened in his embrace. He held her tighter.

"He hasn't slept in this bed. He hasn't come home to this house. He doesn't want this." She tried to pull away, but he tightened his grip.

"Why do you punish yourself, Viv?"

"Let me go, Will. I don't want to talk about it."

"No," He held her tight in his grip, "Tell me, tell me why you punish yourself."

She twisted in his arms. "Let me go. Will, I don't want to talk about it! He didn't want me to follow him!" She tried pushing his arms away. He let her struggle.

"Shhhhhh" he soothed as she fought him. "Shhhhhhh" he would give her this comfort.

"I am not enough." A small sob escaped her, and she began to hold on to his arms instead of pushing them. "I wasn't enough to keep him here."

Her breaths heaved in and out of her chest. Her breathing was rapid, her arms held onto him tightly. But she didn't cry, and he was proud of her for not crying. She shouldn't cry for any man's love.

He brought her down onto the floor in his embrace and held her against his chest while he stroked her wet hair. They stayed that way for a long time. Silent, just resting on the floor of her bedroom.

Will finally broke the silence.

"Why would you think he could stop loving you?"

She paused for a long moment before answering as honestly as she could, "I think because I wasn't deserving of it."

"His love?"

"Any love really, the things I've done..." she shook her head, "I don't deserve the good things."

He felt his muscles tighten and turn hot as his blood boiled under his skin. It wasn't an answer he could have anticipated. His grip tightened on her arm and he pulled her shoulder back so that she faced him. "*That's* what you think?" Fury built in his chest and he allowed a slow moment to gain his composure. His fingers tilted her chin, bringing her face up, "Look at me."

Vivian's confused eyes slid to his. He wanted her to see his anger, to feel it too.

"Because of the things we did, the horrible things that no one else could, you and me, we're the only ones who DO!" The sudden increased volume of his words made her jump.

She tried to look away from his gaze, but he gripped her chin, not allowing her to escape his intensity. "Don't be weak now, pet, don't hang your head for surviving, for deciding who survives with you. We deserve it *all.* Every single good thing should be ours, but they don't give it to us, do they? They want us to spill the blood and hear the screams over and over and over again, so they don't have to. And we get what? A fucking parade? A free sandwich at the gas station once a year? They don't want to hear us scream in the night when the faces come to our beds. They don't want to deal with our drinking problems or drug problems or anger problems or panic problems... no...no... they don't want to see that either.

"You see, Viv, they thank us for the evils we did for them and then shame us when we can't handle living with ourselves for doing it." He spit the words out like venom digging his fingers into her skin. "So, they don't get to decide what we deserve any more. If you want something good, take it, or let me take it for you."

He grasped hold of the wet hair at the back of her neck and pulled, forcing her mouth up to his, and he claimed it. Claimed her mouth for his own.

His lips parted hers, and his tongue plunged into her mouth. He was hot with anger and desire. *She needed him.* God, but she didn't even know how much. *Not here.* No, it couldn't be here. She wasn't ready. She didn't know what she needed.

He slowed the kiss. Put his forehead to hers. "Put your face on. We have art to see." Kissing her forehead with a peck, he jumped to his feet, heading fiercely to her open bedroom door and down the hallway, down into her private cocoon to wait.

The drive to the art display took about two-and-a-half hours. Traffic was light into the city. It was a Wednesday, and most adults their age were at work, not purposely seeking out particular collections of art. The building was mostly empty.

Almost silently, the other art connoisseurs moved around separately of one another. An old man with a cane shuffled slowly from painting to painting, stretching his aching neck to look up, holding onto his balance long enough to feel the pleasure brought by each masterpiece as his old eyes gazed upon them. A pregnant woman in sneakers swayed as she moved. Her face glowing as she rubbed her swollen belly beneath the beautiful paintings brought to life by the talent of famous dead artists. Vivian paid notice to the people enjoying the art as much as she paid notice to the art itself. It was comforting that they could all be in the same space, yet each in their own personal bubble of appreciation.

She stood in a large, inviting room. One section of the wall carved out into small square windows so that sunlight could cascade into the space. She stood in the sunshine as it beat down through the glass, staring up at the hundreds of years old masterpieces of art that decorated the world around her.

One painting in particular intrigued her, trapped her gaze, and pulled her in. Three women. One sitting on a small stool, her naked back with slumped shoulders. A second woman sat on the floor, and she was either putting on or taking off stockings, while the rest of her was unclothed. The third stood atop her clothing in the center of the room, leaning to one side, hands together in front of her. Their bodies had curves, little collections of skin and fat where they bent. Their bodies were real. The moment seemed so natural, so ordinary.

Vivian wanted to be in the moment with the women, allowing her own body to show, her real skin, with its scars and curves. She wanted to stand naked, leaning to the side in the center of the painting hung on the wall of the art gallery for hundreds of years.

Will walked up almost silently beside her to stand in the sunshine. Bringing his own warmth as he stood close to her. He followed her gaze to the painting of the naked women.

"Worth the drive, isn't it?" His hand gesturing to the wall of art, "I told you the Barnes Foundation Collection would be the right choice."

"Oh definitely. But Will?" she turned to him, "Why this museum, this collection? You were so dead set on seeing these paintings. Is there a meaning? A reason? Do they remind you of a long-lost love or bring back memories of a grandmother who taught you to cherish art?"

"You want there to be a hidden secret soft side to me, don't you?" He stood straight and distant. "A romantic place that I keep locked away?" He moved his eyes down to look at her and paused before answering her, "No. There is no love lost or kind grandmama. There is a reason though."

Vivian moved her eyes back to the painting in front of her. The one with the naked women nonchalantly carrying on in the private moment of dressing, or undressing, as her and Will stood watching them. She wouldn't ask him for the reason, as it belonged to him. If he wanted to share it, he would.

A long moment passed as they stood in the sunshine of the large window, staring at the beauty captured on canvas so many years before.

Will finally broke the silence. "It was stolen." She looked up at him as he gestured the paintings on the wall.

"That painting was stolen? Is it a replica?"

"No," He laughed at her, "Oh but I do enjoy you, pet." His fingers reached up to trace down her face before he spoke again. "This entire collection of art was privately owned by a man named Albert Barnes. He was rich, made his money developing the cure for gonorrhea of all things, actually."

Her eyebrows went up with her smirk of disbelief. She didn't speak though, because she wanted to hear the story.

Will continued. "He sold his business right before the stock market crash that led to the Great Depression. Probably had insider information. Anyway, he wanted the collection to stay private. When he died, he left his belongings to his wife, but when she died, she died without an heir. The will specifically stated what they wanted done with the artwork. The government basically said, 'Fuck your will' and stole the art. So, this entire art gallery is stolen property."

Her eyes moved around the room they stood in, the smile dropped from her face, seeing it differently now. "How? How could the state just take someone's property?"

He shrugged his shoulders. "There were a lot of court hearings about the whole thing. Public protests." His hands came up to her face again, pushing her golden hair gently behind her ear. "In the end, though, the state made sure the theft was justified in the eyes of the law." He smiled down at her in wicked delight.

"That is a terrible reason to want to come see this collection, Will."

His laugh echoed through the high-ceilinged room causing the few random art lovers around them to glance over nosily.

"Naive Vivian. It is the best reason to want to see it. All of this beauty, all of it was taken without permission. It was taken without authorization because there was a good reason to take it. Every beautiful painting in this building, thousands of priceless pieces of art, worth billions of dollars, gives us pleasure without permission. Every smile I see on someone's face, every hint of pleasure or happiness I see when they look up at these beautiful paintings, reminds me that every wrongdoing can be justified if it is done for the right reason.

"Think of the thousands, the millions of people who have traveled miles and miles to come walk through these hallways and enjoy this stolen artwork." He snickered again. "We could even take it further. Look at this painting. The one you seem so fixated on with the naked women in the room. That moment was stolen from them by the artist. They were probably whores, paid to go into that room and take their clothes off so the artist could capture the moment and put it on display for the whole world to enjoy for centuries and centuries."

Vivian stared at the women in the painting. Looking at them in a new light that she didn't want to see. She didn't want to see them as victims without power. Maybe he was right, maybe the moment was stolen from them and given to all of us without permission. It seemed so wrong, so devious and disgusting now to look at their naked bodies. Maybe they were whores posing because they were paid to, but Vivian desperately wanted it to be their choice.

"But if they were whores, they were paid, so it wasn't stolen. It was bought."

"That makes it better?" Will seemed bewildered by her observation.

"Yes, because it never belonged to Albert Barnes. Who was only able to buy it because he was shady and sold his business to save his own hide, knowing that his good fortune would contribute to everyone else's downfall." She gestured to the painting in question, "That moment wasn't stolen. Those women profited from man's need to want to capture what doesn't belong to him. Or maybe those women weren't whores at all, maybe they just knew that millions of people would find billions of dollars of worth in that one single insignificant moment of their lives, and so they gave it freely, selflessly, just for the pleasure of everyone else."

"Would you give a moment of your life freely for the pleasure of others?"

"You and I both did. Many moments actually." She smiled now, staring at the painting, seeing it now in her own light. "We both gave ourselves freely so that others could live in the pleasure of safety and freedom."

"Whores, Vivvie, we were government whores." He moved behind her, holding onto her shoulders with his strong and large killer's hands. "We were paid to get fucked. Don't pull wool over your own eyes just to make all the sheep feel better about the tasty safe and free grass they munch on at our feet. Nothing is given freely. You've deluded yourself if you believe otherwise."

He moved around her where she stood, staring at the naked women. She listened as he strode through the hallway of the art gallery filled with stolen paintings.

Vivian stood, wishing she could sit on the floor next to the naked woman.

I wish I could lean my naked shoulder onto yours and rest against your proud breast for a century or two.

The thought reminded her of how weary she was, how heavy her shoulders had become, and how tired she felt inside her own skin.

No, I wouldn't want to get blood all over your beautiful skin and no matter how hard I try, I can't seem to get it off my hands.

Chapter 8

The Male Army Medic Veteran's Apartment

The walls were completely bare all around him. Little cracks in the paint between the window and the ceiling reminded him of veins in the bloodshot eyeball of a drugged out junky willing to drop down to his knees in a back ally to suck dick for meth.

He sat on the couch that Vivian had supplied him, in the middle of the room with the television that she gave him, on the stand that she bought him, to set it on. Over on top of the small kitchen table she put a laundry basket filled with curtains and candles, little paintings to hang on the wall. The fixings of a home.

The two of them had gone out to lunch to finish the official paperwork for his claim a few days before. They had been faced with a conundrum up until that day because the veteran applying for benefits needed an address.

The veteran, Will, didn't have an address, and he refused to use hers, even though she had offered.

Vivian had called him the day before, informed him she came up with a solution to their problem, and asked him to meet her at the local diner. She pulled the finished paperwork out of her briefcase and asked him to sign it.

"Whose address did you use?"

"Yours."

"What do you mean?"

"I got you an apartment!"

Will had sat in silence, staring at her in confusion, but Vivian was looking back at him, smiling in absolute pure delight. Her beautiful blue eyes were gleaming, and she was genuinely happy that she did something to bring him comfort in life. She gained nothing from helping him, nor did she ask anything for helping him. How could she be so completely overjoyed by his fortune at her own expense?

"It's a month-to-month lease, so you don't need to feel obligated to stay, but it's at least a place that you can make a home if you want. At least for now. I've got furniture and decorations, towels, sheets. You have everything you need! Like a starter home package."

"And who paid for all this?"

"I did. It's my money and I can spend it however I want to."

Will didn't know if he should feel guilt that she spent such effort and money on him or feel good about himself for giving her a reason for her eyes to shine.

He decided not to protest her gift or shame her for it. For once, she deserved to feel good about herself. Taking the pen from her hand, he signed the forms needed to start the appeals process. "Let's drop these in the mail on the way to my new apartment."

It was exactly the right thing to say. Vivian beamed at him radiantly. It was the gleaming of one of his mother's diamond rings, catching the sun as she moved. As a little boy, he would love seeing how the sun would throw rainbows and bright balls of light across the roof and on the doors of the car. His mother would notice him smiling at her ring rainbows and would hold her hand up to twinkle her fingers in the sunshine to make more beams of light and rainbows scatter around them in the car. Seeing

Vivian smile at him unguarded the way she was in this moment was rainbows and beams of light scattering across his world again.

Only now he sat in the apartment, alone, wondering if he was being played for a fool. Was Vivian really a plant? A spy from the FBI? Were they on to him, or did they know about the women?

Could she have been placed purposely in his path to watch him and gather intel? Gain his trust to trick him into offering up incriminating information?

Paranoid, he got up and started meticulously searching the furniture. He felt every inch of the couch cushions, ran his hands along the side of the television screen. Lying down on the floor, he inspected the underside of the table and chairs. Fondling every towel and curtain, he inspected every item in the basket before moving to the bathroom to continue nurturing his own unfounded suspicions. Closing the bathroom mirror, his elbow knocked the toothbrush onto the floor and Will swore he heard a noise come from the toiletry item.

This is crazy.

He picked up the toothbrush, holding it up to his eyes to look over.

"Is it though?"

"Who said that?!" He yelled out spinning around the small room. Reaching for the door handle, but realizing someone had locked him in the bathroom. He pushed on it, jiggling the handle, threw his body against the door. "What do you want? What are you doing here?"

"I've always been here, Will. To keep you on track. You know that. Use your head. You're trusting this woman like a fucking pee-pants schoolboy."

Will fell to the floor, holding the toothbrush tightly in his hand. He was panicked now, breathing heavily and sweating. *I've lost my fucking mind. I'm fucking insane.* He smashed his head against the bathroom wall, pinching his eyes together tight.

"Get a fucking grip. Look at you! Jesus Christ, what the fuck has happened? You want to make a goddamn happy little family with this girl? Is that it? You think she would ever give you enough to satisfy you? That's goddamn laughable. You would grow bored with the wallpaper one night and wake up to gut her from bellybutton to sternum just so you could pull out her intestines to re-decorate the wall. I know you."

"No, you're wrong. I want to keep her. I could do both. I could have both."

"Oh, really?" the voice in the toothbrush laughed sadistically. "Fine. Test out your theory, lover boy. Show her then. Show her how to feel it and see if she doesn't run screaming from your life. Get ready to run, though. I bet she heads straight to the cops."

"No one would believe her, anyway. If she did, I'd be able to leave, I'm sure of it."

"You would have to kill her."

"No. She doesn't need to die either way."

"You say that now, but I know you. If she threatens your freedom, your safety, your way of life, you will kill her. Probably kindly because you've gotten sentimentally attached like a broke dick pussy, but you'll end her if you need to."

"Shut up."

"You know I'm right. There is no way for you to know how much she is willing to let you push her until you actually put your hands out and start doing it."

"Ok, I get it. I knew this would come up. I need to push her. It's for her own good, anyway. I know she'll realize it. I know she'll do well. I know it."

"Tell yourself whatever you need to, you sick fuck." The toothbrush laughed again. "How long has it been since you wet your cock? You didn't fuck that anorexic racist cunt on the balcony. That was a fucking mistake, and you've been pussyfooting around this little veteran bitch like she's made of some special gold entwined in her skin. You're going to snap, Will."

"I'll start again. I need a new computer and profile, in order to find some selfish, life draining degenerates to add to my collection."

"You are a fucking moron for not having started that already."

"Let me out of this fucking bathroom."

"Fine, but stop fucking up. Will, this isn't a game."

When he reached for the doorknob again, the door opened. He held the toothbrush in his grip and rushed out to throw on his shoes and leave the apartment. Walking down the street to a fast-food restaurant on the corner, he threw the contaminated toiletry item in the dumpster. With *the crazy* disposed of, he headed to the Walmart, where he needed to get tools to take that fucking bathroom door off, and to buy a new toothbrush.

Back at the apartment, he removed the door and stored it in the bedroom closet. He hung the curtains and all the pretty little paintings on the walls and made the bed up with his own favorite bed sheets that he carried around in his suitcase. The comforter Vivian picked out was nice, a rich masculine brown with patches of deep greens and rustic reds, making an offsetting quilt like pattern. The accent pillows were decorative and gave it a little touch of flare. He unpacked all his clothing, folded everything perfectly the way he liked, and then organized his shoes on the closet floor. The laundry basket fit nicely in the back corner of the room and the bathmats gave color to the drab windowless bathroom adjoining the bedroom, now without a door.

Vivian had stocked the fridge with food. She had thought of everything he could possibly need. She even gave him her login information for apps to watch movies and shows on her accounts. *Why wouldn't she just invite me into her home?*

The thought irritated him. He wanted to be welcome in her home, a permanent fixture to come and go as he pleased. He wanted his clothing to be hung in her closet, for his shoes to sit in her shoe closet by the front door, and his shampoo in her shower, his towel hanging in her bathroom where fucking toothbrushes didn't talk, and doors didn't lock you in. Will knew though, he knew the time had come to test Vivian, to give to her by taking from her.

With his phone in hand, he texted her number. "Coffee tomorrow? Starbucks?"

She agreed. A lamb to the slaughter.

Before putting away his phone, he opened the Uber app and scheduled a ride to the Best Buy. He would buy a new laptop. Although Vivian thought him to be penniless and in need of her money, Will knew he had thousands to spare. He would buy a nice laptop and begin a new dating profile tonight. He'd get started on the itch before getting anywhere near Vivvie.

His Uber driver's name was Zachary. A perfect new name for the next round.

Zach, a prison security guard injured by stopping an inmate from snapping the neck of another guard. There, a backstory to ride on. That's really all you need to pretend a life. One simple story to make up, the rest comes easy.

While he was out, he would get a haircut and a pedicure. Having his feet pampered was one of his favorite things to do. The women would scrub them and scrape them and soak them, and he would remember how horrible they ached in his boots for days on end and enjoy the hell out of his feet being pampered. There had to be a mall somewhere nearby too, a Macy's or something at least, somewhere to buy some fancy body wash, make himself smell good for his coffee date tomorrow morning.

I'll get flowers and a nice new vase too, to put on the table.

She was going to do well. He just knew she was going to do well.

Chapter 9

The Female Army Medic Veteran and the Gift

He held the door open for her like a gentleman when they entered his new apartment building. They had just enjoyed a wonderful coffee date, and he asked if she would stop by to proofread the admission essay he wrote to get accepted into college. He had shocked her with that request.

Will was going to enroll in college.

The thought made her feel embarrassingly proud. He was settling in so nicely to a life beyond just wandering, and she had contributed to that.

Will put his hand gently on the swell of her back, guiding her into the apartment ahead of him. She noticed he put up the curtains she had given him, and it made her smile. His small apartment was looking more like a home and had some permanence after wandering for so long.

The army had done that to him, made him unable to stand still, unable to hold a job or keep his family. The war stripped away so much.

It had stripped her down too, and now here they were, two army combat medic veterans treading water trying to keep from drowning every single day.

She wanted to hold him up.

Selfishly, Vivian wanted so desperately to help him, because he was the same as her, and if he could find a way to be okay, then so could she.

If he could smile again, and laugh again, and become bright again, then she could too.

And he was trying. He was piecing his life back together, one small step at a time.

He had been homeless, but now he had an apartment. It was small. But it was a start, it was a home, she would help him make it a home. He was going to get his life back.

She was still smiling as she stepped through his door...

... and then she was spinning.

Will threw her up against the wall. Her feet twisted underneath her, and her body thumped under his weight. She had no balance, no way to stand. He held her up using the wall, while he pinned her to it with his hips, and tangled his legs into hers to steal her balance. One arm expertly wrapped around her head, the other went straight to her throat. His hand covered both her nose and mouth, cutting off her air with just one hand.

Her fingers reflexively flew to his wrist in a futile effort to break his airtight seal.

She tried to swallow, but his grip was strong on her throat. Her mind panicked, and he saw it. He saw the panic and confusion reflected in her eyes, and he came alive. As if her panic fed him life.

But I trust you. Her eyes screamed out at him, even though her voice could not.

She saw something spark in him, something ignited like gasoline thrown on a fire. He finally got to feel alive.

She tried to think of how to get away. Though she knew she'd been taught how to get out of a choke hold when she was a soldier, and knew she should be able to get away, but he was so much stronger.

She was trained, but he was better trained.

He had been a Ranger, served on special operations missions. He was the elite of the elite.

She couldn't fight him. He would know how to stop any of her efforts anyway, but shouldn't she try to fight him? She needed to breathe.

Why didn't she try to fight him? Why wasn't she? *Fucking Christ*, this couldn't be her, it wasn't her, and it had to be someone else. *This* could not be him. It had to be someone else, yet it wasn't someone else.

"Say no if you don't want this," he said breathlessly into her ear.

But she couldn't say no. His hand over her mouth wouldn't let her speak. He wasn't allowing her say no.

"I know you need this, Viv," he whispered, leaning heavier against her chest. "You need to just trust me. Please?"

No! Her mind screamed. She struggled against him, she needed to breathe, and she needed to break his hand away from her mouth. Air! She needed air!

He simply pressed firmer.

"Please don't fight me. I know how to make this good for you, I promise. I don't want you to fight me." His tongue went in and out of her ear, "... you won't win."

She felt his tongue swirled around inside it. She couldn't breathe, and he was kissing her ear like it was her mouth.

In and out, swirling around, in and out.

"*I need air*" she was in a frenzy for air, she was panicked to find her legs, and to find balance. She wanted to scream. She dug her fingers into his wrists.

In and out, in and out.

It felt so foreign and so fucked up. Her ear hole, not her mouth or her neck. His tongue where it shouldn't be.

He wanted to be everywhere that he shouldn't be. To own the shock and awe. He wanted her to squirm and writhe beneath his touch.

With lungs straining to take in air, she wiggled in panic, and a tear slipped down her face. Then his hand released.

Vivian filled her lungs with as much air as she could, while he licked down her skin over the path of her tear. Closing her eyes, she tried to focus on breathing, to fill her lungs, and to breathe normally.

As she panted, his hands reached up behind her head. He clenched his fists into her hair and used his grip to pull her head back.

She whimpered at the pain and felt his lips smile against her skin as he brushed them to her throat.

She dared to plead, "Please..."

Her head was thrown into the wall and his hand cracked hard against her cheek before all the sound could even reach her lips.

The slap threw her face to the side, and it stung, burning on her face.

But I trusted you? Her thoughts screamed.

She put her hand to where he had struck her, to feel for blood, or to hide it, or to somehow comfort that spot on her body. Or simply a reaction from the stunned hurt. *This couldn't be happening.*

"Take your pants off," he commanded as he backed away abruptly.

She was left standing against the wall on her own. She found her own legs, found her balance. Maybe this was her chance. She could try to knee him in the groin, or try to run past him to the kitchen for a knife, for a lamp, for any weapon.

He was bigger and stronger, making her hesitate in fear.

"Take off your pants," he repeated calmly as she stood frozen.

Her eyes found his, hoping to plead, hoping to find his goodness, hoping he would see her and think "*Oh god I can't do this to her*" but instead he lunged.

Instantly, her face was cupped by his large, warm hands, forcing her mouth up to his.

"I said, take off your pants," he spit into her mouth, "Take. Off. Your. Pants."

Her fingers didn't feel like her own.

"Good girl," he whispered. "Now your shoes."

She stepped out of her flats, making her even shorter than him. He made her feel small.

Then he placed his foot down on the middle of her pants. "Pull your legs out."

She did as she was told. Stepped out of her shoes, and her pants.

His fingers slid her sweater off one shoulder, as his lips placed gentle kisses on her skin. Then he pushed his body against her. Though they had been alone before, and she had been in her underwear with him before, she had never felt threatened, nor had he made her feel unsafe. Why now?

"Take it off," he commanded, tugging on the sweater.

Her fingers went to the buttons... diligently she undid them all, as she was told.

He grabbed the wrist of her right arm, pulling it up, holding onto the sweater so she could pull the arm out... she complied. Her arm fell to her side. He grabbed the wrist of her left arm pulling it up, holding onto the sweater so she could pull the arm out... she complied.

In her tank top and underwear, she stood in front him.

No, *he* stood in front of *her* with her in nothing but her tank top and underwear. She felt so small, so trapped.

She closed her eyes and focused on breathing.

If she closed her eyes, she didn't have to see that this was really happening.

So she closed her eyes, so she didn't have to see him as a monster.

His fingers ran lightly down her shoulders, and her muscles tightened as he touched them. "Open your eyes, Vivian."

She paused a moment. *He is my brother in arms, my army brother. I don't want to see him like this.*

But she opened them, obeying, staring straight at his chest.

"Look at *me*," he ordered.

Vivian moved her eyes to Will's face, his eyes a soft dark green, his lashes long and thick with a darker ring that outlined the color perfectly. His eyes were beautiful and piercing. They were eyes that screamed control and command, but never danger. She had never seen him as frightening. She didn't know to be afraid.

In his eyes she could see he was broken, and she could see he was hurt. But what she didn't realize until this moment was that he didn't want her to help heal him. He wanted her to be hurt with him.

Now, his eyes were terrifying, and her eyes held fear. She knew he could see it and knew it didn't matter.

Or maybe that was all that mattered.

"Come." he sighed as if this were a chore for him. Something he had to do, as if she had begged him and now he had decided to give it to her.

He lifted her hand to lead her through the apartment.

Towards the bedroom.

He was so attractive, beautiful to watch move. When she first met him, he was wearing a black designer suit and expensive nice shoes. His light brown hair was styled in that short jagged messy way that only magazine models seem to be able to pull off. His perfect white teeth smiled beneath his perfectly shaped pink lips, a smile that lit up the world around him.

It was his smile which melted her reservations about being near a strong male stranger. His extreme good looks dismissed any thoughts of ulterior motives. A man like him could walk into a bar and walk out with any beautiful woman he wanted on his arm. Why would a man that good looking want to touch her? He wouldn't want to date her, or love her. Because he was clearly out of her league, she didn't think she had to worry about him ever trying to have his way with her.

When she met him, she couldn't believe he was homeless. It shocked her to realize her own preconceived stereotypes of what someone who was lost should look like. Now it shamed her to realize how she envisioned an old dirty bearded bag of bones smelling of garbage, not this young six foot tall bronzed male god with his perfect smile and his fancy shoes.

But he wasn't wearing those fancy shoes today. Today he wore white sneakers as he walked her through his apartment. White sneakers without so much as a scuff mark on them. Did he clean them after each time he wore them? He must put such attention to detail in all he does.

Meticulous care and planning.

Scrupulous and careful with every step throughout the day. *He planned this,* she thought.

She pulled back on his hand, but he was much stronger. Wrapping his strong hand around her wrist, he simply tugged her into the room before briskly flinging her away from the door.

"Get on the bed." He commanded calmly.

She had to plead, had to try.

Standing far enough away from his slap, in the middle of his bedroom in underwear and a tank top, she looked around. Trying not to panic. "Will, I don't want to get on the bed," her voice sounded so small, her breathing was too fast, too labored from fear.

"Get on the bed." He calmly commanded a second time.

"Will, I..."

He clenched his jaw and spoke with great effort through his perfect white teeth, making the veins in his neck scream. Then he said, "*Get on the bed*."

His beautiful face was losing its composure. This was his game to be played just how he wanted it.

What would he do if she didn't comply? How far would he go to punish her for ruining this?

He had been a special operations soldier. He had killed so many. What would one more be?

She wanted to leave this room alive, and to walk out of this apartment. She couldn't fight him, and she couldn't hide or run from him. Because she didn't want to lose her life in this room, she would play his game by his rules. There would be no pleading, and there would be no appealing to his better nature. There was nowhere to go but on the bed.

I will endure this, whatever this is, I have suffered through worse, and I will endure this too.

She sat down gently on the edge, resting her hands calmly on her knees.

"Good girl." His face smoothed out in evident relief at her decision to comply. He turned away from her and went about the routine of readying himself, ignoring her presence completely. He moved so gracefully for someone so powerful. She watched his every move as he glided across the floor to turn on one bedside lamp at a time.

He left the bedroom door open, so sure that she wouldn't try to run, so sure that he would be able to catch her and bring her back if she did.

Bending down to remove each lace of his perfect shoes, he made sure to tuck the laces in before placing them down in their designated spot next to his fancy, expensive ones on the floor of the closet. Will moved casually, ignoring that she was sitting on his bed half naked with his red handprint on her cheek.

He pulled his shirt over his head, folded it like they do in the store displays, and placed it carefully on the dresser. Next, he removed his pants, then his underwear and with easy methodical motions folded them carefully to be placed in their spots next to his shirt.

She watched as he moved comfortably around the room wearing nothing but his socks. His true self emerged from behind the facade of designer clothes he wore. His bright smile and comforting mask were wiped off his real face, vague and blank underneath. The actual man he had become, stripped down, bared for her to see, as naked as his flesh.

Will's eyes now held the nothingness she had grown so accustomed to seeing in the mirror when it was just her, alone, staring back at herself.

She watched as his muscles moved, each one going through the motions of his direction, watching as they worked to follow each command he gave them.

She knew her body was next.

He plugged his phone into a speaker on the nightstand, as pounding techno music filled the room. One sock, and then the other were draped carefully next to the phone on the nightstand. He stood still for a moment, collecting himself. Breathing in deep, Will exhaled, and then slowly, calmly, walked over to stand in front of where she sat on the bed.

Vivian kept watching his face as he moved towards her. She noticed for the first time how worn he looked around his eyes.

As he neared, she pushed her hands firmly against her thighs where they rested. Her back straightened and her muscles stiffened in anticipation of his proximity. She held her breath as his bare feet slid next to hers, skin against skin. She braced for pain.

He stood still there for a moment, towering over her. Standing so close to her that his warmth radiated off his skin and embraced her before he even lifted his hand from his side.

Why couldn't he just ask me for this? I would give it to him.

Gently he reached up, and her eyes followed his hand, anticipating pain.

She shivered as his fingers gingerly ran through her hair. Slowly, Will lifted the other hand, slowly, tentatively to lightly cradle her head.

Delicately, he began to pet her, dragging his fingers through the long golden strains.

"I knew you would do well. I wouldn't like you all bruised or bloody," he shuddered, "it would ruin your makeup." His fingers slid over her eye shadow, his thumb smudging the shimmering blue and brown colors across the eyelid. "Your makeup is always so pretty."

The fingers trailed down her face, grazing her cheek where his slap still stung. He slid each finger over her mouth, lingering there with his touch, his thumb pulling down on her bottom lip.

"You really don't know how pretty you are. You're beautiful, really, in your way. Your lips are so pink," he leaned down to brush his mouth across hers, back and forth. When Will sucked in her lower lip, she drew in her breath. Gently, he pulled it into his mouth before backing away to study her face. "Your eyes are so blue, like the sky on a pretty summer day. I love that color, and I love those kinds of days. You know the days I'm talking about? Where the big white fluffy clouds roll lazily across the sky and all the color around you shines in the sunlight. That's what your eyes look like." Then he pressed his lips to her eyelids, one at a time. "But they don't shine, did you know that? Your eyes don't shine."

Tears escaped unwillingly down her cheeks. *Not like this.* Not with such sweet words, such tender loving sentiments. The fear mixed together with the feelings of being cherished. They clashed inside her and rumbled in her stomach, falling into a pit of lost dreams.

Will licked at the tears as they fell one by one.

His lips were damp with her tears when they reached her mouth. Unable to move, she sat motionless. Will ran his lips back and forth against hers and she wished it could be love. Oh, how she wished it could be honest and real. Somehow the wish hurt worse than the reality.

His hand came up caressing her neck, slowly and delicately turning her face to the side as his soft mouth slid across her cheek. Vivian melted into him, into this softness, and this gentle pleasure.

He whispered in her ear, warm breath tickling her neck, "Don't scream. I don't like it when girls scream."

Fear prickled up her skin, and suddenly her throat was back in his hand.

Immediately her hands went to his wrist, her mouth opened instinctively, and she cried out despite his instruction not to.

"SHHH," he cooed before spitting into her mouth and whipping her face with his slap, "I said don't scream." He spit again, "You like that?" he smacked her face again, "You like that don't you?"

His grip on her throat was so tight, she tried to wriggle her legs down to fall to the floor, but he caught her up and threw her further up the mattress to straddle her on the bed, and pin her in place. His free hand traced down over her underwear, stroking slow, gentle circles on her intimate areas.

He moved his fingers like a lover, trying to bring pleasure to the woman he treasured.

Expert fingers moved back and forth.

His grip on her throat eased up slightly as his rhythm increased in speed.

She clenched her body to force control, but it betrayed her as it responded to the physical sensations. Not wanting to find pleasure in his touch, she tried to move him off her, to move his fingers off the area where he knew would force her to respond.

His control prevailed. Slowly, moving her panties to the side, rolling along with deliberate accuracy on her flesh, his fingers quick and knowing. When he slid his fingers inside her, despite her fear and panic, her body still responded to being touched. She felt her muscles tense as she tried to fight the unwanted pleasure, but his touch knew how to make it come anyway.

Vivian heard herself cry out in defeat at the physical spasms in the throbbing heat of her orgasm clenching his fingers.

"I told you that you wanted this." He pushed his fingers deeper inside her and smiled triumphantly. "I told you I would make this good for you."

His hand left her throat as he went to his knees to pull her underwear down her clenched legs. He wiggled it past her knees.

Will smirked at her attempt to spite him. "Why do you want to fight it? Hmmm? Answer me, Vivvie?"

His hands slid softly up her legs, over her hips, up her belly, to her shoulders. "Please, tell me why you don't want to feel this. Doesn't it feel good? See how your body loves my touch." Slowly, almost lovingly, he pulled down the straps of her tank top, exposing her bra.

She was choking again, but not by his hands, by her own screams of frustration that were unable to leave her throat. *You are stealing it from me!* She choked on the angry words trapped in her throat.

Her arms bent at the elbow and lay on either side of her head, her hands clenched in fists, her body holding all her muscles tight, watching his hands. Trying to figure out what he would do next, attempting to prepare for the next slap or the next choke hold or the next loving caress.

When his hand came down to her face, she flinched away from it.

"Sweet, sweet, pretty pet..." he held her face gently in his hand and licked across her jawline. Slowly, so slowly, he moved his mouth down her neck to the top of her breast. "I told you, don't flinch away from me again." Then his tongue traced along the top of her bra cup and he said, "I don't want to have to hurt you."

Reaching into the cup of her bra, Will pulled out one breast. "God, you have nice tits. That's what I like about you thicker girls. What are you, a size ten? I mean, skinny girls look better in clothes. It's better to have a skinny girlfriend, to show off, you know? But not to fuck. You curvy girls are better to grab hold of." He seized hold of the exposed breast, "I have something to feel."

Vivian pushed her fists into the bed beneath her, trying to sink into the plush softness of it. She wanted to get away from the pleasure of his mouth on her breast, the thrill of his hand traveling down her stomach touching her hip, and circling down, pushing between her legs. His knee parted her thighs with minimal effort, and his erection fell onto her flesh.

Legs parting legs, hands moving up and down skin, fingers swirling around nipples, pinching and soothing, lips sucking and licking. Warm heat of breath up and down her skin.

He moved to position his cock to go inside her body, and her hands flew to his chest to push him back and away. Then her legs kicked out to hurt him.

"No, WILL! NO... not like this... ask me! Ask me, *please!*"

His heaviness weighed her down. His hands found hers. One at a time he pushed them, forcing them up above her head, pinning them both in one of his large, strong hands.

"Shhhh..." he consoled against her cheek, "You're okay, shhhh-hh" He lay on top of her, stilling her fight. His lips kissed hers gently as she began to panic, unable to move underneath him, her chest rising and falling too fast.

"Hey, hey, hey... shhhhh... it's okay." His legs pushed hers open. "I promise, it's okay, you need me."

His penis slid up and down against her folds... up and down, up and down.

His cock grew hard as he slid over her wet soft flesh, over and over and over. He groaned, and she whimpered.

Though she anticipated him going into her, the unwanted fullness, the invasion of him... yet he just kept sliding and rocking and kissing and pushing her down.

Will's expression distorted with control as he tortured her with suspense. He watched her face, watched as she waited for it. Watched as she wanted it to just be over, but *he* wanted it to last, and last and last.

He wanted her beneath him, clenched and writhing for as long as he could keep her there.

Vivian's arms above her head ached as he toyed with her for his pleasure. He compressed her wrists so tight that her fingers tingled and burned. She was trapped. Weighed down, trapped, and he was torturing her by sliding up and down her body. All she wanted to do was scream and get away.

"STOP!! GET OFF ME!!" she screamed, and pulled up on her arms to buck her hips to move him off.

A smile lit up his beautiful face as she fought him. She heard a crack as he smacked her cheek hard, then smacked her left breast, and then her right breast, and then her hips, one at a time.

He grabbed her mouth, pushing her lips up, pinching them in his grip. "You want to fight? Now you want to fight me? Yeah... " he bit her lips into his teeth until she tasted blood in her mouth.

"Why do you want to pretend you don't like that?"

He licked the blood off. "God, Viv, you know how good it feels. Fuck it." He grit out between his teeth and plunged his cock inside.

She screamed out once before his hand fell back onto her throat, taking her voice away.

He pounded hard into her over and over. Desperate to get deeper, to get more of her, to be further inside her than he could physically get.

Vivian could focus on nothing but the sensation of him filling her, of his hands pressing her down. Her mouth was open, trying to find more air. She could hear herself whimper, could hear his breath quicken. His skin was damp with sweat and his muscles were tight. She thought he was close, could feel him reaching for his pleasure. She felt the relief of having an end come soon. His eyes were closed, his teeth clenched, surely he was close to being done with her... he had to be close.

But instead, he slowed his pace.

Will didn't want to be done.

He stopped thrusting and held himself still over top of her. Holding himself, he tried to regain composure, with his brow resting on her collarbone. His chest heaved into hers as his labored breathing quieted. Slowly he lifted his head to look at her face, to see her confusion, to see her disappointment that he hadn't finished with her yet.

Cradling her head on his arm, holding her by the forehead, he slowly began to move inside her again. While he raped her, he caressed, kissing her mouth, her neck, and her shoulders. He pet Vivian's skin, running his fingers across her mouth as she panted. Losing himself in her, he pushed into her slowly and deeply, and when he finally found his pleasure, he pulled her closer to him and held her there for comfort.

"You feel so good." He kissed her and stroked her neck. "We needed that. We both did. You just didn't know it. You didn't know you needed it."

She closed her eyes as he caressed her and petted her skin. Didn't want to feel him still inside her. By closing her eyes, she tried to control her seething anger, because she had nowhere for it to go.

After a while, his breathing calmed, but he held her still, gently stroking his fingers across her skin. They lay in silence for so long; she thought maybe he fell asleep.

Finally, he broke it. "I know you're mad right now, but you never would have said yes. This was my gift to you, Viv. You and me, we're the same. We felt the same things in the war and now we both feel dead *all the time*."

He pulled her closer to him as he spoke, as if making sure he still had her to hold on to. "I knew you needed to feel it again, that feeling over there. Overseas. You know what I mean. We were both addicted to it, we just didn't know it. The scared mixed with the exciting and a little bit of hate. I know you felt it just now, I felt it too." He kissed her neck. "We can't feel anything, you and me. They made us numb. We might as well be as dead as the patients we couldn't save."

She felt her muscles clench under his touch as he spoke. He was wrong, and he was wrong to do this. He was wrong to think she wanted this. She wanted to hurt him, and wanted to get away from this man, this rapist.

He read her thoughts. "You think you hate me now. Don't hate me yet, just think about it. How did you feel when I threw you up against that wall, Vivvie?" He rubbed lightly up and down her bare arm with his fingertips.

When he threw her to the wall, her first thought was that he must have seen a danger she didn't. He must have been trying to protect her from something she didn't see.

"You are the same as me and we are both dead inside." Will's voice was flat but steady. "We've been dead since the day we came home, and I *knew* when I met you. I *knew.* But I had to show you, I had to show you that I figured out how to feel again. I had to make you feel again, Vivian. I had to give that to you."

She listened to his words because he was still holding her there, and she listened to his words because she couldn't get up and walk away. She listened some more to his words because he was forcing her to listen. She hated listening to his words because he was right.

When she thought of how he made her feel, the anger and fear and the hate, the unwanted exciting rush of adrenaline that flowed through her blood when she couldn't escape him. That it felt good.

He was right. She had felt dead since the day she came home from the war, medically discharged from the military. Ever since that day, she walked around numb, and not wanting to be alive feeling the way she did.

"Talk to me," he pleaded. "Tell me I'm wrong. Look at me and tell me that you aren't a walking, breathing, fucking shell of a person that hasn't felt any goddamn thing on the inside, except guilt and a need for something that you didn't know what it was. Then tell me you didn't just find it when I slapped your pretty little face until it stung. Tell me I was wrong." He leaned her down so he could hover above her face. "Look at me."

Her eyes went to his and in some fucked up way, she could see that he meant it. She could see he meant every word he was saying.

How could he mean rape to be a gift? How could he think something so fucked up?

But God, he wasn't wrong. He wasn't fucking wrong.

She thought of all they had told each other, of how they talked as two veteran combat medics, both with too much blood on their hands. When she confided in him because he could understand the gut-wrenching guilt of having a human life die in your hands, because you weren't equipped and because of the war around you. The twisting feelings of guilt that consume you from the inside out that never let go until there is nothing left to feel, and then you're empty with nothing left inside you. Not hate, or fear, or sadness, just nothing.

And you don't want to die, but you can't stand to live feeling nothing.

Nothing moves you, nothing grasps you, you have nothing left of yourself. You're only alive on the outside for everybody else. You get drunk to feel numb because numb is feeling something. You hold up the people around you to give yourself purpose, though you're treading water every second of every day. Treading water while trying to hold up the world for everyone else, but wanting to drown, to sink to the bottom and let your lungs fill up and burn.

He knew how she couldn't stand to be touched. Couldn't stand even a loving pat on the shoulder. She told him how she sometimes pinches the scarred skin on her stomach where her organs had to come out, how she closes her eyes and tries to relive the pain of it because for some fucked up reason the pain gives her comfort. He knew she found comfort in pain. While he knew she was numb, he knew she needed to feel.

Holy Fuck, he thought he was giving me a gift.

He didn't take off her tank top, and he didn't look at her scars because he knew she didn't want anyone to see them. He didn't stop because he thought she needed to *feel* something inside more than she wanted him to stop.

He did this because he wanted them both to feel again.

Though they were numb, he knew how to make them feel angry and scared, but also excited... how to feel wanted but disgraced... cared about but used... violated but intimate.

And now she lay in his powerful, knowing arms. The only person in her world who knew what it felt like, who knew the emptiness, who knew the guilt and fear. He hurt her and he stole from her and now he comforted her.

She closed her eyes tight as the sobs clenched, stuck in her throat.

"Vivvie, say something," he commanded. "Please, say something," he pleaded.

"I cried," she whispered. "You made me cry."

"Oh Viv, I know. I know I did. I had to." He pushed the tears off her cheek as they fell. "I'm not sorry though."

Pulling her closer to him, she let him. She let her rapist console her, as she fell into her rapist's strong arms, letting them wrap her up in comfort and safety.

"You need me," he kissed her hair. "We're going to be good friends and I won't touch you again unless you ask me to, okay?" He kissed her hair over and over. "I promise."

Vivian allowed his comfort. She melted into the acceptance that his attack was a gift, and let her body relax in his arms. ... *God, how did I get to be this fucked up?*

They both drifted to sleep.

Chapter 10

The Woman Who Wore a Red Shawl
Years Past

Her face was old. The years had warped her into an old woman before her time. The outside layers of skin couldn't hide the weary and broken irretrievable young woman beneath. What stood there was a shell, a shell of what once was a human being. You could see that she was meant to be beautiful, could see she was so much more than this 'emptiness' wrapped in skin. In her eyes you saw the years of worry, the ever spiraling, dwindling of her humanity, and the hate that war pierces into the heart and burns into her soul forever.

The reality that her life had become. Only horror and devastation was overflowing from her soul. To *feel* meant to hurt, yet her pain was so inescapable that she accepted it as part of reality. Inside her she had no more room to carry it all, but she had no way to put any of it down either. The hate, the burning rage, the hopelessness, the loss, it filled up her emptiness until it consumed her.

Maybe her shell wasn't empty, maybe instead it was too full to contain.

Either way, she was lost. Lost in a past that can never be healed and lost in a hopeless future. She had stopped living. Really, her only push in this life was given entirely for the last hope she held tightly in her arms. Wrapped up in his little baby blanket.

She was a refugee of war. They had been forced out of her home with an armed escort.

Again.

Forced back into a country that didn't want them. They had no home, no country. This time they had walked into an American, British, Austrian, Italian, French occupied area... all thrown together into a multinational brigade force aimed to keep the peace after a long mass genocidal war between ethnicities. It was not a place to stay by any means, but at least it was a place to rest.

She found herself at a MEDCAP mission, an American and British run aid station for civilians. After being in lines of hundreds for hours, in freezing temperatures, they sent her into the color-coded area that matched the paper given to her by the soldiers.

She pulled her dirty red shawl closer around her shoulders to gain comfort and stepped into the building.

A man directed her to a small room in the front corner of the shelter.

Entering, she saw a short young girl in a soldier's uniform was removing latex gloves. The girl looked disheveled, but composed. Her blonde hair was matted onto her head in a loose bun with pieces floating around her face, and her short frame swam in the uniform that was much too big.

Though she was young, there was an air of confidence about her. The way she held her head up proudly and her shoulders back, despite the exhaustion that was evident on her weary face.

Next to her on the floor lay a military bag open with medical tools scattered about. Her weapon was propped up against the window with a large, warm winter coat draped over the barrel. There were thick black gloves and a warm hat stuffed into the pockets, and the woman wondered why she wasn't wearing it.

Why in the freezing cold room would she toss such a comfort to the side?

The medic's eyes did not look up as she reached for the paper in the woman's hands.

As the young girl studied all the information written by the triage team, her hands rubbed against her thighs, trying to warm her frozen fingers.

Her face was focused, but the woman clearly recognized the girl's mask of 'togetherness.' She saw beneath her facade into the compassion that the mask was desperately trying to conceal in order to survive this day.

She could tell the girl was still raw to the guilt and the hardship of war, because her eyes still held shock at seeing the harsh reality of a world that had lost all evidence of humanity.

The woman shuddered, knowing that a piece of her horror now belonged to these soldiers, too. It wasn't even their war.

As the young medic looked up at her, with her no longer sheltered American blue eyes, the woman felt a slight embarrassment as the realization hit that the comfort of warmth, from her United States Army issued coat and gloves, must have been discarded for the sake of pity. The soldier didn't want to be warm if they didn't get to be warm, too.

In that moment, she saw in this young girl something she had forgotten existed in this world, and for the first time in years, she felt the smallest twinge of hope shoot up from the pits of her lost heart.

The Young Army Medic

It took a moment for the medic's eyes to move away from the woman's face of a thousand words to notice the baby she instantly held out. He was motionless, his skin burning and his breath labored. With one look, the young Army Specialist knew she could do nothing to save him.

"Go see if Doc can come in here a minute, I want to be sure." she turned away from the woman before whispering to the interpreter, even though her language wouldn't be understood.

The decisions were coming much too easily for her now, deciding who was worth saving, who would benefit from the precious and scarce medicine, and on who it would only be wasted.

The young Specialist and her Doc only treated children. They volunteered every Sunday along with other teams, multinational soldiers, medics, docs, and interpreters set out to provide what medical care they could to the sick and injured.

Their 'clinics' were in old, half bombed out buildings and schools. Their 'treatment rooms' consisted of scattered clusters of lawn chairs, biohazard bags hung off windowsills, and aid bags spread open on dirty floors. All the medics learned as they went and were forced to work well outside their 'scope of practice'.

They were Army combat medics and every one of them took on the job of an emergency room doctor, every one of them held onto false confidence with a death grip, and every one of them knew they had to become what these patients needed even if they had no fucking clue how to do it.

The young Specialist learned the hard way that war blows up all the walls of civilized boundaries. And the aftermath of war is no different.

Chaos swarms the masses and survival becomes a selfish torment that engulfs the souls of all those who survived. Degrees and certifications, medical schools and white coats mean jack shit. The only things that matter in times of desperation are knowledge, the courage to do what's needed, and, of course, the accessibility to drugs.

On her first mission, a young boy, about eight or so, sat down in her chair and unwrapped an arm slashed open, completely consumed by gas gangrene. After swallowing back vomit, she all but ran to the Doc, asking to pass the patient off to him. But his only reply was to give a detailed step-by-step procedure on how to treat it herself.

Staring at him in panic, she stated, "I can't do that."

To which he replied, "Then who will?"

And with that, the nineteen-year-old medic earned her medical degree.

This day wasn't any different. The baby's lungs gargled as he struggled to breathe in her arms.

"He said there are too many," the interpreter returned from the doc, "he said it must be your call."

The young medic didn't want to hold this baby, and she didn't want to see him or feel his life drifting away. The examination was mostly to appease his mother, although she wondered if her actions would only give her false hope.

The mother's eyes watched her every movement over the baby's fragile little body. His lungs were overpowered with the sound of fluid, drowning from the inside. This poor child needed a hospital, a team of specialists and trained nurses; he needed an ICU, and intravenous antibiotics. His mother brought him to the young medic, the only hope he had in this world, a nineteen-year-old glorified EMT with six months of fucking training.

And now here they were. Asking her to save him.

Vivian knew his mother was begging for someone to find a way for her to hold on to what she had left. She needed hope, and she needed that little baby.

"All I have to offer is a goddamn bottle of Augmentin," Vivian whispered it to no one, really. She knew it would be an absolute waste on this baby, who was dead in her arms already. "And you know I can't even give him that." Her interpreter, and friend, touched her shoulder as she spoke.

"What should I tell her then?" He asked in English.

"I don't know." She looked at the child's burning face and felt the helplessness creep up out of his tiny body to nestle into her own soul.

She had set out on this deployment with so much hope, so much conviction, in all that was right and good. She truly believed in goodness and wanted to naively 'change the world.'

Instead, it was the world that changed her. It stripped her down to the reality of hate.

Nothing she believed in was sacred anymore, nothing she put her faith in existed.

But this baby existed, and so did his mother.

And now they were nothingness trapped in the aftermath of a mass genocidal war. They had no meaning, they had no worth, they were nothing and their nothingness tore at her and ripped at her and made her hate them as much as she grieved for them.

Letting go of hope in the face of the cruelest realities is a tragedy. To play God, to decide who is given a chance at life and who is no longer worth the effort, is willingly deciding to carry around the blood of the innocent on your hands for the rest of your life.

As she looked at this child, this tiny faultless baby, she knew his death was now hers to hold inside her. Her stomach churned at the choice. To go against all hope and send him away with nothing was exactly what she needed to decide.

It was the right choice, but she wasn't strong enough to make it. But to give the medicine gave a false hope back to the woman sitting before her and to waste medicine that the rest of the children in line needed to live.

But how could she not try? She was a medic. Shouldn't she at least try?

While panicked inside and drowning in guilt, she could feel the endless remorse begin.

She had to decide. There was no good choice, and there was no right choice. There were only shades of horrible to pick from.

She looked up into the face of the woman. "Tell her he's very sick and the drugs won't help him. Then say to her he needs a hospital. We'll give him medicine to ease his suffering, but it won't save him. Give her directions to the closest hospital and maybe they will take him, if she can get there." Vivian knew even as she spoke the words that this refugee couldn't get there, and it wouldn't save him even if she did.

While the interpreter spoke, Vivian's eyes never left the woman's face. As she continued to rock the dying boy in her arms, and her words were translated, the woman's eyes never left the medic holding her son.

The young medic didn't offer words of sympathy or condolence because there was no place for them here. She watched the face of the mother closely as her last glimmer of life faded out and then handed the small baby back to the woman.

She wrote the medications for pain medicine and fever down on the color-coded pharmacy "trunk" paper and turned away to remove her gloves and add them to the pile.

She didn't watch the woman leave. She didn't want to see her walk away with her nothingness wrapped up lovingly in her arms.

Without a moment's hesitation, she motioned for the next hopeless child to come in.

This day had begun early. Several vehicles had driven in to set up the tables and chairs. They noted snipers in the bushes and called in for a small infantry force to set up a perimeter around the building. It was a half bombed out structure, dirty with shit on the floor. Goat shit, or sheep shit, human shit too.

After the helicopters dropped off the multinational medical staff, they assigned rooms and scooped the shit off the floor with gloved hands before setting up their treatment areas. OSHA would have lost their goddamn minds.

Now, hours later, the infantrymen were grumpy, the refugees were desperate, and the medical team was drained. It was freezing. They were all hungry, and they had been holding their piss for hours. The afternoon drug on, patient after patient after patient.

The dental treatment area was next to hers. Rotting brittle sharp nubs of teeth stuck out of painful, infected gums. The dental team held patients down, pulled the rotten pieces out without Novocain. The children got into fistfights over who got to go next.

The pain must have been excruciating. To live without having their teeth ripped out of their faces must have been worse.

They all screamed.

Hearing the screaming, Vivian put her hand to her mouth, thinking of the thousands of dollars spent on braces just to make her smile pretty. It made her want to throw up.

The afternoon had barely begun when an infantry sergeant came in, decked out as the infantry's poster boy.

"You want to explain to me why you're not wearing your gear, soldier?"

She glanced up from her notepad and glared, "I'm treating patients, Sergeant. My gear is unnecessary."

"There are snipers in the bushes, and you think your gear is *unnecessary*?" The Sergeant was a high speed infantry soldier from a line unit, and was visibly angry, tired, and done.

"Well, if there are *snipers*, I doubt my gear will make much difference when they *snipe* me in the throat or head, will it?" He wasn't the only one tired and out of patience, "Besides, they only want to intimidate the refugees, not us."

"You got a smart fucking mouth," he shook his head, clearly too tired and overworked for this. "Get your fucking gear on. You guys are moving out in ten."

"What? We can't leave. There are still lines and lines of people out there!" She felt pinpricks cascade over her skin at the idea of just packing up and leaving them.

"Birds are coming in ten, kid, and then they're leaving. You are gonna be on one. So, get your gear on."

"But why?" She walked over to stand in front of him. "We can't just leave."

"Hey, *hey*, it doesn't fucking matter, okay? We can't secure this area anymore, word came down, we made the call, you're out. Now get your gear and meet out the back door."

Vivian stood in the spot he left her for about a single heartbeat before turning on her heel to rush through finishing scraping the wart colonies off the little girl's hand.

"What are they going to tell them all?" Milosh asked in English.

"I don't know." They locked sad eyes, the young sheltered American girl with perfect teeth and the war surviving interpreter.

Milosh went to help the doc get his stuff together. Everyone was quickly packing up, loading bags, walking out the back door.

Vivian sent the wart colony child off and loaded her own bag and finally put on her gear to head out. She took too long packing up and ended up standing in the last wave.

The infantry soldiers stood in a semi-circle around the medical teams as the helicopters began coming in. The refugees in line realized what was happening and began yelling. She could see their mouths moving and their arms gesturing, but there was no sound over the chopping blades against the wind.

The helicopters came in for hot landings one at a time. The crew chiefs hopped out to guide the medical teams on before quickly taking back off.

The crowds became more desperate. Many of them came rushing over from behind the infantry's line of protection. Vivian stood there, frozen, as the people converged around her. They pleaded with words she couldn't understand, and they grabbed at her arms, her shoulders. One woman dropped to her knees at Vivian's feet, grasping onto her hands in an iron grip of despair. Someone pulled on her aid bag. Her weapon was slung on her back beneath it and she worried about their hands touching the trigger.

She didn't know what to do, what to say. "I'm sorry."

The people kept pleading as they grabbed onto her.

"I can't help you, I'm sorry."

She heard the shouting of the infantrymen and felt the wind of the helicopter on her face. The wave she was in headed toward the helicopter, but she couldn't just shake people off.

"All I have is an aid bag, and I can't help you." She tried to make them understand.

A tall German soldier appeared before her. His eyes held sympathy as he picked the woman's fingers from Vivian's and pushed the woman away. With strong hands, he pulled Vivian away from the crowd, and into his embrace as they both crouched down and jogged side by side to get onboard their ride. Boarding, they found seats, and then the tall German soldier leaned over and patted her knee. He said something over the noise, something important. He said something meant to comfort her, meant to bring her to the place he had learned to go years ago as a medic, but she could barely hear his voice, barely hear the words...

"Wake up, we fell asleep."

Chapter 11

The Two Army Medic Veterans

She opened her eyes, disoriented in the now dark room.

Will sat on the side of the bed, naked, shaking her shoulders gently. Confusion crept up as she looked down at her own mostly naked body sprawled out in Will's bed. There was a white sheet draped over her. "I don't remember getting under the covers."

Will smirked and laughed nervously. "That's what you say?" He looked down at the floor.

She thought back on earlier that day. The 'good-willed attack,' how he hurt her, how afraid she was, and how good it felt to *feel.* She shivered and closed her eyes.

"Will, I need to go. Am I allowed to leave?" She said it snidely, a hint of resentment flavoring her tone.

"To go where? Home to an empty house?"

There was no malice in his words, but they still stung. She knew as well as he did that her husband wouldn't be there. She glared at him from where he sat.

"I need to know you're okay? I didn't hurt you, did I?" Genuine concern shown from his green-shimmering eyes.

Her thoughts screamed through her head, *No, I'm not okay. You just forced yourself on me and choked me and then made me realize that I'm so fucked up and numb that I liked it. That makes me feel like something is so wrong with me that I can't stand to be in my own skin, but I don't want to tell you because it will hurt your feelings and that is even more fucked up!*

Jesus, how does he do that? Make me feel sorry for him because he feels bad for hurting me?

"I'm fine," was all she said out loud.

"Good." He bounced up off the bed and walked into his bathroom to brush his teeth. "You don't need my permission to leave if you want to go, Vivian. But you know I'm right, he won't be there."

She sat up in his bed, pulling the white sheet up to keep her breasts covered. She knew he was right. Her husband wouldn't be there.

She rubbed her hand across the fabric of the top sheet.

This is so soft, such a soft beautiful fabric, pure and white.

"Will, where did you get these sheets?"

"What?" he popped his head out of the bathroom with a toothbrush hanging out of his mouth. Still naked.

"Your sheets, they're so pretty. Where did you get them?" She brushed her fingers across the fabric, watching as it moved, imagining water in a lake gliding under her touch. "When I was a kid, my dad used to take me to this quarry. I would love to sit on the rock ledge and dangle my feet in the water. These little, tiny fish, Sunfish, or sunnies, I'm not sure what the name was? But they would come up and nibble my toes." She felt a smile light up her face, a real smile, a smile that touched her eyes. She closed them and drifted back for a moment, a little girl, gliding her hand through the water at the quarry. "I loved to just sit and watch how the water moved. It was beautiful."

She took a deep breath, still sliding her hands across the sheets like the water. "So, where did you get them?"

He looked at her, slightly confused. Like he wanted to say something or find something to say, but instead walked back into the bathroom sink to spit and rinse his mouth.

Leaving his task in the bathroom, he entered back into the bedroom to answer her odd question. "This girl gave them to me," he said. "Do you want me to ask her where she bought them?"

"No," she smiled and shook her head, "I don't want you to ask her. Nice girl though, she went all out getting you good quality sheets." *To fuck other women on.*

"Yeah, she has good taste."

"And a lot of money, apparently."

"Well, yes, she was a wealthy girl."

"Like the girls who buy you all those fancy shoes?"

A cute, boyish grin crossed his features. "I have a lot of nice friends."

"Hmm."

He walked back into the bathroom. She waited until his back was turned to grab her bra from the side of the bed. He took it off her at some point, though she couldn't remember it. Her mind tried to remember, a memory of his hand covering her mouth and nose, her breasts bouncing freely as he slammed into her body brushed across her mind...

"Are you sure you're okay?"

She jumped at the sound of his voice. Her cheeks felt flushed, embarrassed for remembering him inside her. She shook her head yes and held her bra to her chest.

"I'm going to go to the gym." He walked over to his closet and pulled out a t-shirt. "You can stay here if you want."

"No, I need to go." She turned her back towards him to put on her bra. Pulled the hooks to the front of her body to fasten them and sliding it around.

Before she could pull the straps up over her shoulders, she felt his warm, muscular chest against her back, his powerful arms coming around her body, and his hands cupping her breasts.

The hands like hers, covered in blood.

"God, you've got nice tits." He kissed her neck before jumping up off the bed again and heading into the kitchen. "Are you hungry?"

Vivian quickly pulled her straps up and found her underwear on the floor. "No thank you, but would you mind bringing my clothes in here while I use the bathroom?"

He didn't respond. She quickly headed into the bathroom and realized he had taken the door off the hinges.

Why would he do that?

Sitting down on the toilet to pee without a door felt so uncomfortable. She sat, pushing her knees together in such a private moment.

Hearing him walk into his bedroom startled her. By leaning back, so the sink would block his view, she tried to hide herself. Peeking over, she watched him handle her clothing, folding it meticulously like it was to be put on display.

After laying her clothing down, he sauntered over and leaned against the door frame of the open bathroom, saying, "I put them on the bed for you." He looked at her nonchalantly, like she was sitting on a bench at the park and not pissing on the toilet with no pants.

She felt her face blush with embarrassment. "Thank you."

He nodded and went toward the kitchen, no uncomfortable vibe in his body. It was as if they had been intimate partners for years, with this level of comfort he assumed walking around in only a t-shirt, his limp dick swinging in the wind.

"What the fuck?" she whispered to herself, putting her head in her hands.

She used his comb to brush her hair, splashed some water on her face, rinsed out her mouth and put her clothes back on. By the time she came out of his bedroom, he had put on gym shorts, socks, and his sneakers, black with grey accents.

Where did he keep all his shoes when he was homeless?

He wore a ball cap and looked boyishly cute in it.

When he noticed that she had come out of his bedroom, he smiled a disarmingly beautiful smile at her.

"I often forget that you're so short."

"Maybe because usually, I'm wearing shoes."

"Yeah, I guess that's why." He reached down to pick up her shoes. "But this is a flat. You shouldn't look taller in a flat than you do with bare foot." His beautiful smile still in place, while he waited for an answer to his odd observation.

"Maybe I just seemed taller because you know I was a soldier. In that role, I stood taller, and now you see me how I really am." She shrugged her short shoulders.

"An afraid little girl." He answered, smile still in place.

"I'm afraid all the time, of everyone, of everywhere." Her eyes welled up, "You make me feel small."

"Why do you wear these shoes?" He held up her flats as if he hadn't heard her. "They're old and worn down. Where did you even get them from, Kmart?"

She shrugged and shook her head, "I don't remember. I've had them for years."

"You need new shoes, Vivian." He handed her the shoes.

She slipped them on her feet and picked her car keys off the table. Will opened the door for her and rested his hand gently on the swell of her back as he led her out of the apartment into the hallway.

At her car, he pulled her into a hug. "I'll see you later."

She nodded and got into the car. Will stood at her door as she put the keys in the ignition, the car dinging that the door was open.

"Remember, we're going to be good friends now." He was beaming with delight as he spoke.

Vivian shook her head in agreement. His face lit up with the disarming smile, the fake one that made him look like the happy guy at a perfect summer's day picnic, with a perfect dog, perfect food, perfect clothes, and perfect hair. But really, it's a picture in a catalog trying to get you to buy something they want to sell for way too much money.

"Good," he shut her door, the dinging stopped, and she drove home to her house.

Will was right, it was empty.

Chapter 12

One Army Medic Veteran and the Lady

When she got home, she drank two shots of Yukon and then sought solace in the bathtub. When her mind wouldn't stop, she would always lay down in the water, letting it fill up to her ears with its stillness. Her mother told her she had loved the water since the day she was born because she was a Pisces. Sinking down into the warm bath water, the thought of her mother's silly beliefs made her smile.

She missed her mother.

The water muffled her mind, muffled her thoughts, muffled the world around her.

She would lay there with the water as high as she could make it, almost reaching her lips. Then she'd imagine what it would feel like to breathe it in, to let the water fill her lungs. The burn would fill her up from the inside out, the burn would consume the crazy, and the burn would stop the faces she saw behind her eyes every goddamn time she closed them.

Trying not to see them, Vivian closed her eyes and imagined just allowing her mouth to sink down. To finally have a moment's peace without guilt or fear. To finally not feel undeserving. To finally be able to put it all down, for just a moment. She laid still. *Just let your chin drop down Viv, just sink into the beautiful stillness of the water. Just for a moment.*

She breathed in a giant breath of air and then put the entire idea out of her head.

After the water got cold, she dried off and grabbed her favorite robe.

She tied the belt on the robe and walked down to her kitchen, poured another glass of whiskey, and went to sit with The Lady.

The Lady in the Red Shawl, a painting her Nana had painted before she died. A naked woman with black hair pulled back into a bun, not a single loose strand falling around her face. She was looking down sitting on a stool in an empty room of colorful shadows, or sometimes on a rock by a stream, dipping her bare feet into the water, a waterfall cascading down behind her, or sometimes on a mound of earth surrounded by emptiness. But always draped in a red shawl falling across her lap and spilling down off of her.

Vivian loved the painting and hated the painting. Since she came back from the war, she became obsessed with The Lady. Who she was, what she was thinking? Why she wore the red shawl. She never dared to ask her Nana the real answer, and then a few years after first hanging it, her Nana died. She would never know. Probably for the best, the real story is usually disappointing.

Vivian sat naked in her plush robe on the hardwood floor, propped against the wall with her glass of whiskey, and stared up at The Lady. She looked at her tonight and saw her face gazing down at the ground, focused on a thought in her own mind. She saw The Lady slouched over on a stool, barely able to hold herself up from falling over onto the floor. The shawl rested over her lap, soft and beautiful, to try and cover her nakedness, to hide her from the world. The colors around her swirled and blurred into the sides of her vision to cloud her reality. To keep her sane. The

Lady was aching, all alone. She sat there naked, and afraid, barely able to hold her own head from falling over onto the ground. The red shawl comforted her tonight.

Vivian sat naked in her robe, on the floor, drinking her whiskey propped against the wall, but she didn't have a red shawl.

"I don't deserve a red shawl," she whispered to the Lady. "I don't deserve it."

The text message alert binged from her phone. She ignored it and stayed sitting with The Lady. The alert went off again and again. Without looking at the phone, Vivian left her spot on the floor, climbed the stairs, and went to lie alone in her bed, hoping for a few hours without screaming nightmares ripping her from sleep.

Chapter 13

The Two Army Medic Veterans
Two Days Post Will's Gift

Will's Uber pulled up, and he jumped out, a familiar backpack in tow.

His face lit up into a smile when he saw her waiting on the porch. It was so genuine and real she couldn't help but smile back.

"I was worried about today. Worried you'd be depressed or upset with me. I'm relieved to see you smiling."

After a restless night of almost no sleep, Vivian had finally looked at her nearly dead cell phone left on the floor with The Lady the night before. There were dozens of missed texts and calls. Will had been frantic. Worried she hated him, concerned she was depressed, or worse. She replied to him simply, *I'm fine. Come over tomorrow for breakfast.*

"I told you I believed you, and that's all there is to be said about that. We don't have to talk about it again." She gestured into the house.

"Then we must work on your cell phone etiquette, Vivvie."

He walked through the doorway and rested his backpack on the floor of the hallway, hung his jacket on a peg on the coat rack, then sat in the corner to remove his shoes. After taking them off, he opened the hallway closet and placed them neatly on the floor next to hers, carefully closing the door before turning to face her.

Vivian stood in the hallway watching him own her space. She looked tired, weary on her bare feet. Her hair was collected into a loose French braid, tucked under at the nape of her neck. Those few unruly blonde wisps she hated fell freely. Her sweatshirt was thin and comfy looking, baggy with the collar hanging off the shoulders in the '80s fashion. The deep royal purple color made her eyes glow in contrast. Her pants were a thin stretchy material that hugged her ass and hips snuggly, but then loosely fell to the floor. They were way too long for her short stature, but they somehow fit her. There was something perfect about seeing her standing comfortably in the sunshine of her cocoon-like house.

It bothered him more and more that he was growing attached to this one. *Why her?*

"Can I get you a drink? Water, coffee, wine?" She politely asked.

He didn't want a damn drink. *I want to be able to share your comfort. No, to be your comfort.*

Shaking his head, he walked directly into her living room and gestured for her to follow him. "Come. Sit with me."

She stood a moment longer before complying.

"Get comfy." He ordered, "I want to listen to some good music."

Reading his body language, she hesitated for a second, but her hesitant assessment did not escape his notice.

"I said get comfy." His bright white smile lit up his face. "Please?"

The irony of him insisting she get comfy on her own furniture did not escape her. It felt good to not be alone, though. To have a warm body next to her, another voice to break through the heaviness of silence that floated through the rooms of an empty home. Some nights she would sit on this couch alone, in silence, just staring at the Lady in the Red Shawl, listening to the nothingness surrounding her. Silence has a sound, a feeling, and it changes after being in war and never stops stinging in your ears. It hums through your blood and tingles your skin. It invades inside your skull and traps you at the root of your own self, pushing in on you all around until you can't stand the pressure of it.

Music began filling up the silence, and instant discomfort consumed her. She became worried that the music would stir emotions she didn't want to feel.

As awful as the silence was, it was better sometimes.

A friend of hers, a marine veteran, couldn't stand to hear his own infant daughter cry. His innocent daughter's cry would slam into his brain and fill his lungs with hot, heavy breath that burned his throat. The baby girl would cry, and his ears would be ringing from the air strike he just called in, and then *they* would be burning again. All the little burning babies walking out of the building. Skin charred and bleeding, and they were screaming and crying in agony.

He would yell at his wife, "Shut her the fuck up!" and his wife would look at him in disgust. The disgust would make him feel good though, better that she looked at him as the baby killer he was than the wonderful father she wanted to see him as.

It drove him insane though, the crying. He couldn't hear his own daughter cry without seeing the burning children. He couldn't touch her infant skin without knowing he called in those children's deaths.

Horrendous burning, screaming, suffering deaths.

He talked to Vivian about it one night while they were drinking. Told her he had cheered when the rounds hit the building. They all had. The building had held a sniper who had picked off two of their Marines from that position. He didn't know the building had children in it when he called in the strike.

To kill the sniper, he burned the children.

They screamed as they walked out of the building and the Marines ran to them. Ran to try to help them. In his mind he screamed, "*God I'm so fucking SORRY!*" But knew he would do it again. Kill the children to stop the sniper.

Only now his daughter cries and he is sorry all over again. She cries and those children still burn and then he burns too and his wife's love for him burns up with them.

Sometimes the silence is better.

"Vivian, I swear, I wish I could follow where you go sometimes."

Will's voice brought her mind back to the room in her house with the comfortable couch and the strong, warm man sharing it with her.

"Believe me you don't."

His thumb brushed her cheek as he sighed. "Come." Leaning back, he pulled her with him so that her body rested against him. "We can lay trapped in hell together."

"I don't want to be trapped in hell with anyone. I think there has to be a way to live with this."

She noticed that his breath hitched at her words and it seemed like he wanted to talk, but stopped himself.

"There is, but at a cost I doubt you're willing to pay."

"Do I make it worse or better for you?" She asked almost hesitantly.

"What do you mean?" He brought his arms around her, holding her tight with her back against his chest while he propped himself up on her array of decorative pillows.

"You must have decided to be alone because it's too hard for you to be around others who understand. Does being around me make it worse for you?"

He chuckled, "I'm not alone because it's hard for me to be around people."

"Then why are you alone?"

"I have my reasons." His finger traced the scar along her neck. "Where did you get this? I've wondered about it since I first met you."

"Iraq."

"Are you going to make me ask every single necessary question to find out about the scar, Vivian, or will you just tell me?"

"Are you going to tell me why you prefer to live alone?"

He surprised her by laughing out loud again. "Oh, but I do enjoy you, pet. I never thought I would, but God, do I enjoy you."

She felt his lips on her head, kissing her hair. Had he realized that he had made a habit of kissing her hair?

"Let's just lay here and listen to the music for a little while. You look exhausted. Your beautiful eyes have horrid bags. I want you to take a nap on me while I hold you. Don't let your mind wander, just listen to my breathing and my heartbeat under your ear. When you wake up, we'll order food and watch a movie."

"Like real friends." Her eyes felt heavy as he breathed steadily under her. Without thinking about anything else, not the complication he brought on them with his gift of rape, or her guilt about her husband, or how she couldn't stand to hear the emotions of music, she focused on his finger tracing down the scar on her neck. She breathed in his smell of spiced pepper and bergamot mixed with the air that swirled around mossy trees basking in sunshine on a mountain hike during a lazy fall afternoon.

She felt herself drifting softly into the warmth of his chest and the lulling of his breathing, while she fell deeply into sleep, held securely in his arms.

He knew the moment she had fallen asleep. Her muscles fell heavier against him and her body lightly twitched. Normally, he couldn't stand being awake while anyone else slept on him. It was annoying. But she looked like she hadn't slept since he'd last seen her and it worried him. She might get sick. He didn't want her ill, and he didn't want her with dark circles under her eyes or black and blue marks from clumsily bumping into things because of her tired state. He panicked at the thought of her tumbling down the steps in the night because she was too tired to be climbing up and down them. She would lay hurt on the floor alone for God knows how long before anyone found her. The thought of her mangled and bruised on the floor made him hold her so much tighter that she let out a little gasp of air in her sleep.

The irony didn't escape him. That this girl covered in bruises made him feel panic, but he purposely wanted to make bruises all over plastic girls to bring pleasure into his own world. This was something he needed to give serious thought to. Just staying in this town was risking his freedom. She wasn't worth that, but she felt like she was, as he held her while she slept.

This is bad, he thought.

Developing an attachment was something he never considered. He needed to end this. There was no other way. She wasn't his, or his problem.

A small little moan released from her lips as she slept in his arms and that little furrow between her eyes creased in worry. Without hesitation, he comforted her. "Shhh." He cooed softly into her ear as his hand smoothed the skin on her face and her neck and her arms.

This is really bad.

She settled into him again as he made his decision. He would stay until she completed his VA claim for her own accomplishment, and then he would disappear. No goodbye, no explanation.

He would leave, and they would both forget each other and move on.

His gut filled with regret as his mind made itself up and he held her tighter. “I’m going to miss you, little pet. More than I should.”

He knew from now on he would treat her a little harsher, try to find the things about her that annoyed him and focus on them. That would make it easier, for both of them.

She would be better off.

He would be better off, too.

“Much better off.” He lied to himself out loud.

Chapter 14

The Two Army Medic Veterans Off to the VA

They walked up to the small coffee shop. It was such an odd place to find one. Fields and fields, cows everywhere, sheep, and then a coffee shop.

He opened the door for her, led her in with the slightest touch on the swell of her back.

As was usual, her eyes went to the ceiling, but here the usual was replaced with an artistic swirl of colors. Blues and blacks, painted to be a representation of the night sky on a clear but starless night.

She stopped abruptly when she noticed the beauty above her. Will crashed into her, having to take hold of her arms to steady them both.

"Jesus Vivvie," he muttered in annoyed exasperation.

"Look up!" She wanted to share the beauty. The ordinary brought to life by artistic, talented brush strokes. It must have taken days to complete. Hours upon hours of the artist straining his neck, always looking up. His arm aching as the blood drained and muscles screamed from being forced to hold the paintbrush high above his head, reaching. His mind would transport him to the memory of some dark night. The image of that memory stored protectively behind his eyes until he could share it through art.

Allowing anyone who thought to glance up the privilege of sharing in the beauty that once belonged only to him.

She stood smiling up at the ceiling.

"You're so fucking weird," Will's harsh grip tugged on her elbow, his eyes never glancing up. "It's embarrassing to be out in public with you."

She brought her eyes back down, wishing he wasn't holding her elbow. The last week, Will had become easily irritated, annoyed by her every action. She was nervous around him, afraid of doing or saying the wrong thing. Yet despite her unease, his sudden change of character felt forced.

"Sorry," she whispered.

Will stopped walking, turning to face her, still grasping her elbow, standing close and leaning down low to her ear so no one else could hear his words. "I told you to stop apologizing. You saying "*I'm sorry*" all the time makes me think you see me as this giant asshole. When really, I'm just trying to help you to not be so fucking *off*." His disarming smile was replaced by honest disapproval. "When I scold you, I'm not wrong, and I'm not correcting you to make you feel sorry. I'm helping to fix you. Now what would you like? I'll buy."

He flung her elbow free.

She stopped herself from apologizing again and walked lightly over the eggshells he placed at her feet to get to the counter.

Standing behind the counter was a bright-eyed young woman with pretty blonde hair pulled back into a cute ponytail high on her head. "Hi, welcome to Bean Brothers!" she beamed enthusiastically, "do you know what you want to order?"

"Yes, I'll have a large regular coffee, please."

Vivian had wanted a latte, but Will was insisting he would pay, and she knew he didn't have much money.

"Sugar and cream, Hun?"

Hun, did she seriously call me Hun?

"No," Will answered sharply, "Only creamer. I'll have a large Caramel macchiato," he flashed his disarming smile at the young girl, "and cream on top if you have it, please."

Of course, the young barista melted deeper with each word that flowed out of his perfect mouth. Vivian stared at him disapprovingly, but not for flirting with the barista, she didn't care about that.

He wasn't hers.

She was irritated that he knew how she took her coffee. She couldn't even remember being with him when she was drinking coffee. Months ago, the first week they met, she had made herself coffee at the meeting while they spoke.

He paid attention to my coffee choice the first time he met me and remembered it?

He briefly caught her glance, lifted an eyebrow and shook his head slightly, warning her not to interfere with his dominance right now. They were in public.

"Um, will that be everything?"

Vivian turned a pretty smile to the young girl behind the counter.

"Yes, thank you."

"No," Will spoke over her, "We'll each have one of those delicious looking pastries." He gestured to a small glass case of baked goods. "Did you make them? You made them, didn't you?"

She blushed, shining in the glow of his dazzling attention, "No, um, I'm not good at baking. I mean, um, I'm the one who makes the drinks." The young barista twisted her hair as her cheeks were burned red by his fraudulent sunshine.

"How long have you worked here," he looked at her name tag, "Hailey? Pretty name."

Vivian rolled her eyes at him as she turned away from his artificial brightness. "I'm going to find a table," she mumbled.

While gathering napkins, she picked a small table away from the other patrons and sat to wait for her coffee. Will still chatted with the young, naive barista. Her girlish giggles wafted through the air.

Vivian closed her eyes, trying to recall the last time she giggled. *I don't think I've ever been a giggler,* she thought. But she had to have giggled at some point in her life, right?

I must have giggled like her when some dazzling good-looking charmer flirted with me, when I was young and untainted by the world, just like that cute little barista.

Her eyes opened, looking up at the swirling blues and blacks of the artist's ceiling tapestry, and she thought back to when she was the same age as the young barista. At that age, Vivian had been sent to war. Before turning twenty, she had already watched death leave the bodies of the lost, already knew what gangrene smelled like, had already felt the guilt of sending babies off to die. The swirls of blue and black from the artist's brush became the tears of the lady in the red shawl, tears enough to drown in.

The girlish giggle pierced through her thoughts.

No, I was never young like her.

She glanced down from the ceiling, immediately capturing Will in her line of sight. He took up the entire room with his presence. A natural air of authority and commanding dominance perforated the space around him as he moved. She imagined him in his uniform, strapped with all that heavy intimidating gear, how menacing and frightening his strength and confidence must seem with an M4 in his grip.

He caught her stare in his. The artificial beauty of his disarming sunshine stripped down to the bare face of a man steeling himself to be able to voice the horrors of war out loud to a stranger, a VA doctor. All to prove he is deserving of compensation.

A civilian, someone who couldn't understand what it takes out of you. Someone with no idea how your humanity bleeds out with their blood to soak through into the earth.

Your humanity bleeds and bleeds until there is nothing left. War bleeds your goodness to death, and it dies inside you.

All so that little baristas can giggle.

Vivian's knowing eyes bore into his as he closed-in on her position.

Will pulled out the chair across from her and sat, still holding onto her gaze. They said nothing, stoic empty expressions reflecting the blankness their souls each became after years of bleeding to death. She could read on his face that he was listening to the barista giggle, surrounded by people enjoying coffee in the cute little coffee shop, and he too was mourning his early loss of innocence. They sat, allowing each other to feel the jealousy that comes after giving too much of yourself for a worthy cause, and it was comforting to know he felt it too.

"Here you are!"

Vivian jumped, gasping in air, blinking to remember the outward artistic display she must paint on her face in this moment. The young barista placed her plain hot coffee with creamer, no sugar, in front of her on the table.

Viv radiated a bright phony sunshine smile of her own at the girl, "Thank you."

The young girl beamed with delight.

She turned to Will, "And here is your caramel macchiato, with cream on top, special just for you."

He kept his eyes locked with Vivvie as she placed his cup in front of him on the table.

"And two pastries." The barista was ear to ear bubbly smiles, so proud to have brought it to him, waiting for him to flirt with her, waiting for his beautiful Indian Summer smile to shine up at her again.

But Will and Vivian stared into each other's eyes, their shared loathing of her innocence seeping out between them.

They both hated the young barista who could still giggle. The girl whose brightness was real, whose smile wasn't fake or used to disarm. They envied her meaningless job, her silly role in this life, her weightless shoulders, and her hands that hold coffee and pastries and not lives.

Their eyes held each other, seeing the bloody mangled bodies, hearing the screams of terror and cries for help, the chaos and smoke, the rush of fear and panic, the horror or war.

The barista stood there, awkwardly. She shifted her weight from one foot to the other. She didn't know what to do, if she should walk away, or wait for him to see her.

Vivvie felt her lips smirk, her eyes dancing to the tension that was now radiating off their little barista. A part of her liked making the barista feel upset, part of her wanted her to feel something bad, even if it was as simple as embarrassment.

Realizing the source of her twisted humor, Will's lips twitched at the corners, his eyes sparkling as well.

He cruelly dismissed the barista, "Oh, you can go... *Hun.*"

Vivian's smile widened. She felt it touch her eyes and looked down at her coffee cup to keep from allowing a little giggle to escape. *I almost giggled.* The thought amused her.

The little barista quickly scurried away.

Vivvie's downward glance grazed over to his specialty drink noticing the delicate leaf drawn in the cream, "Hey look!" she pointed to his drink, "I've never seen one of those designs in real life."

"Really? God, have you been under a rock?" He laughed, "Every coffee shop out in Washington state does these. It's ordinary."

"Well, it's not ordinary to me." She picked up her plain coffee cup. "I've never had a design on my drink."

"Maybe you should travel out to Washington." He took a bite of the pastry, "or work on your smile dazzle, like me."

She laughed at the cheesy smile he put on for her.

"What is it like out there?"

"What do you mean?" He knitted his brow but continued looking at his pastry.

"Are the trees the same? The weather? The people? I don't know, just what was it like?" She held the warm cup in her hands, elbows on the table, taking small sips as he devoured the pastry.

He shrugged, "I don't know, it's about the same as anywhere really, but you get the fancy little designs on all your coffee." He took a sip and realized she was still waiting for an answer. "It's a lot more liberal. No one really cares about trans people or gay people just doing their thing. A hell of a lot easier to get girls, and drugs, too. That's why I came out here. Too much temptation, and I don't trust myself yet."

"You haven't found any, have you?"

"What, girls?" he flashed that boyish grin at her.

Vivian frowned. "No, I don't care how many girls you find."

"Really? It wouldn't bother you to know I'm fucking a bunch of girls?"

"Why would it bother me? You're not mine." She smiled reassuringly at him, "I would rather you find someone who makes you happy instead of just fucking a bunch of girls, but really it's not my place to say what you do with your cock."

"I'm not yours? I can't be your side piece?" His disarming fake smile returned.

"No, you're my friend Will, and you didn't answer me about the drugs."

"I haven't found any because I haven't looked for any." Dazzling smile still in place, "Why aren't you eating your pastry?"

She breathed a sigh of relief, "I'm really not hungry."

"We have been up since 0500 and you haven't eaten anything all day. You need to eat."

"I said I'm not hungry." She continued to speak even though he scowled at her. "I'll eat in the cafeteria when we go back. I didn't order this Will, you did."

He shrugged, reached over, and slid her untouched pastry to his side of the table. Fake smile still in place, he picked a small piece off and popped it into his mouth.

She felt desperate to strike up another conversation, something to take his mind off her lack of appetite.

"What was Ranger school like?"

"It sucked." He laughed.

"Elaborate please." She edged him on.

"I wanted them to wash me out at first," he laughed. "While waiting for my slot, the rangers there made my life hell. This one prick really had it out for me, fucking hated me. I went to the First Sergeant and told him that I wanted to fucking quit. He was fine with it, told me I had to wait to leave, and he'd let me know when. So, I was a complete jack off during that time."

He laughed again, remembering it. "But then Top asked if I wanted to go to expert field medic school instead of washing out," he shrugged. "I was willing to do anything to get away, so I jumped on it."

"God, I can't imagine going to expert field medic school."

"Yeah, it was pretty rough. I was the top of my class though, the *expert* of the expert field medics."

"Wow, *tha*t is impressive." She meant it, knowing what was required of medics to earn that badge.

"What? I haven't impressed you already. Did I tell you I was a Ranger?" he smirked.

Vivvie giggled and rolled her eyes, "Yes, a few thousand times, I think." *He made her giggle.* "So, then what? Did you go back and go through ranger school?"

"No, I deployed with them first. I didn't go through Ranger school until I got back."

"Do you think it helped to have real world experience?"

"I guess. Maybe it changed my perspective about what hard really is. But nobody ever makes it through on the first try."

"You got recycled?"

"Yeah, but only once. Then I knocked it out of the fucking water. I was goddamn awesome, and after I graduated, I used my awesome connections to land a sweet medic slot in a dog handler's unit."

"How come you didn't become a dog handler?"

"I wanted to, I was almost going to, but the Ranger platoon caught wind and pulled my ass back over for their deployments."

"I didn't know you loved dogs so much?"

"I've always loved dogs. I think I really need one. You know, to help with my anxiety issues, and my depression, and my *other* issues."

"The paranoia, you mean?"

He shrugged again, "I guess."

"You know when you go in there to the C & P exam, they are going to ask you for specific events from your deployments that caused your anxiety, depression, and *other* issues."

"Yes, Vivvie, I know. We've talked about this before."

"I just know how much it sucks, that's all, and I want you to get the highest percentage you can."

"Yeah, I'll just march in and tell her all about the time my sergeant popped these two civilians for no fucking reason. I'm there with this guy's brains all over my fucking boots with his wounded wife screaming and crying over him on the ground, scared as fuck of us. She's in pain from being shot, and everybody else is laughing about it, making fun of me for wanting to render her medical care. They made me leave. I left her with some fucking gauze and tape for her gunshot wound that I snuck to her without anyone seeing. Just a woman. She never did anything wrong. I still see that guy's brains, smell it."

"I didn't mean you had to tell me. You don't have to tell me."

"I know, but maybe the more I say it out loud, the less it will mean, you know?"

"Is that when you stopped trusting anyone? Even yourself?"

"What?"

"Your paranoia, thinking everyone has ulterior motives, you know?"

"No, I don't know. Doesn't everyone have ulterior motives?" he leaned in close to the table. "We all have ulterior motives. You, me, all of us. Everyone is out for themselves and anyone who says any different is a liar."

"I think we should go. It's almost time for your appointment." Something about his eyes when he spoke made her want to end their discussion. She wanted to lighten the air that had suddenly become heavy around them. "Maybe you should at least say goodbye to your little barista. She is going to be heartbroken if you don't."

"Good, let her suffer for me. I already suffered plenty for her." He put his hand back on the swell of Vivian's back to lead her out of the coffee shop, barely touching her, the way he knew didn't bother her. "Come on, you can ask me some more annoying questions in the car."

She giggled again as they walked out.

Chapter 15

One Male Army Medic Veteran

Will had packed up the small apartment. He loaded it all into a U-Haul truck and drove over to the small storage unit he rented on the edge of town for his trunk of vases. He had called the storage company to reserve a bigger unit, to fit all the little things Vivian had given him. Maybe he was becoming too sentimental, but it filled him with guilt and sadness when he imagined abandoning the items Vivvie had picked out for him. Instead, he would pay hundreds more to rent a storage unit big enough for a bunch of second-rate items that he never would have settled on for himself. How the hell had he placed sentiment over practicality? But wasn't this what he had been doing with her since the moment he met her?

Since the very *second* he placed eyes on Vivvie Goodwill, he was placing sentiment over practicality.

Why her?

Both beautiful and curvaceous, but Vivvie was nothing special. She had all these quirky little things about her that annoyed him, like how she held her fork. The last time he saw her, they had gone out to eat. Will had spent the entire dinner date focusing on all the things about her that irritated him.

She looked up at the ceiling like she always did the moment she stepped foot into the restaurant and then sat down without allowing him to pull out her chair. Or how when she got nervous and tapped the scar on her throat. He thought about how secretive she was about the scar, how she must not trust him enough to tell him about how it happened. Why should he trust her if she didn't trust him?

He was grasping for reasons.

When the salads came, he noticed that she held her fork resting between her middle and ring finger. She was a grown woman holding her fork like a child.

He was going to give her up because she held her fork wrong and looked at ceilings? Was he going to abandon her to be alone in her little world of warmth and nightmares without him because his own crazy couldn't find a place for her to exist with him? Would he hurt her on purpose, rid himself of her on purpose, because of a fucking hold on a fork? The mounted irritation he worked himself into spewed out as he brought the fork-holding-flaw to her attention.

To Will's own surprise, he flinched as he watched shame blanket her features because of his callousness. It stung in his gut where it sat, feeling heavy and wrong.

"How should I hold it?" She asked hesitantly.

"Like a normal non-mongoloid adult person with basic table manners."

Fuck, I'm a monster

Vivian put the fork down. "Have I done something to make you angry with me, Will?"

This was a conversation he didn't want to have. He didn't want to tell her he was leaving, that he would never see her again. He didn't want to even admit to himself that he was trying to find reasons to make himself not miss her. Trying to find enough flaws in her to make him *want* to leave her.

Only this time, it was beyond just his own wellbeing. He was trying to be gentle with her as well. He wanted her to think him cruel and cold, heartless, and annoyed.

He didn't want her to miss him.

But sitting across from her now, with her wounded blue eyes shining over the table at him, he couldn't bring himself to twist the knife. "Here, let me show you."

Vivvie allowed it. She permitted his petty annoyance to influence her behavior, to change how she had held a fork her entire life. She respected him, valued what he thought, and wanted him to enjoy her company.

Fuck. He didn't want to lose her.

When they parted ways, he kissed her hair. "You're so damn short," was the last thing he said to her.

She *was* so damn short. Short and lovely, and kind, and good, and broken. She needed him so badly. Will laid in his bed all night fighting the urge to call her, beg her to come over, to figure out a way to be in each other's lives. But his rational thought won out in the end. The deciding justification had been that she was married, after all. It was wrong of him to touch and care for another man's wife. The job of taking care of Vivian belonged to her elusive husband. It was her husband's job to take care of her. She wasn't Will's problem.

He needed to just forget her and move on.

Will visited with his girls at the storage unit while he waited for his Uber to pick him up. The beautiful vases he had selected were spectacular. He kept them all carefully stored in a locked trunk wrapped in bubble wrap.

His favorite held Jessa's heart, his first stateside kill, the heart of his new life. The vase was a cream white with gold edging. It expanded out at the top, creating a pointed rim, giving the appearance of blooming flower petals flowing open from the inside. The handles bent down on either side like leaves off the stem of the growing flower. The belly of the statue painted with a flower bouquet array sufficiently beautiful to decorate the foyer of an old English country house parlor. Pinks and whites with purples and yellows, all wrapped in the deep greens of leaves accenting around them. The contrast of gold's eccentricity and nature's natural floral décor made it the perfect piece for his collection. A display of beauty being forced into excess using expensive design.

While examining the delicate vase holding the magnificent organ, preserved in beauty for his pleasure, his phone alerted him to a text. Fittingly, a text from the vessel containing the heart that would soon be housed in one of his precious vases here in the trunk at his feet.

Ms. Olivia Moreen Taylor, Esquire, defense attorney to the rich and entitled. She was beautiful, strikingly so. Shining, sleek, platinum blonde hair cut into a blunt bob resting at her chin-line. Bred from pedigree lawyer stock, she was raised in the luxury of two ostentatiously lavish homes owned by each divorced parent. After graduating law school, paid entirely by her father, she was given a job in his law firm, and paid well enough to purchase her own ostentatiously lavish home in the same neighborhood. She told 'Zach' that she loved his willingness to reach for a higher social status by being bold enough to date his betters. Will wondered how she could believe that a lawyer who worked to keep bad men out of jail would be considered better than a guard who worked to keep bad men in jail. Obviously, he was not a guard, and didn't even know any, but it bothered him that this woman already saw herself as his better based on the accolades of his pretend job compared to the accolades of a job daddy gave to her.

Ms. Taylor's morals were corrupt, and Will was going to put her in his vase because of it. He had an extended stay room ready for him near her home. He would woe her, kill her, and save the world from her brilliant mind working against the greater good for personal financial gain and social standing.

And forget all about Vivian Goodwill.

Chapter 16

One Male Army Medic Veteran, the Lawyer, and the Pedophile

Savannah, Georgia

It wasn't his first time in Georgia, as he had been to Savannah before. It was such a unique gem of a city, both quaint and booming all at the same time. He visited a drag show here years ago with a group of soldier friends just looking for fun. Men as large as him dressed in glamorous gowns and makeup, balancing on high heels while dancing on a stage full of lights and glitz, with loud music and drunken patrons. He had admired the performers for their freedom of expression in such an oppressive world. They beamed in comfort with themselves, and exuded radiance and self-celebration with every wave of the hand on the stage. He respected each of them and was genuinely hurt when he found out later that week that one of the dancers was beaten to near death on the way home one evening.

Their beauty hurt no one, and their love for dressing up into a stage presence to become something 'other' than what they had been born into under their skin harmed no one. Why should they be punished for that? Punished for being different, for walking in heels instead of loafers. Having the life beaten out of them for being brave enough to live. It made him sick, it made him disgusted to be a human being among those who found justification in such acts.

Will's disgust went deeper though as he thought of how good it had felt when he smashed his fists into the face of more than one of the zip tied bound insurgents they had apprehended on missions. He had joined in on the beatings, to let out his own frustration, hate and rage. He threw it into the face of a man whose name he didn't even know how to pronounce. Pummeling him as his flesh swelled up into a purple mound of inflammation. Even seeing in the man's face that he had given up, that he was no longer a threat, Will threw it all into him again and again, until his own fists bled and burned from it.

Now, Will rode in the back of an Uber driven by a man who looked and spoke with the same accent as the enemy he once killed. It hurt him to think about all the killing, all the savagery that seeped out of them. He thought of Vivian as a medic, running past all the savagery towards the sounds of men calling out her name. He knew the face she would have on, the one with the wrinkle that pinched between her eyebrows. Could hear the air gush out of her exhausted lungs as she told them she was there to help them, as she reassured them that she wouldn't leave them. She would look them in the eyes, and she would comfort them with her words, "We are there, sir."

Will's driver popped into his thoughts of medic Vivian giving comfort to the wounded. "It is the big hotel on the left I believe."

Will was jealous of every man, woman, and child her healer's hands ever laid a finger on.

"Thank you. You're not going to try to drive back tonight, are you?" Will asked.

"No sir, I will sleep in the car at the rest stop."

"I'm going to get you a room. Sleep until you're rested enough to drive back. I don't want you sleeping in your car, because there are a lot of bad people out there."

"That is kind sir, very kind."

"Well, kind is my middle name."

Ironically, Will dazzle smiled at him in the rearview mirror.

Chapter 17

One Army Medic Veteran and the Lawyer

The painting on the wall was a Gustav Klimt. It had to be a replica. It couldn't possibly be an original. That would be shameful. To have an original work so beautiful in a private home, hoarded for one person's pleasure. Will recognized the painting, and was sure he had seen it somewhere before. A woman standing, hand on her hip, with a decorated blue dress that hugged her tall body. Details painted by the artist's talented hand to look as if fine beads formed patterns along the exquisite fabric. She was decorated in elegance with the perfect marriage of colors and pop to give her plain face beauty. The elaborate collar framing around her regal face was painted with a flowing floral appearance, and the blue scarf tightly wrapped around her throat looked dreadfully uncomfortable, but fashion is often like that.

"I hate that painting." Heels clicked on the floor, moving through the foyer.

Olivia wore a pristine suit. Black, with a cream satin scoop neck camisole and pearls around her neck. She walked crisply and with arrogance. Will knew she loved hearing the click of her heels that were designed solely for envy echo in the large room.

"Then why do you have it?"

"The decorator told me it gave the room aristocratic ambience. I guess it's by a well-known artist. I don't remember his name."

"Gustav Klimt."

"Look at you Zachary! Well done." She leaned over to kiss his cheek, condescendence dripping off her lips. "What other cultural knowledge do you keep hidden behind that handsome face?"

Will beamed his false, radiant sunshine at her. "Where are you off to?"

"I have a preliminary hearing today. I'm looking forward to it immensely. My client was accused by his stepdaughter of sexual assault. Child protective services found evidence to support the claim, hit him with a PFA. Criminal court, though is a lot harder to prove guilt in, so we'll rip her statement apart on the witness stand. All we need is enough reasonable doubt to sway the jury, and there is no way they could have evidence that her hymen hadn't been torn before this incident."

"How old is the stepdaughter?"

"Fourteen, I believe. She's a healthy fourteen though, looks at least seventeen. Lucky for us, she filled out sizably in the breasts while we filed all our delay tactics. We wanted her to be as old as possible before the hearing, so the jurors won't see her as a child if she doesn't look the part."

"She was thirteen when all this happened?"

"No, she was twelve. She's mixed race too, and it shows a lot more now than it did then. Our client is very white collar with excellent family community ties. His father is an elder in the Masons. I don't see any problems winning this one. The case almost played itself out for me. Minimal work for a sizable fee."

"Do you think he did it?"

"What do you mean?"

"Do you think he raped the little girl?"

"The physical exam showed evidence of sex. He had a history of some 'rapey' behaviors with his ex-wife, but none of that was allowed in the courtroom. It's all hearsay." She waved the significance of the evidence away with her manicured hand.

"The physical exam isn't allowed in the courtroom?"

"The findings are irrelevant. They have no proof he's the one who broke it, no semen, no DNA. Besides, it doesn't really matter if he did or not. Should we really ruin a decent member of society's life over one mistake? She's in therapy, and her mother gets a divorce with alimony. What good will jail time do anyone now?"

"Hmmmm." Will kept his opinion on the subject to himself. Attorney Taylor would find out how much good it would have done for her soon enough. "Would you like me to stay tonight?"

Will could feel the sexual smile that moved across her face. She had just outlined how she would get a child rapist off from all criminal charges, with a dismissive air of wealth superiority over moral obligation, and was now thinking of engaging in consensual sex with him for pleasure. The little girl was twelve when the man, who should have loved her, should have protected her, stuck his penis where it didn't belong, and Olivia was set out to further victimize that child on the witness stand. All to make sure a fat paycheck landed in her own pocket to buy paintings she didn't even like to hang on ostentatious walls.

"I'll take that as a yes."

"Just make sure you're careful about not being seen coming and going. I don't want my father to know."

"You don't want your father to know you're shacking up with a lowly, blue-collar guard?"

"Oh Zachary, you know it isn't that simple."

"I know, Love. I understand." *I understand that you're a disgusting human being.*

"You're so handsome. I wish I could have a painting of you to hang on my wall." She turned him by the collar of his shirt and pulled Will into her kiss. He fought the bile of disgust that rose in the back of his throat as her tongue swept into his mouth. She stood eye to eye with him in her heels. She was a tall woman even without them, slender, with perfectly tanned skin. She had a tiny waist, slight curvature of the hips with a small tight ass. But when he looked at her, Will only saw legs that were sticks holding up her rotten core containing the putrid remembrance of the humanity she soaked in acidic regurgitated greed. Her apple shaped tits were the temptation of eve in the garden and the snake weaved around inside her soul, finding ways to feed off her wretched selfishness.

"Could you drop me off at my hotel on your way to court? There are a few things I need to attend to today."

"Oh really? What could you possibly need to attend to?" Her condescending teasing was irritating.

"I would like to plan something special for you tonight." *I'm going to think up a way to make you suffer worthy of the hell you inflict on the innocent victims denied justice because of your lack of humanity and goodness.*

"Why don't I just let you borrow one of the cars? The keys are hanging on the wall next to the garage. Take whichever you like. Just make sure you're here waiting for me when I get home. I deserve the pleasure of looking at your hot ass after a hard day's work." Olivia slid her hand down his chest to grab hold of his cock. "And touching your hard, hot, toned body all over too. Hard is what I want."

His hands slid along her elbows, fighting the urge to push her away from him. Will took a deep steadying breath and looked down into her pretty hazel eyes, "You'll get what you deserve."

When she left for work, Will followed her.

He didn't look like what you'd imagine a pedophile to look like, but Will knew better than anyone that the outer shell did not illustrate the inner soul of the human. He sat in Olivia's silver Mercedes down the street from the courthouse as the lawyer team walked out, pedophile in tow. Olivia and the male attorneys split off from their client after a brief conversational exchange and walked over to enter their vehicles together. The pedophile walked to his vehicle alone. Will followed.

Justice was such a delicate matter. Who is given the authority to decide what wrongs deserved what punishments? How was that authority issued, and who was worthy enough to determine if justice was to be served, and how? The system was flawed. Not just the judicial system, the whole damn thing. Society, the community as a whole, the values placed on our culture benefiting the rich and powerful while the small get shit on and used up.

They made him into a monster-soldier to trade blood for oil, to use fear and terrorism as a reason to sanction the horrors he inflicted on a country different from our own, and called it patriotism. Flags waved him home with cheers and spews of thankfulness from a grateful nation, and then they labeled him dishonorable for not being able to live with all the blood he carried on his hands. The same nation that rewarded Olivia Taylor for giving a man who ripped open a child's innocence to steal it from her body a free pass.

The army gave him the authority to punish wrongs against Americans. The army trained him to capture the evil wolves of the earth and punish them. They sanctioned his use of force, sanctioned his cruelty to keep brutality from our shores. Only now

Will was home, on our shores, and the wolves walked among us. It takes a monster to fight a monster and Will fit the bill.

After following the man home, Will decided that waiting to approach the pedophile's home until after he had gathered the proper supplies from his suitcase back in the hotel was the practical decision. He had not planned to kill two this trip. Strategy would need to be readjusted, but it was doable and necessary. Rather convenient, actually, a lot less planning involved in the aftermath. No clean up, no hiding evidence, or body disposal. Murder suicide. Improvising could be visited for this particular case. There was about three hours until Olivia was due back from work. Plenty of time for kidnapping.

The pedophile had no cameras or surveillance outside his townhome. The fool didn't even lock the back door. Will simply walked into his home.

He sat in a lazy boy watching the television, whiskey in hand.

"Excuse me?" Will asked.

When the man turned to see what stranger was asking for his attention, Will wrapped him in a hold, rendering him immobile.

Will said nothing more as the pedophile slowly lost consciousness in the grip of his arms. Bending down, he swooped the man into a fireman's carry, snatched his phone and wallet from the counter, and walked out the way he came in.

The drive to Olivia's house was short enough that he stayed comatose in the trunk for the entire ride. Which was convenient for Will, as he had fully expected a fight in the garage. Instead, he simply scooped the man up out of the trunk and carried him into the house, straight to the indoor spa room. The sauna would make a nice holding cell, give the pedophile time to relax before the show.

Laying him down on the bench inside the sauna, Will casually sauntered down to the pool house at the back of the property.

Days earlier he had noticed a door jammer, the perfect way to trap a weak little monster in a wooden box. After jamming it securely under the door handle of the sauna, Will heard the pedophile call out.

"Where am I?" he shouted. "Who are you? What do you want from me?"

Will had no intention of answering. He simply waited there to make sure the door jammer would contain him.

"Help! Help me! Is anyone there? Hello?"

Honestly, the very first thing Will would have tried was to get out of the room. Why was this man just standing there yelling for help? Any idiot should realize that inside a wooden room with thick wooden walls no one would hear you.

"Please, hello? Anyone?"

Will rolled his eyes, *and still, this idiot didn't reach for the door handle.* He didn't even check to see if it was locked. Annoyed, Will reached up to turn the sauna control to the on position. It made him chuckle when the pedophile yelled out inside the box the moment the lights turned on. Finally, he reached for the door handle.

Will stood next to the door jammer as the man threw himself up against the door over and over. Convinced it would hold strong, Will left the spa room to set up the surprise he had for Olivia upon her return home from work.

No sooner had Will finished making everything perfect, than the garage door opened, alerting him to her arrival. Heels clicked on the hard floors following the rose petal trail he left for her, leading up the stairs to her bedroom, where he waited in the shadows of the dancing candlelight. The glass of wine sat on the small table with a little note. "Drink me while you undress" it read, she giggled.

"I know you're here somewhere. I love this game. Very thrilling." She brought the wineglass to her lips as she stepped out of her heels. "Where have you gotten to Zach?" Another sip as she hung her suit jacket carefully up in the walk-in. "It's cruel to make me wait like this. I've missed you."

The glass was back to her mouth, her skirt falling to her feet. She wobbled slightly to the side, while taking another sip. Olivia stepped out of the closet and set the glass down before pulling her camisole over her head. "Oh Zachary? Where are you?" she cooed teasingly, picking up the glass to finish off the red liquid inside.

"You look amazing standing there in your underwear and thigh highs." He spoke up from the shadows. Olivia turned towards the sound of his voice and found herself stumbling into the vanity. "Oh my. Zach, I feel strange."

"You should." He laughed, "I put enough valium in that wine glass to knock out a moose."

Chapter 18

Three Monsters in a Mansion

Will sat in the chair next to her bed, gazing at the scene laid out before him. Olivia was peacefully sleeping on her back, sprawled open for him to see. It was a very pretty view, a beautiful woman spread eagle on a four-post bed. He tied each hand to the bed-posts with her fancy, expensive scarves. It was almost romantic. Her legs, though, he secured using a rope that he had brought for the occasion. He needed her legs very secure. Hands could be wrestled back down, but legs could cause damage if they got loose.

In his hand, he fiddled with the end of the .380 pistol he found in her nightstand. A little weapon made for small hands. Good enough for intimidation tactics or good enough for killing if the bullet was well placed enough. Turning the weapon over and over again, he stared down at the gloved hands he used to maneuver it. Overseas he sometimes wore gloves, issued gloves, without fingertips. The average person didn't realize how fucking cold it could get in the dessert. There were nights he froze his balls off, shivering and shivering, trying to keep focused on watching his post. There were no comforts on those nights. The muscles would ache after a while, all of the muscles you didn't even realize you had. The toes in your boots would burn with the numb tingle that crept up them, and every part of your body would clench up tight to search for some way to get warmer. Every part except your hand holding your weapon. That hand stayed in control, trigger finger extended, in complete control. It amazed him how quickly the body could go from a shivering mess of contracted muscle to a controlled fighting machine following the muscle memory needed to survive.

"Ohhhh." Olivia moaned from the bed. "Ohhhhh."

Her cries were pitiful. Slight little noises communicated in medication induced confusion. Muscle memory. Will watched as her muscles moved, taking over in her brain's inebriation. One arm pulled up, then the other. Her head turned from one side to the next, her voice moaning as her body moved. Both knees flexed this way and that, sliding against the expensive cotton sheets.

The human body amazed Will, how much it could withstand, how hard it tried to salvage life. When a patient would go into shock, their body would pull the blood in from all extremities, it would sacrifice the use of the limbs to preserve the use of the vital systems at the core. The body was practical and systematic, and it didn't give up easily. Will respected the human body immensely. It was the human conscious he had lost tolerance for. Especially Ms. Olivia Taylor's conscious, or lack thereof one.

As she began to stir, Will decided it was time to move forward. He sighed, getting up from the chair, anticipating the thrill of the next few hours.

Without even a single glance in her direction, he headed down towards the in-home spa.

Thank fuck he stopped screaming.

The pedophile had finally given up yelling for help. Will had dropped by every hour to turn the sauna timer back on and every single time he heard the futile efforts of the horrible man inside begging for help. Will opened the sauna door. The pedophile had stripped down to his boxer shorts and was lying on the floor in the fetal position, panting or crying. Will couldn't tell which. It was a kind of a weird in between panting and crying like chest heaving. Either way, it was completely induced by self-pity and it disgusted Will.

"I do not believe I ever got your name, sir?"

The pedophile startled at Will's voice.

"Please, please don't hurt me." His voice was horse, almost whispering at Will's feet.

"Don't hurt you?" Will laughed. "I asked for your name. What is it?"

"Mi, Mi, Michael."

"Well, Michael, I feel you have calmed down enough now here in the sauna to be willing to comply with my orders. Do you agree?"

Michael stared up at Will in confusion, appearing about to cry.

Will kicked him swiftly in the stomach, and Michael screamed out in pain.

"Do you agree?"

"Yes! Yes!" Michael cried.

"Wonderful. Please stand and walk with me down the hallway. No blubbering or begging, it's unnecessary. We are simply joining our friend in her bedroom." Will gestured with a smile for the man to stand. "Go ahead now, stand up."

Michael slowly moved to a sitting position.

"I would like to make it clear though Michael, that I do have a gun, and I will shoot you if you try to disobey or annoy me." Will shrugged, "Either or. So please just do as you're told."

"Okay." Michael sobbed again, "I will do whatever you want, just don't, don't kill meeee."

Instantly, Michael had annoyed him beyond all levels of annoyance. He gestured for him to rise and moved out in front of him. It was almost comical seeing this grown man cowering in his boxer shorts as he fell all over his own self moving down the hallway.

Will sauntered behind him with the gun hanging down by his leg.

Michael had to have fallen at least ten times before reaching the bedroom. How do men like that live with themselves?

As they walked into the room, Will realized that Olivia was alert. "Oh good. You're awake. Olivia, you remember Michael. Michael, you know Olivia."

"Zach? What the hell is going on? Did you drug me? Untie me! Untie me right now!" Then, "Please, please just let me leave. I just want to go home. I won't say a word to anyone, just let me leave."

Will took in a deep breath and shut the bedroom door. He gestured for Michael to move over to the corner of the room at Olivia's head. He, of course, complied, and Will casually moved over to the comfortable chair, set up to block any escape to the door.

"Well, I feel it's only fair that we begin with a proper introduction. My name is not Zachary, and I am not a prison guard." He waved his hand in Olivia's direction. "I apologize for lying. It wasn't well done of me, but necessary."

"I don't know who you are, but I can pay you. I can pay you anything you want."

Will quickly put up a hand to stop her. "No, no Olivia, this isn't about money. I don't need any of your money. No, this is about character. A test of character, and you failed. You both did." He looked over in Michael's direction to include him in the conversation. "I've never needed to really explain this to anyone. It's a little awkward, isn't it?" Will shined his dazzling white smile at them. "Well, I was a special operation solider in the war. Killed a lot of bad guys, so I know bad guys when I see them, and you are both bad guys."

Will paused, waiting for either of them to argue or plead. Neither spoke.

"So, we are all here now together, and we need to decide what your punishments should be."

"You will never get away with this. I have security cameras everywhere in this home. They will find you and you will be the one punished."

"Oh, my, well, that would be unfortunate. But I disabled all the security cameras the first night I was here, Olivia. Deleted any footage I could have possibly been in. I even got all the dating profile information off your phone. I mean, not that it really mattered, it was all fake. Your concern for my future though is endearing. However, what I'd really like to talk about is how you both are okay with men who rape little girls not being held accountable."

"Oh, my god." Michael quietly sobbed in the corner.

"Yeah, see up until this morning I had only planned on killing Ms. Taylor." Olivia glared over at him. "Olivia, you deserve it. You are a self-righteous, self-absorbed, horrid human being. Plastic on the outside and putrid on the inside. I didn't go ruin my life in combat to preserve your ability to use everyone to get ahead. You shit on everything I fought to defend."

"Zach, please, I can change."

Will held up a hand. "I told you, my name is not Zach, and there is no begging, or promises, that will change my mind. Punishment will be delivered. However, now that there are two of you, well, I feel it only right that I allow you both a minute to discuss what you feel your punishment should be. We can either go with that punishment, or my idea for a punishment. Now, I'd like you both to consider this, because I assure you, in fact, I cannot express to you enough, how much you will not enjoy my version of a punishment."

Will got up from his chair and walked to the doorframe. "Go ahead, talk amongst yourselves." He moved with his back to them, leaning against the wall on the other side of the hallway.

He listened to their scared mumbled conversation while hoping against hope that this pedophile motherfucker would have the balls to try to attack him or attempt to run. Nothing would give Will more pleasure than just one little, tiny single reason, to strip himself of his composure and go animalistic on these pieces of shit.

"Excuse me."

Will closed his eyes. *No balls.*

"Yes, Michael, what did you decide?"

"Well, Olivia would like for me to untie her and allow her a blanket to cover up while we decide what to do."

"Oh, would she?" Will asked calmly, "Do you think the little girl today at the court hearing would have liked to have had a nice blanket to cover up behind while Olivia tore into her about the validity of the worst moments of her life? The worst moments that you, Michael, gave to her in the first place?"

Will moved slowly back into the bedroom to sit in the chair.

"It's just, I don't know what you want us to do."

"What I want you to do is to decide what you deserve for the things you did. Kind of like how I left Olivia here naked on the bed, so she feels vulnerable and exposed, just like she makes the victims feel when she verbally tears them apart, to defend their perpetrators."

"Yes, I do feel like that," Olivia cried. "I feel just like them, and I swear I won't defend a pedophile. Just let me go."

"Honestly love, do you really think you feel *just* like them?"

"No," she began to cry. "I don't want to die Zach."

"Shhhhh, now Olivia, Michael here is going to decide if you die, right Michael? Do you want Olivia to die?"

"I, I don't want her to die, and I don't want to die either."

"So, what if I told you, just one of you had to die? What would you decide then? What if I made it completely your decision, Michael?"

"I don't understand."

"What don't you understand?" Will chuckled. "I will shoot you in the head, or I will shoot her in the face. Who would you decide? Be honest now, I'll take your recommendation to heart."

"No! No Zach, please! Let it be my decision!" Olivia yelled.

"I would pick me." Michael answered abruptly.

"Olivia, I'm not speaking to you. If you're rude again, I'll have to hurt you, and you don't want that. Michael, you would pick yourself to live?"

"No, no, I couldn't live with myself if I did that."

"Ah, so you would do the honorable thing and allow her to live." Will looked between the two of them. Enjoying them in their moment of fear.

"But I don't want to die." Tears fell from the pedophile's eyes, snot dripping from his nose.

"Hmmm, well what if I said that I would allow you both to live if you made Olivia feel as bad as you made that little girl feel."

"I don't know how to do that."

"Oh, but don't you?"

"He wants you to rape me, because he's a sick fuck!" Olivia screamed from where she lay restrained on the bed.

"Sick fuck?" Will laughed out again. "Yeah, but a sick fuck with a gun. Tell me, Olivia, if I had the money tomorrow to pay you enough, would you defend me in court for this?"

"No! You're an animal!"

"But he's not? You're an adult, and how does it feel to think of him being inside you without wanting him there?" Will used the gun to point at Michael. "That's what he did to a child, Olivia!

A fucking child! And YOU defended him! *You* are the sick fuck here, you are both the sick fucks in the room, and now I am your accountability!"

"I'm sorry." She sobbed the words with her head to side. "I'm sorry."

"No, but you will be." Will settled back into the chair, regaining his composure. Reaching into his pocket, he pulled out a bag of pills. "Here," he tossed the bag to the pedophile. "You'll need those probably considering that she is a lot older than what you usually like to get off to."

"Okay, okay. I'll do it." Michael opened the bag of pills and swallowed two. "There see... see I'm going to do it." Michael moved over to the bed and climbed up between Olivia's legs. "I'm sorry Olivia, I truly am, but sex is better than death."

Will watched as Olivia sobbed naked on the bed in her restraints. Michael ran his hand up her thigh, grabbing hold of the flesh as he climbed. Leaning down, he lined her belly with uncomfortable kisses leading up to her small little breasts. She pulled on the scarves, trying to get free. She didn't protest with words, which surprised Will as he observed. Slowly, Michael moved his lips across her nipple. He nipped at it with his teeth. Olivia whimpered as the nipple released from his bite.

"It's the best way, Olivia." Michael rationalized to her before sitting back on his heels to wipe sweat off his face. He sucked in a harsh breath before leaning down to run his mouth along her breast again, but he was turning pale, sucking in air in an exaggerated way.

"I don't feel like I can keep going." Michael rested his face against her breast, closing his eyes.

"What's that Michael?" Will asked.

Michael stayed leaning over the top of Olivia's naked flesh. His breathing became shallow and rapid. "I can't breathe." He was gasping for breath as sweat beaded across his body.

"Probably not." Will chimed in. "Those pills I gave you were PCP, not Viagra. I'm sure you assumed they were Viagra, but I figured if you decided you'd rape her to live, then you deserved it."

"My heart is racing." He fell over onto Olivia's side, gulping for air.

"What is happening to him?" Olivia was frantic, trying to move away from Michael as he clung to her for comfort, for help. Olivia began screaming as Michael began to seize.

"He's having a seizure. His brain is probably too hot. I don't know why you're screaming. He was going to rape you." Olivia continued her screams as choking foam filled up in the pedophile's mouth. "You'd think you'd be relieved."

Pulling himself out of the chair, Will moved over to where Michael lay, seizing on Olivia. Piss began running down his boxer shorts over Olivia's legs and her scream turned to hysterical sobbing.

"It's normal. Most seizure patients lose control of their bladder. It's just piss, Olivia, not battery acid." Will rolled his eyes at her reaction. "Hold still. I'll move him off you." Putting the gun down on the night side table, he rolled Michael off the bed onto the floor. "Olivia, pull yourself together, Jesus Christ." Will stepped over Michael as he lay choking on the foam in his throat. "You and I need to decide what to do here." He cupped her face in his large killer hands, forcing her to look into his eyes.

He smiled at her reassuringly. His beautiful face was such a convincing lie, the smooth glide of his lips across the perfect white teeth, the twinkle in his shining eyes. The way they glistened when he tried to be endearing reminded him of the deadly Anglerfish luring prey in with their luminous glow before devouring them. Up close to her, he could smell her adrenaline and fear. It aroused him. He leaned in to breathe in the scent on her sweet long perfect throat.

"Zach, please just let me go." She begged, "I promise I won't tell anyone."

"Kiss me." Will hovered his mouth over hers. She was quick, desperate, to lift her head up from the pillow. Reaching for his mouth with hers, she sucked in his lower lip, and he could taste her tears. Olivia was gorgeous, and wicked, and naked, tied up on her bed in complete fear of him. Will had been fucking her every which way all week, but in this moment, when he should have wanted to devour every ounce of her fear as he stole her life. Will didn't want to be inside her. *What the fuck?*

He snapped up off the bed, resisting the urge to kick Michael on the floor. "I don't understand it."

"You don't understand what?" She sniveled like a child who had been crying for too long.

"I want to punish you, and hurt you, and that should give me the most intense pleasure you could imagine, but it's just, not."

"Maybe you care for me."

"No, it's not THAT. I truly think you're a monster." He told her nonchalantly, as if it should be common knowledge to her already. "Like even more of a monster than any other person I've ever killed."

She began crying again.

Will rolled his eyes and put his face in his hands. "You know what, just hang tight. I need to make a phone call."

He got up from the bed and began walking around the lavish four post bed she was tied to for the door.

"Whaat? You need to make a phone call?" Her voice was exhausted, confused, and she sounded so beaten already. *Girl has a long night ahead of her, better get a second wind while I step away.*

"Yeah, I won't be long." He patted her foot as a goodbye, as he walked beside it and then out the door.

Will went down to the Mercedes to get his personal phone out of his backpack. Will pressed Vivian's name, and the phone began to ring. No answer. He pressed her name again. It rang and rang. No answer. He called a third time. Straight to voicemail.

Answer the fucking phone, Vivian. Fuck.

He knew she was sitting there, alone, looking at her phone light up with his calls. He called her from the hotel when he first got to town. Told her he decided to leave. He could tell that she was hurt, that he didn't think she was worthy of a goodbye. Her voice revealed her sadness, and the sadness whispered that she thought she had meant more to him. She had no idea he was leaving her *because* she did mean more to him. Much more, too much.

He hadn't answered any of her texts or phone calls since. He wanted her angry, not sad. It broke him to think of her hurt because of him. But fuck, he needed her now. He pressed her name again and listened to the rings. As soon as it went to voicemail, he pressed her name again. On the ninth call, she answered immediately.

"What!? What do you want!?"

Her venom filled him with a warm swarm of happiness. "You're angry with me." Because she cared, he thought.

"You left without a word, acted like I was an asshole when I questioned you for it last week, and now just stalker called me over and over because I didn't want to answer your call."

"I did not stalker call you." He chuckled at her over reactive display because she was mad.

"Non-stalkers realize after like the second try that someone is purposely not answering their call and don't just keep calling and calling to force the person to answer."

"How could I force you to answer? I'm not there."

"Yeah, I KNOW you're not here. Because you just up and left."

"I'm sorry."

"Me too."

He laughed. "Well, that didn't last long. I tell you I'm sorry and you just concede?"

"No, I mean I'm sorry that you made the choices you made, too."

"Vivvie, that makes no sense." Will realized that he was cheesy smiling into the phone.

"I am saying that I'm sorry with you. As in, I acknowledge your self-realization, and I too regret that you are an ass!"

He laughed again. "You're sorry still makes no sense."

She humphed dramatically, and it genuinely amused him.

"Why did you stalker call me, Will?"

What was the reason? Oh yes, Olivia. "I needed to ask you if you think there are some things beyond redemption."

There was silence on the line.

"Viv? Are you there?"

"Yes, I'm here. Just trying to wrap my mind around you and how unbelievably pompous you are."

"A pompous stalker huh?" He was laughing again. How did she make life so enjoyable? "Do you really miss me that much, Vivvie?"

"Yes."

"Yes, you miss me. Or yes, you think there are things beyond redemption?"

"Both."

"That's it? That's all you're going to say about it?"

"I think redemption is like a catch-22. You know, like if you are good enough of a person to realize you did something wrong enough to need it, then you'll never forgive yourself, anyway. So, nothing you ever do to earn redemption will be enough to actually be redeemed. But if you think your wrongdoing should be forgiven, then do you really deserve redemption for it? So, I guess there are some things that just aren't redeemable."

"Those who are worthy will never think they are worthy." He agreed with her explanation.

"Exactly."

"Your insight is eye opening. Thank you." *Kill Olivia.* "And missing me?" he asked.

"I hate that I miss you," she admitted.

"I really am sorry, Vivian. I hope that's enough."

"You're okay though, right? You're not having thoughts of self-harm or anything, right?"

"I have no intention of killing myself if that's what worries you."

Will could hear her audible relief at hearing him say those words out loud. It confused him. Why on earth would she think he would kill himself?

"I don't think you should call me for a while then, Will. It just reminds me that I'm not enough to keep anyone around." She laughed, but he could hear the sincerity in the words.

"Viv, that's not why." Will heard a loud thud from upstairs. *Shit.* "I need to go. We will continue this conversation another day."

"No, no, I don't think we should. It's okay Will, just take care of yourself. Okay?"

"Vivian."

She hung up.

Will put the phone in the backpack and hesitantly mounted the stairs. He heard heavy, panicked breathing and bumbling, frantic movements. Olivia must have gotten free. At the top of the steps, Will put his back to the wall and just waited for her to come flailing around the corner.

Sure enough, the moron came rushing right to him.

She screamed as he wrapped her up in his arms.

"You really have no natural instincts."

Olivia tried to wiggle and fight, screaming out in terror.

"You come straight for the main staircase of the house, making as much noise as a drunk sneaking in after curfew." The thought amused Will. "You really thought running down the hallway for the door was the best choice? I mean, the damn gun was right next to you on the nightstand." He kept her wrapped up in his hold, picking her up off her feet, to hold her firmly against his chest. With minimal effort, he slowly sauntered down the hallway.

"And you just completely left Michael. Fuck him, right?" The amusement turned to snickering disgust. "You knew he was alive, and you could have grabbed the pistol to defend him, to ensure you both lived. Instead, you abandoned him for your own life. At the turn of every single corner in your life, you make the choices that benefit you no matter what the consequence to others. You are just an undeserving horror."

He passed the bedroom door and headed toward the spa room. Olivia continued screaming and twisting. When he reached the door, Will kicked it open and threw Olivia into the room. She went stumbling in, naked and thrashing around.

"Don't touch me, stay away."

"That's not what you said this morning, or last night, or the night before that." Will shut the spa room door. "You wanted to hang me on your wall, I believe."

"You are going to fry if you touch me."

Fry, huh. "Does Georgia have the death penalty?"

"Oh yes, you didn't know? Yes, we do, and I know the prosecution team is *really* good. You don't want to risk that." Olivia was arguing her case from a different angle.

Prudent of her. A valiant effort. He could use this to his advantage though since she ruined his plans by getting out of the bed restraints.

Will put his hands out in front of him with his palms up. "I do not want to face the death penalty. How can I access money to get away if I let you live?"

"Yes, take the money. It's in the safe in my bedroom, just take it all. I have thousands in there and some jewelry. Take it all." Olivia started crying again. "Just let me live."

Will paused, giving her a chance to even bring up the fate of poor Michael. He acted as though he was considering her deal. Will had already taken enough money from her, she just didn't know it yet, and he would not be taking anything from the safe alerting police to a third party involved in this tragic crime scene. But he was trying to give her the chance to show *some* kind of concern for the man lying on her bedroom floor.

"I'll stay here. I won't try to run, I swear it."

No mention of Michael. "Hmmmm, I will need time to get away. Could you do me the favor of stepping peacefully into your sauna? I'll put the door jammer on, go deal with Michael, and then alert someone to come find you when I'm far from here."

"Yes. Yes, I will go into the sauna and just wait. I won't even try to get out." Olivia was already rushing over to get into the safety of the wooden box. Even hearing that he planned to go kill her client, Olivia still was ready to jump on the deal, promising her own life.

"Thank you for being so compliant. I'll even turn it on to warm you up. You must be cold, having been naked all this time." Will dazzled his disarming smile at her to convince her the ordeal was over. "I'm sure it has a safety timer, correct?" He obviously already knew the answer. He just wanted to reassure her enough to keep her calm.

"It does. It does. Just put me in there and go. I won't try to get out or follow you. I'll be fine for the night. Thank you. Thank you, Zach."

Olivia sat down on the bench, hugging herself around the chest to cover her breasts. She brought her legs up on the bench and cozied in to finally relax. Will shut the door and put the door jammer in place. He turned the sauna timer on and walked down to the bedroom to check on the pedophile.

Michael lay on the floor on his side. Will couldn't tell if he was passed out or sleeping from the drugs and seizures, but he was completely confident that he was still alive, yet not in any shape to go anywhere.

Leaving him sprawled out on the floor, Will walked back out to the pool house to gather more supplies.

He had time.

Sitting at the kitchen island, Will couldn't help but allow his thoughts to drift to the situation he had created with Vivian. She was hurt, and it was his doing. How had he allowed such an emotional mess to breach his life? Now he was feeling guilty, like a real shitbag, for making her think she was unworthy of the actions woman like Olivia received from men.

Will had waltzed into town and spent the entire first day setting up the most perfect date that any woman could ever dream of. He put effort into every small detail of the date, down to his own belt choice and cologne. Flowers were selected based on what he believed Olivia, specifically, would like. He bought tickets for a river cruise with special wines and cheese before dinner. All because she had mentioned, once, loving the water. He researched the top ten most romantic restaurants in Savannah before even considering making a reservation because he felt he wanted to impress her. Granted, Will had done all those things with the sole purpose of murdering Olivia, but nevertheless it bothered him that he never once thought to do anything like that for Vivian.

Here he was dedicating his life to punishing women for expecting entitlements they never did anything to deserve. While the one woman he knew who *did* deserve them had never been valued enough by any man to experience them.

Vivvie would have been at war when most young women were being wooed by young men. She wouldn't know what it felt like to get asked out on a special date planned by a man wanting to impress her. No doubt her husband left her for a woman like Olivia, or Serena, or Jessa.

Who took care of Vivian?

Hell, no man even held her damn doors open for her.

Vivian earned all the good things and yet all the men went to be with women who never did. All the men were drawn to the women who need to be taken care of. All the men flocked to the pretty hair, and the glossed lips and the well put together outfits, and they planned fancy dates to match their fancy style, and no one bothered with pretty little Vivian in her Walmart shoes.

Well, unless they needed comfort, of course. Unless they needed someone to land on when they fell. *Fuck.*

They all used her for the wonderful things she gave them without any expectation of anything in return, himself included. She was a doormat. She knew it, and she held them up anyway. Vivian held her shoulders back instead of melting them into the arms of the man next to her and for that, she was seen as being self-contained, self-preserved, and strong all on her own.

Did she want to be held up?

She must just be so tired. Hell, Will had seen it in her eyes. He had felt her in his arms just begging to be allowed to rest there.

Shit, what the hell, why was any of this even bothering him? She was just a damn woman, and women were a dime a dozen.

Will sighed and took the last bite of the delicious turkey sandwich he made for himself. He had been upstairs twice to turn the sauna back on. Michael was strapped to the chair in the spa room now, Olivia secured in the sauna, and Will knew he got moody when he was hungry. So he decided to make a sandwich and drink some milk before proceeding. He still was not completely sure what he planned to do.

Not having sex with Serena while killing her was a mistake. He had lost his own mental composure and made questionable decisions afterwards that he regretted. He had formed emotional attachments to Vivian because of those questionable decisions, and now that was causing moral conflict. Was that the reason for his inability to perform upstairs? Having feelings for Vivian?

It hadn't blocked him from sexually performing all week with Olivia. What had caused it to feel so wrong earlier?

Maybe it was the fact that he felt nothing while fucking Olivia all week. It had been part of the strategy. He had planned to feel the thrill and the pleasure tonight. To feed off her adrenaline, to get off on knowing she was being punished.

No matter where they dwelled from, these moral feelings were preventing him from getting the rush he was craving and needing.

What the hell was he going to do now?

Will couldn't help but remember the feeling of wrongness that filled him up the first time he ever killed someone in the war. To cope, they all praised each other for the kills, laughed about things like bodies that twitched and fluid seepages. They did these things to disconnect emotionally from the guilt and dreadfulness that invaded their souls when faced with the reality that they were ruthless enough to partake in the repulsive behaviors of war. After a while, those feelings disappeared, and eventually all feelings disappeared, during consciousness at least. The nightmares allowed all the sentiment to invade at once, shocking the soul into devastating torment, and trapping it there. That was why Will kept himself in control of his emotions. That was why Will was so baffled by his noncognitive surrender to Vivian. That was why he needed to take control back with Olivia and Michael.

Will sighed again and moved his empty milk glass and plate to the sink to wash them. He put his gloves back on and wiped down all the surfaces he touched. Walking back up the stairs, he felt the thrill start to build inside, knowing he had made a new plan. If this plan did not renew his thrill, he feared nothing ever would.

The first stop had been the bathroom was to methodically remove his clothing. He folded every item and placed them on the sink. Entering the spa room, Will was dismayed that Michael was still too out-of-it to proceed. How could a little bit of phencyclidine knock this man out for so long? He took a long, steadying breath. It was fine really. He still needed to speak with Olivia on the new plan. No reason to get flustered already. A change in plan is bound to have minor hiccups. An extended time hack truly isn't the worst thing that could go wrong.

Opening the sauna door, Will walked in and sat on the bench stark naked.

"Oh, it really is nice in here." Olivia looked up from where she sat hanging her sweat drenched head trying to breathe.

"You said you would leave." She barely whispered her words, and she looked on the verge of passing out.

"Oh, Olivia, let me get you some water. You look absolutely parched."

He almost bounced off the bench and jumped out of the sauna to retrieve a glass from the bedroom. Filling it with water from the bathroom sink, he rushed back, hoping that she had at least tried to get out while he was away, only to find that she hadn't even moved a single muscle.

"Here."

She took the glass from his grasp almost instantly, and instinctually with desperation.

"You truly have never had to spend one single moment of your life in a state of discomfort, have you?" His dazzling smile lit up his features, "It's usually polite to say thank you when someone does something nice for you, like say, I don't know, jump up to go fetch you water."

"You have tortured me, locked me into a sauna, and lied about leaving. Why should I thank you for anything?"

"Well, it just might behoove you considering that your dramatic assessment of torture, and my more worldly definition of the same term, differs vastly. Tremendously actually, as I will soon demonstrate on your client. However, that is what I came to discuss with you."

"What are you going to do to me?" If she hadn't been bone dry of fluids from the lengthy stay in the sauna, there was no doubt she would be crying yet again.

"See, Olivia, you still aren't getting it. I tell you I'm going to torture your client beyond your wildest imagination and you start getting all weepy about your own plight." Will rolled his eyes in frustration and shook his head in his hands to gather himself. "I am trying my hardest to negotiate with you, Olivia, for your own best interest. Please, please try your hardest to keep my irritation to a minimum, hmm? Shake your little head if you agree?"

Olivia slowly moved her head up and down in compliance. "Good girl. See, I had not planned on having two of you when I set out on this journey. Now I've had to evaluate who I believe is a more evil soul. You or him. I have adjusted my punishments accordingly."

"But you said you would leave, and I would just get to stay here until they find me."

"I lied. I needed to stash you away for thinking purposes. Plus, I needed a sandwich." He shrugged apathetically as she began to make little sobbing noises. He ignored them. "Anyway, so you now have a choice. You must really give it some consideration here because I do not want you remaining all blubbery and weepy every blasted second. It is annoying as *fuck*."

Will took a deep breath in the warm dry air to collect better control over himself. "So, I have decided that Michael is going to die, he deserves it, and I'm going to make sure that his life ends before leaving this residence. Nothing can change his fate. You though, Olivia, you have two choices. You may die as well, here in your home, before I leave in any manner of your own choosing. Or, you must have consensual sex with me while Michael is dying, and anytime afterwards for the duration of our time together, and when I have decided I have had enough, I will let you go."

There was a long silence in the hot sauna. "Are you thinking about it?"

"You want me to have sex with you while you kill him?"

"Yes, and anytime thereafter, until I let you go."

"What is wrong with you?"

"That my dear is a weighted question that I simply just do not have the time to divulge tonight. I should probably add to the list that you are not permitted to ask me ridiculously stupid questions."

"How will I know if it's a stupid question or not?"

"If you think it up in your ridiculously stupid mind and it threatens to pass over your collagen injected lips, then it is more likely a stupid question and you shouldn't ask it." He dazzle smiled at her again, dripping with loathsome condemnation. "I'm impatient Olivia, you've only even had this long to consider my proposal because our pedophile is still waking up from his little drug trip, and we need him alert for what comes next."

"What comes next?"

Will fought the urge to reach out for a fist full of her sleek blonde hair to bash her skull off the wooden bench. "Dear, sweet, stupid, Olivia, you're still not thinking before you talk. What happens next is up to you, remember? You decide if I kill you tonight, and how. Don't forget the how, because I doubt very much you'll enjoy my choices. Or you can agree to consensual sex while Michael dies, and anytime I request it, until I decide to let you go."

"You will let me go, though, right? It's not a trick? You won't lie?"

"I will let you go."

"I will do whatever you want until you let me go."

"Without the blubbering and crying and fighting and stupid questions?"

"Yes."

"Knowing that if you annoy me too much, or try to fight, or run, I will kill you?"

"Yes."

"And if you do not follow every command I give you, I will kill you?"

"Yes, and then you'll let me go?"

"I already answered that question, Olivia. Does my patience look intact enough right now for a second asking of the exact same fucking question I already answered?"

"No."

"No, is correct. Now get up. Let's go out and test our newfound arrangement. Shall we?"

Will got up from the bench and opened the sauna room door. "Ladies first." He motioned for Olivia to move in front of him. "Please bring your glass." She immediately leaned over for the glass she had placed down on the bench, and then hesitantly moved through the door. "Good. Now, walk yourself to the upstairs bathroom, use the toilet, fill your glass, drink it all, fill it again, and walk back to me."

"Okay."

"Olivia? You do realize this is a test, right? Tell me you understand."

"I understand."

"And that if you try to get away, you won't get far. Do you believe that?"

"I believe it."

"Good girl. Now head to the bathroom while I get things ready."

Olivia moved naked out of the doorway. She walked hesitantly down the hallway as he watched her move towards the bathroom as directed. Will knew she was scared enough to comply. He just wanted her to feel his eyes on her for a moment, to ensure that her fear was adequate to keep her from trying anything stupid. Once she reached the bathroom, and he heard the door click shut, he resumed his preparation.

Will found the control box for the tanning bed, used some tools he had retrieved from the pool shed to remove the temperature safety features. He had looked up how to do this on the computer downstairs. It was amazing what you could find out how to do on the internet. Michael was moaning, beginning to move around, so the timing was absolutely perfect. Will carefully untied him from the chair and removed the underwear he had piss soaked earlier.

With the pedophile now naked as well, Will opened the tanning bed lid and helped Michael inside it. He casually leaned against the tanning lid to wait for Olivia to return.

Upon her arrival, the pedophile was coming back to reality. Confused at where he was and why he was there as his brain caught up with him.

"Olivia, drink the glass of water please and then grab the straps that were used to hold Michael down to the chair."

She did exactly as she was told.

"Now, secure the tanning bed handle down to the bottom of the bed so it can't be opened."

Olivia began to breathe heavily as she moved, but she complied.

"Good. Make sure it's tight. Give it a good tug before you step back over here to me."

Olivia again did as she was told.

"Go lean over with your face into that little space of an opening next to Michael's face. Reach your fingers in and stroke his hair while trying to calm him down a little."

Olivia complied. "Shhhh," she cooed. "Try to take some breaths, Michael." Tears streamed down her face as she attempted to comfort him. Then she reached her hand into the opening of the bed, running her shaky fingers along his face, but jolted them back in surprise when she felt Will behind her, moving his hands down her bare ass.

"Go ahead Olivia. Keep comforting him."

"Let me out of here." Michael slammed his knee up against the tanning bed. "Open it! Let me out!"

"Calm down, please. Please calm down." The sobs almost began again from her.

Will grabbed hold of the flesh of her ass and paused. "No blubbering, remember?"

Olivia took a deep breath to compose herself.

"Now turn it on," he ordered.

With a shaky hand, Olivia reached over to turn on the tanning bed.

"NO, no, why are you doing this?"

"Say nothing." Will commanded. "Arch your back and allow me to play with you while we wait for this to heat up."

Will's hands slid up her back and down over her ass a few times before moving his fingers inside her. "You see Michael, you are a thief." Two fingers slid in and out. "You stole from that little girl. Your fucking step-daughter." Four fingers. "You hurt her physically, and you robbed her of her own body." Will moved his hand around inside Olivia pushing on the wall of her vagina until he heard an unwanted moan leave from her lips. He pulled his hand in and out slowly, inching a little more inside as he moved. "You used your power, and your money, to hire this woman, to get away with it, and it worked." He pushed his entire fist slowly in, spreading her open, little moans escaping her as he moved. "Until now."

"Oh, my god. Oh, my god." Michael was panicking, flailing around as Olivia let out little screeching noises at the fullness of Will's fist rolling around inside her body. He pushed further and harder, pulling back slowly and then throwing his fist into her again, lifting her ass off the ground as he got faster and harder with his fisting. She began to scream out as he moved.

"There is no god where you're going," Will chuckled. "But why count on the biblical promise of ramification for immoral actions? Let's bring Hell here, shall we? Olivia, turn up the temperature on the tanning bed."

Olivia didn't respond. She was too focused on the sensations inside her.

"Olivia," he paused his fist, "reach over and turn up the temperature on the tanning bed."

"NO! No, Olivia, don't do it! Please! Please don't."

She rested her face on the edge of the tanning bed, catching her breath before slowly bringing her hand over to the arrow that controlled the bed's temperature. She pressed it up a few times, to the maximum setting, and stopped.

"Keep going."

"But that's the highest it goes, Zach."

He pulled his fist out of her suddenly and landed his hand hard down on her flesh. The slap rang out through the room as she yelled out with surprise more than pain. "I overrode the safety Olivia, now turn it up."

She pressed the arrow one higher and stopped. His hand smacked down hard onto her skin, this time to hurt. "Higher."

Once more she pressed it, another smack. "Higher."

She whimpered, but pressed the arrow higher.

Will began thrashing her skin with both open palms over and over, hitting her ass, back, sides, and her thighs. She screamed out. Michael screamed yelling for help, and Will spoke between gritted teeth as he hit and hit. "Keep going higher, higher!"

Olivia hit the button frantically, sending the temperature of the tanning bed to one unsustainable to human flesh. Michael's screams began to change to those of insurmountable pain.

"Put your hands on top of the bed."

Olivia stood still, afraid to move, afraid to do the wrong thing.

"I said, PUT YOUR HANDS ON TOP OF THE BED!" Will commanded louder.

As soon as her hands hit the lid of the tanning bed, he slammed his cock into her. Olivia leaned into the bed as Will rocked his hips in a harsh rhythm that forced her breasts to bounce against the space where Michael's face could still be seen.

"Fuck, it's getting hot in here, huh?" Will laughed as he pushed hard into her, throwing her body against the bed. Michael tried to put his hands up to push the lid open, and he slammed his knees into it repeatedly, desperate to get out. Each time his flesh touched the hot lights, a sizzling sound accompanied his feral, tortured shrieks.

"I'm sorry," Olivia began to hyperventilate, "I'm sorry."

"Shut the fuck up, Olivia."

The skin began to blister, and the pedophile thrashed without hope. He screamed in guttural pain as Will increased the intensity of their sex over top of the burning box.

Will could feel the thrill beginning to build, and his blood prickle inside his veins with the excitement of panic, pain, and fear. The smell of her adrenaline mixed in the air with the pedophile's burnt flesh.

With his eyes closed, he could feel the power in his hands again bringing him to ecstasy. He threw his pleasure as deep inside her as he could get, and then collapsed down onto her body, pinning her to the top of the tanning bed. His hands wrapped up into her hair as he caught his breath, and Olivia began to scream and wiggle. "It's burning me! It burns!"

Will smiled big against her neck. "I'll bet" he chuckled. "Must be what Hell feels like huh?" Leisurely he moved off her, allowing her to step back from the burning on her belly.

She stood there naked, shaking, and staring at the blistering, seeping, screaming man burning alive in her tanning bed. She couldn't take her eyes away from him, nor could she even bring her own hand to cover her mouth and nose from the smell. Her chest heaved air in and out too quickly.

Will stood behind her, his breath slowing down as he composed himself, sexually spent.

"That's what he's always looked like, you know. That little girl saw it, her mother probably saw it, and I saw it. You were just blinded by money and power, and you couldn't see the burned-up man standing before you. He did not deserve to get off on that charge any more than he deserves to get out of this tanning bed now."

He turned her around and pressed her up against his chest into a hug. "Shhhh," he soothed, rubbing circles on her back. "Shhhh Olivia, you did well. You felt so good. Only a few more days now, and then I'll let you go."

She sunk into his embrace, exhausted and in shock. She sank into him, accepting his comfort and sobbed. He stood rubbing her back and cooing to her in a soft voice while Michael's screams subsided into moans. "Come. We will get a shower, put clothing on, and head out."

"Whe...where, where will we go?"

"Careful Olivia. I've cut you some slack because you pleased me tremendously just now. Don't ruin it."

Will slid his hands down her arms and grabbed hold of her hands to lead her out of the room into the bathroom for a shower. He was beginning to get used to showering with his girls. It had a certain comfort to it. He may need to do this more often.

Chapter 19

One Female Army Medic Veteran Alone with Her Thoughts

The air was chill. Not cold enough to see your own breath, but cold enough to make your shoulders pull up on their own to hold warmth into the body for reserves. Vivian walked slowly around the small man-made lake on top of the mountain, surrounded by state game lands. She loved coming up to these woods to walk. There was something so comforting about being among the large trees, feeling the vastness of the wilderness, thinking of how many years these trees stood against the brutality of weather and human activity. It made her feel awe inspiringly small. Insignificant in a good way, a way that allows all your own worries, and angers, and sadness to become unworthy of presence.

She had walked around the easy little hiking trail a few times now and decided to sit in the cool sand for a while with her shoes off. Let her toes dig into the coldness.

They roped off a small area of the lake for swimming and would truck in sand every year for the summer. A small booth opened by the bathrooms where they'd sell ice cream, snacks, and hot dogs. There was even a lifeguard stand, the coveted teenage summer job within a 100-mile radius. The man-made beach, at the man-made lake, becomes a special retreat for the land locked residents of the area in the summer.

Today though, it was empty and cold. She sat alone, staring at the water, remembering the last time she had been there. It had been a late summer evening. The days were still relatively hot, but the evenings brought in a chill reminder to everyone alerting them that summer was over, that winter was creeping in. Jason had asked her to go driving with him that day. They loved going driving, blaring all different genres of music, sharing a bottle of vodka passed between them. They would take turns picking songs, singly loudly, with the windows down. Vivian loved putting her arm out the window, feeling the resistance of the air as they drove. It always reminded her of what she used to enjoy about flying in helicopters. The freeness of whipping through the air at speeds that made the air sting if it hit your bare skin.

The two of them laughed together at the old songs they picked and relished being on the move, attempting to outrun the demons for a few hours. Moving, driving, not sitting still. For a few moments they could escape it all together, and be happy.

Then they would park the car, and the two of them would be instantly found by reality again.

There was no real escape. Vivian knew that now.

One of those drives had brought them to this place, this little lake in the woods. She sat at this exact spot with Jason as the chill in the air surrounded them while the sun disappeared. Everyone else had left for the day. The lifeguard stand stood empty, and a few little buckets and shovels lay abandoned on the sand.

They sat together without speaking. Devoid of reason or explanation of intent, Jason stood up and pulled his shirt over his head. He reached down, removed both shoes, socks, and pants. Standing in his underwear, he glanced down at Vivian and smirked. Her lips hitched up at the corner and she removed her clothing as well. Jason helped her up from the sand, and they held hands as they silently walked into the water together while the sun set.

Goosebumps crawled over her flesh, but the water felt warmer than the air around them making it a relief to sink down under the stillness of it. The two of them lay floating on their backs, watching the sky turn into a thousand colors all blended together. The brilliant golds, reds, and pinks painted the scene above them as they allowed themselves to float silently around the empty lake on the mountain.

They held hands but said nothing to each other. Their hands touching spoke of everything they needed to say. They never needed words, they only needed to be near one another. She could understand his soul just by seeing his eyes or hearing his voice.

Jason could see her just as clearly.

The two of them only needed to know that the other was on the same earth to be as close as any two people could ever be. When the sun disappeared and the colors were gone, Jason put himself upright in the water. He swam around Vivian, putting his arm under her back to pull her upright into his embrace. As they tread water together in the lake, Jason pulled back so he could look into her face.

"Marry me, Viv?"

Vivian was caught completely at a loss. "What? Marry you?" She laughed out, "Why on earth would we need to get married? We have lived together for years, we own our home together, and we sleep in the same bed. Why do we need a license for it?"

"Please." He looked lost, broken, as if marriage might put him back together. "I want to get married. Please, please marry me."

His intensity concerned her, "If it matters that much to you."

"Is that a yes, then?"

"Yes, Jason, that's a yes. But I don't understand it."

He pulled in a deep, relieving breath that filled his lungs all the way up as he patted her shoulders.

"Good. That's good."

As quickly as he had jumped up, he lay back down to float in the lake on his back, holding her hand again.

Vivian pushed the confusion and concern back to the far corner of her mind to chew over later as she too lay on her back to float next to him. They stayed there until the night fell and their fingers pruned. She shivered when they got out of the water. Rushing to put on clothing, the two of them ran to the truck and warmed themselves up with swigs from the vodka bottle on the way back to their house.

Two days later, Vivian walked into the kitchen and found a jewelry bag on the kitchen counter.

"Jason, what's this?"

"Oh," he yelled from the living room. "That's your ring. Open it up, see what you think."

Vivian stared at the bag as if opening it might burn her fingers. "You were serious then? At the lake?"

"Yes, I was serious." His voice was closer as he moved to stand next to her in the kitchen. "I'm dead serious, Viv. If you don't like this one, we can return it and get a different one, but I want you to have something from me that is beautiful and precious. I want you to know what you're worth and I want it to be on your finger every single day, reminding you. Every time you glance at the ring on your finger, I want you to think, 'Wow, I am worth being decorated with beautiful diamonds because you are. You are the best person I have ever known."

"You don't need to prove to me that I'm special to you. I already know I am. You don't have to marry me. I'm not like other girls. I don't need marriage to know you want to live this life with me."

"I understand that, but I want you to be my wife. Please Viv, it's important to me."

"All of a sudden, it's important to you?"

"Just open the bag, see if you like the damn ring."

The same uncomfortable concern crept up into her spine and settled into the back of her neck as she opened the bag. This didn't make any sense. His sudden desire for marriage didn't make sense. What they had together already worked for them. It was enough. What on earth would possess him to suddenly want her to be his wife? Why would he think she needed an expensive ring to wear around on her finger to remind her what she was worth to him?

Reaching inside the pretty bag, she removed the tissue paper and pulled out the little box. Gingerly, she opened it, and immediately stopped breathing.

The ring was gorgeous. Beyond anything she had expected. A white gold setting that sloped up with an intricate pattern of swirls only seen from the side to hold the diamonds on top. The setting reminded her of the eloquent borders in the doorways of old Victorian homes owned by rich 1800 Lords and Ladies. Old fashioned beauty. On top of the setting sat a halo of little diamonds rounding one brilliant large sparkling diamond in the center. Two rows of diamond-halos circled with leaf shapes on either side. Next to the delicate leaves were rows of more little stones tucked into the band.

Looking down on the ring, it resembled a delicate open rose that bloomed with pure artistry.

"Jason." She couldn't think of what to say. "This is too beautiful. It's too expensive. I don't need something so lovely."

"Why not? *You* are that lovely, *you* are that beautiful. You are worth the expense. Put it on. I want to see it on you."

Vivian looked up at him in shock. "I can't. It must have cost two grand. I don't deserve it."

Jason laughed, "It was three."

"Three thousand dollars? Oh, shit Jason." She closed the lid of the ring box and put it back in the bag. "No, no, there is no way I'll wear it."

"Oh yes, you will." He took the ring box back out of the bag and opened it again. "Here. Take the beautiful ring, put it on right now, and never take it off. I want you to wear it always. Please Viv, I just need you to. Please?"

Reluctantly, she pulled the ring out of the box and slid it onto her finger. It fit perfectly.

"That really looks good on you. Like it belongs there." A real smile lit up his face, looking at the beautiful ring on her hand. "You should have been dripping with diamonds already. You are worth all the diamonds hanging from you. I hate that you don't know that."

"I've never owned anything this expensive, or beautiful. It truly makes me feel special. Thank you. I don't know why it matters to you, but I'll wear your ring. Always."

He reached out and pulled her shoulders into him for a hug. He rubbed her back and held her where they stood in the kitchen. "You are worth it. You have always been worth it."

Vivian felt sick in her gut. It all felt so wrong to her, like he was hiding his reasons. She couldn't understand why he needed this. None of it made sense, but she held him in the kitchen with her new big diamond ring on her finger because he asked her to.

Two months later, they had a small winter wedding. Vivian wore a cathedral veil of lace. The dress, an ivory mermaid gown with floating lace applique and a soft shift blossom at the bottom. Vivian's sister served as the maid of honor. Jason's best friend from the Corps drove four hours to be his best man. Their colors were ice blue and silver, with sparkling snowflakes, white Christmas trees, and candles decorating the reception hall. A few of their family and friends gathered happily. The food was superb, toasts were given with fine champagne, and Jason and Vivian danced in each other's arms to all their favorite car driving songs. They laughed when he smushed wedding cake into her face and the night ended with the new husband and wife running through bubbles to get to their decorated truck.

They took a short honeymoon to Atlantic City, ate at the fancy hotel restaurants, and he taught her how to cheat at poker. They walked together for hours on the beach, just watching and listening to the ocean.

Every night they would begin kissing as soon as they reached the hotel room, but no matter how the sex began, he always turned it into lovemaking. It was so new to her. He had never been interested in being in-love before, had never looked at her so deeply, or held her face so gently. He worshiped her body with his, left kisses up and down every inch of skin, grazed fingertips along every scar, and caressed her face so delicately that he made her feel that he worried holding her too tight might shatter her to a million pieces.

"Do you know how much you mean to me? Do you know how appreciative I am to have you in my life? Do you know how much happiness you have given me? Do you have any idea how beautiful you are?" He would ask her these lovey-dovey questions as she bounced on top of him, her golden hair flowing freely as he filled her with enough praise for a goddess in all her naked glory above him.

In the morning they would lay naked in the white sheets, tangled all up in each other. His large killer hands would pet her head, stroke her shoulders, and slide along her breasts so softly. He would twirl the rings around her finger and then bring her hand to his lips to kiss each one. He would breathe in the scent of her wrists and slide his lips along the delicate flesh there.

Committing her smell to memory.

He would pull her hand to his face and encourage her to stroke her fingers through his beard. Committing her touch to memory.

He would bury his face into her neck and rest there with her arms holding him against her chest.

Vivian was so taken by his need to love her. He was the most loving he had ever been since she first met him years before. She had never seen him so in need of comfort, either. He couldn't stand to be without her touch, couldn't sleep without her in his arms, and couldn't be more than an arm's reach away from her at any time. He seemed afraid to be without her at his side. It melted her heart, but it frightened her at the same time, because it was less like love and more resembling desperation. Vivian had never seen him desperate or afraid. It worried her, while it made her want to hold him tighter and kiss him more.

On the last day of their honeymoon, they went down to the ocean's edge so Vivian could collect a few shells before they left. She was holding her yellow dress up in her arm to keep the hem from getting wet as she walked with her feet in the water, searching for the pretty ones. She reached down for a shell worthy of taking home and grabbed it. Holding it up, she turned to show Jason, but the smile fell from her face as she saw him standing there staring at her with unrequited pain in his eyes. Vivian dropped the shell and rushed the short distance between them to pull his face into her hands.

"What is it Jason? What's wrong?"

He smiled down at her, taking her hands into his and kissing each palm. "My Viv, you're my best friend. Do you know that?"

"I know, I *know* I am, Jason. Please, tell me what's wrong. Please?"

"I'm just tired, Viv. Just so damn tired."

"Let's go home. Come on, let me take you home. You'll feel better once we're home."

Jason shook his head reassuringly and leaned down to kiss her there on the beach.

Not long after their honeymoon, Jason decided to leave. And so Vivian sat alone on the man-made beach, at the man-made lake, wondering why she hadn't been enough to keep Will around either. She wasn't so naive to believe that Will loved her, but Christ, she thought that he at least valued her enough to want to be around for a little bit longer than he was. She thought that maybe he would have at least found her worth a conversation about why he was leaving, that maybe he might think her worthy of an explanation. That maybe he had been a real friend.

Wrong again.

Looking out on the little lake with her feet buried in the cool sand, Vivian decided that she wouldn't allow herself to think about it anymore. She would shut it away with all the rest of it, lock it up, drink it down, and ignore all emotions related to it at all. Forget his name, forget his eyes, his laugh. She would forget his phone number and refuse his calls. He would no longer even be a passing thought in her mind, and she would stick her head in the cool sand, like her toes were now.

"What does it matter, really?" She said out-loud to the lake, "I am insignificant after all."

Chapter 20

One Male Army Medic Veteran and the Lawyer

Thank whatever fucking God may be that Olivia had finally stopped crying. The entire car ride to Missouri, he had been wishing he'd left her in the tanning bed with the pedophile. He wanted to find a trunk locker to put her in and lock it up. She was rather tall though, and there was no way she would fit. *If I cut off her feet, she would fit.* The idea amused him, and he laughed out loud. She stopped her blubbering to look over at him. Will waited for her to speak, for her to ask him what was funny, but she held her tongue.

"Don't you want to know what amused me?" He asked her without taking his eyes from the road.

"No, I don't need to know." Her voice was meek and demure.

"I realize you don't need to know. I asked if you wanted to know."

"Do you want me to know?"

"Holy fuck almighty, you are making me want to bash your skull in with a hammer." She immediately began crying again, prompting Will to begin smacking the shit out of the steering wheel. "I was thinking of cutting your feet off to make you fit in a trunk, which made me laugh. Now you're crying again and it's not fucking funny anymore. Stop the fucking crying! *Stop it!* Do you hear me? Stop!"

She sniffed and breathed deeply in near hyperventilation, trying to control herself.

"Finally, you understand." He worked to control himself as well. "Fuck. We are nearly to the house. We've rented it for the duration of my stay here. The neighborhood is not anything you're used to, but I've been told it's decent. Now don't ask me how long that will be or how long until I let you go. Engage me in normal conversation and we will get along much better."

"What is the neighborhood called?"

"See," he beamed a smile to her, "that is exactly the right way to go on. However, a truly moronic question. I don't really know that the name of where we're staying matters. Now, the woman I'm here to ruin lives in a neighborhood called Sunset Hill, or something like that. Her house reminds me a lot of your house."

"Why did you rent a house and bring me along when you could have stayed with her?"

"There is a child. So, I won't stay there, and as I mentioned before, I had planned on killing you. Would you prefer I killed you?"

"No"

"I didn't think so." He laughed again. "So, you will stay at the house I've rented until I figure out what to do. Unless you want me to decide now, which of course would be to just kill you."

"I'm sure the house will be fine."

Will chuckled, "I bet it will."

"You just go around the country killing people?"

"I don't kill them all. Some I just ruin, as I mentioned with this woman here. She's why we're in Kansas City at all. This area of the country holds no appeal to me." He rolled his eyes, "But I feel as if her daughter will be much better off without her as an influence."

"So, you won't kill her because she has a child, but you don't want her to raise the child?"

"Correct. It would be cruel to the child to have to mourn her mother's death. I'm not a monster, Olivia."

She said nothing.

"You want to disagree with me, don't you? Only you won't because you're frightened, and rightfully so." Will chuckled a little at how crazy she must think him. There was no way she could understand. There was no way a mind like hers could ever wrap around his reasons.

"I do empathize with you. Having to be a part of something horrible for the greater good can seem evil when you are in the thick of it. So, I can understand how I might appear to be a monster after the other night." He peered over at her from the corner of his eye to see if she had any reaction. She continued to stare ahead stubbornly. "Stop and ask yourself though, who in this vehicle is putting the wellbeing of the child involved first, and who in the vehicle allowed one to get fucked for money. Just something to think about, princess."

The house was fully furnished. He had used some good old-fashioned chloroform on Olivia so she would be sleeping in the car before they met the homeowners to get the keys. It was an Airbnb rental, and he booked it for the month at about sixteen hundred dollars, all under a fake identity. The house was a two-story baby blue sided home with a nice little front porch and big bay windows on the side going up both floors. It was sleekly renovated, with hardwood floors and exposed beams on the ceiling. Large sliding barn doors separated the rooms, impractical but stylish. The color palate was grey and white, and greyer and whiter, and different shades of grey and white. Very bland but very easy to decorate and upkeep. Smart business decision since this was a year-round rental. Will wondered how the owner made constant money off a rental located near nothing special. All he could think of was that people rented it for visits to the city. It was almost depressing to think anyone would want to spend a vacation in Kansas City.

The house was a good decision. Originally, he had booked the house because he was simply tired of hotels, but now it was a huge convenience. He had not expected to have Olivia to restrain while away, which wouldn't have been possible in a hotel room. Things would go much more smoothly now.

Will carried Olivia into the house first, put her up on the bed to sleep while he brought in their bags, and looked around the house. The upstairs bathroom was the best place for securing Olivia while he was away. There were no windows and a loud fan with the ceiling light fixture. He could strip her down in the bathtub and zip tie her hands and feet. But he would have to figure out a way to secure her to the wall or the pipes, something permanent in the bathroom. Though he could rig something up tonight and make a quick trip to the nearest store for groceries, and something to restrain Olivia more permanently for his long visits with Crystal.

After stripping Olivia down, he carried her to the bathtub and zip tied her arms behind her back and ankles together before wrapping her up in a blanket-and-duct-tape cocoon. She had wiggled herself out of restraints once before, so he was taking zero chances with her ability to do it again. If Will was being completely honest with himself, he thought her fight factor was why he was keeping her alive. Besides, it was comforting to have someone around he didn't need to be fake with. He would be able to tell her about his dates with Crystal, bounce ideas off her for his plans to ruin her. Maybe it wouldn't be horrible to have her here, inconvenient, but not completely horrible.

Her appearance would need to change in case someone saw her. If they ordered a pizza and the delivery man caught a glimpse, it might trigger his memory of the platinum blonde bombshell. Photos were no doubt all over the news since her disappearance was reported. She would look good as a redhead, maybe a dark rich auburn red.

Will was gone for a few hours and returned to Olivia screaming for help as he entered the front door. He rolled his eyes at the audacity of her thinking he would have left her in a place he thought others would be able to hear her scream. He put the perishable items away in the kitchen before mounting the stairs to see to his loud captive.

"You'll be very unhappy to learn that your screams are completely suppressed by the bathroom walls and fan. I couldn't hear even the slightest noise outside the house."

"My hands Zach! They're burning!"

"The zip ties had to be tight. I took the liberty of getting a more comfortable method of restraint while I was out. I'll set it up and then release your hands."

"Please. Please do it now. It hurts so bad."

"You're overreacting, Olivia. I made sure that they were loose enough for blood flow. You're going to have to learn that your body can endure a lot more than you believe it can."

She cried out, "I can't stand it!"

"Olivia, women have babies every minute, not to mention what the female veterans endure, so you can stand zip ties." Will chuckled in response as he scooped her up, still in her blanket cocoon. Slicing down the tape, he peeled it away from her upper body enough to cut the zip ties around her wrists.

Olivia sobbed in relief and Will laughed.

"Keep your tears coming, girl, because you're *really* going to cry over what comes next." Will reached in the bag and pulled out the department store boxed hair dye.

Chapter 21

Unenthused Ruination

The entire day had been spent with Crystal and Ada. The absolute loathing that dripped off Crystal anytime she saw her daughter smile made Will's stomach churn. How could a mother ever feel in competition with her child? If Ada stood near Will, or attempted to claim any of his attention, Crystal would put her hand on her shoulder, pretending to be a loving embrace, but Will knew better. He saw the well-practiced hidden wince the child exhibited as her mother's fingernails dug into her flesh.

After dinner, the girl's grandmother came to pick her up so Crystal could 'have a break.' As if the child, who never so much as breathed heavily without permission, put a strain on her mother enough to require a break. As soon as Ada left with her grandmother, Will took the opportunity to question Crystal about the girl's father. He learned that Crystal used the girl to bleed money out of the father and loved it. She kept the kid to torture the man. He owned a small but successful construction company, dressed in jeans, and wore a beard. He used chewing tobacco, which disgusted her, and bitched at length that he had taken her camping without a camper. Will questioned why she ever dated him in the first place and Crystal smiled with pride in her eyes, "eighteen years of income."

Will was uncharacteristically beaten down by this one. It bothered him because he felt so bad for the child being used by her mother for money. The worst part was that the man actually wanted to be a father, but Crystal kept him away. Unlike his own selfish fuck of a father. Will couldn't remember his father ever putting effort into him ever, he would throw money at him, expect him to look the part of a good son, but he never wanted to have his children for anything except showing off.

After the horrible day spent with Crystal, Will went straight upstairs to get Olivia out of the bathroom. He had her ball gagged and handcuffed, chained to the pipes around the toilet with a padlock. Her box job red hair was trashy looking, and he loved it on her. He had her in a neon green lace camisole and matching blindfold. The porn store attached to the strip club on the outskirts of the city had proven to be one stop shopping the day before. Handcuffs, blind fold, camisole, and a ball gag, all in one stop. He also got a few other adult store products for Olivia that would allow him to let off some steam. She should realize she was only alive as a diversion. He wanted to make sure she knew what was required of her, to make the inconvenience he tolerated for her worth it.

"Hello Olivia, how was your day?"

He reached up to remove the blindfold and then the ball gag. She moved her mouth around but said nothing.

"No, tears today. You are learning endurance, good girl." She needed his praise so he could mold her.

He uncuffed her and pulled her by the hand into the bedroom. "There is a glass of water for you over on the end table with some cheese and grapes. Help yourself, I already ate."

Will sat on the edge of the bed while Olivia ate as much as she could as fast as she could. "I'm glad you like the spread. You have my sincere apology for leaving you worried and hungry for so long. It was poorly done of me. I'll try not to be that insensitive again.

Today was hard to endure on my end too, I assure you. I wanted to gut this selfish cunt and instead I had to sit and plan a trip with her like we are lovers going on vacation. Of course, I'll be paying." He rolled his eyes. "Well, she thinks I will be. What she hasn't realized yet is that I took out several credit cards in her name and have been racking them up with everything she thinks I've been buying for her. It's actually comical if you think about it."

"Is that how you'll ruin her?" Olivia asked very quietly between bites. She was much more demur now, and he preferred her this way, almost liked her. Almost.

"No," he snickered, "credit card debt is just a little added bonus. My plan is to get her arrested and for the little girl to go back with her father."

"You're going to get her arrested? For what?"

"Well, you're the lawyer. What's the best way to get the kid taken from her?"

"Abuse, neglect. I don't know Zach. Attempted murder."

"Olivia, that's brilliant! I could set it all up to make it look like she planned on killing the little girl for a life insurance policy and then report it. It's perfect and it won't take long to set up. I'm tired of being here."

"Where will you go after you leave here?"

"You mean where will *we* go when *we* leave here?" Will stalked slowly over to where she sat eating the grapes. "Olivia, Olivia, and you had been doing so good, and then you had to go and ruin it with one of the forbidden questions."

"But I didn't. I didn't ask."

"Oh, but you implied. That's the same thing as asking, isn't it? Seeking out the answer to a question. You were trying to figure out when I'd be letting you go." Will shook his head exaggeratedly and ran his thumb along her jawline. "I love your hair like this you know. You remind me of a back-alley hooker. Now, lay on your belly."

She instantly did as she was told. She was pleasing to look at and he did want to reward her for the vast improvements she had made in their short time together. He climbed up onto the bed to straddle around her thighs. Reaching up to massage her shoulders and back, he ran his hands down over her bare ass as he rubbed. "I've rented the house for another month. Then I want to buy a cabin. After you help me find one, close on it, and decorate it, then I'll let you go."

He focused his attention on her ass, kneading as he spoke. "I know it seems like a long time to you. But don't you want to help me get this little girl to her father, who loves her and doesn't want to use the shit out of her for money?"

"By framing her mother for attempted murder?"

"Yes. I do so love being able to discuss plans with someone else."

"You do?"

"I really do. It's nice having someone to talk to again."

"Again? Did you used to have someone?"

"I did."

"Was she actually special to you? Did you kill or ruin her?"

"I never said she was a female. I mean, she is a female. Though I didn't kill or ruin her, I just left. She wasn't one of you. Wasn't like you or Crystal or the others. She is deserving of good things that I don't have it in me to give her. She was actually my friend."

"So, you miss her. Can't you just call and tell her you're sorry and you miss her?"

"I've tried. I've been trying to call her, but she won't answer." He rolled off Olivia's legs and flopped onto the spot next to her. "I've texted and called and called. She just doesn't want to talk to me, I guess."

Olivia flopped her head over on the pillow to look at Will where he lay. Hesitantly, she reached her hand over to move a piece of his hair across his forehead. He allowed it. "Tell me about her. I mean, if you want to. Maybe I can help figure out how to get her back, as your friend."

Will draped his leg lazily over Olivia's legs. "Her name is Vivian. She was a medic in the army, like me."

"You were a medic?"

"Yeah, I was an army ranger, though. A lot more killing than saving. But technically, my MOS was medic. So, I went to meet this horrible woman named Serena, to kill her, and happened to see a flyer for a veteran's meal. I decided to go, and Vivian was there." Will leaned up on his elbow. "Is this pillow talk?" He smiled at her genuinely, one of his genuine smiles.

'Yeah, I guess it is. I like your smile, you know. I haven't seen it before."

"You've seen me smile a thousand times, Olivia."

"But not like this. Not a real smile. Do you smile like that at her?"

"I don't know. What does how I smile matter? Or explain why she won't answer my calls?"

"It matters. You aren't trying to get anything for it. I know because I do the same thing. I flash whatever I need to in order to get what I want." She shrugged. "I think that's probably why she isn't answering your calls. You didn't want anything from her and maybe she feels stupid for loving you now."

"You think she loves me?"

"I don't know her, so I'm not sure, but people don't usually not answer calls unless they're hurt. If you're mad you answer to yell, 'Fuck off,' or something mean. You *don't* answer if you're hurt, and you can't be hurt by someone you don't have feelings for."

"She's married."

"Really! That's scandalous. Well, maybe she was just using you for sex."

"No, it wasn't like that. We only had sex once. Vivvie wouldn't use me for anything. She isn't like that, and they aren't together. He left her. I think it just bothered me that she belonged to some other man, because she could never be mine if she's already his."

"Did you ask her?"

"Did I ask her what?"

"If she wanted to leave her husband and be with you." Olivia was slowly running her fingers through his hair as they spoke.

"No, there is no way I could ever be with her. I need *this*." Will gestured around the room.

"Maybe you wouldn't if you had her."

"I'm afraid that it won't be enough, that she won't be enough, and I'll end up hurting her."

"Kind of like you already did?"

"Hmmm. I see your point." He was being honest to Olivia, enjoying the conversation about his true emotions. "It was better for me to leave her, though. She doesn't understand how I keep myself sane."

"You call this sane? You kill people and keep me locked up in a bathroom."

"In your mind it doesn't make any sense, but in mine, it's justice. I'm taking back from you what I earned for you by going to war. Vivian would understand."

"Then why didn't you tell her what you do, Zach? Is it because you think she will stop you?"

"My name is Will, actually. I want both. I want the comfort I get from her." Will sat up and got off the bed. He walked over to the bag he had brought in from the porn shop. "But I want what I get from you, and Jessa, and Serena, and Michael, and Crystal and the others too."

"What do you get from us?"

"Redemption."

Olivia gazed off towards the window, and a somber look fell over her features. "You know, I didn't realize. I didn't understand that it was wrong to use the law to get guilty people off. I justified it. It's what I was taught my whole life. My father, I just wanted him to be proud of me."

"You knew. You just didn't care. There is a big difference in the two, Olivia. Maybe when you were a child, you could use that excuse. But as an adult. No, you knew. What I'm doing is the opposite. I care way too much that what you do is wrong." Will stood confidently in the words he spoke.

She surprised him with a retort. "But you know what you do is wrong too, and then you justify it by saying it's redemption. When really, it's because you need the thrill of it to survive and you're afraid your Vivian will see right through that."

"I guess you're right." Will laughed sardonically. "We are both monsters." He took the dildo out of the bag and brought it over to the bed. "Bring yourself up onto your knees. I enjoyed this little conversation, thank you. I'm also going to enjoy a little sexual tryst with you now. Is that alright?"

"Please don't hurt me."

Will rolled his eyes. "I'll only hurt you for pleasure, not for punishment. You'll enjoy it. Cross your ankles and open your knees wider."

Chapter 22

One Female Army Medic Veteran Alone Again With her Thoughts

She lay with her face against the hardwood floor. Her phone lit up on the floor next to her.

It was Will calling. *Again*.

She didn't have anything to say to him yet. She really wasn't mad at him, it's not like they were a couple. It was more that she felt like they had connected in a way that few would understand, and she believed it mattered to him. She believed she had mattered to him. Only the truth was she was expendable. She had been expendable to everyone who she ever cared about.

Vivian didn't want to hear his voice. She didn't want to hear anyone's voice.

She just wanted to be alone in her house, still and unfeeling. So, she lay on the floor in her robe with the bottle of vodka next to her. She could hear the silence. Could hear the stillness of the air that didn't move into the lungs of soldiers anymore. The thump of a heart that gave up. She could hear the moment when the screaming stopped.

The stillness had so much to hear, so much to fill up inside her. She didn't want Will to hear it in her voice and worry.

The burning started to fill in her throat as the stillness surrounded. Another pull from the bottle to meet the burn was the only defense available. She lay her face back down on the floor, surrounded by the empty places where sounds should be.

She felt lost without her face pushed onto the floor. She didn't know where she had gone or how to get back. Her mind remembered a child's song her granny used to sing. It crept up into her mouth and filled the stillness around her without even meaning to. The words just kind of slipped out in desperation to be somewhere other than where her mind was always trapped.

"Where oh where is sweet little Vivvie,
Where oh where is sweet little Vivvie,
Where oh where is sweet little Vivvie.
Way down yonder in the paw paw patch.
Picking up the paw paws, put them in her pocket.
Picking up the paw paws, put them in her pocket.
Picking up the paw paws, put them in her pocket.
Way down yonder in the paw paw patch.
Come on boys, let's go find her..."

No, her eyes closed as the burning filled up her throat again. "No, please don't find me. Please. Please, don't find me." Vivian cried alone on the floor in a burning heap of stillness that nobody heard, and nobody saw, and nobody knew. She crawled on her belly across the floor to find The Lady, so she didn't have to sob alone. "Please don't let them find me. I'm sorry, I'm so, so sorry."

In that moment, she wanted him. She wanted Will.

If she could replace alcohol in her life with a person, it would be him. Everything she sought from the bottle she gained from him.

Inside his arms she found security, a shroud of brief escape into the warmth and steady absolute conviction of safety that his body *forced* into her when he was there.

With her face pressed against his chest and her head tucked under his chin, with his hold so secure engulfing her in his arms, she was never afraid.

Or was that how she felt with Jason? *Fuck, I can't remember.*

Was it Jason, or Will, who gave that to her?

But Jason wasn't here. *Neither was Will, though.*

Vivian craved that moment against Jason's chest. In that moment, she never feared herself.

His voice calmed the panic that forever stirred under her skin. He commanded it to be still with booming authority.

But Will's mere proximity comforted the anxiety that had held her. Even the anxiety that held her with the sharp sting of tight barbed wire wrapped around her internal self since the very moment her boots grazed the earth of the god forsaken countries they visited.

Or had that been Jason, too? She could barely even see his face anymore behind her eyes.

Near Jason, her senses were able to relax, her racing thoughts slowed. He simply commanded her body to be 'at ease' when he was near, and her body complied without protest. Only, as wonderful as his smooth burn may have been, he was also the damaging crush that alcohol brings as well, because he was no longer there.

Neither of them was here.

Not Jason.

Not Will.

Not anyone else.

Only The Lady.

Which was probably better, because standing near either of them was like standing too close to the edge of a cliff.

Vivian decided it was better that they were both gone. Maybe they were the same as the vodka in her bottle, both the best thing she could feel and the worst thing she could ever do to herself.

Chapter 23

One Male Army Ranger Medic and the Lawyer

Will looked over at Olivia sitting on the couch in her new pink latex garter dress. He liked hearing her move in it. The stiff scrunching sound reminded him of visiting his great aunt's house as a kid and having to sit on her plastic covered couch.

This latex dress that he bought for Olivia with Crystal's credit card was see-through. He could see her tiny tits smushed up against the fabric. They really weren't that much fun to play with.

Will let out an exaggerated, audible sigh.

He really wished that he wasn't getting bored of her and her tiny titties, but he couldn't help but admit to himself that he was. There were things about her that he still enjoyed. She was intelligent enough to carry on a conversation with. That was an unexpected delight, being able to discuss things with another person. He was also quite pleased with how adapted she had become to her new submissive role. She had molded herself to him in a way he hadn't expected, almost as though she *wanted* to make him happy, and she wanted to please him with her own suffering. What was it they called that, Stockholm syndrome?

Will had found a helpful website to overnight a few items. The hammered steel coffee table-cage was the most expensive, but the best investment by far. The steel bars were welded, probably why it cost so much, but with a simple padlock he no longer had to worry about her escaping. Olivia didn't even protest getting into the cage anymore. He still put the ball gag on her, but it was more for his pleasure to see her silenced than to actually ensure her silence in his absence. It had only been two months, and he honestly believed she would sit silently in the cage if the police were knocking on the front door calling her name.

"I thought I would feel better today than I do." He admitted to Olivia.

She looked over at him from the couch, confused. "But it all worked. The entire plan."

She was right. Will had taken the life insurance policy out on little Ava from Crystal's bedroom computer. He planned an island vacation with her and had her sign the life insurance policy, unknowingly, by telling her it was a needed document for the travel insurance. He set the entire plot in motion the day they left for the airport.

It had taken minimal effort to trick Crystal into believing that something "from work" had come up suddenly and that he would need to meet her at the resort. She whined about traveling alone at first, but Will was able to appease her by telling her that the night flight didn't have any first-class seats available last minute. The thought of flying coach if she flew with him had her instantly agreeing, with a fake pouty lip, and Will left the airport to go set the scene without issue.

Crystal hadn't realized that nothing in the trip had ever included her companion, and the resort was a singles resort. The credit cards used to book the entire thing were all in her name, and his name was not on one single document.

After leaving the airport, Will drove her car back to her home to inject antifreeze into all the apples in the fruit bowl using a needle and syringe, ordered with her credit card, of course. Crystal was the one who had put the apples in the bowl, so her fingerprints would be on them. Her prints would be all over the antifreeze bottle too, since he decided she should know how to service her car and taught her how to replace it in her vehicle the week before.

He also had her call her mother that morning to instruct her to bring Ada to the house after school and insist she eat the apples for a snack, so they wouldn't go bad while she was away on her trip. Will even had her write a note to Ada on the counter, making sure she was aware of what to eat while 'mom was away.'

Her own damning diary was left laying out on her bed. The entire thing detailed how much she viewed the child as a paycheck and never really formed the loving relationship she should have with her. Her own awful words would seal any doubt anyone ever had that she was an unfit mother.

After setting the scene, an anonymous tip was called into child protective services, and the police were sent out to investigate. It was proven that the apples were injected with antifreeze, and the grandmother confirmed her daughter had emphasized that the apples were for Ava. Even the note on the counter was in Crystal's handwriting, more evidence stacked against her. Then the life insurance policy was immediately located.

The girl's biological father was given emergency custody and Crystal was arrested for attempted murder, among other charges, the moment she stepped foot off the plane. Of course, she cried and pled that it was Zach who was responsible. Only Ada had only met Zach once two months before and no one else had seen him. His name wasn't on any of the travel plans and the authorities believed Crystal was just searching for any plausible fall man to clear her name. When they tried to call Zach, the number she had for him was out of minutes, and his dating profile had been deleted. Any email or text communications they once shared were gone from all her devices. Crystal never even knew his last name. There was no trace of the man that Ava remembered spending the day with once, two months before, but hadn't seen around since. Crystal's own mother told police she believed her daughter wanted to get rid of the child and was just trying to blame a fake boyfriend for the entire scheme because she got caught.

Will decided no further involvement was needed on his part. Crystal would probably get a slap on the wrist legally. However, the main goal was accomplished. Ada was in the loving custody of her father and would no longer be used to bleed money for her mother. Crystal was shamed and would need to, at the very least, get a job to pay for legal fees.

It all had gone fantastically to plan. Way sooner than he thought possible. Olivia had been surprisingly helpful in the entire process and had become a wonderfully compliant submissive. They no longer needed to stay in this boring city, and he had already found a cabin to buy. Yet he still felt unsatisfied. *Maybe because I didn't kill her? Maybe because he very much doubted the attempted murder charge would stick because of some lawyer like Olivia?*

"Yes, Crystal is punished, and the little girl will be raised by a good man, but it just feels so anticlimactic."

"Everything can't be exciting, Will." Olivia scooted in her latex dress and it made the scrunching noise again. "There are a lot of positives that came out of being here."

"That statement seems ludicrous coming from you."

Will opened the new laptop he purchased to start the cabin search the week before. He had already put an offer on the perfect find. A hunting cabin on fifty-seven acres. It had a two-mile-long gated dirt drive and couldn't be seen from any road. It would need some serious renovations, but he could pay the asking price in cash, and would still have plenty left over to make the home become exactly what he had in mind. The Cape Cod layout couldn't be more perfect either, an upstairs playroom where women could be detained. With only one entry or exit point on the second floor, he wouldn't have to worry about escape. There would be a lovely downstairs to fit his needs of having a permanent and comforting home around him.

Most importantly, it was also only a twenty-minute drive to Vivian's house.

"I've purchased a home in Pennsylvania. It's more remote than this one and smaller. We will be traveling there as soon as I take care of our vehicle situation. So, I'll be going out tomorrow to purchase a vehicle large enough to fit comfortably the coffee table and other items we have accrued. Your car will be sold to some interesting individuals I had the pleasure of meeting when I ventured into the city for purchasing the sex store items."

"Can the police identify it as my car if it gets found?"

"I wonder if you hope I'll say yes or no. Don't you want to be found, Olivia? For me to be caught? Fried in the electric chair I believe is what you warned me of." Will looked up from the laptop to dazzle smile at her where she sat perfectly straight in her light pink latex dress and box dyed red hair.

"I don't want you to get caught now. I like belonging to you."

He studied her for a brief time. "You realize that is pathetic, don't you? You enjoy that I dress you up like a skank and lock you in a cage? Fuck you however I want, with whatever I want?"

"But I belong to you now."

"If that's how you want to look at it." He waved his hand around flippantly in her direction. "I would like you to help me renovate the new cabin, but after that I'll let you go, as promised."

"That should take a long time, though, right?" Olivia appeared to be holding her breath.

"Yes, it should take some time."

She let her breath out in obvious relief, "Oh good."

Will was instantly put off by her neediness. He would need to think up ways to make her not so keen on belonging to him anymore.

The idea perked him up from his disappointment slump. This could be a thrill inducing endeavor. An experiment of sorts.

If he took her farther and farther into the world of punishment, would she become more attached or begin to hate him again? A worthy divergence while he focused on renovating this cabin.

"Unfortunately for you, that means a long day in the cage again, so I will allow you to sleep in the bed with me tonight. We will secure only one wrist to the post. You've earned that." Positively enforcing her compliance had seemed effective beyond measure so far. How easily she would be able to sneak away tonight, but she won't. She won't even try because she wouldn't want him to be upset with her. The realization made him snicker. It was mentally fucked up, but also so very interesting.

"First, though, we'll play a little."

By play, he meant that he would flog the shit out of her ass before fucking her, to make it sting while she lay on him just so he could rub his hands over her beaten flesh gently, to soothe the very sting he put there. She would be so grateful for his comfort and attentive behavior, forgetting entirely that he was the reason she needed it. This was an amusing little turn of events. Not a long-term way to handle his internal demons, but it would suffice long enough to set up a permanent location and to decide how he wanted to proceed with Vivian.

Vivvie's plush tits would look so sexy pressed into that pink see-through latex garter dress. He had only seen them once but remembered that her nipples had been so delicately pink, they would almost match the pastel garment. God, how he wished he could see how they would pop out after being touched and rolled between his fingers or sucked on through the fabric.

Not like Olivia's nipples at all. Olivia had dark saucer nipples with her little breasts around them. The tight latex hugged around Olivia's slender legs and her tight little ass fit so perfectly above the garter. It fit her like a glove, but that wasn't the point of the dress. This dress was supposed to make the woman appear to be bursting out of it. He wanted to see a peak of a big ass hanging out of the bottom as the fabric stretched tight across the ripe rump of luscious hips.

Will could envision Vivian's big thick thighs smushed together so that the latex scrunched against itself with every tiny movement. She would look edible in that dress, like ribbon candy painted all pretty and delicate. He would want to put his mouth all over her, run his hands all over her, and taste the sweetness. Vivvie, in that dress made him want to pleasure her with love, not punishment.

Will looked over at where Olivia sat. Her thighs didn't touch.

Will sighed. "Come." He closed the laptop and moved it over to the end table before standing up and motioned for Olivia to walk ahead of him up the stairs. "Get that black flogger out of the bag, rest your forearms down on the mattress with your ass in the air, the flogger laying over your arms, to wait for me."

Even though Olivia immediately did as she was told, Will left her there as he closed the bedroom door for a moment of privacy out in the hallway. He took the cell phone out of his pocket and slid down the wall to the floor.

He tried calling first.

It rang and rang again, going to voicemail. He tried calling again. "Come on, Viv, answer the phone." Voicemail. Fuck.

He tried texting.

I just want to talk to you.

Will waited and waited. Then texted again.

Please answer the phone.

No response. He tried calling again, but it just rang and rang and rang again going to voicemail. Will bashed his head into the wall behind him and he shut his eyes. Why wouldn't she answer the phone? What the fuck was she playing at?

Still on the floor, he carefully folded up each sleeve of his black sweater. It was driving him insane that he didn't know what Vivian was doing, who she was with, if she was okay. Maybe she was sick or hurt or losing her mind.

Or completely moved on already.

Moved on from what?

They weren't even dating, just friends, and he left her so he could go off and feed his own needs.

Only somewhere along the way, she became part of his needs.

Now he was left wanting to lie with Vivian wrapped up on him, holding her in the shower even in underwear, smelling her, kissing her hair, having her make him laugh.

Meeting her made him realize that he needed that, the comforting she brought him, all of it. Only he needed to have writhing, bleeding, and crying beneath his hands, too.

How did he get to have both? How did he feed the monster and the man?

More importantly, why the fuck wouldn't she answer the phone?

Getting up from the floor, he walked into the bedroom where Olivia lay perfectly as she was told to. Will took off his pants and folded them carefully to place on the dresser, the underwear folded on top. His shirt and socks he lay over the top of the chair by the window before turning his IPOD on to his trademark techno music.

Walking over behind her to start the flogging should have made him feel enthralled, excited, but all he felt was tired.

Picking up the flogger, he gave her ass a good strike.

She jolted forward and cried out.

Will moved to the other side and hit her again. She yelled, but he felt nothing.

"It's no use, Olivia. Go turn off the music."

Will plopped down on the floor cross-legged and put his face in his hands like a child.

Slowly, Olivia moved over to turn off the music, confused, sad even. Her dress scrunching as she moved. She stood awkwardly by the window, shifting from one foot to the other, not sure what to do with herself while he sat naked on the floor.

"What should I do now?" She finally got up the nerve to whisper into the silence.

Will looked up at her standing there by the window.

"I don't know, Olivia, just stand there and think of a way to get me interested in you enough to make it worth dragging you around everywhere and buying all this expensive shit for you." Will was annoyed. Irritated. Only not with Olivia, he was upset with Vivian. No, not even her. He was irritated with himself.

"You were excited to hit me downstairs. Then you said we could sleep together tonight."

"Well, unless you think of something enthralling, I will be jerking off in the shower and you're going back in the cage."

Olivia continued shifting from one foot to the other where she stood, the latex dress stiffness annoying him. Will shut his eyes and imagined Vivian in the dress, rubbing her thighs together. He thought of how she would probably be smiling, but she wouldn't be afraid of him, afraid to move around him, afraid to touch him. Vivvie would be over standing behind him, running her fingers through his hair right now. She would be pulling his face against the latex. He could lean his face up and suck on her nipple through the garment by going up on his knees. She wasn't afraid of him. She should be, but she wasn't. With his eyes still closed, he felt something hot and wet on his bare big toe. His eyes flew open.

"Olivia, what the fuck are you doing?" She lay on her belly on the floor, her face turned to the side, his toe in her mouth, and she was sucking hard. Her tongue slid along the side of his toe.

"Reach back and grab hold of your feet." He commanded.

She complied. She lay on her belly, holding her feet in her hands, and she sucked on the big toe of her captor without even being asked to do it. "God, you're fucking pathetic." Will kicked her hard to get her off his toe. "Disgusting."

Blood flew from her split lip when he kicked her off and she yelled out.

Her hand shot protectively to her face. But he threw it away as he flipped her onto her back and straddled her head.

"You want something in your mouth? Hmmm?" Will put his cock into her mouth. "Keep it open."

Her hands came up to control how much of his cock went into her mouth, but Will grabbed her wrists and brought each hand down under his knees. He kneeled on her wrists and pushed into her bloody mouth. The blood was warm and slippery, and he came alive in it. He levered himself over her face and pushed deeper down her throat.

Olivia's feet scuffed across the floor, trying to get traction so she could push away from him. She made a horrible gargling noise as she choked on the blood and spit and his growing member thumping down her throat hole. He pulled it out and grabbed hold of her hair, flipping her over so she could drool out all the fluid. "You like having me in your mouth. Down your throat. Feels nice to have me there, doesn't it?"

She was still coughing, her eyes watering and red. Will kept her hair fisted in his hand and pulled her over to lie on the bed. Tossing her down onto her back, keeping her head hanging off the end of the bed, Will stood on either side of her face, leaning over to pin her wrists to her sides. "Open your mouth, Olivia. Tell me to fuck your mouth."

She complied the first time he commanded her to. "Please fuck my mouth."

It was pleasing. "Of course you may have it. Oh yeah, all the way down."

Will fucked her throat. The blood from her lip all over her face, all over his balls and thighs. He bent down to get deeper in her throat as she began to struggle beneath him for air. "I could kill you just like this. Suffocate you with my dick down your throat." She squirmed harder, pulling up on his grasp in desperation. Her eyes wide and bewildered, her throat gagging around him as he thrust into it. "God, I'm going to cum."

He slammed deeper as his hot seed shot down into her gut. Vomit coming up around his cock in her throat to mix with the blood and spit and cum. He pushed deeper once more before whipping it out and flipping her over so she could breathe. He stuck his fingers in her mouth to help clear out the airway from the throw-up now coming out all over the place. Chunks of dinner and bodily fluids dripped from her chin and her hair. It was everywhere, all over both of them, sliding over the pink latex dress. Olivia was crying as she coughed, vomit coming out of her nose.

"Holy Fuck Olivia, that was amazing. Come here." Will pulled her into his chest and held her there while she sobbed and coughed up all the shit up from her throat. "You surprised me with that." He rubbed his hand down her hair. "Did I hurt you?" His fingers gently pulled her face up to look at him, her lip swollen and split. "Oh baby. Ouch." Lightly he leaned down and pressed a feather of a kiss on her broken mouth. "Come. I'll wash you. We are a mess together, aren't we?" He dazzle smiled at her, making them a team with his words, as if what they just did was theirs and not his. Kissing her and sending gentle caresses down her hair, her neck, and her shoulders. As if the pain she felt wasn't because of his hands to begin with.

Olivia leaned against him as he led her into the bathroom. He peeled the latex garter dress off her vomit-soaked body and had her step into the bathtub. When the water first came out of the shower head, it was cold and she screamed out. "Shhhh. Olivia, it will be warm in a second." Will jumped in with her. "I'm sorry about the water. I honestly didn't mean for it to be cold." He moved her into the water stream first, "But I apologize for nothing else. You really pleased me in there. Well done."

"Really? You are happy with me?"

"Well, of course. I had decided to give up, to sleep alone, and instead you thought up that delightful way to make our sex alive. I know you didn't enjoy the act itself, but how did you feel, just now, learning that you pleased me?"

"I feel proud."

"See, that's what it's about. The fine line of pleasure and pain, not all the pleasure is about the sexual act itself. Most of it is about crossing boundaries that just normally aren't crossed. It aroused me to have your blood and vomit all over my hard cock. Most people would find that grotesque. But most people don't realize the ownership it brings to have another's insides all over you." Will reached for the shampoo and squeezed it into his hand, "May I?"

"Please." Olivia smiled up at him as if he just proposed marriage. She closed her eyes and relished in the sensations of having the lather worked into her scalp by his large hands.

"You will sleep with me tonight. With only one foot tethered, and tomorrow you may pick your own travel clothing for the day. Rewards and punishments. It's exciting, isn't it?"

What he left out from his words was the irony that he was rewarding her with choices he took away from her in the first place. He comforted her from punishments he bestowed on her, and he did so without permission. He took her life from her because she didn't deserve it.

Her choices made on her own, before him, had her scratching the belly of evil. When her life belonged to her, she used it to reward the unworthy and to punish the undeserving. Really, she brought all of this on her own self and Will didn't feel the tiniest bit of guilt for his role in helping her to redemption.

Chapter 24

The Cottage House in the Woods

The cabin had good bones. That was really all he needed, something to start with. He would set up Olivia's room first so that when the construction teams came in, he had a place to hide her. That room would have to be set up by him alone. Olivia could help, but no one else could ever know the room existed. The hardest part would be attaching beams for securing chains to, and he would also need to put up some form of sound proofing.

The bed he ordered had already been delivered. The frame had restraint hoops attached to the steel frame in all four corners. The thick posts were square and canopied over the mattress, and the top rails had restraint hoops, too. It claimed to be squeak free and built as strong as a tank for the roughest bondage.

The damn bed cost him a couple grand. All the attachment chains and ropes were sold separately, and he spent another couple grand for restraints and toys. He had a ridiculously hard time deciding between a ball gag and blindfold harness or the full slave hoods with a snap-on gag and blindfold. It bothered him beyond measure that just one small, trivial choice had gotten him so worked up and angry that in the end he splurged on both options.

Spending the money to make this room efficient was important to Will, but surprisingly, it was Olivia who could not wait to get it set up. She seemed genuinely excited about the medieval dungeon and wood hand-stocks he purchased. One of them hung by adjustable chains from the ceiling, a wooden board with wrist holes that clamped to force the detainee to dangle with their arms in the air. The chains could be lowered to allow feet or knees to touch the floor, or lifted, to really punish. The other stockade, simply a wooden board with clamp holes for the ankles and wrists.

Will allowed her to help pick things out, including some outfits, but he was beginning to regret the decision. He wasn't sure anyone but her would be able to wear them, because he didn't plan on allowing any of the girls, after her, to be this close to him. She had become so involved in the lifestyle that what Will had meant to be a punishment, was something she enjoyed. He was already beginning to dread how awkward it was going to feel when he decided to get rid of her. Like putting down the family dog or something.

Will did admit, though, that he was looking forward to trying out most of the new toys with a willing partner. It would be so much easier to learn how they all worked without having to deal with screaming or crying or fighting.

As soon as the room was set up the way he wanted it, then he would start on the rest of the house. Once the home was sorted, then he would work on wiggling his way back into Vivian's life. Eventually, he would bring her here, and show her what he created for himself. Not the upstairs room though, that would never be for her. Vivian would be the comfort in this space, and he would worship her for it. *Getting ahead of yourself, Will.*

"What do you think of a garden?" Olivia's tentative voice broke through his thoughts.

Will was taken off guard. "What?"

Olivia spoke up, assuming he hadn't been able to hear her. She sat on the edge of the bed that would be hers. The dungeon bed, the one to which he'd restrain her to while she slept and while he fucked her, but also the one he allowed her to pick out what sheets and comforter she wanted and so she called it 'her bed.'

"What do you think of a garden? In the back."

"It's not really something I had given any thought to. What kind of garden?"

"I don't know, just flowers. I just thought it would look pretty."

He thought of the empty flowerpots lined up on Vivian's porch. She must have had a plan for them. Had she just thought they would look pretty for everyone else to see or for herself? She wouldn't have purchased them or placed them on the porch if she hadn't intended to make them pretty for someone. Maybe Olivia could help him understand why she stopped, why she only placed the pots but never planted the flowers.

"Would you make the garden to pleasure yourself or others?"

Olivia hesitated.

"Answer honestly, not what you believe I want you to say." Will reassured her by sitting back, allowing her to have time to relax a little.

"I thought it would please you if I made something beautiful for you to look at."

"You thought that I would like flowers to look at? Don't women usually enjoy flowers?"

She dropped her gaze to the floor.

"I'm not upset with you, Olivia. I'm simply trying to understand your thought process. Explain."

She hesitated again. It annoyed him, but he held his tongue. "Please?"

"I guess that I thought if you saw pretty flowers, it would make you happy, and if I were the one who planted them," she shrugged, "then you would think of me when you looked at them."

Maybe that was why Vivian had stopped. She had wanted to make the house beautiful for her husband, wanted him to walk up to the front door and be filled with happiness to be home. Only she realized it wouldn't make him think of her even if she did plant them, and so she stopped. Or maybe there had been flowers in them, but she let them die.

Will remembered Vivian smiling so sweetly at a painting at the Barnes Foundation. A Renoir painting of a woman gardening. The lady in the painting wore a hat and was kneeling, bent over, tending to the dirt in her dress on the garden path, surrounded by beautiful flowers. Will had never seen the painting before, and neither had Viv. It wasn't a very famous piece, but she had paid it a particular amount of attention. When he asked her why, she had said it reminded her of being a child in her great-grandmother's garden.

"You will make me a list of everything you'll need to plant a garden." Will thought of how Vivian would smile when she saw the garden that resembled the painting. "I will choose the flowers and give a blueprint of how I want it to be set up." He would search the Barnes Foundation webpage and study the painting. Olivia could make it as close as possible to the painting. "This will give us something to occupy our time while the construction crews are here over the next few weeks. We will make a garden while they fix up the house."

"Thank you Will. I was nervous about bringing it up."

"As you should have been. I'll allow it to slip this once, but don't make such an error again."

Olivia looked at him, baffled. She looked at him as if she had completely tricked her own mind into believing they were lovers, and this was their home to share together. Will had heard of psychological responses like this to traumatic circumstances, but never expected his pedigree lawyer to fall victim to such rudimentary emotions.

"Olivia, remind me? When you were in your 20s, what were you doing?"

She hesitated. The annoyance was beginning to outweigh her worth. "You were in college, weren't you? On your daddy's dime. And after college, what did you do?" He paused, hoping for her to chime in. She hesitated. "You got a job with your father making shit tons of money defending horrible monsters and keeping them out of jail. Until what stopped you?"

Will paused again. Waiting for a response. Waiting for a response. "What fucking stopped you?" He screamed.

"You." She whispered the words, sobbing, keeping her eyes on the floor.

"That's right. Me. Now you want to cry? Now that you've been caught and held accountable?" Will shook his head. "You know what? My father had money too, Olivia, a lot of it. He would buy my love with ski trips every year.

I actually enjoyed hitting the snowboarding slops as a young man, but when I became a man, I saw what my father was in truth. He tried to buy my love, which makes him a solicitor of prostitution and me a whore, Olivia. You thrived as your father's whore and you fucked anyone you had to for your own benefit. I joined the military and went to earn my own path and to defend those who were too weak to defend themselves against monsters like you. Now you want to plant a fucking garden? You want to plant a fucking garden and play pretend with me here like you aren't the very scum I set out to rid this fucking world of?" Will laughed. "Plant your garden, Princess, but don't forget for one second why you're kneeling in my dirt."

Three months. It had taken three months for the crews to be done with all the renovations that the cabin required. It was more of a cottage now, though. Fireplace, custom bathroom, an addition for the master bedroom with exposed beams and a skylight, like the Kansas City house. The kitchen was completely remodeled kitchen with recessed lighting and all stainless-steel appliances, and of course, a superb security system with cameras and motion detectors.

Olivia really had made a beautiful garden, very similar to the painting he showed her. They worked on it mostly together. He provided all the heavy lifting of bags, poured rocks, and dug the holes for bushes and trees. It was pleasant doing a home project with her. Will had seen real pride on her face when the garden was complete.

"Is this the first time you've ever made something with your own two hands?"

"It is. I've never worked so hard on anything." She took a sip of her lemonade as they sat on the adorable bench she picked out and had him place in the center of the garden labyrinth. "The best thing about it is its self-sustainability. Almost everything we planted is perennials and they are all in the correct sun or shade needed to prosper. With some weeding and new rocks, when needed, this garden should be beautiful without much work." She beamed a smile at him.

She appeared so genuine there on the bench with her lemonade. The red hair had faded tremendously since he first dyed it with the box-color. The sun had faded it into an almost pink color, and her roots were growing in dark blonde. Much darker than the platinum blonde she bought for the years and years at salons before crossing paths with Will.

He bought her a few dresses to wear while the construction crews were working in the cabin. The one she had on today was the one he thought fit her best. It was a short cotton dress, green, with little flowers all over it and ruffles around the bustline and the cap sleeves. Without makeup, she looked less cold, and the little bit of sun she had gotten on her face gave her a glowing look that he hadn't noticed on her before.

"What job would you have picked for yourself if you didn't have the means to go to law school?"

"I'm not really sure, Will. I spent my entire life being groomed for what I became." She shrugged. "I loved winning and nothing else mattered. I never wanted to have babies or get married or bake or garden. All I wanted was more and more winning and money. I think maybe I became addicted to it."

"Maybe. I feel as if you've changed a great deal over the past few months. I'm almost sad to have to let you go."

"You don't have to, you know. You could keep me here, with you. I wouldn't be a bother. I'd stay up in my room or be in the garden. You would never have to take me anywhere or worry about me running away, I swear."

"Until you grow tired of it. Until you decide you want more. Or become jealous."

"Jealous? Jealous of whom?"

"The other women I go to spend my time with." Will laughed. "You think I would have a relationship with you? That I would be exclusive?" He laughed again. "My god, even kidnapped submissives have fidelity expectations."

"No. I would not be jealous of you going to kill anyone."

"What about to fuck? Or even to love? What if I want to bring a woman home to my house?"

She stayed quiet. Her silence made him feel the need to explain. "Olivia, we are not in a relationship. I found you to kill you."

"But now I belong to you."

"No, your repentance belongs to me. That is what I have claimed from you and even that is not a relationship."

"You don't have any relationships though, Will. None. You don't call anyone or text. You never go out or even check on family."

"I have family. I have Vivian too."

"Vivian." She rolled her eyes in annoyance. "She won't answer your calls. She disobeys you when you tell her to call you back and she doesn't take your feelings into account at all. You have told her you're sorry for leaving, but she doesn't care. I hear your voicemails to her. You beg her to call you back, to let you know that she is okay. Vivian has no heart, or loyalty, at all."

"Careful Olivia. I'll forgive your nastiness because I can see that you are jealous of my genuine regard for Vivian. You have no idea what you're talking about when it comes to her. She's confused and alone and hurting, because of me and because of so many others. She would never hurt me. Hell, in her mind she probably believes that by not calling me back she is allowing me a reason to be angry with her instead of feeling bad for leaving. Or she is distraught and doesn't want me to feel obligated to disrupt my life trying to comfort her." *That's it. That's what she is doing.* Will put his head into his hands. "My god, that's it. Fuck, I've been an idiot! *That's* why she has been ignoring me!"

"She doesn't love you, Will. How could you think you matter to her after ignoring you all this time?"

"Come in the house now, Olivia. I need to plan."

"Will, I want to tell you that I have fallen for you. I think we could be something."

"You can't possibly be serious." He jumped to his feet and grabbed hold of her hand to walk her back into the cabin. "How could you ever feel that way, Olivia? You are a chore to me. At best, you're someone who sometimes scratches an itch I can't reach.

True, you amuse me at times, and can be useful to throw the occasional idea off of, but overall, I view you the same way I do the luffa that hangs in my shower. Nice to use for my own comfort, but completely unnecessary to fulfill any of my needs. Then, when it's no longer tight and easily lathered up, I can throw it away and pick out a new one."

He placed his hand delicately on the swell of her back to lead her through the door. "Now, go up into your room and change into the green jumpsuit, the one with the holes cut out where it matters. I want to enjoy you, and then go discretely observe the comings and goings of my Vivvie."

Chapter 25

The Stalker

Finally, she emerged.

Will had been parked down the street from her house for the second day in a row. He spent hours watching and waiting for the opportunity to go into her home to bug it. She went out through the garage, which was disappointing, as he had hoped he could have gotten a good look at her.

When she drove off, he moved in.

Will walked up to her front door and simply turned the handle.

"I told you to lock the goddamn door, Viv."

Moving into the unsecured house, Will removed his shoes, not wanting to track dirt through her home, as that would be rude.

He moved into the living room first. She had a book open, lying face down next to a plush velvety blue throw blanket with fringe on the ends. A coffee cup with a tea bag string hanging over the edge of the mug sat on the floor beside where she had been sitting. He could see the scene in his mind. Vivian curled up in the corner of her sofa, the blue blanket wrapped around her body, a book in one hand, her tea in the other.

Will picked up the book, *Leaves of Grass, Walt Whitman*

The page she had the book open to was all marked up with underlines and highlights, little stars next to certain lines of poetry.

He turned the page back to find the name of the poem she seemed so invested in.

The name of the poem made him smirk, *The Wound-Dresser.*

This one page in the book, found lying open on her couch beside a warm soft blanket, was all the confirmation he needed to know without a doubt that he had been right. She was struggling in her own mind, hurting, and completely alone. She was so desperate that she was reaching into the mind of a medic from the civil war for comfort.

Of course, she would connect with this poem. The poem that speaks of the preciousness of blood and mercy. The poem that stresses the sense of duty the medic feels towards the wounded. How treating their wounds force the medic to turn off all their own emotions. To have such a duty asked of you over and over again... it burns inside you, just as Walt says.

"She needs me." Will whispered the words to the empty room. She wasn't ignoring him. Because she was burning, she was protecting him.

She didn't want him to worry, and she didn't want him to hear her voice and know that her insides were enkindled. Vivian was hiding in her home so that no one who loved her had to be hurt, seeing that she was incandescently glowing with the burning guilt and sadness consuming her.

He put the book back the way she had left it, but picked up the mug and carried it to the sink. Will pulled the used tea bag out of the cup and walked over to the garbage can to throw it away. Under the lid, two huge bottles of vodka sat empty in the can. A few K-cups of coffee and banana peels, but that was all she had in her garbage. She wasn't eating, and she was drinking herself to death, just to be able to feel.

"Oh Vivvie, you need me soon." Will closed the lid and took the small spy bug he purchased out of his pocket. He could listen to her talking, and figure out who she was speaking to, if not him.

Before leaving, he ventured upstairs to look around. The closer he moved to her bedroom, the stronger he could feel her. Being there evoked a strange feeling in his chest. *Longing.*

When he reached her room, Will stood at the foot of her bed, frowning at the realization that this woman had become someone he missed. He craved her voice, her smile, to watch the little ways she moved that only belonged to her. She flipped her fingers around on the air as she talked and had this annoying way of resting her hand on her chest and tapping her scar when she was anxious.

Walking over to her closet, he grabbed one of blouses off the hanger and put it up to his nose to smell. It was clean, but didn't smell like Viv. She probably hadn't worn it in some time. Maybe she didn't have anywhere to wear it to. Will walked over to her bathroom, picked up her hairbrush. Next to the brush were a pile of the hair-ties she used to put her hair in that horrid bun she forced her golden strands into. He put them all into his pocket and laughed, thinking of her confused dismay when she couldn't find them.

The hamper in the corner was full, and she needed to get some laundry done. Will sifted through the dirty clothing, trying to find some evidence that anyone else's clothing might be in there, too. Everything belonged to Vivian. He picked up one of the dirty tank-tops to smell. Breathing in the scent of her body was like closing his eyes and nuzzling his face into her neck.

God, what the fuck! Will, pull it together.

Throwing the shirt down, he rushed to leave her home. He needed to get out of this space, her space. To clear his mind. How had this girl become so important? He bought a house to be near her, for fuck's sake. For what? She wouldn't even answer his phone calls.

Maybe he had gone too far when he forced her to fuck him. She wasn't ready to understand how sexual extremes were the only way that either of them would ever be able to feel anything in this postwar existence. Maybe she needed *some kind* of emotional sex first? Something to make her feel that they had *some kind* of amorous relationship before jumping into the rape-ish thrill attack he knew that they both needed.

When she met with him after, she said she understood, but maybe he should have shown her that she also meant something significant to him, too.

Walking back down the street to where he parked the jeep, Will wondered if *he* had even realized she had meant something meaningful to him before leaving.

As he sat in the driver's seat waiting and watching for her to get home, he reached the only conclusion viable. He had to act on his feelings. He just couldn't have a life without her in it. He would have to figure out what way he wanted her in his life later, but for now, he was going to need to make it a possibility.

First, he would need to weasel his way back into her good graces, get her to trust him again. Trust that she could lean on him, that he wouldn't just disappear on her again, like her husband.

Fuck, I did the same thing to her that he did.

He would have to show her she could lean on him instead of the vodka. Then, he would need to get her to believe that she mattered to him, and the lunacy of it was that she really *did* matter to him. What was worse was that Will wanted her to see the real him and to matter to her as well.

He wanted her to see past his looks, past his dazzle. He wanted her to see the raw him.

It was out of character for him to want to show anyone his true self, but he honestly wanted Vivian to know him, to see him. He wanted her to love him. To find him worthy of her love.

Secondly, Will was going to need to find and kill her husband.

Chapter 26

A Sudden Vacancy

Walking into the cabin, Will immediately ran up the steps to talk to Olivia about what he discovered at Vivian's house. "We're in business. The bug is in place."

He unlocked the door to her room and found her sitting cross-legged on the bed, reading a magazine. She had on a cute little white baby-doll nightie with a pink ribbon that almost matched her faded red hair.

"Why would I want anything to do with your preposterous venture with Vivian?" She flipped the pages aggressively.

Will smirked as he leaned lazily against the wall, arms crossed. "Are you angry, Olivia?"

She said nothing. Only continued flipping the pages of her magazine.

"Although amusing, I don't want you in this state of jealously while I'm trying to help a friend in need."

"Is she a friend? Is that all she is?" Olivia threw the magazine across the room. "I am doing everything you want! I changed everything about myself, for you, and all you've cared about the past couple of days is helping this twit who doesn't even call you back!"

Will surprised her by laughing. "Oh, but how entirely fitting that you're experiencing unrequited love."

Olivia's lip quivered. "It's not unrequited! You do love me back! You do! Or you wouldn't have kept me alive. You wouldn't have meals with me and conversations or have worked to build our garden with me. You love me Will. Maybe you didn't at first, but you do now." She jumped up off the bed and was moving towards him across the room. Her baby-doll nightie barely touched the top of the fluffy thong undies that matched it.

"Olivia, I assure you with one hundred percent clarity that you are absolutely delusional." He laughed again, "But isn't it reassuring to know that you do have a heart under that thick layer of money you've wrapped yourself up in all these years?"

She moved closer to him slowly, her arms at her side giving away her shrouded fear of being so bold with him.

"I know you love me, Will. I can feel it when you look at me. When you touch me, I can sense that your feelings have changed." Reaching where he stood, tentatively her hand reached out to graze along his jawline. "I want us to live like this forever. I want to be yours forever."

Will sighed, standing up to his full height in front of her. He looked down at her briefly, calculating how to handle this new impasse they seemed to have reached. As he brought his arms up to gently grasp hold of hers, Olivia's eyes met his, gazing into him with a languishing need for vindication.

"Listen to me carefully. There is nothing about you I have ever loved or could ever love. Before me, you were a shrewd savage who preyed on the misfortunes of countless victims while they begged for justice to punish the unimaginable cruelties your clients bestowed on them.

After meeting me, you have willingly tossed aside every shred of dignity and honor you might have harbored for yourself by becoming a willing strumpet for my pleasure and a puppet for my games." Will ran his thumb down her face. "You disgust me now more than you did then for falling in love with a man who only wanted a warm place to deposit into for a while." Leaning close to her face, he softly placed a kiss onto her cheek. "So, now my dear, it is time to let you go."

With fluidity and swiftness, Will pulled her through the doorway of the room and flung her down the steps. Her body crashed into the wall before it tumbled down, feet flying over her head, arms flailing. On the second crash, he watched her leg snap like a little wafer cookie. It made him want to drive back out to the grocery store to buy some vanilla wafers to eat with tea while reading the copy of *Leaves of Grass* he had picked up on the way back to the cabin earlier. The last few steps, she slid down on her back before stopping at the bottom. Will hadn't even taken his first leisurely step out of the doorway before she had flipped over onto her stomach and began trying to slowly low crawl herself across the floor.

"I'm proud of you for attempting to get away." He took each step casually, allowing her time to feel successful in her efforts. "A rather pathetic attempt, but at least you're not just lying there crying and begging."

After coming down from the last step, he moved over to where she laid, prone on her belly, hands in fists, dragging her legs as she struggled to get to the door. Will shook his head in gentle regret as he reached down for a fist full of her hair. She screamed as he dragged her by the hair down the hallway into the kitchen. "I had hoped to kill you gently by putting something into your tea or give you an injection to make you fall asleep before I killed you. I figured you had at least earned that."

"Will, please! I don't deserve to die anymore!"

"I didn't burn you in the tanning bed. That has to count for something."

She reached her hands up, clawing at his arms. One of her nails caught his skin, and the instant sting caused Will to let go of her hair, while her head smashed to the floor. "Fuck! What the fuck did you think scratching me would do except piss me off?" Blood surfaced to the scratch on his forearm. Will put the cut up to his mouth to swipe the wound with his tongue, stepping on her fractured leg as he walked over to the sink to put water on the scratch. She bellowed out in agony.

"Do you think you love me *now,* Olivia?" Will laughed, "I can't believe you'd be stupid enough to talk shit on the woman you know I actually care for. You could have lived a good deal longer and had a painless death." He put the plug into the sink and let the water continue to fill it up. "Vivian was a medic like me you know. If she could see you right now, she would crawl over shards of broken glass to get to you, just to treat your wounds for you, and *you* had the nerve to question her loyalty?"

Olivia whimpered where she lay on the kitchen floor. He caught resemblances of apologies and pleading between the hushed crying.

"Now I have to figure out how to kill you on a whim because you just couldn't keep your mouth shut about your fucking feelings. Everything had to be about you. Even as a prisoner in the attic, you still thought so highly of your own damn self that you couldn't just respect those who deserved it."

Straddling her where she lay on her belly, Will bent down to knead her ass with his hands. "I made a mistake when I didn't fuck the last girl I killed while killing her. It led to some really bad judgment errors on my part. So, I'm afraid you are going to have to endure." He stood up to remove his pants and boxer briefs, sighing heavily as he laid them both neatly over the kitchen chair. Naked from the waist down, he sauntered into the hallway and up the steps to retrieve a pair of wrist cuffs from Olivia's room.

Returning to the kitchen, Will pulled both her hands into the swell of her back to restrain her before jumping up to turn off the water he had left running. "Oops, looks like we are about to have an overflow."

"Will, I will be respectful. I promise. Please don't kill me, please. Just punish me. I deserve it." Olivia pleaded as Will rolled her over and sat her up. As he moved to pull her up onto her feet, she screamed out in agony. "My leg is broken!"

"I know. I watched it snap when you hit the first stair." Will chuckled a little. "It's a pretty nasty fracture. Come on, move over to the sink." He had to pick her up to move her. Bruises were beginning to show up on the skin from where she hit on the fall. "Just lean over the counter here and let me punish fuck you and then we'll clean you up, okay?"

"Okay. Yes, punish me. Will, I'm sorry. I'll do anything you want me to."

"I know." Will pushed her against the sink and bent her hurt leg up to put her knee on the counter. "Here, rest your leg up here. You're tall enough and the fracture is low enough." With her leg up on the counter, he admired how spread open she was for him. "I truly am sorry you're in pain while we do this, but I promise, you'll feel better in a minute."

Pushing himself against her, Will guided the head of his cock inside while bending her down, forcing her head into the sink full of water. She instantly tried to bring her leg off the counter to fight, but he had angled himself in a way to prevent it. She had nowhere to go, so she could only thrash around in the water with her head as he held her down. Her bound hands grasped hold of his shirt, trying to pinch or scratch him as he thrust slowly in and out of her body while she drowned. Bubbles surged up from the water as she tried to scream. Her torso twisted, her legs shaking this way and that way, trying to gain some kind of stronghold to be able to get her head out of the water.

It was useless.

Will held her head firmly under the water with one hand, while his other held her shoulder in place so he could slide in and out of her easily. The sloshing water from the full sink, her muffled water screams, the way she tried to twist around in desperation as he fucked her, heightened his arousal. It was the thrill he yearned for. It was the exact adrenaline rush he was chasing. The substance he hungered for to fill up the empty hole inside of himself.

It was bliss.

A slow, languid pleasure while just pushing himself into her bent over body against the sink. It didn't even need to last long or be a thought-out event, using toys or disturbing outfits. He could find pleasure in just loving the feel of her around him, almost like a normal couple. Only in this couple, he was the only one who could feel it as the life left her body.

Without even needing to speed up his pace, Will found his pleasure in a roar of adrenaline, collapsing down onto her bent over back. He rested his weight on her to catch his breath while her shoulders heaved with the gulps of water her lungs finally sucked in.

After her body went limp and stopped twitching, Will pushed himself out of her and slid her body gently to the kitchen floor. Her wet hair splayed across her face as a pool of water formed all around where she lay. He stood over top of her looking down for a minute, wondering if he should miss her movements, her voice, the life in her eyes.

Only he didn't. He loved her for the first time, seeing her still, laying there dead with her baby-doll nightie soaked against her skin, knowing his sperm dripping out down her leg was the only living part of her anymore.

Will whipped his shirt over his head and went to grab his box of special tools. The ones he used to remove what he wanted from the girls.

From Olivia he wanted something different, from her he wanted her hands. He loved the hands that tended the garden with him in the back of his cabin house. Those hands were the only part of her he actually felt any kind of respect for. The rest of her was selfish and cruel. Why keep any of that for his collection? He would cut them off and burn them out in the garden using the ceramic chiminea he bought to have fires in on cool fall evenings. The ashes would go into a vase with flowers on it, to remind him of the only good part of Ms. Olivia Moreen Taylor, Esquire.

Chapter 27

One Female Army Veteran Rejoins the Living

Vivian's phone rang again. It was the third time that hour that Lauren was calling her. *Maybe it was an emergency.* The thought guilted her to answer the phone.

"Hello, are you alright?"

"Oh, Viv, I was so worried about you. I haven't heard from you in months, so I called a bunch of the girls and no one has heard from you or seen you on any social media. Can I come over?"

"You want to come over? Now?"

"Yeah, is that okay?"

"Um, I guess so."

"Great. I'll be there soon!"

Vivian hung up the phone, a little confused about what prompted Lauren to have this sudden care for her wellbeing. She had always been a good friend, but had never really put much interest into Vivian or her social scene after high school. If it had been anyone but Lauren, she would be suspicious of the motives behind the visit, but that wasn't the kind of person Lauren was. She was genuine and good-hearted. Slightly naive, actually a lot naïve, but sometimes it was good to be around someone like that.

Not an hour later, her friend was already knocking on the door.

Vivian answered, and Lauren wrapped her into a hug. "It's good to see you."

"You too, come on in. Have a seat."

The two women walked into the living room and sat down on the couch.

"Can I get you anything?"

"No, I just came to talk you into coming out to girl's night tonight. Now, before you say no." Lauren paused with her hand up. "Your mom called me. She begged me to get you to go do something, anything. She said you're practically a recluse these days. Please, please just say yes. All the girls are going."

"Lauren, I don't have any *girls*. You are my old friend and that's about it."

"Come on, Viv," she rolled her eyes. "You do to have friends. Kaitlyn is coming with Shelbie, I mean you don't know *her*, Shelbie, I mean, but you'll like her. Then Alexis is bringing Larissa and Jensi said she would meet us there too.

Kaitlyn had her baby last summer, and it's really the first time since little Brock was born that she's going out and I told her 'we should get all the ladies together' and she was like 'we really should' and then we listed off everyone we thought should come and she brought up you. I told her I didn't think you'd come, and we dropped it, but then your mom called me yesterday and I just knew that was a sign that I was supposed to come talk you into coming."

Holy fuck, that was a lot of words all at once.

"It's really nice of you, but those are your friends. I don't even like most of them."

"Well, they like you, and you haven't seen any of them in years. I mean, I guess I understand why. No one is mad at you or anything for it, it's just... Honestly, Viv, you make things so difficult sometimes. You don't need to be alone all the time." Lauren took in a big sigh. "I feel like we never got you back, you know."

"Where exactly are you going?" The guilt on Lauren's face, the innocence of not understanding that she was right, they didn't get her back.

"The Cottage."

Vivian made a face.

"Don't make that face, Viv, you used to like going there for the bands."

"I'll go."

"Really?" Lauren squealed in girly delight.

"Yes, but you have to drive so I can get drunk enough to deal with it."

"I can drive, no problem! Oh, I'm so excited. Larissa said there was no way in hell I was going to be able to talk you into it, and really it didn't take that much convincing at all. Oh my gosh, what do you want to wear? Let's go up and look in your closet. Your hair looks terrible in buns, and I always tell you that. But I know you like them, so I won't pester you about it, unless it will matter, of course.

I really have missed you, ya know. But I just didn't know how to be around you anymore and," she paused midsentence in a sober silence as they walked over to the steps together. "Viv, you look horrible. Have you seen yourself?"

"Oh, thanks so much Lauren, fuck."

"Well, you have no makeup on, and your clothes are just hanging off you. Grab your coat. We're going to my house to get ready. I have plenty of awesome 'going out' clothes and I can do your hair and makeup and Chester will love to see you again."

"I still cannot believe you married a man named *Chester.*" Vivian laughed, a real laugh. "Did Kaitlyn really name her baby Brock?"

"Oh, Vivian, you're terrible."

She grabbed her purse and left with her old friend.

The women had known each other since high school. They stayed close until Vivian left for her second deployment. After being blown up, and coming home wounded, she lost most of her friends. They all tried to comfort her, tried to include her, but it was as if their lives were going on and Vivian's was standing still. She couldn't move past it all. She didn't know how to come home to them. Maybe a night out with old friends would help her. Maybe it would remind her how to breathe again.

She couldn't breathe.

Please don't follow me. The words were echoing in her mind. The words that clenched her fate. She sat with her head resting on her hands, elbows on her knees, inside the women's bathroom of the bar.

"Viv, open the door."

Her friend's words drifted through the closed bathroom door as Vivian sat on the closed toilet seat with her beautifully painted face. She was wearing Lauren's clothes, a blue delicate lace shirt with cap sleeves tucked into a heather grey skirt with buttons going down the front.

Lauren knocked gently again. "I'm sorry, Viv, this was supposed to be fun. What should I do?"

The hell if I know.

She needed to pull herself together. What she needed was the damn rescue pills from the VA. She reached into her bag and pulled out the familiar white bottle labeled with the suicide hot-line number on top.

Please. Don't follow me. Words written by hand on a sheet of white paper, covered in brain spatter.

She sighed.

The VA was trying. Her family was trying. Her friend was trying. Everyone was trying to help.

What should I do? She wanted to know what she should do. The VA wanted to know what they should do. The loved ones wanted to know what they should do.

She swallowed two of the pills in the bottle that came to her in the mail.

Please don't follow me.

With a deep breath, she opened the stall door. "It's fine, I'm fine now."

"Oh, Vivian." Lauren had such kind eyes. Such a genuine blind soul. "We can go if you want. Do you want to go?"

God, this world could eat Lauren alive. It would pull her goodness out by her fingernails as she screamed for mercy.

"I really don't mind if you just want me to take you home."

Home to an empty house? Home to sit alone again with The Lady? I can't keep hiding with her.

"No, we can stay. I think I need to stay. I just heard someone say the wrong words, that's all. But I'm fine now."

Lauren's kind smile was laced with her pity. She could never know how cruel the world outside was, and she should never lose her pretty eyes with the pity and kindness. *I'm glad she doesn't know.*

They walked out into the crowded bar. The group of women that came to mingle for their girl's night all sat at the table together. They looked at Vivian awkwardly as she returned to take her seat. This was why she never wanted to do anything with them. She remembered almost instantly after walking into the bar. They always looked at her awkwardly. Like she was tainted with the experience of being blown up, or maybe simply because she served in the war at all.

That, and that she never knew how to react to their silly girl talk about boyfriends and husbands, their cute stories about toddlers, and childbirth, and motherhood strife, or discussions about the new popular television series and Hollywood heartthrob scandals. Vivian just didn't fit into their worlds anymore.

When she first walked in with Lauren, they all jumped up from their drinks in their fancy outfits and the compliments flowed about how pretty Viv looked and how she had lost weight. It sparked an instant conversation about diets and how many amazing recipes you can get off Pinterest and the struggle to accept your new body after having children and being over thirty. Vivian's face hurt from keeping the smile in place and nodding to keep up with the conversation. She was relieved that none of them seemed to notice she never answered when they asked how she lost the weight.

I've been drinking vodka for lunch, and dinner skittered across the inside of her mind.

"You okay, sweetie?" Jensi asked from behind her fake eyelashes with fake concern. Jensi had been the first to congratulate her for her weight loss when they first walked in. Like it had been an award worthy accomplishment. In her defense, to Jensi it probably was a true compliment. She valued her figure as her own accomplishment and had probably viewed Vivian's extra pounds as something to be ashamed of.

Jensi went to the gym daily and posted selfies in her designer matching work-out uniforms to every social media outlet she had. She was a beautiful and well put together woman. Her fingernails were always so lovely, her nails displayed art, always a different color and design. She had brought Vivian for a manicure once a few years ago, and the process amazed her. The nail professionals worked with the chemicals and materials and tools to create such delicate details of perfection and beauty. It was an art.

Jensi's entire body was art, really. The artistic way her hair highlights and low lights were precisely arranged to flow together, no matter how she wore her hair. The layers of eye shadow that matched the outfit she wore, the contouring makeup that made each facial feature appear flawless. The straight line of eyeliner that aligned perfectly to the shape of her eyelid, stretching it further and longer to add to her features. She put so much effort into how she was seen, how she wanted to be seen, and it never faltered. Vivian couldn't help but wonder what she would look like disheveled, covered in sweat and dirt and sand and blood.

She couldn't picture it.

"I'm fine. Sorry about that, I get uneasy sometimes in loud places. It's really no big deal."

The sympathetic smiles washed over the features of the women around the table.

They look at me like I belong in a loony bin.

She wanted to hide, to melt into the faces of people around her.

To be one of them, laughing and comfortable around each other. She wanted to hear the music, laughter, and casual conversations around her as the normal hum of being in a social setting.

To see the faces all around as a hue of happiness and good intended human interaction.

To feel the energy in the room and allow it to make her feel excited and alive.

Jensi's eyes suddenly got wide as her focus settled in on the space above Vivian's head.

The hairs on the nape of Viv's neck prickled. Then the empty space around her was replaced with warmth that traveled up her arm caused by the large male hand sliding up to rest on her shoulder.

Killer's hands, she thought.

Vivian turned toward him slightly as his face came in to kiss her cheek. His soft lips melted into her skin with a familiarity that implied intimacy.

"Vivian, it's good to see you." The breath his words flowed on stirred her hair as he spoke them softly into her ear.

Jensi's mouth dropped open across the table as the handsome dreamboat rested his lips on Vivian's neck for a second greeting.

"Will." His name fell off her lips in surprise at his over-familiarity in public. "What are you doing here?"

His hand on her arm tightened. "It's a bar, Viv." He laughed, allowing a hint of his anger to roll off him and float away with the false sunshine of his beaming, brilliant, radiant smile. "You haven't seen me in months and that's what you say?" He paused briefly, smile firmly in place, hiding the disappointment at her greeting. "I'm a single man. What do you think I'm doing here?" He laughed again and the women at the table giggled in swooning girl tones.

But he doesn't drink. He has no one in this community to come back for. She wanted to say it, but didn't.

"Pull that chair up for him, Vivian. Don't be rude. He should join us." Jensi pointed to the chair behind her at an unused table and gave her the needy girlfriend look. The *Oh my God, why didn't you tell me you know such an ornament, and don't you dare let him walk away* look.

Jensi was almost bouncing at the chance to get to know this new flavor. It irritated Vivian slightly that her *friend* wouldn't assume he was someone that she was trying to date. But only slightly, considering he was the kind of man who dated women like Jensi, not Vivian.

Will's hand fell from her arm as she got up to follow Jensi's direction and provide him with a chair. Turning, she looked up into his face for the first time in months.

His hair was longer than it had been. He had it styled tonight, parted to the left with clean cut precision. His face was cleanly shaven, showing off his sharply etched jawline. He wore dark jeans with a light blue button-up shirt, ironically the same color as Vivian's, rolled meticulously to rest below his elbow. His collar buttons were open at the top, showing a hint of his smooth chest and making it visible to see his throat as he swallowed.

He took a step closer to her, speaking low above her head. "You don't do my heavy lifting."

"And you don't drink." She shot back.

"I was bored," his shoulders shrugged. "I wanted to be around people."

"Did you know I would be here?"

"No, Vivian, how would I know? I haven't heard from you in months."

Her neck prickled. She couldn't think of a way he would know.

"I'm sorry. I'm sorry I haven't answered your calls. And I'm sorry I questioned you being here." She shook her head and smiled up at him, "I'm just, I'm not comfortable here. I'm really not enjoying being around people right now."

"So, why are you here?"

"Do you know the author, Virginia Woolf?"

He nodded, trying to follow where she was going with such an odd question.

"Well, she filled her pockets with rocks and walked into the river. That's how she died."

Her eyes slid away from his, focusing on the bursting life around them, the laughter and the voices wafting in the air, the feel of being alive, of being a part of life. She closed her eyes before turning her gaze back to him.

"I'm pretty sure I understand why she did it." She shrugged and snickered, taking in a deep breath. "But too many people would hurt if I found rocks, so here I am. A *fun* night out with the girls."

His hand reached out and tipped her chin to force her to meet his gaze. "You will not let them see you, do you hear me?" His face was void of emotion, his voice flat and hard. "Smile at me right now." She turned her lips up into a complying smile.

"Jesus, Viv. What have you done to yourself? Fuck." He sighed, his eyes scanning from her head to her toes, as if annoyed at her emotional state of disarray and weight loss. "Come back to the table with me. Be social."

They rejoined the table of women.

"So, tell me," Jensi's piercing voice drifted loud over the noise of the room, "How do you two know each other?"

Will chimed in without so much as a glance in Vivian's direction. "We met at a veteran event for medics."

"Oh, you were in the military with our Viv?"

Our Viv? Jensi was ferociously on the hunt. It made Vivian let out a slight snicker. Will pretended not to notice.

"Well, we served in the same army, but I was a medic with the 2nd Ranger Battalion, 75th Ranger Regiment."

Vivian rolled her eyes at his cocky Ranger, bragging as each woman at the table swooned a little further. She wondered if Jensi's panties would be able to stay up long enough for them to be alone. The thought made her laugh louder.

Will's eyes slid over her in perturbed unease. He probably thought she belonged in the loony bin too. Vivian in the crazy house and Jensi on his arm. They would make such a pretty couple. Perfection.

The conversation drifted on around her as Viv swirled the ice in her drink. Giggles from the women at the table swarmed up into her ears as her mind focused on the ice cubes moving around each other in almost a dance.

"Viv. Vivian?"

She blinked back into the moment. The faces around the table were suddenly sullen, and she saw pity again in Lauren's lovely eyes. Will looked embarrassed, waiting for a reply.

"I'm sorry, what?"

"I asked if their husbands were friends with your elusive husband." His embarrassment was an obvious annoyance. "I meant it in jest, since I have yet to meet the man, but now I'm confused?" His irritation at being confused evident in his face.

The eyes around her all focused on her. The noises surrounding them were louder. The people all around were closer. It seemed to crush against her in a wave of fire as she burned where she sat. Vivian smiled nervously, her breathing getting away from her for a moment before pulling her shoulders back and taking in a deep breath affording her the ability to reply.

"My husband isn't living, Will." Her eyes darted to the women sitting around the table. The uncomfortable moment creeping up her body and seeping into her skin.

"So um, but Jensi isn't married. Are you seeing anyone now? The banker." Her hand went up in a nervous wave of recognition. "Are you still dating him?" Her face was hot, her lungs feeling heavy. She couldn't look at Will. She couldn't stand to see what his expression would say. She stared at Jensi begging her to save this moment. But Jensi sat in silent confusion, as if Vivian were speaking Greek.

"Oh Viv," Lauren's lovely giggle broke through throwing a life raft, "The banker was like five boys ago, wasn't he Jensi? What was his name... Aaron. He ended up having a weird obsession with finger smelling, remember?" She nervously laughed again.

"Oh, yeah." Jensi picked up on the lifeline, finally. "We would go out to these fancy restaurants and there we would be at the table and he would smell his fingers between courses. The salad would come, and we'd eat, and the waiter would show up to take the bowls away and there he would go, fingers to his nose with a whiff." The women all laughed as she went on talking about the banker, the last man Vivian could remember being on her Facebook feed.

Will sat still and quiet beside her.

The conversation continued as Vivian swept herself gingerly off her seat to walk over to the bar. She would go get a shot or two, allow them to gossip about how her husband had swallowed a bullet over three years ago. Fill Will in on the gruesome details of how she found him in the garage, his brains all over the wall. The note he left, *Please Don't Follow Me.*

I wouldn't shoot myself, she thought.

It was horrible to find him that way. He always had such a perfect mouth.

But he blew it apart.

Rocks in the pocket was the way to go. Virginia had the right of it. Simply allow the water to swallow you up, pull you down into it. The burn would ignite death as it filled up in her lungs.

She flagged the bartender over and ordered two double shots of gentlemen jack.

Immediately, she threw back the first shot and rested her hand around the second. A bearded man in plaid spoke up next to her.

"Two double shots? Rough night?"

She gave him a placid smile.

He put his hand down on hers. "What could possibly drive a pretty girl like you to double fist gentlemen jack?" He was flirting.

The thought almost made her laugh.

Well, first there was the mass genocide, and then I think getting blown up in Iraq next to my best friend, who had to be scraped out of the vehicle probably contributed. Oh, and my husband, a Fallujah Marine, who I only married because he felt obligated to take care of me, blew his brains out, and right now my table of friends over there are all talking about it.

But before a word could leave her mouth, another hand was resting on the swell of her back.

"Everything alright here?"

Will's other hand reached down to grab hold of the shot glass, taking it from her fingers as the bearded man in plaid quickly pulled his away.

With his face, Will communicated with the man that it was a smart move. He held the shot glass up, using his other hand to push against Vivian's back, guiding her to move in the direction he was leading. Walking toward the table of women, he handed the shot to her. "Take it."

They stopped briefly, long enough for her to throw the burn down her throat, and then continued back on their path. "I'm taking you home."

They reached the table. "It was a pleasure to meet all of you ladies, but I think Vivian and I would like to catch up if you don't mind."

Lauren was over to Vivian in a flash, hugging her, speaking into her ear, "Do you want to go with him?"

Viv felt herself nodding with a smile as the relaxing burn warmed up her veins as it sailed through her body all at once.

"Okay, if you're sure."

Vivian nodded again.

"I'm glad you came out. I miss you, Viv." Her words melted as she spoke genuinely.

“I know.” She smiled at Lauren’s kind face again before turning toward the door. Will was at her elbow in a half step. He said nothing as they walked toward the doors. Relief washed over her with a rush as she pushed out into the night air and breathed in deep, enjoying that the music and hum of people were no longer mingling inside her head.

His hand was on her back again, leading her as they walked. They moved in silence through the parking lot.

He drove here.

The mix of alcohol was beginning to buzz inside. She thought of how many drinks she had before she took the double shots back-to-back. She was glad she didn't drive, and that Lauren wasn't going to have to drive her home.

“You bought a car?” She asked, wondering now how he got to the bar.

He didn't answer. She slowed her pace in confusion, suddenly realizing they were walking towards a brand new slate grey Jeep.

Realization hit her. She stopped dead in her tracks.

“You got it!” Her face lit up into a genuine smile.” 100% right? All the back pay. I knew it. I knew it would work!”

He still didn't talk.

Was he angry with her? Well, let him be angry. At this particular moment, she really didn't give a flying fuck if he was.

This night fucking blew.

She just wanted to go home and take her clothes off and sink onto the floor to drink some more with The Lady.

He opened the passenger door of the Jeep and all but lifted her up into the seat. “I'm not drunk. I don't need you to put me in the car like a child.” Vivian snapped at him.

“Good to hear, because I don't fuck drunk women, and as sure as hell don't fuck children, and I plan on fucking you tonight.” He slammed the door.

Vivian sat in the passenger seat, shocked into frozen stillness. The thought of his hands on her body pricked through her mind... his hand on her throat.

Will jumped fluidly into the seat.

He didn't put on his seat belt. It bothered her.

No music played as the vehicle turned on. The engine hummed, and the dark interior lit up with the florescent light of the dash.

"You said you wouldn't force me again." Her words barely made a sound.

"*Again*? What do you mean, force you again? Did I or did I not tell you to say no if you didn't want to?"

Her mind was beginning to slosh, she thought back to him, pinning her to the wall.

"Did I, or didn't I? Answer me."

"Yes, but..."

"But nothing. You can't rape the willing, Vivian. And now I find out you aren't married," he chuckled, shaking his head, "you're a fucking widow. All this time," He ran his hand through his hair messing up the precision of its style, "All this time I've been beating myself up for sleeping with a married woman. I disappeared because of it! Do you even realize that?" He turned to look at her while he yelled. "You weren't mine, so I left."

"Wait, you left because of me?"

"Well, partly. Why didn't you tell me? I asked specifically if you were married."

"No, you stated that I was married. I never said I was *still* married."

"You wear a fucking ring, Viv! Why wouldn't you want me to know you were available?"

"Because I'm not *available*, I will never be available. I don't ever want that. Ever!" The thought of him dating her made her laugh ironically. "Besides, why would you want to be with me?"

"*That's* not your decision to make. It's MY decision!"

"Just like who I fuck is mine! It's my decision, and you stole it from me!"

"YOU didn't say No!"

"I told you I didn't want you to, not like that!"

"You didn't know what you wanted and still don't! There is a serious fucking disconnect in that confused drunk mind of yours between what the fuck you want and what you need, and you're too fucking self-destructive for me to allow you the liberty to decide either one. So just sit there with your mouth shut and be grateful I like you being on this earth with me!"

"Well, I'm not grateful to be on this earth. I'm not grateful for any fucking thing and you don't want me. You pity me!"

"Vivian enough!"

"No! You pity me because I'm just like you, with blood all over my hands. We both know how warm and silky it feels running through our fingers until it begins to get sticky and the smell seeps into your nose so you can taste it like metal in our mouth and it steams in the cold off of them while they scream!"

He reached over and grabbed hold of the back of her hair.

"I said ENOUGH!" He yelled, slamming her head back into the headrest.

Her breath hitched as her neck lashed back and a slight whimper escaped her lips.

The ride continued in silence as they both sat stewing.

At the very moment he pulled in front of her house, she hit her seatbelt release to get out of his new fancy vehicle as quickly as possible.

Anger burned through her veins.

Her door flew open, and she hopped out of the jeep, and range-walked as fast as her heels would take her up to the house.

As fast as she could, she turned the unlocked handle to open her into the dark, quiet house.

Instantly, his hand was on the back of her neck, pushing her in.

"AND you didn't lock the door."

Will threw her into the hallway, causing her to stumble down onto her hands and knees. Her purse flew open onto the hardwood floor, spilling its contents. She flipped around onto her butt, her knees up, feet flat on the floor.

"It broke you, Viv. All of it." He shut the door behind him, locking it. "The war, the wounds, your husband offing himself."

"I'd like to think it made me stronger." Her stubborn chin held up, eyes watching his predatory movements.

"You're not strong. You just put on a good show for the people who need you. Really, you're fragile." His hands picked up a delicate, ornate vase from the hallway table, running his fingers along the curves of it. "Fragile, like a beautiful broken vase that was carefully glued back together, and everyone looks at it and thinks 'oh how amazing that all the pieces went back together and it's fixed' but really, it's still broken and just held together by a thin layer of glue. It can never be useful again, and can't hold flowers or water, it's just empty. Sitting there so other people get to look at it, but the tiniest brush of wind will shatter it to pieces again."

With one swift throw, he smashed the vase against the wall as hard as he could and was instantly down on the floor over top of her. "That's how I see you. This fragile, beautiful vase held together, so no one has to be sad that it broke into a million pieces. It makes me want to steal it away, hold it in my hands to hide it so no one ever gets to enjoy its beauty again."

Flipping over onto his back, he pulled her down against his chest. Grasping her wrist, throwing her arm over top of him, he swung his leg over top of hers, locking her against him in a cuddling position on the floor.

His chest heaved up into a deep breath as he settled into holding her, his free hand finding her hair, stroking it down through his fingers. She could hear the air moving in and out of his lungs as his strong heartbeat slowed inside his body.

"But why?" she whispered. "Why would you want to hold me? Why would you want to hide me away?"

"Because none of them ever did a goddamn thing to earn the right to look at it. Don't you get it? They are all stupid sheep who want to latch onto things that don't exist, like God, and prayers, and hope, and dreams, and fate. They want to see you as the *strong veteran* who was shattered but put back together so they can all feel good about your hope filled story of faith and perseverance. When really, you're just a pretty shell that was pieced together with glue but will never be able to hold anything again. Just empty and scared *every second* of falling over again. And they will never get that. They have no clue what it takes out of you. For what?... Fuck, I don't even know why I'm even trying to talk to you about this. You're a fucking sheep too."

Irritation laced his words again.

Her tone mimicked it, "Why? Because I still believe in goodness? Because I'm hopeful that good things can still happen?"

"Yes!"

"Well then yes, I'd rather be a sheep than seeing *everything* as beyond saving!" Unafraid, Vivian yelled right back.

He pushed her over and hopped up to his feet gracefully.

"I'm going home. I can't stand being with you anymore."

"Fine. Maybe stop at the thrift store on your way and find a pretty vase to look at!"

"What did you say? I'm sorry, I can't understand your sheep talk."

"Sheep talk," she laughed, "You know what? No! You can't label me a sheep. I've at least earned the upgrade to like a llama or something."

"You are infuriating. Stop talking." He was at the door, angry.

"Do llamas bah? What noise do they make?" He turned to glare at her, intimidate her.

It didn't work. She sat on the floor smiling.

"I'm sorry Will that I put you in a baaaaad mood."

She giggled as he slammed the door.

Will stormed out to the jeep, jumped in, slamming his own door out of anger. He put the keys in the ignition and turned on the quiet engine before leaning back in the chair, resting his head against the seat and blowing out his breath. He began replaying their words in his mind and a burst of laughter escaped him.

"Stop by a thrift store." He said out loud to the empty space of his quiet jeep. He shook his head. *Why on earth did I come back here?*

A sigh left his lungs. "So stupid."

His mind answered, *you wanted to be near her.* "Fuck." He hit the steering wheel with his fist. Will knew he was taking a chance going to find her at the bar. When he eavesdropped on her conversation with her friend earlier that day, he knew it was a chance to see her again. Though he knew that he wasn't ready, and hadn't planned or thought it out. He knew it would be a shock to her, knew her suspicions would trigger.

Only none of it mattered.

He just wanted to go be with her again. Any fucking way he could, he just wanted to be near her. Then when he was near her, walking up behind her where she sat, all he could think about was getting his mouth on her. He limited himself to one kiss. Maybe he had taken liberties with two, but he had been obsessing about all the damn emotions surrounding her for so long that he suffered a temporary lapse in control, for just that one moment.

The rest of it he had handled so well. He was being such a good gentleman. Charming her friends, being a normal veteran buddy that happened to run into her at the bar.

Then the bombshell.

All this time, she had been a fucking widow. It infuriated him. Why hadn't she told him?

Will put his head into his hands on the steering wheel.

"A fucking llama." He snickered in the empty darkness.

Vivian stayed lying on the floor where he left her when he stormed out. Her mind foggy from the alcohol, she couldn't stop herself from revisiting her paranoia from earlier in the night. There was no way he just happened to run into her at the bar.

"Stalker." She whispered into the silence.

I like that he found me.

The thought brought out a hum of sadness in the dead quiet. Lying alone on the floor of her empty house, she admitted to herself that she was warmer with him near her. She had become so isolated, so alone all the time. Tonight, she had hoped a night out with old friends would fill some of the emptiness that was eating her alive inside. She had thought that being with those women would fill even a small piece of the giant abyss beneath her skin. Instead, sitting at that table, it felt even larger.

Until Will stood behind her, until his hand brushed her skin, his lips found her neck. She didn't feel the void when he was near.

Vivian looked up as the door opened and Will stepped back through. Rising onto her elbows, she pointed at him with an accusatory look of disappointment, "*You* didn't lock the door!"

Dropping her finger, she smirked as he fell to his knees beside her.

He came back.

Will stared down into her eyes as he moved so his legs straddled over her on the floor.

He was angry, and we fought, but he came back.

Slowly, he leaned down close to her face, a serious and determined air surrounding him. "I told you, locking the door is the only way to keep the monsters out."

Vivian sucked in her breath.

"Maybe I don't want to keep them out."

"Do you think I'm a monster?" he asked. Eyes boring into her soul, searching for an answer.

She didn't hesitate, "Yes," sorrow lacing the words, "but so am I."

The only perfect answer there was.

"Do you hate me for taking from you?"

She turned her face away to answer, but his fingers pushed her chin back to his gaze.

"No." She spoke it firmly.

"Why not?"

"Because I believe you. You meant it as a gift, to make me feel. I don't feel anymore. I don't feel anything."

"Do you want to? Do you want me to show you how to feel?"

Her breath hitched in her chest. Looking up at him, she could feel his intensity, could feel that he was restraining himself for her to decide.

"I thought you didn't fuck drunk girls?"

Moving his face closer to her lips, his arms bulging from suspending himself over top of her, his words came out sultry and heated, "Is that a no, then?"

"No"

"I didn't think so." Will sucked in air as his perfect lips delved into hers.

His hands hurriedly pressed against her flesh feverishly. He slid them up her leg to penetrate under her skirt, to find her wetness with his fingers.

Wait. He paused his hands. *I need to ask her. I don't want to have her any other way.*

Will broke off the kiss suddenly. "Do you want more? Please tell me if you want more from me."

"I'm kissing you back this time, Will. Touching you back." She gave a little chuckle, reaching her mouth up to find his while pulling at his shoulders, trying to bring him back down on top of her.

His tongue plundered as far into her mouth as he could reach. Her compliance was all he needed to unleash.

Without hesitation, Will grasped her arms hard, pinning her down as he pushed his weight on top of her. The air rushed out of her lungs and his cock twitched.

"Wait." Will stopped himself again, putting his forehead to hers, catching his breath and his thoughts.

They were both breathing heavily.

He felt his own hands release. Her body was let go. He gave her the opportunity to turn away from him, to crawl away if she wanted to. He wanted her to know she meant something more to him, but he didn't know what that more was. She needed to know she meant more. How was he supposed to make her feel something that he couldn't define himself?

"I'm not... normal. I enjoy this differently, Viv. I need you to know, I am not. I'm not gentle."

"Will, I'm already broken. You said it yourself."

"I don't want to break you more. I want to be the one who holds your brokenness."

"Then hold it."

"You're sure?"

She nodded, but he could see she was nervous. He didn't want to make her nervous. Will braced himself again on his knees, as he slid his hands around the back of her neck, cradling her head.

"Vivvie, God, I don't want to fuck this up. You see because, I've missed you and I hated it. I don't want to miss you again. I want to show you, to make you feel what I do, but I don't know... " Her eyes were grey blue, not their bright blue. She had been sad without him.

They were grey because she was sad.

"Fuck, Viv, I don't know how to..." Fuck, he was fucking this all up. He was bumbling like a moron.

She brought her hand up to touch his lips, to quiet his words. "Will, I trust you to know best."

"You do?" His forehead knitted in confusion. "But you look at me like you're afraid?"

"I'm terrified. But I want it anyway."

He paused for a brief moment, considering her words. This was Vivian, with her knowing blue eyes, her annoying quirks, and her medic touch, telling him she wanted him, even though she was afraid.

"Come."

He took her hand and led her up the stairs to her bedroom. The hallway floor wasn't the ideal place to make her feel all the pleasure he wanted for her. She trailed behind him as he pulled her up the steps and down the hallway, dropping her hand only once they entered the room.

Leaving her standing alone in the middle of the bedroom wearing her friend's pretty outfit, her golden hair a mess around her face, he hadn't expected the intense satisfaction he would have seeing her standing there anticipating his touch, nervous for it, hoping for it, wanting it. It filled him with something warm, something foreign, something all-encompassing inside of him. It was overwhelming.

Boldly, he walked over to where she stood, bringing her chin up so he could sip on her mouth. He walked her backwards as he enjoyed her lips, sucking them, tasting them, nibbling them. She moaned softly, and his restraint faltered.

Will's careful control floundered as he ripped the pretty blue shirt open, kissing the mounds of her tits before pulling what was left of the shirt off and releasing her from her bra.

"You broke Lauren's shirt."

He opened the top button of the skirt with his fingers, popping the rest apart brutally with his hands. "Her skirt too." Will added.

She giggled at his comment. The sound of it made him smile. His real smile.

He pushed her hard enough to have her plop onto the bed. She lay in her underwear with her breasts and scars bare to him, and he wanted her.

Not as a chore.

Not to punish.

He wanted to pleasure her, to find pleasure in her. He whipped his own clothing off in uncharacteristically feverish haste. No control at all. No folding. They fell onto the floor wherever they landed, and he climbed beside her onto the bed. Leaning over where she lay, Will ran his hands up her skin.

"You're beautiful."

Her brow knitted together. "Don't lie to me." She chastised him with a pleading whisper, "You can do anything you want to my body just, please, don't lie to me."

"But I'm not lying, Vivvie." His mouth swept along the inside of her arm, up to her neck. His lips brushed her throat. "You are beautiful. Like sunshine when it reflects off stained glass, that kind of beauty. The kind of beauty that has to be felt." She sighed as his hands moved up her leg, his fingers finding her clit. Slowly, he moved circles with his hand while sucking and kissing gently on her flesh. "Beauty, like seeing the stars shining crystal clear on the darkest, coldest night of war."

"Will," she whispered. "Give me more."

His mouth smiled against her skin. "Flip onto your belly." He helped her to move, "just like this." Will positioned her legs. Crossed her ankle over ankle, knees spread apart. His warm skin slid across her back as he pulled her up onto her knees, forcing her to brace herself on her arms. "Oh yeah, just like this. Beauty, like your perfect ripe ass, splayed open before me. Stay."

He climbed up onto the bed, one leg on either side of hers, and leaned down to ease her undies down as far as they would travel on her legs. With the fabric out of the way, he reached down with both his hands to hold her open to him as he slid home. Slowly, inch by inch, far enough inside her that his arm's reach could extend close enough to her body so a hand could wrap around her nose and mouth.

She wiggled under his hold, a whimper escaping through his hand.

"I won't suffocate you, Vivvie. I promise."

Standing on her bed, with one large hand enclosed around her face and one pulling on her shoulder, he sped up his pace, pushing and pulling against her over and over.

Releasing his hold on her mouth, in order to hold her trust in the future, Will pounded faster and harder. The bed bounced hard with their movements, and she cried out. Not from pain, but with pleasure.

The sensations were overwhelming for him, new to him. He felt her muscles quiver inside as he filled her up with his girth and power. His thighs burned as her pleasure finally released. She was exquisite, in the throes of pleasure. Her moans and spasms became the air filling his lungs.

He slowed himself, enjoying her as she came to pieces around him. Her body collapsed down, breathing in gasps as he stepped off the bed. His cock still throbbing, desperate to burst.

Gently he crawled next to her, and he moved her to enter a new position, but she pulled away.

He was momentarily dismayed by her refusal. Until he realized she was rising onto her knees, sliding the underwear the rest of the way off her legs, and straddling him.

Keeping his eyes locked with hers, he felt her as she reached down to position his cock, guiding him into her again. Her eyes closed, her head falling back as the full length of him settled. Slowly, she began to move, rising over top of him. Her hips held him as her breasts bounced heavily with her motion. Leaning back with her hands firmly braced on his thighs, she bucked forward steadily, and the sensation was amazing. The view was amazing. He threw himself up to meet her movements, thrusting to fill her, wanting to find his pleasure with her this time.

It hit him hard, raced through him without any control. Noises he didn't know he made coming from his own throat. It was feral.

Will was lost in her.

His hands grasped her thick thighs, holding on hard enough to bruise as his control dissipated and his pleasure burst high up inside her.

Vivian fell down on top of him. Her breath heaved as the pulses of desire subsided. Will's own breaths matched hers.

Fully exhausted, he felt stated and relaxed. Her forehead rested on his shoulder, their bodies still connected, and his arms holding her plastered onto him.

"I'll get a washcloth." She spoke softly into his neck, but his muscles flexed, holding her tighter before she could move.

"Wash the sheets." Will locked his arms and legs around her, trapping her to him where she lay. He could feel the warm trickle of his seed spilling out from between her legs, but he wasn't bothered in the slightest. Moving her down, Will pulled her over to his side. Tucking her into him like a comforting piece of the blanket. Drifting to sleep while holding onto her plush softness protectively, or maybe ensnaringly, was going to be a delight. Something he couldn't remember ever enjoying before. Will wrapped as much of himself around her as he could and settled in for the night.

Slowly, gingerly, she moved her hand up to rest her fingers against his forearm where he caged her. She touched him so gently with trepidation, but he felt her body give way to comfort one small piece at a time. Finally, she allowed her head to rest heavily onto him, and he could feel the moment sleep took her. He didn't dare move even a muscle.

Will was so pleased by her, happy even to have her in his arms. He would allow her to feel warm and safe for the night. Just one night without being afraid of the monsters in her own head, because Will knew that none of them could compare to the one she now rested on.

Chapter 28

One Dead Marine Veteran

Vivian woke up before him. The morning sun peeking through the curtains rested over her closed eyelids. Before she opened them to the sun, she realized how hot she was. Her face felt flush from being so warm, her hair plastered to the side of her forehead from sweat.

She had woken up covered in sweat from nightmares a million nights since the war, but this sweat was from the heat cocooning around her off of Will. He was a furnace of warmth, and even in his sleep, he clung to her.

Tentatively, she moved his arm of hot coals from around her body. Slowly, she crawled out of his hold climbing off the bed. She stood in her bedroom, completely naked, while looking down at him, all nestled up in her covers. He looked too large in her bed. Though he looked so peaceful, with his sleeping face resting serenely on her pastel pillows, and completely at ease. Bared in the morning sun, he lay there with his perfect skin stretching across the taut defined muscles over his back and arms.

Will was nothing like her husband had been. Jason had decided to grow a full beard the second he got out of the Marine Corps. Tattoos covered him in ink, painting every inch of his arms.

She loved when Jason would lie sleeping in their bed with the sun hitting his beard, highlighting all the red hairs that she loved to tease him about. The hair on his head, and all over his manly fur-covered body, was deep brown, but his beard, his beard grew in with ginger red lace through the brown.

She teased him relentlessly and pulled on the red hairs every chance she got.

Jason's beard was the first beard she ever remembered touching. Beards always looked so coarse and prickly she wondered why men liked to keep such harsh décor on their faces. When they first met, she asked permission to touch his beard, out of curiosity, and was surprised that it was soft to her touch.

After that, his beard reminded her of him. The harsh and coarse looking man, secretly soft to the touch. There he would stand, with Marine killer's hands and stern eyes that scared away the gentle sheep that grazed in peace because of his willingness to do horrible things on their behalf. Vivian could see him beyond who he had become, and looked past the facade he forced to line the outside of his shell to protect what weak and broken pieces still lay shattered beyond the sheath.

Soft.

She loved touching his beard after that, to feel its softness, to see him allow her the intimacy he normally turned away from.

Jason hated having his face touched. Hated being vulnerable in any way. Yet when Viv would run her fingers through his beard, and then over his eyelids, and cheeks, and across his lips, he would close his eyes and lean into her touch. He'd forget how it felt so good to be delicately caressed until the moment her soft skin would run along the areas of him that he had closed off to all comfort and pleasure. He had such a fear of feeling too much that instead, he chose to feel nothing at all.

With Vivian, though, it was different. With Vivian, she was allowed.

Every time she would reach out and touch Jason's face, he would jerk away like she had burned him with hot iron on his skin. His combat Marine would stare out through war trained eyes until he realized the touch on his face was healer's hands, soothing his wounds, and then, instead, he would melt into her touch. Desperate for her reprieve, Jason carried such heavy pain with every step he took. He never put down the heaviness of war. He never took off the protective gear, or dropped the weapon that kept him alive. Instead, he ran with heavy boots through the burning sun and held the breath of a thousand Marines in his lungs without ever exhaling all those years.

Trigger finger was always at the ready.

Jason looked so disheveled when he slept, and then he'd wake up confused and disoriented. If she had to wake him, she would stand at his feet and barely touch his toe while saying his name softly and delicately. "Jason, it's time to wake up," she would whisper and he would whip his body up, ready to take on the unknown threat that faced him. Vivian would back away, announcing with her hands out in front of her that it was just his Viv come to wake him.

He'd look so frightening and dangerous as he registered that it was her, and not a threat. His fists would unclench, and he would reach for her with his mean face unchanged, pull her into him, and he'd growl like an angry bear as he sought to pull her into his protective embrace.

She loved that noise, the low rumble in his chest when he got her into his arms. Every time he touched her, every comfort she gave him, he purred like a huge cat trapped in the body of a burly mountain bear. When he would kiss her mouth, the passion would build up in his chest and he would rumble with such a feral boundless desire for her that the grumble would bellow loudly out of him as his sexual need overwhelmed him. Vivian missed that noise. She missed the deep roar of his comfort and love, and how safe she felt in love with him.

Will lay where her Jason should be.

Sadness crept up through her veins and settled into her heart as she compared the two men, knowing that none of their differences mattered except that one was dead and rotting under the earth, and the other was alive and laying in his bed.

Jason was dead.

She had to remind herself of that harsh reality from time to time. When she felt too sentimental or started reminiscing. Sometimes she would sit and try to think about what it was exactly that made her miss him so much. She would wonder if maybe it wasn't so much that she missed him, but more that she missed who he made her when he was beside her.

But Jason was dead.

He was dead and there was no sense in trying to hold on to him, or anything he had given her. It was gone, and she would never feel it again. One thing she had learned with complete certainty through her experiences was that some things were worse to feel than feeling nothing at all.

Two months after their honeymoon, she found her husband dead in the garage.

It all made sense in hindsight. The precious ring he gave her, so she would know how precious she had been to him. Insisting they marry, so she would legally be his wife and could collect all the benefits a wife could receive that a live-in partner could not.

He knew he couldn't stand it anymore in this life, even with her by his side. He just couldn't stand it.

She understood better than anyone that it wasn't that he wanted to die, that wasn't why he killed himself. He didn't want to die. He just couldn't stand living with it all anymore.

Death, to those who had taken life so freely, was so easy. Death seemed to have no permanence in war. There was no capacity for mourning in combat. No leisure to allow the permanence of death to sink under the skin and bury into the soul. They could not process loss, could not begin the stages of grieving, they were unable to process it at all. None of it was *allowed* to be felt until years later, and then they felt all of it. All at once, all the time.

Death was so easy. Life was harder, and her Jason just didn't want to fight anymore.

Vivian wasn't even angry with him for leaving. She was simply sad that she didn't get to feel his comfort anymore, that her love wasn't enough, that she couldn't bring herself to be selfish enough to join him.

Jason was dead.

Vivian moved away from where Will lay sleeping in Jason's bed. After going into the bathroom to find her robe and brush her teeth, she wanted to go downstairs have a cup of coffee and some cereal, throw a load of laundry in the washer, and begin the day. The night before had been unexpected and emotionally confusing. Time to think alone with her thoughts was needed.

What on earth happened to make Will suddenly want her? He had kissed her throat in the bar, had put his hand on the swell of her back to guide her through the people. He wanted her the moment he stepped foot in the bar. It didn't make any sense at all to think the unbelievably attractive hot ranger would pick her, plain and plump, when he could go home with Jensi or any other woman in the place. It didn't make any sense at all that he would even be back here in her town.

Jason used to say he hated the town. It was small with nothing to do, but he stayed because of her. Maybe it was as simple as that, Will wanted to be near to where she was. Jason thought she was enough of a reason to be there.

Until she wasn't.

Vivian put her toothbrush back in the holder and turned off the bathroom light to wander downstairs.

Jason was dead.

Chapter 29

Two Army Medic Veteran's Reveille

All the lights were still off from the night before, but the kitchen glowed with the brightness of the sun breaching through the curtainless windows. Will was drawn to it like a moth.

The soft yellow color of the wall reflected a golden hue across the small room. It created a certain safety in the stillness that normally evaded his surroundings. The feeling of comfort and warmth sunk into his skin as he stood in the glow of the sun, throwing light into her small little kitchen. He couldn't remember the last time he felt comfortable anywhere.

She was comfort.

Her skin was comfort. Her eyes touching his skin warmed him the same as the sun in her kitchen.

A blue towel with yellow swirling patterns laid spread across the counter next to the sink. A freshly washed bowl and coffee cup sat upside down on top of it. Almost absentmindedly, he flipped the mug over to stand it upright and traced his fingers along the rim where her mouth would have been. It was clean. She used it and then washed it. Her hands would have submerged it into a sink filled with hot soap and water. She would have scrubbed the rim with a sponge, dipped it inside to swirl around where the hot coffee had contaminated it. Her hands would hold it delicately, knowing how fragile the mug was, and would cradle it protectively in one hand, but the other would scrub it clean. It needed force to be cleaned. It was fragile but needed strength to make is usable again. He wrapped his hand around the coffee mug, fingers through the handle.

How much pressure would he need to apply to crush it?

His forearm flexed as his strong, large hand squeezed.

Hands of a killer wrapped around a porcelain mug.

He pressed harder. Turning his knuckles white as the sun kissed them through the window glass.

"Oh, do you want me to make you coffee?"

She swept into the room as brilliantly as the sun, with her golden hair reflecting rays as vividly as the wallpaper.

"I'm sorry. I should have had some ready for you before you came down. I'm not used to entertaining anymore." She laughed nervously and began bustling. He couldn't remember the last time he watched a woman bustle around a kitchen.

His sister, at Thanksgiving dinner, the year she moved into her own house and wanted to make a home instead of the sterile catalog-display-home they grew up in together. She bustled around her kitchen the same way.

"You believe I'd be properly entertained with coffee?" He released the pressure on the delicate mug.

Vivian snickered at his comment while continuing her bustle. Golden hair sweeping around her head as she moved, oblivious that she blended into sunshine.

"I meant that I should have been polite and offered you morning coffee."

"No," *I know what you meant,* "I don't want coffee."

She stopped midmotion, disappointment painting her features. "Oh, okay." A fake smile lifted her lips but didn't touch her eyes.

She wanted to serve me coffee. Vivvie wanted to be able to offer me something so she could serve me.

Turning to search in her fridge, she asked, "Is there anything else you want? Fruit? I have cantaloupe."

His mouth hitched up at the corner. "No, Vivian, I don't want you to entertain me. I want you to be comfortable with me in your home with you." He wrapped his hand around her arm, gently pulling her back from the open refrigerator door, pushing it shut with his foot. "If I want something, I'll help myself."

A stray lock of hair lay over her eye. With his free hand he brushed it away from her face, allowing his fingers to trail down the golden strains as he guided them back over her shoulder. He allowed his hand to follow the strains back, curling his fingers around her neck.

So delicate, like the coffee mug.

He squeezed gently.

How much pressure would it take to crush her? The thought aroused him. He took in a deep breath to calm the excitement trying to crawl through his veins.

"We're friends." His false sunshine smile matched the sunshine in the room. "Friends don't need to entertain each other." He cocked his head to the side, wanting to say more, wanting to squeeze more, but a jar on the counter behind her caught in his line of sight.

"Vivvie, what the hell is that?"

Will moved her to the side so he could get a better look at the large jar. There were jagged holes that had been slashed into the metal lid. Some of them seemed to have been pried up to allow more airflow. Inside stood a branch, a few green leaves still attached with one large leaf curled in on itself, hanging down.

"It's a chrysalis," her words came out defensive, "Actually, I'm pretty sure it's a Luna moth."

Will wanted to burst out laughing. He felt it surging in his chest.

"Why the hell do you have a fucking moth cocoon in a jar on your counter?"

"When I saw the caterpillar slinking through the yard a few days ago, I could tell he was headed for the big tree, but a large swarm of birds came in and sat above him. I didn't want them to eat him." She shrugged, "So, I got this jar out and put him in it." She moved away from Will's touch and walked over to lean on the counter, elbows down, backside out into the open kitchen so she could put her eyes cocoon level. "I looked up pictures online and I'm pretty sure it's a Luna moth. They are very beautiful, and rare for humans to ever get to see."

You're beautiful and rare.

The thought invaded before he had time to digest what that meant to him.

"You're so fucking weird," were the words that he allowed to be heard.

She laughed out loud. "I'm excited about it."

"Is that how you cut your finger?" Will reached out and delicately pulled her finger up to his eyes for a closer inspection.

"You noticed I cut my finger?"

"Well, we were relatively close the last few hours, don't you think?"

Her cheeks blushed red. "Yes, I sliced it, making the holes in the lid, so he could breathe."

"I don't like you bleeding."

"Well, I didn't like thinking he would get eaten before becoming a beautiful moth." She pulled her hand back. "It was just a small little cut, so don't be so overprotective."

"I'm not being overprotective. I just don't want you to bleed. Even if it means something beautiful gets to live."

"I love that I have him here, safe on my counter." She brushed off his concern.

"And when it hatches? Will you keep him in your jar?"

"Oh no, as soon as he hatches, I'll set him free."

"You could keep it in the jar and when it dies, put it in a picture frame on the wall."

"Like the naked ladies in the art museum?" She looked at the cocoon with sad eyes for a moment. "No, I'd rather him die where I don't know about it."

"You'd rather be blind to the realities of life?"

"I'm not blind to them. I just see them so much with my eyes closed that I'd rather not see them with my eyes open too."

"So, you kept the birds from a nice caterpillar meal, and cut your finger slicing holes in the lid of a jar, ruining a very nice lemonade pitcher I'd like to point out. Subjecting yourself to having to look at an ugly, gross pod taking up real estate on your counter for the next three weeks because you don't want to face the realities of life anymore? All for a moth that only lives about a month, if it's lucky."

Vivian stared at the cocoon. A million thoughts racing behind her eyes. He could feel all the feelings and words dashing from one side of her mind to the other. A part of him wanted to just hug her, pull her into his chest and hide her eyes, tell her he understood what she wanted. Tell her a part of him wanted it, too. Promise to shield her from anything harsh or unpleasant or real for the rest of her life.

I could hide her away. Keep her in my house in the woods.

"No, my reasons are purely selfish, actually. I just want to get to see the beautiful outcome for once. I saved that caterpillar and want to see the beauty that comes out of it."

"How can keeping it safe in a jar knowing you'll release it once it's hatched be selfish, Vivian?"

"If I wasn't selfish, I would have simply picked it up and walked it over to the tree. Or waved a broomstick at the birds, giving him time enough to move to where he wanted to go." She smiled sadly, still holding eyes on the cocoon trapped in the jar, "But then I wouldn't have gotten to see the rare and beautiful moth he will become. So, I trapped him in a jar for my own wants."

She wants to trap the beautiful things just like me.

Will smiled inside as he thought of his vases. The beautiful delicate vases he had lining the walls of his cabin house. The different colors and designs, the different sizes, all arranged perfectly against the wall. Some already filled with the precious beauty he knew was now resting inside them. Some still waiting to be filled.

He could never put her in one of his vases.

She was the vase. She was the breakable vase, and he belonged inside her.

Maybe it wouldn't be horrible to have someone around all the time. Maybe she would understand his needs, understand what makes him feel alive. She endured his assault and still agreed to more.

He wondered what it would be like to possess her, to lock her into his home like the cocoon in her jar. Her golden hair dancing in the sunlight as it shone through *his* kitchen window. He could sit on his bed, admiring his wall of vases, and listen to her hum the private tune she sings when she is all alone, the tune she allows to swirl around only herself.

He would be able to lock her in when he leaves for his trips, keep her safe from the world, make sure no one gets to stare at her, and nothing breaks her any further. When he got home with the key, he could open the door to her and touch her all over for the comfort of her softness. He would touch his finger to her scars and trace them along her pale white skin, wishing he could be edged into her as permanently as they are.

His body was filled with the desire to wrap her up in a cocoon of plastic wrap, hang her from the rafters of his loft style living room, her golden hair free to catch the sunlight as it beamed in through the windows. His house would be her jar and she would stay there showing her beauty and rareness only to himself.

"I need to get ready." She stood up straight as she spoke.

"Ready? What do you mean, you need to get ready?"

"I'm volunteering at my nephew's school today. They are having a spring festival, and I'm scooping out Italian Ice for the kids and their families."

He stood up straighter, feeling betrayed by her announced obligation.

"You have a nephew?" The words clipped and cool.

"And four nieces." She shook her head, smiling, "I try to be a good aunt when I can be."

"I didn't know you had family around here."

"Well, you never asked."

"I also didn't know your husband was dead until last night, either."

"You never asked."

"Where does your family live?"

"My sister lives about two hours away, and my brother about five minutes away. My parents live with him and his wife, and their kids. That's why I stay here, in this town."

Will hated them. Instantly, he hated them all. Her brother, her sister, their kids, and spouses. He hated her mother and father. He wanted them all bleeding and still on the floor with their organs in his vases on the wall. He hated she belonged to them, and that she stayed for them.

Holding herself together wasn't for her, it was for them.

How did they deserve it? How did they allow her to suffer for them?

Without warning, he reached out and grasped the back of her head, pulling her into his chest, gripping her hard. Her face buried into his chest, he could just hold her tighter, push her face into him with a little more force. Just a little while and she would be still.

But I don't want her still.

Pulling her hair, he pushed her face back, holding her in place so he could lean down and bite her lip. Her breath hitched as he sucked in on her mouth, digging his fingers hard into the back of her neck, bending her back, molding her into his body as he moved forward. Her arm came up, fingers splayed on his chest, pushing back slightly, a plea to slow down, to ease up. The action irritated him and aroused him. Reaching his hand up, he gripped her wrist and twisted it back like a prison guard controlling an inmate for transport. She whimpered.

"Will," Vivian tried to speak against his lips.

"No, no talking from you." He moved forward, forcing her to take steps backwards. "I want to wrap you in a cocoon and put you in a jar."

"I won't turn into anything beautiful." She talked anyway.

His hand came up to backhand her across the face, but stopped before making contact. She flinched, closing her eyes, anticipating the slap that never came.

"Shhhhhh," he cooed, brushing the back of his hand gingerly across the skin he had almost hit. "I said no talking from you."

His hand slid under her robe, holding onto the bare flesh of her back. Moving his head down, he grazed his mouth down her neck, biting little bits as he went. She jumped at the pain when his bite went deeper, her hands instinctively moving to his head. His tongue swiped over the place he bit into sensitive skin before he righted himself.

"Do you care for me?" he whispered in her ear.

"What kind of a question is that? Do I care for you? Of course, I care for you."

"Do you love me?"

She paused, really considering his words as he moved his hands down her bare skin.

"Maybe someday, but I don't know that I can be in love." She paused again, gathering composure, or courage. "I don't know if you'd be deserving of it if I could."

Courage. He smiled against her warm skin, grazed his teeth along the sensitive place on her shoulder. "Why not?" he asked.

"Because I fear you, too. I care for you, but I'm afraid of you." Her breath hitched as his teeth wrapped around, sinking ever so slightly into the flesh again.

"I can't be in love with you either." His face turned into her throat again as he spoke, slowly gliding his nose along her bare skin while.

"I know." Vivian let the words out on the breath she hadn't realized she had been holding, swallowing hard as the warm moisture of his breath trailed along her bones.

He paused his movement for a moment, keeping his head bent, breathing in the scent of her skin, deciding on honesty too. "I'm glad you're afraid of me. You should be. I can't see or touch anyone anymore without wanting them to feel hurt.

"I want every happiness to sting." He looked at her as he spoke. Seeing her standing in the kitchen light, her golden hair shining. Rocking back onto his heels he lifted himself upright to his full height. Stepping forward, lightly brushing his fingers down either side of her neck, slowly beginning to squeeze, "every touch to stir fear under the skin."

Will leaned down to her face, bringing his lips to hers, and gliding across her mouth then down her jaw. "Every single pleasure to hurt." Her lips parted as his mouth found her, his teeth bit down hard on her ear. A whine of pleasure and pain escaped on her breath.

"Don't go today." He bit down again as he moved his hands down her body to find her breasts. "Stay here with me."

"I can't" She was breathless.

"Yes, you can." He reached his intended destination, his hands grabbing hold of her breast, his fingers swirled around her nipple. "Come with me to my house. Let me take you there."

"You bought a house?" Vivian yelled out, halting their mood. Her hands shot up to steady his as she stepped away, away from his control. "When? Where?"

He was bewildered, shocked that she was taken aback by his admission. "It's a cabin, really. Just a small cabin out in the woods. It was stupid to pay rent."

"I can't believe you!" His Vivvie was angry. "You disappear for months! Then show up out of the blue, finding me. Which I don't think for one second was a coincidence. In a new jeep all angry but wanting me *all-of-a-sudden*." Her eyebrows drew down, creasing her forehead. She stepped back further away from him. "I don't get it, Will. I don't know where you went or why, and I don't know why you came back here. You have nothing here. Now you tell me you bought a house. Why?"

He was enjoying seeing her angry with him. Her golden hair glowed in the sunshine. He loved seeing it out of that horrible bun she wore, out of any resemblance of control. It flowed freely around her and framed her face so sweetly. If he could paint, this would be how he would paint her.

But the face she wore now, the serious confusion. She was scattered.

He wondered if that was how she looked running into bombed out buildings to find men with blown off legs. The scared, serious look of confusion that screamed out bravery through the scene of danger and horror. It would have contorted her face. Her lips would have been parted and dry as she sucked in hot desert air. Her golden hair would have been pinned back in that moment, secured behind her head in the bun she used to control it. The pieces that flew away would be plastered down by sweat and dirt and oil from not being washed in days. Her Kevlar would encase it all, trapping the golden locks away from the glow of the sun.

She would drop to her knees beside the screaming men, covered in blood and burning with pain. Then her hand would touch their foreheads, calming them with the feel of her soothing hands of goodness. Her eyes would shine the blue-grey hue of life saving beauty and it would give them hope an angel had found them there in their hour of need.

But they wouldn't get to see the brightness that surrounded her face when the golden locks gently flowed freely with her movements. They only got to have her in the shadows of need.

He didn't want her there ever again.

"Go get ready for your ice cream social." He needed to plan. To decide what he wanted, to decide how to get it from her. "I'll let myself out." He turned to walk out of the kitchen filled with light and the smell of vanilla.

"Will. Don't go. I didn't mean for you to storm out." Her arms flew down to her sides, her shoulders falling. She looked exhausted and small there with her shoulders slumped in her bare feet and golden hair escaping all around her.

"How did you get wounded?"

Her chest expanded with the air that she sucked in with shock at the question. Hands flew instinctively to her stomach, remembering the pain.

"I need to know." Will pleaded. *I need to understand how they broke you.*

She stood straighter now, shoulders back again. "IED."

He waited for her to elaborate, but she didn't. It was all he would get for now.

"I like having all four seasons. I wanted a place I could always come back to."

"So, you picked here."

"So, I picked here."

He smiled with his fake Indian summer smile. "Just so happens you are also where all four seasons are. Knowing you were near... " Will confessed. "It's comforting."

"It killed the driver. When I opened my eyes, he was already dead. He was my friend."

"And you? How bad were you?"

"I died that day too."

"Go serve your ice for your nephew. I'm going to relax a little. Maybe get a shower before I leave."

He walked back up her stairs, climbed back into the sheets that smelled like their sex, and fell back to sleep.

Chapter 30

The Female Veteran Army Medic and the Ice Scooping

The sounds distract the ears once you've heard them in another place on another day. The loose gravel rocks under the tires of a golf cart transports the mind to the adrenaline of a patient-transport racing through camp to the main hospital on the back of a make-shift ambulance.

It sticks inside your ears and presses down on your chest, crushing your breath and pulling in all your focus. Your mind settles on it, the sound. It settles and stands there. The people around you don't hear it. They talk and laugh and continue about their normal day while you sit, frozen, trapped on the back of a make-shift ambulance in a war zone.

Then you look down at your hands, serving flavored ice, and can't help but think that these same hands were inside bodies. These hands were covered in the blood of heroes, and now they scoop a fucking cold treat on a hot day. Inside your mind, all the sounds there remind you of other places. So, you just smile, but in your head, you hear the screams and cries of the dying.

"What flavor is the best flavor?" The woman behind the mobile cooler was asking for advice about the Italian Ice. She was about the same age as Vivian, and a little child held her hand. Her hair was sandy blonde with dark lowlights scattered through it. She had heavily eyeliner covered eyes behind designer framed glasses and fashionable arched eyebrows to match.

Vivian’s mind felt torn. As if one part of it stood in front of the ice cooler, but the other was weighted down by heavy gear rushing into the danger to steal life back from death. The time escaped her as she processed which emotion to focus on.

“Excuse me. Are you ignoring me?” The woman was annoyed by the lapse.

“Oh, sorry, I'm not really sure. I guess Cotton Candy seems to be popular.” Vivian tried to seem normal. To keep her face from showing that really she wanted to scream at the woman with the yellow dress and denim jacket with perfectly sculpted eyebrows, and the cute little boy holding her hand. She wanted to scream in her face, telling her she didn't give a fuck what flavor ice she wants.

Instead, Vivian took a deep calming breath and tried to relax into the entirely civilian situation.

The woman seemed irrationally irritated. “Shouldn't you know more about the product you’re selling?”

“Well, I'm not selling this to you. It’s free. I'm volunteering to help, but I'm not a fucking ice girl.”

The woman's perfect brows flew up as her mouth fell open. “Did you just swear in front of my son?”

Oh fuck.

“Look. I'm sorry. Just tell me what ice you want.”

She rolled her eyes and blew air. “Maybe you should have made better life-choices if you're so unhappy you need to swear at young children.”

“Maybe you should pull the stick out of your ungrateful ass and just pick a goddamn ice flavor.”

The woman froze in shock. Her mouth open in exasperation.

Vivian knew she didn't look like a combat veteran. Even if she did, even if she were a male wearing a harsh beard and covered in military tattoos, this woman wouldn't be able to see the weight of it all. Vivian knew it was pointless to try to make this woman understand the swirl of realities that co-inhabited inside her mind every second of every day.

She didn't see the blood that covered Vivian's hands as she scooped the ice.

This woman had never seen it. She didn't know it was there, all over the hands of the combat veterans.

This woman didn't know that it soaked into their skin and stained them forever.

To this woman, in this moment, Vivian was horrible for being a disgruntled worker who just said 'Fuck' in front of her son. The thought almost made her laugh. *How wonderful that my explicit language will be the worst thing that boy must endure today.*

"You know what, never mind." Angrily, she grabbed up the little boy's hand and pushed him away from the ice cooler. Vivian watched as Ms. Perfect Eyebrows stormed over to the PTO president standing near the edge of the basketball court. Her hands dropped hold of the little boy to fly around as she spoke dramatically, painting the ice scooping volunteer out to be a monster that wronged a mother and son on their fun day out.

I bled for you.

The words sat in the back of Vivian's throat, choking her, as the woman complained to the mom-gathering that now stood around hearing her disgruntled feelings.

Vivian took off the apron provided to her for clothing protection and laid the ice scooper into the water bucket. She wouldn't say goodbye to her nephew or brother. She wouldn't want their images to be tainted by association. She would call later and explain to her brother.

As she range-walked to her car in the crowded parking lot, her head began to feel heavy where it sat on her shoulders. She was exhausted to her bones. She needed to rest, to sink into sleep and escape this 'family fun day.'

Reaching her house was a relief. As soon as she walked through the door, a sense of calm washed over her. She was drained and relieved to be home. The night with Will, the early morning encounter in her kitchen, learning he had moved back here permanently, then the ice queen. A nap seemed like the best escape. Even if only for a couple of hours, a nice nap was in order.

Lying down on the couch, she pulled the pillow under her head and fell asleep.

Chapter 31

The Journey Home

The air stung inside her eardrums as a flat ringing overwhelmed any comprehension of reality. Her eyes scrambled for some sort of orientation.

Metal frame, radio, seatbelt clip, boots, blood.... blood, my blood? She thought quickly, running her mind over the sensations of her body.

The smell of fuel and carbon and burnt rubber was overwhelming. Smoke and dust and heat swelled inside her nostrils. Still disoriented, she desperately tried to get a handle on the confusion rattling in her mind, but the ear-piercing sting still consumed even her reactive self-preservation. Her legs felt too heavy. Like lead had been poured into her veins, the feeling was alien, but still not registering with what her mind could piece together. She desperately tried to lift her body, but there was crushing metal that pinned her knees and lower legs against the rubble. Metal shards stuck into her stomach.

I was blown up.

Her brain slowly collected itself.

We were blown up.

"Blaire!" she screamed out with a raspy, throat-burned voice she didn't recognize as her own.

Her ears still rang with stinging stillness as she frantically searched the scene beside her. Blood pooled and splattered around a mangled mess of metal and flesh and army boots. The rest of Blaire sat still, completely motionless, his lifeless head hung irregularly, one of his arms mutilated and burnt. The other snapped backwards. Blood soaked the fabric of his uniform. His body, held up only by the structure of his gear, was limp. He was absent of all movement except the steady stream of escaping blood.

"No, No!"

***

Will had just walked through the door of his cabin. He heard through his spy bug when Vivian slammed through the door of her house and plopped down onto the couch in her living room. He couldn't believe she would be back so soon from her day of serving ice to little school children.

He laughed to himself that she must have been tired from their night together. She wasn't used to being kept up by the sexual prowl of an ardent man such as himself. He was smiling as he sauntered into his bedroom to don new clothing.

After changing, he ventured to the bathroom to brush his teeth and style his hair. He was deciding what he should do to find out why Vivian left the child function early. She had told him it was something she volunteered to do for her nephew. He imagined her nephew must have some kind of weighted importance to her on a familial level or she would not have agreed to give her time to go be around a bunch of asshole civilians in their natural habitat.

"No!" The word was barely a whisper, but he heard it loud and clear from her lips.

Will dropped the comb and ran to the listening device.

Did she just say 'No'?

Who was she saying it to? His breath held in his chest as he stood listening hard. Trying to hear what was going on in her home that would have caused her to say 'no' out loud.

He grabbed the phone to call her, but no answer.

"*Get him out*!" Her words were clear and crisp, floating across the room through the bug.

"Jesus Christ." Will threw his feet back into his shoes and ran out to the Jeep, part in protector mode, part in exacerbation. Either way, he needed to go make sure she was all right in the house.

Turning out of his long lane, the realization that he didn't lock her damn front door when he left hit him in the chest like a battering ram. He did it to be funny, but fuck, what if someone had gone in? Lay in wait for her?

Fuck.

He drove fast, a lot faster down the mountain roads than was safe. Rushing to her house.

When he finally pulled into the driveway, he jumped out of the vehicle and ran to her door.

"It burns!"

The whispered words *screamed* out from her lips the moment he stepped through the threshold. He held his breath, rushing the corner to find her.

Oh Vivian.

Her forehead was furrowed and pinched between her eyebrows as she lay sleeping on the sofa. Will fell against the doorframe, grasping his chest, catching his breath.

It was a dream.

Leaning into her wall, Will laughed. His hand found his own forehead, pulling his fingers down his face. He couldn't understand himself. The thrill he felt over being so worried about this girl was the wrong kind of thrill. It was panic; it was worry.

This was... *a concern*.

Why did he care for this girl so? Why her?

Will walked over to where she lie sleeping, golden hair wisps on the pillow.

God, but she looked so troubled in her sleep, so afraid. He wondered what her dream was about. He had read somewhere you shouldn't wake people in nightmares.

But her breathing was hitched and labored. Her hands clenched into fists. Muscles tightened down her entire body. How could he leave her trapped there?

He touched his fingertips to her cheek.

I know where you are.

Her arm twitched violently. He could *feel* her fear. Could sense that her adrenaline had spiked under her skin. There was no reason for it physically around her, no reason for the fear, no reason for the panic outside of her body. But inside, inside her body, she was fighting a war. Under her skin, her body was in the thick of it, enduring the horror and intensity all over again. He could sense it radiating off her, could see it racing through her veins, making her pulse soar. He dropped his fingers to her neck to feel her heart race. It boomed.

I want to be there with you.

Leaning down, Will dropped to his knees, and put his nose to her throat where his fingers had been. He wanted to breathe her in deep, in an attempt to inhale adrenaline off her skin. He wanted to taste her fear in his own mouth and feel it in his chest. He longed for his heart to boom as hard, to soar as fast.

Didn't he just feel it for himself, though? Thinking she was in trouble, believing she needed him to save her?

"But you need me to save you, don't you?" Ever so slowly, Will slid his lips to her ear and whispered. "Viv, wake up."

She whimpered out loud.

Gently, he shook her by the shoulders.

"Vivvie, open your eyes."

Her hands shot up and grasped his forearms as her eyes opened wide. Confusion was reflected in the speed and depth of her breaths. "Hey, hey. You're safe." He kissed her nose, her cheek. "I'm here." He kissed her other cheek and then her lips. Before he even understood it, his mouth was parting hers, and ever so slowly, he was kissing her softly. Her hands held onto him as he deepened his kiss, pushing his tongue lightly past her lips on an exploration to meet hers. He was delicate with her, tasting and sipping. Her eyes shut again underneath him, but her sigh into his mouth assured him she would see nothing but *this* kiss on the other side of her eyelids.

Gingerly, Will moved his body over top of hers where she lay. Never breaking his mouth from hers. His elbows bluntly supported his weight as he leaned in, his heaviness pinning her into this moment here with him.

She could feel nothing else, only him. Only his touch, his pleasure, his pain, his joy. Only his needs and wants. He would fill her up with it, fill her so full of him she had no room for anything else. He would overwhelm her and devour everything she held inside. That is how he would save her from the terror, from the nightmares. That is how he would drag her out of hell.

Will broke his mouth from hers and moved his kiss down her neck. Sucking and nipping on the delicate flesh there. She sighed at the sensation, pushing her fingers harder into the forearms that she still held onto.

When his lips found her collarbone, she pushed her hips slightly up to move against his body and he growled. The sound from his own chest was shocking. He felt savage.

Gripping the top of her shirt collar, he ripped the fabric apart. It was the second time he ripped her clothing to get to her. Will smirked at his own loss of control. It was counterintuitive in his lifestyle to ever be out of control. Only hovering over top of Vivian, with her moans and whimpering, he was victim to his own passion.

Christ, he thought, even with all this passion he should be in control, but without even a thought to what he *should* do. Will was pulling down her bra to expose her breasts. His mouth was on her nipple in a heartbeat.

"My fucking God, I love your breasts." Will's hands gripped them both, pushing them together for him to lick both nipples at once. "I want this to be for you. Just lay back."

It had been a long time since he had felt the desire to simply give a woman pleasure without taking anything in return. Only that was exactly what he wanted in this moment. He wanted to feel her come apart at the seams under his touch.

Will moved down her body desperately, pulling her pants down as he went. His mouth settled against her thigh to start small sensual kisses towards her pleasure. Moving her panties to the side, he sucked in the delicate mound of her bud before moving his tongue around it. She moaned as her hips flexed up to meet his motions. Reaching around, Will grasped hold of her hips to steady her where she lay. It did not take long for her to surrender herself to the sensations he was delivering. For her to become lost in the physical feelings of her body, thinking of nothing else, nothing more than the pleasure he was giving to her. She reached down to weave her fingers into his hair, to hold on to whatever she could of him as her hips slowly moved against his mouth.

He could feel the quiver begin to build, so he slowed the pace of his tongue while reaching down to pull off his own pants, releasing his hard cock from its cloth prison. Will needed to experience this with her. He thought he could be satisfied with just her pleasure in his mouth, but he was too greedy, he needed to cum with her.

Her pussy was so wet. God, he loved tasting her juices on his tongue, he didn't want to stop but his cock throbbed. It begged to be there feeling the moist heat between her legs. He wanted her love to hold him, to bury himself into her, to find a way to ease the burning he felt now building inside.

Her muscles quivered as she neared her own release. His Vivvie lifted her head off the couch, her lips forming a cute little circle, her eyes wild with bewilderment at the luxury his attention brought to her. She whimpered when his mouth left her.

Actually whimpered.

The adorable pitifulness of the sound had him smiling again as he stood up from his knees. Will quickly positioned himself between her legs and buried himself deep into her with one swift thrust. Vivian's head flew back further as racking waves of pleasure ravished through her body. She cried out loudly, her tits bouncing in the sunshine as he surged into her over and over.

Watching her naked brightness while he fucked her brought Will to a place he had never been to with a woman. He wanted to keep her pleasure going and going. He never wanted her to come down.

He moved slowly inside her lavishly to gather his control again.

"Oh, please," she begged.

The sound of her words was foreign to him. How soft and sated her voice sounded. How the words melted velvety off her tongue.

"Please what, Vivvie?" Will smirked as he stilled inside her, hoping for her to cry out to him for more.

"Please, never stop. Please never leave my body. Please *move* again!"

He chuckled and languidly complied. "Feels that good, huh?"

She signed, flexing her hips to push into him faster than he had been operating.

"You wanton minx." Taking the hint, Will picked up his pace, bringing her to the edge of pleasure again.

"Oh Will. Oh, I'm going to again. I can't, it's too much."

"No, no Viv, I've got you. Let it come, don't fight it." He buried himself in her. The veins in his forehead bursting with his focus and control for wanting her to feel all his fullness, wanting her to have all that he could give her.

For once, it wasn't just about his wants.

For once, it wasn't about the thrill or adrenaline.

For once, it had nothing to do with pain, or the need for control.

For once, it was not for punishment.

This was driven by the desire to give everything good about him to her. To be rewarded only by the little sighs and moans that slipped out of her lips. To have desire cascade through his veins, simply by feeling her fingertips digging into the flesh of his forearms, his shoulders, his back. Her touch was like silk rubbing against his skin. Her hands were love on their own, she didn't even know it. She had no idea the love that swept through her fingers when they passed over his body.

God damn him, but he never wanted this to end.

How had she created an escape for him without writhing in pain?

No, she had not created an escape. She *was* his escape. Not to the thrill of war, but to the towel on a beach. Lying with warm sand adhered to the saltwater kissed skin of the body that had just relaxed down from an afternoon of jumping ocean waves, laughing with excitement as the power of the tide lifted him up with the bursting power of water over and over. She was the escape to being pleasantly exhausted, resting on the dry towel in the sand with the hot sun beating down with relaxing warmth to engulf the body in transcendent contentment.

Will grit his teeth as he pulled slowly out of her, only to push gently back in. He felt her body hold him with every slow-moving inch as he glided inside her wet, slick heat. He moved her knees apart further and leaned down over top of her, resting on his own forearms placed on either side of her head.

"Open your eyes." He stilled over her face as her eyes opened compliantly. Will's brow pulled together as he basked in his own bewildered confusion at the building tenderness that he felt filling him up with every movement. His breath came out heavily as he held control, holding still inside her body as he stared into her sky-blue eyes, shimmering with pleasure. His thumb came up to brush the wisp of gold away from her forehead. "Fuck, but you are so much more than I saw before. Even this morning. God, but I didn't see it."

Vivian stared up at him, lost in her own escape. Not at war, but *in* him.

They had escaped together.

He brought his lips down to gently kiss her mouth while he slowly moved again inside her body. But he no longer wanted to breathe in her frightened adrenaline, now he wanted all her glorious pleasure sighs and little catches of life-giving breath. He cradled her in his arm, pushing down on the top of her head to bring himself further into her warmth. Vivian's voice leaked a small weep into his mouth as he felt her muscles clench again and it filled him with the desire to join their pleasure together.

"I want you to cum with me." His words a desperate whisper, foreign to his own ears.

She cried out as he kissed her and pushed faster in and out of her body. As her back arched up, he held her firmly in place against him, to hold all of her opulence, to have it all in his grasp. "Oh Will, Oh please," she begged again as he pushed through her, as he molded himself into her body to join them together in the same escape.

"Yes, Love, let go with me." He yelled out as he felt the thrill of untainted bliss pour through his loins and into her quivering over-exaltedness.

Will collapsed down onto her. Both of their chests heaving, grasping for air to settle them down from the heights they reached.

"Will, what on earth was that?"

Her voice breathlessly spoke in his ear as she wrapped her arms and legs around him. Embracing him with every surface area she could.

"Coming home." He thought aloud.

The hot water flowed out of the shower head onto her skin while she tried to understand what had just transpired with Will. He disappeared without even an explanation and then returned months later with an insurmountable appetite for her. It didn't make sense that she would not be what he wanted before he left, but then return and want her to be his lover?

There was no reason for it. He was still unbelievably hot and desirable. Hell, Jensi was beautiful, and she would have fucked him on the table at the bar if he would have asked her to. It couldn't be that he was desperate or hurting for a willing sex partner. So why the sudden sexual interest?

Part of Vivian didn't want to understand. Part of her loved the comfort of him, the pleasure he brought to her body. She could melt into him, allow the pieces of her that no one else could see or understand to rest under Will's skin.

However, there was this other part of her, the intuitive part, that couldn't shake the enigmatic circumstances that stirred the air around him every time he was near her.

With her hair lathered up, the smell of her shampoo momentarily stilled her thoughts with its familiarity. She closed her eyes to allow her mind to rest. Her fingers slid through her soaping strands floating the fragrance around her and then silently her hands were replaced. Adept fingers plundered the silky feel of lather through her hair without any alert the shower had even been breached.

Killer's hands.

"Let me do this."

Vivian let her hands fall to her sides without protest. He massaged his fingers through her hair, moving the golden strands around her head to wash with excess. Gently, he tipped her head back into the water stream to rinse the soap out.

"Thank you. I can't remember the last time I have had my hair washed for me."

"You don't go to the salon? Get pampered?" Will picked up the body wash, squeezing way too much onto the purple loofah. "Now having your body washed, this will be something you aren't used to. A luxury for both of us."

He dropped to his knees on the floor of the shower and began washing her feet. Up her calves and knees, her thighs. Swiftly, he stood to continue washing the top half of her.

"Will? Why have you become suddenly interested in me?"

"Suddenly interested?" His bare hand slid around her breast, over her shoulder, around her neck. The other lathering her skin with the loofah as it moved. "I've always been interested in you, Viv. Since the very first time I saw you."

"I don't mean interested in a friend capacity. I'm thinking of the sudden interest you've recently showed in an emotionally sensitive and sexual regard."

"You're wondering about what just happened downstairs?"

Vivian humphed because she couldn't express what she was trying to say. "Not just that, although that was a confusing development. I'm sure for you as well, what I mean is." She sighed dramatically, "I don't know what I mean."

Will reached for the conditioner, pouring it into his hands before smoothing it down her hair. "I know what you're saying, and I honestly, I don't know how to answer that Viv." His fingers were back plundering through her hair. "I just know that when I'm not with you, I want to be, and when I'm near you, I want to be closer. Only then, when I'm closer, I want to find a way to be even closer, and then closer still. I sometimes think that I would pull you inside my body and keep you there if I could, but then I realize that if you're inside me, I wouldn't be able to see you or touch you, and I panic."

He leaned her head back into the water to rinse her off. She was clean from head to toe.

"Is it alright if I wash you?" Vivian asked him hesitantly.

She noticed his shoulders straightened a little, but he handed her the luffa and turned his back to her without verbal protest. Vivian leaned her chest into his back, reaching around his body to wash the front of him as she slid against his skin.

"I'm so afraid of you." She rested her face against his back, dropping the luffa. "I feel you surround me, and I want to just rest against you and trust that you'll keep me warm in the dark when it's cold and empty, and I want to, and I think I can, but then I see the little white bloody bits of his skull that skittered all over the floor and the walls." Tears fell from her eyes as she held her face against his strong back in the hot shower. "I will never be enough to hold you, and I don't want it to surprise me when you realize that."

Slowly, Will turned around to pull her to his chest. "Ah, but Vivian, you are mistaken." His hands stroked down her back. "I don't want you to be my everything. I'm way too fucked up for that." The thought made him laugh. "No, no don't cry, pet." His thumbs brushed the tears off her cheeks. "I only want to be everything to you. Come live with me?"

"What?" Vivian was caught off-guard. "You want me to be your roommate, in your new house?"

"No." He laughed again. "I don't want you as my roommate, Vivian. I want you to sleep in my bed and bustle in my kitchen. Because I want you for me. I want you there with me, always. You won't need to worry yourself with anything else in this life, ever. I'll be everything you need."

He put his hand up in front of her face, his finger to her lips. "Don't answer me right now. We can talk about it slowly, and think up all the logistics together, come up with rules if you want. I'm not asking to be your husband or even your significant other. I just want you to belong to me in some way, to know it's possible to always have you. Tell me it could be conceivable for you to give this to me? Is it possible you could be that willing?"

She was so confused. "Will, I don't understand any of this. I don't even know what you're asking me to be to you."

"We don't need to understand it. We can think about it together, we can answer questions as they come. Just tell me that it is something I might be able to have. Tell me I could have you even if I need to conquer it by bits. Please."

Was this something she was willing to agree to? Ever? He wasn't asking her for love or friendship. He was asking her if she would allow him to put her in a jar on his counter.

Would that be so horrible?

Right now, she was living every single day as the caterpillar trying to get to the tree. She had the beauty of the yard all around her, had the open sky and the constant longing to reach the tree, but it was an impossible and horrible journey to make alone. He could be the cocoon she wrapped herself up in, and she could hide away behind his skin.

"It is."

Will smiled as the water cascaded down around them. "I knew it would be."

After the shower, Will pulled her over to the bed. They lay on the bed naked in the daylight. He lazily traced fingers along the edges of her scars.

"What happened today? To make you rush home?"

"One of the moms got to me. I know I shouldn't have taken the bait. To be honest, I don't even think she realized that she was baiting me. She just was standing there with her little boy talking down to me, being a condescending jerk."

"You left because one of the moms' there was rude to you?"

"No, I swore at her, so she went off and made a stink with the PTO. I didn't want my brother or nephew to be involved or recognized as being associated with me. So, I left." Vivian shrugged her shoulders. "Which reminds me, I need to call my brother."

Will pushed down on her shoulders when she tried to sit up. "Oh no, we are cuddling lazily. You will not be getting up."

"But I need to explain to him why I left without a word."

"Don't you think if he was truly worried about it, he would have called you?"

"Maybe he is on his way here right now to check on me."

"Hmmm. Good point. I'll get your phone for you. Stay."

Will held his hands up and jumped off her bed to rush downstairs and retrieve her phone. He was desperate to hear more about this story, more details about the woman who made his Vivvie feel that way.

His Vivvie, had a nice ring to it.

He handed Vivian the phone and lay back down next to her to slide his hands up and down her ripped apart flesh while she selected the number from her phone.

Will heard her brother when he answered on the other end. He sounded worried and his words were rushed. Apparently, the brother had been looking all over for her at the festival and his son was worried. They got nervous that something happened to her or she got sick and then no one could reach her on her phone.

"I'm sorry," she explained. "I had to leave because one of the moms got upset because I swore at her."

He heard her brother asking who it was.

"I don't know her name. She had a little boy, and was pretty, with perfect eyebrows and dark eyeglasses. Her hair was a long dirty blonde with brown shades all through it. Oh, and she was wearing a cute yellow dress and a jean jacket."

Her brother asked if the boy looked to be the same age as her nephew. Vivian confirmed he was, and her brother said it was probably Yvette Landis. She fit the description and was always complaining about one thing or another. He told her not to sweat it.

Will made a mental note of the name. *Yvette Landis.*

"I felt terrible, though. All those women were gathered around. She probably told them I was disrespectful to her son. I wasn't trying to be, but I just got distracted in my own mind, and she was acting like I was supposed to be an Italian ice expert or something."

Her brother interrupted. He went on to say how that woman shouldn't make her feel bad at all. Her husband left her years ago because of how self-righteous she was. He only knew this because he was friends with the boy's father. Yvette's ex-husband hated sharing the child with her because of how she used the boy to punish the father for leaving her. She was a nasty woman who thought her own shit didn't stink and cared more about drama than she did about her kid.

Will decided he might like her brother after all.

"I'm sorry I left without saying anything. But I just didn't want you to be associated with the drama. I love you."

God, but she gave those words to her brother so freely, so honestly. He told her he loved her too, and they hung up.

Instantly, Will was filled with the desire to obtain two things. First, he irrationally wanted nothing more than to beg Vivian to say those words to him. For her to look him in his eyes and to say that she loved him as sincerely and comfortably as she just said them to her little brother. The craving was insanely new and awkward for him to want.

His second desire, however, was familiar. He wanted furiously to find Yvette Landis and punish her.

Chapter 32

Operation Requital

This was going to be a challenge.

Not the physical kidnapping of the woman, that part would be rather simple.

It was the kidnapping a woman in a town he bought a house in, without getting caught, that posed the hurdle. He would need to find a way to get her out of this town, away from this area, and then take her. Simply waiting for her to leave for work seemed the most logical way to achieve anonymity, but still too risky.

Maybe just murdering Yvette would need to suffice. Sneak into her home at night and make it look like a suicide or accident. It wasn't his usual style, but it seemed to be the smartest way. Absolutely zero connection to the murder.

Will had already found Yvette's house. It was a basic bland house lacking any character whatsoever in a cookie cutter neighborhood. The first day he went to stake it out, the little boy Vivian had mentioned was playing by himself on the front porch. He drew an elaborate chalk drawing on the sidewalk and begged his mother to come look at it several times. She never took the time to see it. Instead, she yelled for him to come in for dinner and Will could see the boy's little soul crash further inside himself.

Vivian would have gone to look at the chalk drawing. She would have studied it with as much interest and attention as she gave to the masterpieces hanging on the Barnes Foundation walls. His Viv would have found every little creative detail to focus in on. Then she would have asked questions that she really didn't give two fucks about, just to engage the mind of the little boy who wanted to be praised.

Will watched as his mother came to the door to spit orders at the little boy who begged her to come praise him.

This woman, this boy's neglectful mother was the woman who made Vivian feel like a piece of shit for swearing in front of her son.

Will looked at her, and even from a distance could see that behind her façade of the perfect suburban mother of the year, Yvette was the real piece of shit for the unearned entitlement she spewed out around her. She threw a public fit over Vivian showing a glimpse of frustration in front of her son, implying that his wellbeing was her overall concern. When her *real* problem was having her social status confronted by someone she saw as being beneath her. Yvette's son was not a priority to her, since he spent his time at home away from his mother, out of her way. It made Will disgusted and angry that Yvette was a revered member of society and Vivian was looked down on for using swear words.

Vivian will never be a mother. The war stole her uterus. The thought hit him hard in the gut.

She will never get to hold the hand of a little child to go get an Italian ice. Nor will she ever get asked to look at sidewalk chalk drawings. Vivian gave all of that away so that this woman could neglect her child and use him as a society ladder to climb up. Will was instantly filled with the urge to slice Yvette apart and take her uterus for his vases, the uterus she used to bring the little child into the world that Vivian would never be able to love.

That night, Will drove away from the fake happy home of Yvette Landis. In this state of agitation, he couldn't kill her because he'd make too many mistakes. He needed to thoroughly plan the best way to punish her, but ensure that he wasn't caught. It would need to be one of the few nights that the child was with his father, but that would be easy enough to figure out.

Tonight, though, before he saw Vivian again, Will needed to find a replacement girl for his cottage.

Chapter 33

One Male Army Ranger Veteran and the Disloyal Friend

He drove three hours to find a city club scene far from his mountain home. No one here would remember him leaving with a girl. As he walked through the door, there was a small part of his conscious that felt bad about picking a victim without knowing for sure that she deserved it. But the need was mounting inside him to punish, to hurt and control. He didn't trust himself to be around his Vivvie without knowing he was in control. He had to meet that need inside himself. There had to be someone to put the rage into.

Part of him wondered if this made him no different from those he punished. Had he become what he hated?

"Oh my god, Will! Do you remember me?"

Fuck.

Slowly, he turned around to face the perfectly white and pearly beaming smile. One of the girls from Vivian's group of friends at the bar.

Fuck.

His fake smile beamed back at her. He had no idea what her name was. She wore a skimpy little sparkly pink shirt that showed her belly and skintight black pants. Her makeup was the kind that didn't smudge, and everything about her was as if perfection was vomited down on her from head to toe.

Her skin was flawless, her stomach flat and smooth, her legs slim and flowing up to her neck. She wore her hair straight down with perfect highlights and layers around her face.

"Vivian's friend, right?"

She excitedly slid her hands around his bicep. "Yes, I can't believe I ran into you here! I knew she wasn't your type!" She bounce-giggled.

Will felt his face twitch. It was nothing this girl would notice. His stoicism still held firm, but he felt it. It began in his jaw. A twitch of anger tickling down from the vein that jumped a tiny bit harder as it rushed through his neck and across his chest to fill up his lungs with heat. Then fumed out from his mouth like stone, but his calm words masked the lava that stewed beneath his skin.

Will dazzle smiled his fake sunshine down onto her face. "Why did you think that?"

He knew why. He just wanted to hear it from her mouth.

"Well, you are just gorgeous. Like a tall, chiseled drink of water," she looked him up and down like a snack she wanted to feast on, "and Viv is just," she shrugged, "you know, ordinary and *off*."

He wanted to slap her for that. "What if I were dating her exclusively?"

She went up on her toes and sipped on his lower lip. "I won't tell. That girl needs a little charity, but I know what *you* need."

Her tongue was in his mouth in the middle of the loud, feverish club. His mind was scattered as his hands went up to hold her in place while she stood on her toes, violating her friend by kissing his mouth.

How poetic that she sealed her own fate with a kiss. It was going to be her. Though it was rash and fueled by anger, but it needed to be her. Slowly he pulled his mouth down the side of her neck, grazing his lips along her flesh. Sliding up to suck her ear into his mouth, he whispered, "your name?"

"You don't remember?" She pretended to pout. "I should have been unforgettable to you compared to all the other girls that night."

"Maybe you can make me unable to forget you tonight."

She was giggling again. "Do you want to get out of here?"

"On one condition. You don't tell anyone you're with me." Will stood up tall beside her, touching his finger to the center of her lips and dragging them down. "Promise?"

She nodded, licking her lips wantonly where he had touched them.

He wrapped his hand around her tiny little waist.

Killer's hands.

"Come." He commanded after receiving her nonverbal compliance. He weaved her through the crowded dance club toward the doors.

Once out into the night, Will tucked her tightly under his arm as he walked her down the sidewalk, making it impossible for her to use her cell phone as they moved. Her heels made her the same height as him, and it annoyed him to have her head next to his. It bothered him horribly as they moved so near to each other. Her face being tall enough to bob next to his as they walked, was an intolerable annoyance. When they reached his Jeep, he opened the passenger door and almost threw her up into the seat to get her face away from his as quickly as possible.

Shutting the door, he rushed over to the driver's seat. He didn't want her to have enough time to get her cell phone out. He smiled at her across the jeep as he hopped in. "Let's go find a hotel room to move our own little party into."

A short fifteen-minute drive produced a decent hotel.

Will had Vivian's *friend* stay in the jeep while he went in to book the room. She hadn't noticed him take her phone out of her purse when he leaned over to make-out with her before getting out. He slid the phone into his pocket as he walked towards the front desk to book a room using one of his alias names and credit cards.

When he returned to the vehicle, she was franticly searching for her phone.

"Hey, what's wrong?"

"I lost my phone. I know I had it at the club. We have to go back."

Will opened her door and leaned down to help her look under the seat. Pulling her phone out of his pocket, he held it up as if retrieving it from the floor. "You mean this phone?"

"Holy shit! I can't believe you found it. I checked under the seat at least a million times." She automatically reached for it, but Will moved it up and out of her reach playfully.

"Oh no baby, you're going to need to earn it back."

She giggled again and beamed her perfect white smile at him before settling back into the comfort of the seat. "I will beg, on my knees."

He chuckled. "We shall see."

Shutting her door, he walked around to move the vehicle before escorting her up to their room to beg for the phone he had no intention of giving back to her.

After parking, she was back on his arm. Her tallness irritating him again, especially in the hotel hallway. Walking through hotel hallways always put his senses on alert. All the closed doors where anything could be behind them. The narrow pathway with disorienting patterns swirling around on the carpet in vibrant eye-catching colors. Walking through hotel hallways fucked with him.

She wrapped her hand around his bicep. Her fingers were long and slender with beautifully manicured nails painted pink with patterns grazed in silver glitter, swirling like the carpet on the hotel room hallway floor. As they walked, the walls seemed to move closer to him, while her face bopped closely next to his. He felt his shoulders tense, his breathing accelerate. In his mind, he saw the doors of insurgent's homes from the corner of his eyes. They were kicking them in.

Clear! They weaved through the rooms. After mounting a staircase, the explosion rocked him backwards down the steps and into the wall. His ears bled. With a high wailing ringing, the sounds became muddled and thick around him. He got back to his feet and rushed to the body of his team member. It was mangled, with rips through his flesh. His blood pooled on the floor, steaming in the cold air.

Where the fuck was the room?

Will wanted to throw her hand off him, to throw her into the wall. His breath hitched in his throat and he finally saw their room. He put the key card in and pushed the door open, grateful to be enclosed in a space that wasn't in that long mind-fuckery of a hallway. He ushered her through the doorway quickly and bolted the door closed to lock his sanity back inside.

"Go lay on the bed." He commanded to the girl whose name he couldn't remember.

She let out a girlish giggle. "What makes you think I'm just going to do what you ask me to?"

"Well, because if you don't, I'll make you." He smiled when he spoke, leading her to believe he was playing some kind of role-play game with her. How to make her understand he was in charge now? Walking towards her, he took her slender little hand into his and gently bent it behind her back. Pressing down slightly on the top of her hand made her wince as her wrist felt the pressure.

"What's your name, kitten?"

"I told you, you'd have to work for it." She did this odd little side smile and smoldered her eyes. This game was tedious and completely wasted on him. Will pushed down harder on her wrist.

"Your name?"

"Ow, Jensi" she cried out.

He let up on her wrist. "Oh, now I remember you. The one with all the boyfriends?"

"You really didn't remember me?" Her playfulness subsiding momentarily.

"No, I really didn't. I told you, I was there for Vivian."

"Yeah, but..."

"But what? You're prettier than her?" Will laughed out as he walked her towards the bed. "Maybe slightly, in a manufactured kind of way. Prettier isn't brighter, that's something that all your sparkles and glitter and painted lines can't gain you. You'll never be brighter." He pushed her down, so she was sitting on the bed. "There, now you're doing as you're told." His dazzle smile lit up his face as he reached down to grab her ankle.

He unstrapped one heel, removing it slowly, then throwing it across the room. Immediately repeating the same process with the other shoe. With Jensi sitting on the bed in bare feet, Will removed his own footwear meticulously and then placed them near the nightstand, tucking in his laces. She watched as his socks came next. He folded them one at a time before laying them down beside the lamp. Next, his shirt was over his head and folded on top of the socks, with his pants following. Will stood there in his boxer-briefs, looking at the girl on the bed who thought she was prettier than Vivian.

"You must have been frightening as a soldier."

Will laughed. "What an interesting observation, Jensi. Why do you think so?"

"You aren't even in a uniform or armed, but your face is dangerous. Like you don't even need any weapon but your hands to defeat an enemy. It's hot."

"It turns you on that I've killed people?" Will walked over to where she lay, leaning down on either side of her. "You like to think of me as dangerous?" He leaned back on his knees, grabbing the hem of her sparkly shirt to pull up over her head. "It makes you feel safe, doesn't it? To know there are men like me to fight off evil for you."

He reached to slide her pants down her legs. "And what do I get in return? Have you ever wondered what men like me get for keeping you safe and sheltered?" Will hopped off the bed again to slide his own boxer briefs off, folding them to go on top of his pile of clothing. He was naked, standing next to the bed with Jensi lying in her underwear. She looked confused, almost afraid. He liked that look on her. "You are very beautiful, you know."

Slowly, he crawled back onto the bed and began kissing up her leg. "You have long slender legs and such a nice round little ass." His hands grabbed hold of the flesh of her ass, and she let out a gasp. He slid his fingers underneath the cups of her bra. "Do you want this, Jensi? Do you want me?" *Even though you know your friend is in a relationship with me. Do you care so little for her that you want to take me from her?*

Jensi sat up in a sitting position, keeping eye contact with him while removing her bra. Lifting her hips, she slid her underwear down, flinging them across the room. "Does that answer your question?"

He looked down on her perfectly smooth skin grazing his fingers across the places Vivian's skin was ripped apart and then forced back together by a surgeon's hands. "Flawless," he whispered. She assumed it was a compliment and smiled before leaning up to reach his mouth with hers.

Her kiss was pliable. He could mold her and contort it into anything he wanted it to be. Then, leaning her down onto her back, he brought his mouth to suck her nipple. Pushing her tits together with his hands as he sucked and nipped at them, his tongue running along one and then the other as she moaned.

Her body was pliable too. He pushed his fingers up inside her, moving them back and forth, causing her to writhe beneath his touch. The pleasure he gave brought compliance, allowing him to mold her and contort her body into anything he wanted it to be. Sliding in closer, Will brought his tongue on board to help his fingers bring her pleasure, tickling her shaven twat firmly until she was bucking her pelvis against his mouth and cumming around his hand.

Before she could catch her breath, Will flopped down on his back beside her. "Get on," he commanded.

He could command her to do anything, and she would comply.

Jensi moved to ride his cock as he instructed. She eased herself down onto his hard length, her mouth opening wide as she felt him fill her up.

"Oh my God." The words fell from her tongue as she moved on him, bouncing off his pelvis. He bent his knees with his feet firmly on the bed so he could thrust up with every bounce she made, getting deeper, her breasts smacking harder against her own skin. The sound was erotic. He had to admit, her body was hot to watch. Her face was beautiful to see in different expressions of passion. Reaching behind her, he grabbed a handful of her hair as he took over the thrusting from beneath.

She weighed so little, he could lift her up from the bed to pound into her from where he lay. The shock of it caused her to cry out little wisps of noises that got higher and higher in pitch as he moved. His thighs were burning, sweat drenched his brow. With a hard buck, he threw her off him. She rolled onto her belly as he moved over top of her on the bed. His hand smacked down hard on her ass. Once.

She cried out. Twice.

Jensi twitched with the pain of it as he threw himself into her from behind. Without reservation, Will pounded. He moved fast and hard into her, pushing her face down into the pillows to muffle her moans. She tried to gain some leverage on the bed by scooting her knees up, but Will pushed them out further. He pinned her down flat on her belly.

One hand held her firmly by the back of the neck, and the other pulled her ass cheek open so he could get in deeper. Will pounded until he felt himself release with pleasure. Fuck if it didn't feel good to pour himself into this pleasure box of perfection.

As soon as he was done, he fell off her onto his back. Jensi rose on her knees and rolled over on her side. "That was intense. Like no other, really."

"Go wash me off your pussy so you don't smell like my cum all night."

Will moved off the other side of the bed and went for the bottle of water sitting on the table. He grabbed the remote and turned on the TV, flipping through channels as he chugged the water.

She still lay on the bed where he left her. Looking briefly over in her direction, he met her gaze and used his eyebrows to convey his previous order. Without having to repeat himself, she was up off the bed, headed to the bathroom.

As soon as Will could hear the water running, he ventured in after her.

"Pass me out a washcloth and soap, would you?" Will commanded.

"Oh, well, you could get in with me."

"No thank you, just the washcloth and soap, please." He was brisk with her. She would need to realize that he was no one to trifle with from now on.

She did as she was told. "Good girl." He complimented before washing his dick off in the sink.

When she turned off the water, Will was still in the bathroom drying himself. The shower curtain opened to her standing there in model body perfection, the steam coming off her skin, just as it came off the blood pooled on the ground around the body of his friend. The water dripped down her skin in lines. She was beautiful.

He was going to enjoy her immensely.

"Have I done something wrong?" She was nervously asking him. Almost as if she thought he hadn't enjoyed their coupling.

Will grabbed one of the towels and wrapped it around her shoulders. He put his hand out to help her step out of the tub and began drying her off where she stood. "Oh Jensi, why ask such a stupid question?" He smile dazzled up at her. "Come, let's get some sleep."

Bringing her out to the bedroom area, Will grabbed a couple complimentary alcohol bottles from the room refrigerator. He handed one to her and told her to down it so they could have a fun round two. She giggled and threw it back. He instantly handed her a second. Again, she did as she was told. Will opened a third.

"Will, I feel pretty good still from the club. I don't need anymore." Smiling, he moved over to stand in front of her, pulling her against him, and pressing his mouth to hers. He ravished her with his tongue until she moaned and then grabbed her mouth with his strong grip to tilt her head back. Her eyes opened wide, her hands grabbing his forearms as he walked her backwards against the wall. With her body pinned, her mouth open and her head tilted back, he poured two more small alcohol bottles down her throat. She struggled.

"Swallow it." He commanded as she struggled. Little bits escaped out of the corners of her mouth. Will reached over for another. "Don't fight me, Jensi. This will help you sleep." She tried to kick out at him, and Will chuckled. Pouring more whiskey down her throat, he shut her mouth and held her face tilted back with her nostrils pinched shut until she swallowed.

He walked away, letting her fall forward onto her own wobbly feet.

"What the fuck is wrong with you!?" she screamed at him. Then she headed over to where her bra lay on the floor and gathered it up with her underwear. "Why would you force alcohol down my throat, you fucking weirdo?" She bumped into the chair when she went to grab her pants and shirt from where they were thrown.

Will laughed as she stumbled to the edge of the bed to put on her clothing.

"You didn't think I was a fucking weirdo while you were riding me a little bit ago."

Putting the undergarments on was difficult for her as the booze settled in, and she was swaying back and forth where she sat. "Yeah, but that was before."

"Before what?"

"Before you poured that down my throat." She pointed to the bottles on the table.

"I didn't pour anything down your throat. You must have been dreaming."

Jensi stopped what she was doing and looked up at him, confused. "You made me drink those bottles."

Will laughed again. "Why on earth would I ever do something like that? You wanted to have more fun. I was trying to take the bottles away from you." Her eyes were struggling to stay open. She was completely smashed now.

"Come on silly. Lie down, sleep it off. You'll be fine in the morning." Will laid her down on the bed and tucked the covers in around her securely. "Hush now," he cooed as he climbed in next to her. She rolled herself onto his chest with her wet hair lying like cold noodles on his skin. She passed out almost instantly from all the alcohol in her system. Will put a cooking show on the television and settled in for the next hour or two. He needed to wait until most everyone else would be sleeping before removing her.

Right before dawn he would dress her, then sleepily walk her down to the jeep and strap her in. They would drive to some drug ridden whore lined section of the neighboring city where he would toss her purse. Someone would take it, and use the credit cards and phone. When her friends or family finally noticed she was missing, the police would think she ended up on the wrong side of town and met a disastrous fate at the hands of society dregs.

After dumping her stuff, they would drive to a remote area where he would knock her out and hogtie her for the ride to his cottage. Will would have a nice ride through the mountains at sunrise and get back to his home with enough time to properly secure Jensi and then have a good nap before meeting Vivian for the evening.

To top it all off, he got an unexpected bonus from this evening. He was learning how to make the most perfect waffles on the hotel room cooking show. He would need to purchase a waffle maker before meeting with Vivian. Surprising her with it, he could stay with her at her place tomorrow night, and then make her waffles in the morning. Lying on his chest, Jensi snored softly in her intoxicated slumber. Will crunched his nose up in disgust before pushing her off him and getting comfy again to learn how to make Vivian breakfast.

Things were looking up.

Chapter 34

Dr. Jekyll and Mr. Hyde

The colors were his favorite part of the mountains, especially the different shades of green. Ferns and moss covered the forest floor. Vines and leaves canopied the crown. All versions of dark and light. It made him smile to see how the morning sun rising slowly into the day would reflect off the colors, making them shine through the trees as he passed by in the vehicle. This was starting off as such a peaceful day, a drive through nature with all its baronial majesty reining over any mood a person could individually hold on to. It was impossible to remain separate from the peace of the mountain on a bright morning such as this.

Muffled moaning emerged from the backseat.

Will rolled his eyes. He had expected the alcohol and blow to the head he gave her to have kept her unconscious for a lot longer. It bothered him more than he thought it would to hit a woman that hard with the intention of knocking her out, but he hadn't brought any medications or chloroform. So he clocked her. Tied her hands to her feet and threw her into the back of the Jeep. It was a tactical error on his part. He would not overlook such a detail again.

He didn't have time to plan anything different though, because he had to hurry back to the cabin and secure Jensi. Then go meet Vivian to accompany her on a night out with the same nosy group of women she had been with when he stalked her at the bar that first night. Well, minus one.

Arranging the dinner had been Will's idea the night before, after Jensi had dozed off in her alcohol coma. He texted Vivian and pressed her and pressed her until she agreed to ask her friends and their significant others to meet them out somewhere. He had been obsessing over it after learning that Jensi had thought that Viv was not his type. His irritation at the assumption had quickly manifested into a zealous need to set the rest of them straight. He wanted Vivian to be able to walk into a restaurant or bar with him, show them all that he was still at her side.

In what way he was by her side, he didn't know yet. All he knew was that it bothered him that they would think he didn't want her by his. How could anyone who knew her think she wasn't as nobly majestic as the sun shining through the shades of green that canopied the forest, highlighting every bit of its glory for all to see? She belonged by his side, always, as his sun highlighting the world around him.

Is that what she was to him now? His sun? How could that be defined in his life?

What was he to Vivian?

He had not asked her to be his girlfriend, he really hadn't even thought of her in such a menial capacity. They had been spending almost all their time together, and he was still enjoying her. She made the air around him cleaner to breathe, and was exactly like the sunshine through the forest on his drive today. The colors were beautiful, but when the sunshine hit them, they were brighter.

Humans across the ages wrote poems about holding sunshine in their hands and made art to reflect the feeling of having brightness underneath their skin. They sang songs of the warmth they felt when light kissed their lips. Will didn't know what Vivian was to him, but he did know that having her near him meant understanding every poem, art, and song ever created to describe the feeling.

Driving over the mountain roads with the window down and the fresh air flowing through his hair, and thinking of Vivian while seeing the beautiful scene of nature all around him made Will smile. He knew better than to think he could have a typical relationship with her, but he didn't need anything typical. He just needed her with him in *some* kind of way for this emotion to stay with him. Having Vivian was the same as having bright shining sun through the trees of the green mountain scene on the early morning spring day.

"Please, please, I'm hurt."

He rolled his eyes again.

"I know you're hurt, I hit you." Will spoke out to Jensi. "Lay back there. Be still and quiet or you'll be hurt more."

She started crying. Always, the crying. He wondered if Vivian would cry if she were kidnapped. The idea made him laugh. There was no way she would cry or beg. No, his Viv would think and calculate. She would probably lay silent and still in the back seat, so that he would believe she remained unconscious. Then attack when he stopped the vehicle or when he opened the door to get her out. He could imagine the exact face she would make while calculating her escape, with the furrowed brow she got he hated seeing on her face.

Then her Viking warrior look would come out for the fight. The thought made him laugh.

"Just let me go." Her words were slurred. "I won't tell anyone it happened. I can give you money."

Her sloshy voice was impeding on his thoughts of brightness and Vivian as a Viking warrior. Will let out an exasperated sigh.

"Every time you open your mouth right now, it makes me want to hurt you worse. I won't let you go. I don't want your money. If you keep talking to me, I'll pull this car over and beat the fuck out of you with my coffee travel mug until you can't talk."

The crying continued, but the talking stopped. It was at least an improvement for the hour drive they still had before them. In hindsight, he should have hit her harder, or at least brought a ball gag. It was mainly his fault for poor planning. Granted, he had not expected to kidnap Jensi particularly, but he had planned on kidnapping someone to replace Olivia. He brought the zip ties, but not a ball gag, which was turning out to be a horrible mistake. He blew out air to let go of the annoyance and get back to his thoughts.

The labeling of what he was to Vivian was bothering him. When they walked into the bar tonight to meet with her friends and their husbands and boyfriends, what would she call him? He planned on placing his hand on the swell of her back as they moved inside together. Ordering her drinks and sitting close enough to lean against her at their table would showcase their intimacy. There would be no shying away from touching her or moving the wisps of hair from her forehead when they fell into her eyes. He would whisper in her ear and brush his hand across her thighs under the table. When they left, he would hold her elbow out into the parking lot and push her back against the door of his jeep to kiss her mouth.

So, what was she to him? She wasn't his girlfriend. He didn't even want her to be something so trivial. He wanted her to just be his. For him to be able to say that she was *his* Vivian, just as he told people that this vehicle was *his* jeep.

Only really, he didn't want her to be out with other people at all, because it made her nervous. He hated how agitated she got out in public, how she looked up at the ceilings for comfort. When she did it, he couldn't help but notice. Her eyes would scan the room and then go straight up to find the emptiness above her. Will hated when she did it because it made her look off, and because he wanted her to find enough comfort in his presence to not need to do it. Tonight, he was going to try something new. When she looked up at the ceiling, he was going to wrap his arms around her, and wrap her up in his strength.

Will blew out air in audible exasperation. This obsession with Vivian was ridiculous.

There had to be something deeper going on inside his own self that made him think that he needed Vivian. It couldn't be that he was actually in love with her, or that she was something special.

Only she was something special, and maybe he might be in love with her.

The crying from the backseat turned into hyperventilating.

She was special enough to go through all this trouble to torture the shit out of Jensi for saying that she wasn't. Will couldn't help but laugh at himself over this entire situation he had gotten himself in.

Turning down the lane to his cabin, he was hit with a sense of serenity that he had not realized had developed over the past few months. This driveway with the beautiful green trees and the little birds flying around the bright blue sky. The sight of his little cabin with the garden in the back. It made him feel as if he actually had a home, a place that was familiar, and a house he wanted to come back to.

Parking as close to the back door as he could get, he left Jensi in the vehicle to go inside the house to grab the clozapine and injection kit. The one he should have brought with him in the first place. Running back out to the Jeep, he hopped into the driver's side backseat to have access to the ass end of her.

She immediately began screaming and yelling for help. Thrashing around in her zip ties, unable to do anything but rock back and forth.

"Jensi, no one can hear you. I have no neighbors for miles. I realize you're worked up and scared, but I promise that screaming and ripping your own skin open trying to get away is entirely useless." He spoke to her calmly as she continued to scream and rock.

Will rolled his eyes at her while drawing up a syringe of the clozapine. "Lucky for you, I was a medic, not sure if you remember me telling you that or not, not that you entirely care at this particular moment. Although you should, considering that I am about to dose you with clozapine." He chuckled as she fought harder to get away from him in the Jeep. "I'm going to use it to calm you down. It's a neuroleptic drug, and you probably know them as tranquillizers, but originally they were made to combat things like schizophrenia."

He reached over to expose the rump of her ass. "It's going to make you feel lethargic, probably dizzy, and confused. I doubt you'll be able to talk for a while, and you'll probably drool." He wiped an alcohol pad on the spot he intended on stabbing. "Don't be embarrassed about that, though." The needle pushed down into her flesh, slowly plunging the medication down. "I do apologize for the burn. I've heard it isn't pleasant, but that you won't care for much longer."

Will chuckled to himself before jumping back out of the Jeep to allow the medication to take hold. He ran up to Olivia's room to put new sheets on the bed and by the time he returned to the Jeep, Jensi was fast asleep where she lay, drooling. Sliding her out of the vehicle, he threw her up over his shoulder. "Lighter than a goddamn duffle bag."

Walking her up the steps, he gingerly laid her down on the clean sheets.

"We need to get you into something more comfortable while you sleep this off." He spoke to her as if she were conscious. "I want to keep you rather healthy for as a long as possible. I don't want to go through the hassle of finding a replacement for a while. It's tedious anymore."

He grabbed a knife from his drawer of tools and cut her zip ties off, throwing them away in the trashcan he kept in the room. He sucked in air when he saw the skin under where the zip ties had been. "Ahh. Stupid girl. I told you all you would do was hurt yourself." Will ran his thumb over the raw skin on her wrist. "I'm going to need to clean and bandage these. Make sure your restraints don't touch them, either. We might need to get a little creative."

He pulled her clothing off and put them in a pile near the door. Those would need to be burned. The shoes he had tossed out of the vehicle about a block down from where he dumped her purse. She lay naked and passed out on the bed, though a small moan escaped her lips. "Don't worry. I'll get you all healed up and comfortable."

He left the room to return with supplies for cleaning and dressing her wounds. Lying on the bed naked with her hair flowing all around her, she looked gloriously stunning. Like a beautiful painting. He was thoroughly happy with his choice. She was a heartless and selfish friend to Vivian, but absolutely gorgeous to look at.

Deciding to leave her naked for the time being, he sat her up on pillows, so her head was elevated enough to keep her from choking on any vomit. He attached leather straps to her upper arms and thighs, locking them in place. Then he wrapped a strap around her waist as well, securing it to the bedframe. Her wrists were left exposed so they could heal, trapping her forearms to the bedframe instead. Her ankles he secured above the wounds as well, to allow healing but still securing her legs. Finally he made sure her head was able to turn in case she vomited, but there was no way in hell she would be able to release herself from the bed. He considered retrieving a comforter from the closet to cover her to keep her warm, but thought better of it. Instead, he turned the thermostat up for warmth and left the room to go catch a nap before his night with Vivvie.

He was excited for it, actually. After being in the company of Jensi for the evening, and all day, he longed for the elaborate intricateness that floated out all around his Vivian.

He needed to float around her, too. He wished he didn't need to keep women like Jensi chained to beds for his own sick needs, but he did, and he would.

Didn't mean he couldn't float too.

Chapter 35

Dog and Pony Show

Vivian had changed her clothing three times. Not one of the three outfits made her look as she hoped to look.

She was happy with her makeup, but only because she had watched makeup videos online for hours to get her face contoured and painted. She was happy with her hair in loose curls around her head. Each lock perfectly in place and shiny from all the fancy products she had purchased to mimic the luxury women who Will normally took out on dates.

When it came to clothes, however, she sat defeated on her bed, in her underwear, thinking of what she needed to say to cancel on Will.

She could tell him she wasn't feeling well or had a headache. Those excuses seemed reasonable.

Vivian couldn't understand why he had been so adamant for them to have a 'couple's date' with her friends, anyway. The entire thing made no sense at all. It was ridiculous.

Sitting there feeling hideously flabby, and not at all the type of girl that should be on Will's arm, she felt him before she looked up to see him. "I forgot to lock the door again."

He snickered from where he stood, leaning against her bedroom door frame. "You did."

She peeked up.

He stood in cocky confidence, leaning in a pair of brown pants, a dark blue jacket unbuttoned over a dark slate shirt. He had a scarf around his neck, grey with a dark blue swirling pattern. His hair was tousled in the nonchalant way that drove woman wild, trying to get their fingers into it. He hadn't shaved in a day or two, and the scruff on his face was a shadow, but a clean well-kept one. It was purposely there for effect. The sleeves to his jacket were pushed up on his forearm, exposing an expensive wristwatch on one arm, a silver KIA bracelet on the other.

"Who do you wear your bracelet for?" She asked without meeting his eyes.

"Why aren't you dressed?" He ignored her question entirely.

"I'm not going. I don't look good in anything I wear." She waved her hand across her closet, "and you look so, well, you look unbelievably attractive. I didn't even know men wore fashion scarves."

She felt the smile light up his face. "God, but I enjoy you, pet."

He sauntered across the room to where she sat in her underwear. "Your makeup is stunning."

"Don't do that," she looked up at him, "I am not stunning. Nothing about me is stunning. Why do you want to go with me, Will?"

Very softly, he placed his hand under her chin, forcing her to look up at him. She met his eyes with hers.

"You are more beautiful than any woman I have ever looked at. Not in the way you think, Viv." He held up his hand to stop her face of indignation. "Just hear me, please. You're different Vivian. When I look into your eyes, I see the entire sky on a summer's day. I can feel the warmth of the sun and see the colors of the flowers that dance on the breeze. I fall into them every time. I look into your eyes and I know that every man who died under them saw that summer's day before he died, and I am so relieved to know that they were allowed to fall into your eyes to die."

"Staff Sergeant Fuller," He held up his KIA bracelet, "I wish he could have died looking into them, instead of mine. God fucking knows I would jump into death if I got to do it staring into your beautiful blue eyes." Will stopped a moment to look over the rest of her face. "Your cheeks sit so perfectly above your lips, with a constant glow about them that makes me wish I could just sit in the same glow you do forever. And your lips," He pulled his thumb down to touch over her mouth, "they are pale and naked and delicate. I want to sink my teeth into their plump pinkness until I taste the blood pumping through them."

He fell down onto his knees. "You are so beautiful, Vivian, and I want you, every time I look at you, laugh or worry, I want you. Every time I see you glance up at the ceiling, I want to wrap you up in my arms and never let you go. I don't know what you are to me or what I am to you, but what I know is that I want you touching me all the time. Every day. I want your touch on me. I want to have your sunshine on me every moment I am alive. Do you think I deserve that?"

Vivian felt like her insides were going to melt and sink down onto the floor at his feet. Her hands reached out to touch his perfectly chiseled jaw before leaning into his lips with hers. Delicately, she toyed with him, her tongue parting between his lips to plunder his mouth with the pretty words. She sank off the bed so that she was in front of him on her knees. Needing to hold him, kissing his mouth feverishly, hoping that she could make him feel how worshipped he had made her feel with his proclamation.

Caught off guard, Will fell backwards onto her floor, laughing against her mouth as she crashed down on top of him.

"Vivian, we need to go meet your friends for dinner." The smile lit up his face, the boyish grin making him look less fierce.

She straddled him on the floor, kissing him, "What friends? I don't know of these friends you speak of?" She trailed kisses down his neck, toying with his ears and his hair with her hands as she rocked against him in her underwear. He was still smiling, a genuine smile of happiness, not the fake one he used to throw false sunshine out into the world.

Before she could even gasp in surprise, her forearms were in his grasp and she was in a controlled fall down onto her back. He leaned over top of her, pinning her, looking down in awe.

"God, what you do to me." He kissed her lips gently before pulling his head up again. "But we are going."

With a deep inhale in, he jumped up to his feet and reached down for her hands to help her up. "What's the problem here?"

She relented. "I look awful in every single piece of clothing I own and shouldn't go out in public anywhere near a man like you."

"Vivian, that's horrible to say about yourself." Will scolded her.

"Fine. You find something that will make me look like I should be standing near you in your man scarf." She waved her hand like a wand across all the clothing hanging up.

"I will then."

Walking over to her closet, he examined her options. "Good god, where did you find this disgraceful frock? The bargain bin at the Dollar General?" The comment made her giggle.

"That's not funny Viv, I'm being serious. Burn it."

She laughed more at his serious hatred toward her clothing.

"Let's make a pile actually, a 'burn it' pile."

With her laughter, his followed. He threw clothing off her hangers onto a pile on the floor.

"This is disgusting and looks like gangrene leaked all over it."

He threw another onto the pile.

"Ew, Vivian, is this large flowery polyester nightmare formally your grandma's favorite shirt?" He threw it on the pile.

Moving the hangers speedily in disgust, he finally reached a dark blue suit dress. Pulling it out of the closet, he discarded the jacket onto the pile. "The jacket looks like an old episode of *Law and Order*, but the dress under it, with your curves... " He eyed the dress holding it out. "This is what you're wearing."

He handed her the dress before searching down on the floor for shoes. Digging into her closet, he found a pair of beige heals she had worn once to an awards dinner years ago. "Here, these will do."

With the dress laid down on the bed, the heels beneath it on the floor, he waved his hand over his selection. "See, this will be perfect."

Vivian glanced at the dress and shoes skeptically. "Why don't we just stay in tonight? Every night."

He blew out an annoyed breath of air. "Put the dress on, Viv, and the shoes."

She stood next to the dress, looking down at it, deciding if she should defiantly tell him that she wouldn't get dressed, that she wouldn't go, and he couldn't make her. Only before her mind could even complete the thought, Will was moving in closer, looming over her.

On occasion, he had a sense of danger that dripped out of him and pooled at his feet to encompass his prey. His face held the same composure, his voice the same welcoming tones of conciliating comfort, but Vivian swore her feet were planted in the center of a minefield where she stood. There was a part of her that knew she should fear him, part of her that warned her off from him, but away from him she was desolate.

Desolate was worse.

Being near Will was... almost dropping a tray of expensive glass dishes, tripping on the steps and catching yourself at the last moment, running toward the explosions. Under his looming stature, she felt her heart accelerate and her blood move under her skin, making her feel alive again.

"I want your friends to know I am with you."

"What do you mean *with me*?" A smile crept across her features sweetly. "Will, I don't care what they know. You don't have to pretend this, whatever it is, to protect me from what anyone thinks."

He stared down at her. His mind was moving, but she couldn't feel what he wanted to convey.

Blowing out the breath he had been holding, Will side stepped where she stood to pick up the dress from the bed. Without a word, he slid it over her head.

"I'm conflicted, Vivian. I want to hide you inside my skin so that I may feel you, but no one else ever gets to hear you or see you or need you again. Only I also want the entire world to know that you are beautiful and wonderful and make me smile when I thought that I couldn't anymore."

"You think I'm wonderful?"

Will nodded his head. "And beautiful."

Vivian stepped into her shoes. "Well, I guess we can go to dinner just this one night, then."

"Annoying, I forgot to add that you are annoying."

"And you are smiling."

"I'm going to spend the night with you here after our dinner party." He took her elbow into his hand to move her down the hallway of her house. "I'm going to wash you again and then we are going to lie in the bed naked together so I can show you how beautiful you are to me."

"You realize we have not determined *why* it is important for my friends to know you're still with me because it doesn't matter to me."

"When we walk in this evening, you will say 'I'm sure you all remember my boyfriend Will,' that will suffice."

Vivian laughed as they moved down the steps. "You want me to tell them you're my boyfriend?"

"Yes, why is that amusing to you?"

"Um, because you're not."

"To that effect, why aren't I exactly?"

"Will, this is absolutely ridiculous." Vivian laughed as she moved around her home, turning off lights. Grabbing her purse from the hallway table, she paused to look up at Will, where he stood still in the hallway appearing wounded. She paused in front of him when seeing his expression. "You're being serious? You want to know why you aren't my boyfriend?"

His head cocked slightly to one side at an upward angle, indicating a 'yes' response to her question. She obliged.

"I, I guess I didn't realize you wanted to be."

"I don't. Fuck." Will crossed the space between them with two long strides. He put her face in his hands. "Vivian, I don't want to be your stupid boyfriend. But I do want to have a label for us. What are we? It doesn't make any sense in my own mind either." Will pulled her into his chest to hold her. "I just know that there is this aching need I have to define what we are, and I don't know how to."

"See, we should just cancel the dinner and go on the couch and remain comfortably undefined."

"God damn it, Vivvie, can you just call me your boyfriend tonight? Can you just allow me to have that?"

She giggled. It snuck out. "I'm sorry. I don't mean to laugh."

"Then why are you laughing?" Will burst out in laughter with her.

The two of them were smiling as they left her house. Her eyes beamed at him as he held out his hand to help her up into his Jeep like an old-world gentleman. On the drive, he kept looking over to see her sitting in his passenger seat. The dress hugged her hips perfectly when sitting. The fabric pulled tight across the thickest part of her thighs, hung loose at her abdomen, and then tight again across her luscious breasts.

She kept glancing over and smirking at him all the way to the restaurant. When they reached the parking lot, he instructed her not to move. That he would be over to her door to assist her to the ground.

Vivian's blue eyes were sparkling when he put his hand out to help her down. She could have easily hopped out of the vehicle. After all, she had jumped out of so many on her own accord, but he wanted to make her feel delicate, taken care of. With his large hand offered out to her, his carefully designed outfit resting over his perfect physique, a half-smile lifting the corner of his seductive mouth, he was so beautiful it was predatory. She slid her hand into his anyway.

He had told her he wanted to show them all he was still at her side. Wanted to be introduced as her boyfriend.

Everything he expressed aired a desire for him to belong to her, not the other way around, as he professed to be true.

In her heels, walking beside him, she felt tall and desirable. When they walked into the restaurant, she could feel all the eyes moving over them. The women in the room all wanted to be her on his arm and all the men wanted to be him on hers. She felt beautiful.

Her hair bounced as she walked to meet the woman who had been at the bar the night he stalked her. All of them looked at her in surprise as she moved to her seat. It seemed the women were struck with her change in appearance, or maybe it was for his continued presence. Vivian greeted them all with a smile as they reached their seats.

"You all remember my boyfriend, Will." She kept herself from snickering at the undefined title and reveled in the little gasps and surprised raised eyebrows that flooded guests.

All the women looked happily surprised for her.

All the women except Jensi.

Jensi hadn't bothered to come.

Chapter 36

Breaking Her Will

The night had been splendid. Vivian looked amazing, and her friends swooned at the prospect that he was hers. After dinner, he brought her up into her house, straight up into her bathroom. Without speaking, he stripped her of her clothing.

As she stood before him naked, he had intended to put her into the shower. To soothingly wash her under the warm water and then dry her off before placing her under the covers of her bed. Instead, she stood there, beautiful blue eyes looking up at him behind a painted face meant to please him. He pulled her naked body against him and lifted her ass right into his hands to move over to the sink. Spinning her around, he bent her over and slammed into her until they both found pleasure. After sexually gratifying their mutual needs, Will took a shower with her. He washed her hair and smeared the perfect makeup off her face.

He liked her better that way.

They left the shower and climbed beneath the sheets of her bed. He pulled her against him and rubbed his hands against her skin until she was near sleep.

"Vivian, I need to run home for a short while. I'll be back before morning."

She barely acknowledged his proclamation before drifting off to sleep against him. He lay for a long while just feeling her, rubbing his hands over her body, lightly dragging his fingers along the scars dominating her abdomen. Her breathing was rhythmic when he finally emerged from the bed and put his clothing on to leave her. He didn't want to leave, but he knew he had left Jensi on the bed in a comatose state and was obligated to check on her wellbeing.

After reaching his cottage, he decided to make a sandwich and brush his teeth before dealing with his new girl. He had a thought that maybe he should pack a small bag of things to keep at Vivian's house. It would be nice to have a toothbrush and deodorant. Thinking about what he should pack in the bag to bring back to Vivian's house, and what she would think about him having a toothbrush there, Will causally mounted the steps up to Olivia's room.

Opening the door, he heard the voice from the bed inquire, "Hello?"

He said nothing. He stood there looking at where she lay. Her body was sexy. Every inch of her was flawless and bronze kissed. She had every curve and every tightness a woman would crave to possess. Even laying in restraints, her body flowed in a seductive form. She had rounded hips but slender legs that went a mile up her body. Her waist curved in and her bust was voluptuous. Her breasts sat perky on her chest, even lying down. She was a good choice.

"Hello? Please, please help me." She called out into the darkness again.

Will walked into the room without speaking. He stood looking down at where she lay, helpless and beautiful. She was physically perfect, and she knew she was perfect, but she tried to pleasure her own vanity by hurting her friend. Will could not forgive her for that.

"Who is there? Please," she sobbed. "Please, please tell me who is there."

Will sighed heavily as he sauntered over to the bed. "It's just me, Jensi."

Her crying increased with his admission.

"I had the most interesting night." He sat at the side of the bed as she dramatically flailed away from his proximity as far as she could against the restraints. "I hope that once you have stopped with all this dramatic flair, you'll be able to talk to me about what plagues me. Vivian has been your friend for a while, and I had hoped you have some sort of useable insight."

Jensi pulled at her arms and ankles, screaming and wriggling to be away from where he sat.

"Stop."

He commanded, but her reactions were out of control.

"Stop. Jensi, stop screaming."

He was trying to calm her, to touch her. To gather her composure for a conversation. She bucked and spun in her constraints. Her voice screaming, and her face flailing from side to side.

Will stood up from the bed, watching her flail for a while. Her screaming filled the room as she tried to thrash her hips from one side of the bed to the other. She thrust herself up into the air, causing her breasts to bounce with her motion. Standing beside her, he folded his arms against his chest, hoping that eventually she would tire herself out.

Slowly, her hyperventilation decelerated and her movements decreased. Will moved to sit next to her on the bed again.

"I do hope you are quite done." He spoke the words quietly and calmly. "I won't be here much longer, and I would like to meet your basic needs before leaving you again." Reaching forward, he pushed the hair away from her forehead. She screamed out in response.

"Jensi, you will need to stop that. You are in a cabin in the woods, locked away in a soundproof room. No one even realizes you're missing yet. Hell, I just came from a dinner with your closest friends who all believe you are off on some cruise in the Bahamas. I honestly don't know where that came from, but damn if it doesn't suit my needs."

Her screams subsided, turning to sobs of grief. Will brushed his hand over her forehead again.

"I am all that stands between you and death." He stroked his fingers down her face. "Now, are you calm enough to talk to me?"

Jensi sniffled, coughed, and choked on her composure. She shook all over her body, but eventually answered him with a collected head nod.

"Good. Are you in any pain?"

She answered him with nodding yes.

"Well, if you have pain, you need to tell me."

There was a long silence before she finally spoke.

"My feet. My feet are numb, and they sting." The sobbing breaths began again as soon as she spoke.

Will snickered at her bravado.

"Well done, Jensi. You're conveying to me you believe the leg restraints are too tight. I'll loosen them."

He got up off the bed and loosened one restraint and then the other.

"There." He moved back up to her face. "And you must be thirsty."

Looking down into her eyes, he waited for her to acknowledge that she was thirsty.

"No? I must have been mistaken."

Will moved away from the bed, and instantly she cried out.

"Yes! Yes, please Will, I'm thirsty."

He smirked, "Of course you are. Let me get you a drink."

Leaving her there tied up, he walked down through his home, intent on retrieving a glass of water with a straw to bring to her.

After returning with the water, he sat back on his spot next to her, placing the straw between her lips.

"Drink," he commanded.

She sucked down the water through the straw. She drank every bit of liquid from the glass without protest in any form. When the water was gone, Will set it down on the floor and sat still, waiting for her to settle herself.

"What do you want from me?" she asked.

Will sat still, thinking of her question. What did he want from her? He had almost everything he could ever want from Vivian. He loved her, thought she was beautiful, desired her sexually, wanted to please her, and she made him happy. What did he want from Jensi? What need could she fulfill that Vivian couldn't?

Suffering.

Looking down at her laying on the bed, he knew the answer was that he wanted her to suffer. To watch her pay for all he had done, for all Vivian had done, for her. She never did a damn thing to deserve all the suffering they endured for her. Now it's her turn. Will looked down at her and felt the intense urge to burn her, to make her scream out in pain. He decided to give honesty.

"I want you to suffer, Jensi." He stood up from the bed and moved to the closet next to the door. "I want you to suffer as bad as I suffer, as bad as Vivian suffers. I want you to have even the slightest comprehension of what people like you ask of us." Tears poured out of her at his admission, and her body shook all over. He could hear her teeth chattering as he walked into the large closet where he kept all the supplies for the room. Retrieving the bedpan to bring over to the bed.

"Lift up your ass."

She didn't move.

"This will be the only chance you get to relieve yourself without a mess for quite some time. I suggest you take it."

Jensi did as she was told and lifted her hips so he could slide the bedpan beneath her.

"Good girl. Piss in there, and I'll go get a wipe." He walked back over to the closet, listening as the little trickles pinging in the bedpan became a steady stream. With the pack of baby wipes in hand, he returned to the side of the bed. "Open your legs." He commanded while pulling a wipe out of the package. Sad sobs escaped her as he wiped the pee off her ass and legs before removing the bedpan. "Don't cry about this pet. Using a bedpan is the least embarrassing thing you're going to endure in my care. You're going to have to come to terms with what you are now. From now on, you are my orifice. I know the literal definition of the word is an opening, or hole. However, in our case, I'm using a little literary freedom in stretching the meaning to convey more of an abyss, or collecting ground if you will, for whatever I need to get out of me."

After pulling the bedpan from under her, he walked it over to dump and pour disinfectant into the pan before placing it back into the closet. Retrieving a box of tissues, Will sauntered slowly back over to where she lay sobbing on the bed. Pulling one from the box, he wiped her face as she tried to avoid his touch, even with the tissue between her flesh and his.

"I believe orifice is the perfect word for what I'm trying to convey to you. You will be the dumping place for my pleasure, my anger, and my frustration. You will be filled up with whatever I need to unload into you. In turn, I will care for you, give you affection when deserved." He ran his finger along her leg. "I made the mistake with my last orifice of treating her more like a pet. She grew attached in this sick, pathetic way, and believed she loved me. It was painful for me when I had to kill her. Like the little boy in Old Yeller having to shoot his dog. It bothered me immensely and I don't want to go through that again."

"You killed her?"

"Well yes, Jensi, follow along, please."

"Will you kill me?" Her words shook.

"That was brave of you to ask. I'm proud of you for finding your voice again through all this. It's a lot to accept. I killed her because she gave me reason to. If you don't give me reason," Will shrugged, "then I won't kill you."

"I don't want to accept it."

"See, now that is going slightly too far with being brazen. I appreciate your honestly, however, I did not ask for it. Do you get the distinction? Tell me if you understand?"

"Yes."

"Yes? Explain to me what I meant."

"You only want me to speak when spoken to."

"Close. I only want you to tell me what I ask you to tell me. Now, when I ask you a question, I expect honesty, depth even, but not whatever the fuck you *want* to make known to me. Mainly because I don't really give a fuck what you want, and partly because it fills me with the overwhelming urge to cut your tongue out of your whore mouth and *that* would be extremely messy with a long healing process. Not to mention it takes away your tongue, which I plan on having run up and down my cock on occasion."

The thought of thrusting his cock into her mouth was brought to the forefront of his mind. "Hmm, we don't have time tonight. I need to get back." Will walked back over to the closet. "I need to figure out how to leave you. I'm not sure when I'll be able to get home."

The uncontrollable sobbing began from where Jensi lay on the bed again. Will rolled his eyes. "Are you crying because you don't want me to leave?" He laughed after he said it. "You don't have to answer that. I realize you're very emotional right now and probably trying to think of ways to get away. This is part of the reason why I must keep you bound. I don't want you trying things that won't work, anyway. You'll end up hurt or trying to hurt me and then I'll have to hurt you unplanned. Planned pain is one thing, unplanned can get ugly messy."

"It's going to be difficult enough to heal these wounds you've given yourself trying to burst out of the zip ties." Will chuckled to himself again. "Seriously though, you thought you could *saw* your way through them? I guess I commend you for trying *something*, but was that the best choice?" He pulled the coffee table crate out from the closet and set it up in the center of the room. With Jensi still sobbing, he moved around, setting up the room for her to be without him for a few days. Turned on the TV and put a comforter in the crate for her to curl up on. Like a little dog.

"I asked you a question, Jensi."

"I don't know." Her words came out between hyperventilation sobs.

"You do know. The answer is no, it was not a smart choice." Will rolled his eyes as he walked over to where she lay. He roughly grabbed her face in one of his hands and brought her to look at him. "I'd prefer not having to drug you again, but it would require your cooperation. Would you be willing to do as you're told to move off the bed and into the crate, so I don't have to drug you again?"

"Yes."

"Good." He dazzle smiled at her before reaching down to unstrap her from the bedframe. She lie still, her muscles twitching from shock and being cold. Pulling the restraints away from her body, he ordered her to lie still as he collected the straps to put away in the closet. As soon as he turned his back to her, she was rolling off the mattress and on her feet. Will shook his head back and forth in disappointment. "Jensi, Jensi, Jensi. This isn't going to go well for you."

Naked on her feet, she was wildly trying to plan her next move. Her arms were out wide as she crouched into a stance that would allow her to run. Will threw the straps into the closet and shut the door, waiting to see what she would do. The only way out of the room was behind him.

"Let me out!" She screamed. "You let me get out of this room, you sick fuck!"

He leaned against the wall, silently observing her. It was amusing to watch, to hear her yell like her words had some sort of power. He said nothing and remained still and calm as she moved from one side of the room to the other. She picked up the lamp from the end table. He assumed to use as a weapon, but she didn't unplug it and it crashed to the floor when she tried to move to the far corner of the room. She abandoned it there. He wondered what the hell she was doing moving from corner to corner. Maybe looking for another way out? Did she know what she was doing? Will didn't react.

"There has to be another way out of here." She was mumbling to herself as she moved in a frenzy. Pushing the side table over beneath the window, he assumed she was planning to stand on it to try and get out of the window. He watched her stand up on the table, trying to reach high enough to touch the glass. But she wasn't tall enough. Even if she was able to touch it, there was no windowsill to grab hold of or to stand on. Will felt his eyebrows knit together in a silent "what the fuck" face as she jumped to try and gain height. He watched the table wobble under her.

"There are steel shutters bolted on the outside of that window. I just thought you'd want to know before you go to all the trouble of trying to reach it." His words seemed to not register, and she jumped again, only this time when she landed the table leaned off balance and she tumbled to the ground.

"Are you done yet?"

Jensi rocked from side to side, naked on the floor. She was crying and holding her knee to her chest. "My knee!" She screamed out in pain. Will left his spot against the wall and lazily walked to where she rocked on the floor in pain. He had intended to help her over to the bed, to examine her knee and see if she needed him to immobilize it. Only when he leaned down, she kicked her legs up into his chest, trying to knock him off balance. The force of her kick was enough to expel the air from his lungs, but he barely even swayed backwards.

She was trying to roll quickly onto all fours to stand, but her efforts to knock him over had failed and he simply pushed down on her back with his body, pinning her down onto her belly. He wrapped his forearm around her neck and pushed pressure on her airway, effectively closing it off.

"This is unacceptable." Her hands went to his arm, where he clamped off her air. Her fingers dug into his arm, panicked. "I warned you, I calmly explained how all of this would work and you blatantly ignored me. You broke my lamp and my end table and have forced me to spend longer at home than I had intended."

Her legs wiggled and moved under his body as she tried to get away. He could feel the fight in her decreasing, she was near black out. Will didn't want her to black out, as that would be too kind. He wanted her to feel the burn in the back of her throat, to know the panic of trying to catch air after having it denied for precious minutes. His arm released, and he jumped off her, leaving her writhing on the floor, trying to breathe and cough and cry all at the same time.

He walked over to the closet where he had thrown all the restraints to collect them again. After gathering them up, he tossed them over to the floor beside the bed. Without speaking a word, Will moved over and grabbed a fist full of her hair. She screamed and grabbed hold of his arm as he dragged her across the floor.

"I'm sorry." She screamed. "I'm sorry!"

Throwing her belly-down onto the bed, he pushed down on the small of her back as he secured the waistband around her, attaching it to the bedframe. He grabbed her ankle and wrapped the restraint around it, securing it to the frame. Repeating the action on the other leg.

With both legs secure, he moved to her arms. With little effort, he pulled each arm up to wrap her wrists and secure them. As he moved around her, Jensi was in hysterics. Screaming crying, begging him, yelling that she was sorry. He ignored her cries. After he was sure she was trapped to the bed, he walked over to examine the end table and lamp she broke.

"I really thought this lamp was a beautiful accent to this room."

She sobbed as he collected the pieces of the broken lamp off the floor. Taking them down the steps, he tossed them into his trash can and got himself a glass of water.

Standing in the kitchen, he fumed. She had ruined his plans for the night. All he wanted to do was come back to check on her. Allow her to use the bathroom, give her some water. He had planned on removing her restraints and allowing her to lie on the plush comforter in the coffee table crate. He wanted to put the television on a channel she enjoyed, set the camel back on the wall with the straw within her reach so she could take sips when she was thirsty.

Drinking his glass of water, he glanced over at the clock to catch the time. Fuck. He had planned on being back in Vivian's bed by now. This was not where he saw this night ending.

He wanted to punish her. To hurt her beyond her own comprehension for her disobedience, but also didn't want to have to search out another girl. He calmed himself as he drank his glass of water and decided to beat her bare ass. He would beat her bare ass until his hand stung. But no, he didn't even have time for *that*. He would simply leave her there without a second thought before he returned to check on her. He would let her piss and shit all over herself begging for pain medications, water, and food.

Will placed his glass in the sink and returned to the bedroom above stairs where Jensi lay sobbing.

"Will? Will, I'm sorry. I'm so sorry. I was just scared."

He said nothing. Without a single word, he stood next to her naked body, laying belly down on the bed. He checked to make sure she was adequately secured and moved over to the television set to turn on a channel. "You won't be able to see it, but at least being able to hear it might be comforting. Do you like animal shows? Most people enjoy a good educational program about animals."

Her breathing hitched up as she tried to collect herself. "You, you're not mad at me?"

Will set the remote down on the floor next to the television since the table was broken. Standing upright, he cracked his neck before stalking over to where she lay pinned to the bed.

"Oh, sweet pea, I am seething and pissed at you." His hand came down gently to stroke her hair as she silently cooed to herself trying to control her crying. "But it's late, and I told Vivian I would be back well before morning." Will trailed his fingers down her back gently. "I assure you that you will regret your outburst in a few hours. Lying flat down with your arms stretched out and your legs stretched out, restraints wrapped around your open skin. No water, no food, unable to stretch or wiggle at all.

You'll hold your piss and shit as long as you can, but eventually it will come out and you'll lie in it, having no idea when I'll be back, or if I'll clean you. Maybe I'll just let you fester in piss and shit until the bacteria gets into your open wounds and you rot with sepsis. I have rubber sheets on the mattress, so I'm not especially worried about getting your fluids everywhere. I'm sure the stench will bother me when I first return, but that can be remedied easily enough.

When I do return, eventually, it will be to hydrate you, so you don't die. But I believe I'll treat you to a Ranger IV." Will snickered at the thought. "I'll get the supplies while I'm out. I'll put a tube up your asshole and lay an enema bag filled with water on your back. Gravity will allow the water to flow slowly down the tube and your anal muscles will absorb the fluids to hydrate you."

Moving his hands down, he kneaded the flesh of her ass under his grasp. "You'll learn all that your body can endure, realize you can survive so much more suffering that you think you can, and then you'll appreciate all the kindness I give you. First, I'll give you back the privilege of drinking your water from a straw and pissing in a bedpan. Then I'll show kindness by allowing you to eat some soup or nutrition shake, and clean and bandage your wounds again. Every little thing you have ever felt entitled to, you'll need to earn."

Pulling her ass cheeks apart, Will rubbed his thumb against her asshole as she tried to clench her cheeks together. "Hmmm. Then, I will give you opportunities to earn comforts, privileges." Bringing his hand up in the air, he smacked her ass hard enough to shake the frame of the bed and she screamed out but couldn't move. Walking slowly around the bed, he checked the locks on each restraint. "I'm going to leave now before I hurt you. I want your punishment to be realizing you *want* me to be pleased by you." When he reached the other side of the bed, Will raised his hand up again, smacking down on her ass hard.

"Please don't leave me here. Please Will, I'm sorry! I can't stay like this. Please!"

"God Jensi, did you not hear anything I just fucking said to you? You *can* stay like that and you will survive it. Think of all the horrific things we had to endure in war, and imagine what that was like while you lay there. Perspective." He chuckled as he walked out of the room, but he wasn't amused, he was deeply pissed. He had to walk out of the room to get himself calm before driving back to Vivian.

Will went out his back door to pace in the garden where Olivia was buried. He was trying to unclench his muscles, but the anger was just filling him up from his toes. The longer he thought, the angrier he became. He was aggravated over her little outburst and the broken lamp, but his newfound rage was born from the realization that he had told Jensi that he planned on going back to Vivian and she didn't even yell at him to stay away from her friend. She never screamed for him to leave Vivian alone. Jensi knew he was a monster. She was suffering his sick torture and didn't even give the tiniest of thought for her friend. Not one thought for Vivian's fate, no attempt to prevent her friend from being harmed like she was. Her tears and concern were reserved only for her own selfish self.

She deserved to lay up there and suffer for a day or two.

Please, please, she begged and begged for herself, but didn't even offer one tiny little inkling of sentiment for Vivian's well-being. Did it really surprise him? After all, the entire reason he picked her was because she felt entitled to steal her friend's man, because she saw herself as better.

He sat down on the garden bench. Jensi was a thief of entitlement others earned. She wanted the pleasures of life without doing anything to deserve them.

Looking up at the stars, Will sucked in a deep breath of the night air. He thought of Vivian smiling at him when he offered her his hand to help her down from the jeep. His Vivvie didn't even feel entitled to a simple act of chivalry.

He stretched his legs out looking up at the dark sky. "I have a purpose," he told the night. "To make two women get what they deserve."

Chapter 37

Two Army Medic Veterans Kitchen Discussion

Opening Vivian's front door, Will realized he was tired, bone tired. Putting his hand on her door handle was a release of what he had been holding. Not in a way that made him want to punish for having to carry it, but more like it was dropping off him at the door. As if the air inside her home pushed it away, refusing it entry into the home with him.

He was going to mount her stairs and strip his clothing off as he moved before crawling naked underneath the pink comforter that he knew she would be curled up in. Even the thought of being there with her, in her bed and feeling her skin, was calming.

Opening the unlocked door, he immediately noticed the kitchen light on. Knowing the light was most definitely off before he left, Will walked cautiously down the hallway, almost tactically, to investigate. As soon as he could look around the doorway, he saw her standing with her elbows down on the countertop, the red throw blanket from the couch draped around her, a glass of amber fluid in her hand.

"Vivian, it's three in the morning. What are you doing?"

Her lips slipped upwards, and though it was slight, there was genuine happiness seeing him.

But her eyes, her eyes, were tortured.

"What's happened?" He was over to her as quick as he could get, lifting her chin up to look at him. His hands instinctually rubbing her arms up and down along the soft fabric of the red shawl she wore for warmth in his absence.

"Nothing's happened Will, it's just nightmare hour." The blue summer's day in her eyes was grey. "Don't you get them still?" She wondered out loud.

He sat thinking about her question and how to answer it. Of course, he had nightmares. He had them so bad he turned to meth to escape sleep, ruined his career and marriage, became so angry at beautiful self-serving women that he began torturing and killing them. All because of the nightmares.

"I haven't had them bad in a while."

"How did you get them to stop?"

He looked over at where she stood and wished he could tell her the truth about how he got that to stop. He wished he could tell her he put his torment into those who deserved it. That the only way to get rid of it was to pass it on to someone else. To allow someone else to own it. She would never agree to it. She wouldn't open her mind to see that her decisions in the war were already made for her before she made them.

There was never any good choice, there was no right choice, and it was all horror. They had all been patriotically wrapped up in the American flag to blind them with words like 'honor' and 'glory' used in place of words like 'immoral' and 'inhumane.' There was no honor or glory, was only political gain and power exchange to benefit the rich and self-motivated.

Vivian clung to her actions in the war just as he used to, clung to the guilt and the screams, and allowed them to swim around in the blood as it pumped through her veins. She still believed it belonged to her because it was her eyes that saw it, her hands that held it or allowed it to slip through her fingers, as life often did in combat.

Will couldn't remember the last time he had one of his bad nightmares. Giving his torture to the women had given him peace. Sleeping with Vivian, he didn't get nightmares either. How perplexing? Neither did she.

"Viv, you haven't had a single nightmare the nights we have slept together." Will cocked his head to the side.

She took a sip from her drink, glancing out the window into the night. "I've noticed that too. Maybe with you holding me here, my mind can't go back there." She shrugged, "You won't let me, but Will, it doesn't belong to you. Me having a nightmare or not having a nightmare, it's not your responsibility."

"Like hell it's not." He crossed the space in a few short strides, wrapping her up in his arms. He buried his face into her hair, breathing in the scent of her while rubbing fingers up and down her back.

Almost hesitantly, she exhaled a deep breath and grasped hold of him. He felt her weight give in as she became pliable in his arms.

"Vivvie, what was the nightmare? Tell me what it was about, and then it won't be just yours anymore."

She hesitated.

"I said, tell me Vivian."

"Burning. They were all on fire and screaming and I kept trying to get to them and couldn't get there. I would run, and my lungs were hot, and I couldn't breathe, and I'd keep trying to run to get to them. Only the path would never bring me to them. My bag would get heavier and heavier and push down into my boots and I couldn't lift my legs to move and I had to just stand there reaching."

"You dreamed of a fire?"

"No, that's what I never understand. There is never a fire, only civilians and soldiers laying on the ground with burns going up their skin. Charring up their skin, crawling, and I'm never able to reach them to help."

"Vivian, I'm sorry I left you."

"It's not your fault. You don't need to feel like you're responsible for me, or my nightmares."

He pulled her face away from his chest and kissed her forehead.

"I know I'm not, but I want to be." Will sighed heavily. "Come. I'm tired and you look exhausted. Let's climb into bed and sleep without any burning."

Will decided as they walked up the steps that he needed to get Vivian into his home. She needed to belong to him, sleep in his bed, so she never suffered nightmares ever again. It was possible, and it could happen. He could keep his upstairs room separate from their lives. He could keep Vivian's family away from them. They could visit on holidays, maybe. She could stay there while he was gone, he could lock her in.

"Thank you for coming back." Her voice was so uncharacteristically demure.

"I will always come back to you, Viv. Sometimes I need to go, but I will always come back."

It would work. He could really make this happen. Her family might be an issue, but he could make it so there was an understandable reason that she needs to sell her home and stay away from them.

Yvette Landis!

She was the perfect way. He could kill her and plant rumors that it was Vivian. No evidence, of course, nothing solid for the police to stand on, but any kind of suspicion in a town this small would get tongues wagging.

Vivian would feel the pressure of the unfounded suspicions and run to him. He would hide her away in his cabin in the woods and slowly introduce her to his lifestyle. She would understand eventually.

"What did you have to go do when you left, Will?"

"I told you, I had to run home."

"Well, I know you went home, I just wondered why you had to go."

"I have a pet. I needed to make sure she was fed and watered."

Vivian stopped walking and turned to stare at him, a shocked and confused look on her face.

"You got a cat?"

Fuck, now he would need to get a goddamn cat for when he had her over. "Yes, a pretty little pussy to keep me company when I'm home." Things are getting more and more complicated. Maybe just kidnapping Vivian was the way to go, lock her up in the bedroom, or add an addition to the back of the cabin. He could make her a beautiful little apartment even, with a terrace and flowers and everything she could ever want. She would only need to be in there when he had to leave. The rest of the time she could just live with him, and they could have dinner every night and grow a vegetable garden and go for hikes in the woods.

"Poor little thing is probably so sad when you leave."

He could give her the cat to love when he had to go away to kill, or to find a replacement.

Will thought of Jensi tied down on the bed with her piss pooling around her, getting cold right about now. She was probably sobbing and shivering and yelling out for help. She definitely wasn't sad that he left. The thought made him snicker.

"She didn't seem to mind. I don't think she's attached to me."

"Well, you have to give it time, Will. Eventually, she'll realize you are there to take care of her and that she's alone without you. One day she'll know you love her, and she'll love you back."

"I don't want her to love me, Viv, I just want her to keep me company. Something warm to pet when I'm all alone." Someone to torture, so I don't have horrendous nightmares like you.

Vivian crawled into her bed and Will crawled in behind her. Pulling her against him felt so right, having her tucked so perfectly against him, she fit into him like her curves belonged pressed into him. He felt himself sigh and smile as he closed his eyes.

Tomorrow he could plan on killing Yvette and making people think it was Vivian.

And tomorrow, he could think about how to break-in Jensi to her new life.

Tonight, he was going to hold Vivvie, and smile, and breathe her in to comfort himself, and to comfort her.

Who said a man couldn't have it all?

Thrill of murder, comfort of love. Punishment and pleasure.

Vivian whimpered in sleep, sliding closer into him to irradicate her slumberous fears. He held her tighter, cooing softly into her ear, commanding her to relax into him. His lips smiled against her hair as he relished the feeling of her submitting to his will.

Thank you for reading Book 1
The Lady in the Red Shawl

Now check out Book 2
The Lady Draped in White

After years of experiencing life with Vivian Goodwill in it, Will must decide between his need for retribution and killing or making a place for her at his side. Her unwavering morality, and hold on her past, challenges Will's strategy for setting up an existence where he can possess both the ability to continue his mission of punishment and his Vivvie too.

Will's mental stability bends as emotion instead of rationale overwhelms decisions and actions, leaving him wondering what in his life is real and what is a manifestation of his war-torn mind? Venturing through the roles of murder, veteran, and lover, Will must answer the internal question of whether or not the vengeance was worth the price.

This book is rated R; not appropriate for readers under 18 years of age; contains elements of graphic sex and murder.

Order now from:
https://books2read.com/u/49ve90

About the Author:

Nicolle Vaughn is an Army veteran who now lives a quiet life in the country with her husband and children. No longer interested in a life among society, she finds solace in animals and sitting on the back porch watching the leaves move with the wind.

Authornicollevaughn@gmail.com

fb.com/100069261782021

Ingram Content Group UK Ltd.
Milton Keynes UK
UKHW040706170523
421890UK00001B/74

Dishonorably discharged, ex-Army Ranger William Hartmann, has been home from war for years now tormented by the daily life of a man who was asked to kill at the expense of his own humanity.

Highly trained in predatory hunting, Will's mission to seek thrill and retribution continues without pause until he is drawn to a medic's group invitation. Desperate to have one night surrounded by other veterans, he attends and finds himself unprepared for the contrast in beliefs he finds living and breathing in the mind of the short, blonde, beautiful combat veteran standing at the coffee station.

Too intrigued to leave her alone, will Vivian change the trajectory of Will's post-war existence? Or will he drag her down into his hell?

An erotic thriller filled with sex, torture, murder, and romance seen through the minds of elite military veterans trapped by the war they lived through.

The Lady in the Red Shawl, Book 1 of a 2-book series.

This book is rated R: not appropriate for readers under 18 years of age; contains elements of graphic sex and murder.

ISBN 979-8-201-68751-9
90000
9 798201 687519